BLAND ENCOUNTER

Bland Encounter

Donald Wightman

Matador
9 Priory Business Park,
Wistow Road, Kibworth Beauchamp,
Leicestershire. LE8 0RX
Tel: (+44) 116 279 2299
Fax: (+44) 116 279 2277
Email: books@troubador.co.uk
Web: www.troubador.co.uk/matador

ISBN 978 178306 098 6

Front cover illustration: Joe Evans: http://quirkyjoe.com

British Library Cataloguing in Publication Data.
A catalogue record for this book is available from the British Library.

Printed and bound in the UK by TJ International, Padstow, Cornwall
Typeset by Troubador Publishing Ltd, Leicester, UK

Matador is an imprint of Troubador Publishing Ltd

MIX
Paper from
responsible sources
FSC
www.fsc.org
FSC® C013056

Dedicated to service men and women everywhere.

An Appeal

If you would like to show your support to our armed forces, then please think about making a donation to either:
Help for Heroes or The Royal British Legion

Introduction

When my friend and work colleague Dave Bland asked me to take on the role of ghost writer for his memoirs, I anticipated writing a very dull and dreary tome indeed. It seems to be a tradition amongst railwaymen when putting their experiences into print that the book becomes more a detailed journal of their work routine. You know the sort of thing:

'It was Friday 14th March 1989, the weather was overcast with the odd shower if I recall correctly. I happened to be working the 8.22am stopping service to Welsall, which wasn't the job I had been rostered to, but fellow driver Ken Higgins had wanted to swap turns so that he could take his wife to the dentist to have an abscess lanced.

Anyway, on arrival at Welsall we had twenty minutes before our return journey, so I was just about to tuck into one of my sandwiches – cheese and pickle if I recall correctly – when I was asked by my control to couple up my unit – a three car 182 – with another unit, a two car 194, already in the platform.

Now I expect those readers in the know are already in fits of mirth and merriment, it being common knowledge that the coupler on a 182 is quite different to the coupler on a 194, and therefore incompatible with one another. My! How we laughed at that one! The very thought of it kept me chuckling for the rest of the day, nay, the rest of the week even.'

Now this sort of minutiae may be alright for the true devotees of railway trivia, but my guess is that it would leave the average reader bored rigid. To my great relief, Dave wanted to relate a completely different side of his life to you readers.

As Dave explained to me, books telling of a railwayman's personal experiences seldom ever delve into the weird and wackier world of life between the rails. Dave has set out to try and redress the balance by concentrating on just one extraordinary period of his time within the industry.

Like many of the Mr Averages of the world doing an average job, Dave would be the first to confess to having had, for the most part, a fairly unexciting time in his chosen career. He fully takes the blame for this state of affairs, having never been very pro-active in the thrill-seeking department. For Dave, the idea of seeking out challenging situations was, well... rather *too* challenging.

There was, though, he assures me, one period during a hot-blooded eager-to-please phase of a passionate new romance, when Dave acted completely out-of-character, masterminding a series of events that took him on an adventure previously unimaginable to someone of his nature; motivated entirely by the desire to retain the love, affection and respect of the woman he loved. (The same excuse used no doubt by many an accused man over the centuries to explain an out of character act that resulted in them being brought before the court!)

Luckily, Dave's actions did not result in this form of legal redress, though as the story unfolds, you'll see it comes pretty close at times. During this time, Dave discovered an impulsive, reckless side to his nature that had previously lain undiscovered, (though after careful reflection, he tells me this may be something of an overstatement.)

He describes this period as a journey full of high adventure, combining slapstick, skulduggery and salacious sex in roughly equal amounts. Plenty of humour too! (Exactly the right ingredients for a ripping good yarn, I hear you say, readers.)

Yes, Dave has many a good chuckle whenever he recalls the amusing situations that occurred and the people he got involved with at the time. A keen sense of humour has always been a big part of his make-up, his own brand being much like his favourite Rioja – very dry!

The events described in this story happened several years

previously, and not always with the author present, so it would be impossible to portray exactly what was said, when, and by whom. Therefore, in consultation with Dave, incidental dialogue has been added to recreate an accurate picture of events as they took place.

It was also Dave's wish that his memories of that time should read like a proper story, with him being just one of the characters appearing in it. (There's modesty for you.) This modesty, though, did at times present a barrier to portraying the real Dave Bland, warts and all. Persuading him for the good of the story to be candid and reveal the full details of the many funny and embarrassing situations he found himself in was difficult enough, but getting him to reveal his innermost feelings at appropriate moments was probably the hardest concession I extracted from him. In the end, though, confess all he did.

So what follows is a blow-by-blow account of one period of Dave Bland's life on the railway (i.e. the interesting bit.) Non-railway enthusiasts will be pleased to know that all mention of class 68 locos, rolling stock movements, special workings and other railway jargon have been specifically deleted wherever possible. Reference to them will be made only if strictly necessary to the story.

Donald Wightman
Bridgnorth, June 2013

Chapter 1

Like the D Day invasion of Europe, Dave's mission had been meticulously planned. And like the invasion, luck would play an important part in the mission's success. Although he knew fate to be a fickle mistress, Dave had reason to be optimistic when he entered the car park and found it almost devoid of vehicles.

He took a moment to consider his options. A position close to the entrance would have been the logical place to park, but he knew a vantage point nearer to his quarry was vital if he were to bring the evening's mission to a successful conclusion.

A line of willow trees caught his attention. Spread out along the riverbank, their weeping canopies almost reached down to the ground. The ideal place to conceal himself in he thought. He headed towards a tree on the water's edge where he used his car to part the curtain of foliage and gain access to the empty space within its shroud-like interior.

From his covert location, Dave made a quick check of the riverside before removing the binoculars from their case. Bringing them up to eye level, he focused the eight times magnification lenses on the prominent landmark situated over on the far bank. As yet he could see no one fitting the likeness of the woman in the photograph.

Her most likely approach route, he guessed, would be the riverside walk so he slowly panned along the path's route hoping to locate her. On his return pass, some movement close to the water's edge caught his eye. Dave adjusted the focus to bring the

1

outline into sharper detail. Immediately he recognised the characteristic brown fur coat; the one he'd seen fleetingly a few times previously. The features looked identical; he was sure it was the same female.

With the light fading and a mist now rising off the water, surveillance was proving difficult to maintain. He lost sight of her once, then just as quickly found her again – this time crouched down in the long grass as if sensing some kind of danger. Dave realised he would not get a better shot than this, but he had to be quick, she might flee at any moment. Discarding his binoculars, he hurriedly lined up the cross hairs of his lens on her body and, keeping a steady aim, squeezed off two shots in rapid succession.

Noise reverberated through the car. Damn it! He'd forgotten all about the silencer – why hadn't he remembered? He opened the car door to listen. The volume of sound coming from the exhaust confirmed his suspicions. He sighed, got out of the car and crouched down to look underneath. Just as he thought, the rear silencer had again come adrift from the exhaust pipe. Now hanging loose and almost touching the ground, the vibration from the idling engine was causing it to knock loudly against the car's bodywork.

When the exhaust first came apart a week or so ago, he'd managed to mend it using some wire and a heat resistant bandage, confident that it would all hold together until he could source a cheap replacement; his eight-year-old Vauxhall had cost him a tidy sum in repairs already this year. It seemed his confidence had proved misplaced and, having neglected to obtain the necessary replacement, the broken silencer would have to be repaired all over again.

He was sure the cause of this latest mishap lay with the speed bump situated at the car park entrance. He'd only remembered it at the last moment and despite braking hard, had gone over the obstacle back-wrenchingly fast, fatally weakening the repair in the process. Dave judged there was little he could do about it now, not without another straightened-out coat hanger and a large jubilee clip to replace the perished bandage. He just hoped the exhaust would last long enough in its precarious state to survive the journey home.

Pushing aside such concerns for the time being, Dave picked up the camera from the seat and examined the photos he'd just taken. He was pleased to see the elusive creature perfectly captured in both shots. Although he'd seen the otter on several occasions before at this spot – once with her young cubs in attendance – he'd never been fortunate enough to capture the animal on film.

He returned to the business in hand and checked his watch. Although there were still some minutes to go before the appointed time, he decided to break from the routine of previous visits and anticipate the arrival of the woman he'd arranged to meet here – the walk would give him a chance to plan the format of the evening.

If she was in agreement, it would be a stroll to the nearest pub and then a maximum of two drinks – unless she offered to buy a round. But most importantly, avoid all mention of food. He'd foolishly allowed himself to be conned once before into buying a meal for a woman he'd only just met.

It was their first date together and he was making every effort to be the attentive escort. As they relaxed with a drink at the bar, he wondered if his ladyfriend might like to share a packet of nuts with him, so asked her if she was feeling peckish. The woman seemed surprised by the question and said how nice it was to meet the generous type for a change. Dave thought perhaps she was being sarcastic, but before he could point out he only meant peanuts – not the more expensive cashews – the woman launched into a lengthy explanation of how she'd been too busy getting ready for their date to have lunch and needed a little something to keep her strength up, so his offer was very much appreciated. And while she was tempted to have the sizzling steak platter from the Specials Board, in her opinion the supersized meal deal on the main menu was probably the better option as it included a choice of pudding as well.

He was left reeling at the cheek of the woman. A half share of his Nobber's Nuts he considered more than reasonable on a first date and was tempted to say, "If I'd really wanted your opinion on how to spend my money, I'd have asked for it." But not wanting to appear too miserly in case it ruined his chances of a successful outcome to the evening, he reluctantly accepted the inevitable – though it was all to no avail, he later discovered. The memory of that evening still sent a cold shiver through his wallet.

Two hundred yards later, Dave realised the binoculars were still hanging around his neck. He stopped to think for a moment. It could give his new ladyfriend the wrong impression about him if he were to turn up wearing them on a first date. She might mistake him for some sort of voyeur – a trainspotter even. They would also get in the way should she want to embrace him at some point during the evening. Dave knew it an unlikely scenario given his previous experiences here, but hope springs eternal, as they say, so placed the binoculars under the car seat for safekeeping before setting off a second time.

On reaching the midpoint of the bridge, he spotted a female sauntering close by their agreed meeting place but quickly dismissed her as being too young and, he guessed, almost certainly too attractive for his assignation.

Arriving at the granite monument, Dave paused to peer up at the familiar figure of the World War One infantryman, his Lee Enfield rifle held rigidly at the side. Did he really just detect an acknowledgement from him? Dave had used this same meeting place so many times before, he could almost imagine the old soldier greeting him with a nod of recognition at each of his appearances.

Dave checked his watch and looked around. With still no likely-looking female in sight, he decided to use the vacant time to think up some original lines of conversation. He set off on a slow circuit of the war memorial to help stimulate the creative juices.

Five circumnavigations later, he was still facing a blank page. He went to look at his watch again, then double-checked it with the clock on the church steeple. Both confirmed the fact that she was now late. From experience, Dave guessed the problem was one of orientation. Making arrangements to meet on either the west, or east side of the river caused nothing but confusion in the other ladies he'd met here. It seemed to him that the female mindset was unable to distinguish one from the other.

Strolling over to a nearby shop, he glanced idly at the window and noticed a series of picture postcards. Dave studied one of the elegant bridge, sitting incongruously posed between wisps of steam emanating from the twin cooling towers of the more recent coal-fired power station situated just up river from it. He couldn't help but wonder why out of all the places to build a power station, it was constructed in a position where it would spoil one of the most pleasant vistas along the river. A more popular decision for Ironridge folk, he guessed, would have been to bless the sprawling, modern conurbation of nearby Tealford with the benefit of those huge concrete cooling towers.

A figure in the bottom right-hand corner of the postcard then caught his attention. A figure at once familiar to him, wearing clothes he instantly recognised: they were his own, the very ones he was wearing today.

"I don't believe it, who had I arranged to meet that day?" he muttered to himself. It looked to be late spring or early summer judging by the foliage on the trees. Casting his mind back a few months, he tried to remember who the lady he was pictured waiting for could have been, Jan... June... Jane. It was something like that.

Analysing the pose, Dave regretted he hadn't been standing a bit more upright when the photographer had taken his shot, it would have disguised his thinning hair a bit more. He appeared to be looking down in the picture so guessed he was probably checking his watch at the time; it prompted him to do the same now. Dave sighed and wondered once again why his dates – that is the ones that actually bothered to turn up – were never on time.

The picture postcards suddenly gave him an idea. If he were to buy a pack of them and send out one to every prospective dating partner, together with written instructions on how to find him, it could well bring about a dramatic improvement in their orientation skills.

For good measure, he could add a dotted trail leading to his own figure in the picture, highlighting himself with a circle drawn in thick black ink. This would also have the benefit of masking that glint of sunlight being reflected off his balding head.

Storing the thought away as a suitable remedy for all future geographically-challenged females, he wandered back to the war memorial. Once again he perceived an acknowledgement from the veteran infantryman as he sauntered by. In need of some mental stimulus to help pass the dragging minutes, he attempted to recount the names of the soldiers inscribed on the column from memory.

"Hiya!"

Startled by the sudden interruption, Dave automatically shot a look up to the granite soldier before sensing a living presence behind him. He turned around to see a flustered, overweight woman advancing towards him, one hand flapping a greeting, her paces restricted by the over-stretched leggings pulled up over her sizeable torso.

"Hi!" she repeated. "Are you Dave?"

He was about to answer...

"Sorry I'm a bit late, I meant to park this side of the river, but somehow ended up..."

"The wrong side?" suggested Dave, finishing off an explanation he had become all too familiar with.

"I don't understand all this west and east," she said, ignoring him. "Why didn't you just say the left or right-side of the river? It would have been much easier."

"Yes, well it all depends on which direction you are approaching the river from," pointed out Dave.

"Sorry?"

He explained. "Look, I've come from Bridforth, so I've travelled from south to north to get here. For me, this is the right-side of the river. You would have come from the direction of Tealford so have travelled from north to south. That means for you this is the left-side of the river. The directions left and right are all governed by your orientation whereas east and west are constants that do not change. Do you see now?" Dave could see by the look on her face that she did not.

"Well there's no need to get funny about it, you just didn't explain it very well."

Dave's eyes rolled up in their sockets to meet the soldier's face once more. Did he note a matching look of exasperation in those finely-chiselled features? Undoubtedly as a World War One infantryman, he would have understood the vital importance of being able to distinguish an easterly direction, from a westerly direction; though it could be argued that if the generals from those times had possessed the same grasp of geography as the woman now stood before him, then hundreds of thousands of innocent lives could have been saved; due in no small part to the two great armies not being able to find one another.

He let out a sigh, an acknowledgement of defeat, before turning to face the woman now awaiting his response.

"I'm sorry Pam – it is Pam, isn't it?" He felt a sense of panic when her face failed to register acknowledgement of her name. Was Pam the one from last week?

She corrected him. "It's Penny *actually*," she announced coldly, emphasising the actually.

Dave quickly rectified his mistake.

"I'm sorry about the confusion, er... Penny." He called up a well-rehearsed line, "It's good to see you though – you look great; that outfit suits you." Then glancing down, "Are those er... leggings new?"

She glared back, now even more hostile. "Are you being sarcastic?"

"No, not at all," he replied, not understanding the reason for her accusing tone.

Penny stood glaring at him, her arms folded tightly together underneath her ample breasts – accentuating their size. Her nipples appeared to stiffen in the cool evening breeze – closely matching her attitude. Dave sensed her increasing hostility.

"Look," he said, abandoning his script and trying another tack. "I'm not very good at meeting like this. I didn't mean to sound sarcastic. I just felt a bit awkward and was trying to make conversation, that's all. Look, can we start again?" he pleaded.

As soon as he'd said it, he had to query his reasons for wanting to do so. He realised that although she was large, Penny exuded a sort of earthy sexuality. His desperate need for carnal fulfilment was overcoming any reservations he had about her size should events ever lead up to a satisfactory climax, which at this point in time looked extremely doubtful.

Dave's pleading tone obviously won him some sympathy as Penny's face softened, and she removed the underpinning from her breasts. One hand was sent on an errand to titivate her hair. Somehow realising his more conciliatory approach was having a positive effect, Dave continued in the same vein.

"Anyway, you made it here okay and that's the main thing. I must say you look a lot like your photo," stated Dave. Well the head and shoulders did, he thought. The rest of her body had been partly obscured in the photo by the garden fence she was leaning over. At the time he had thought it a strange pose to take up. He could see why now.

"Thank you, and you do too – I like tall men."

Surprised by the unexpected compliment, Dave studied her face expecting a put-down to follow. It never came.

"Er… thanks Penny, as you can see I do have a less startled look in real life – you know these police photographers are always in a rush… though I did manage to delete the number I was holding in front of me before sending it to you."

His well-practised jokes seemed to be having the right effect. Penny was now smiling.

"You are joking, aren't you?"

"Of course Penny, of course. So what would you like to do then?"

"What did you have in mind?" was her somewhat suggestive response as she leaned against the grounded rifle of the soldier, the carved stone barrel rather inelegantly separating the cheeks of her ample bottom. Noting her ease at having her thighs parted by a rigid instrument, Dave was prompted to say, *Would a fuck be out of the question?*

He actually said, "Why don't we go for a walk, and then perhaps a drink somewhere?"

Penny dominated the conversation as they strolled down the street, explaining how due to her children, dog, car, etc, she had been delayed in her preparations for their date. During her few brief pauses and feeling that a response was expected from him, Dave chipped in with an acknowledgement or two.

After walking half the distance Dave had originally intended, he spotted a pub in the near distance. This gave him reason to break into her monologue and suggest they take their refreshment sooner, rather than later. Dave was sure she must be in need of a drink by now, he certainly was. Leading the way inside, he promptly ordered himself a pint of bitter, Penny, in contrast, erred on the side of indecision. Dave reeled off a list of drinks to help her choose, while the barman filled in the time by drying a tray of glasses. Penny eventually chose a white wine spritzer – his very first suggestion.

Dave picked up the two glasses and gestured her towards a quiet corner seat. Being an early mid-week evening, the pub was only lightly attended. It had he noted, been refurbished in the current vogue for chrome fittings and fake leather seats, finished off with a lavish display of beech melamine. Assembled by the bar were the customary chalkboards offering the usual badly-punctuated pudding's and special's.

Dave found that Ironridge was an ideal venue for these assignations. The pretty cottages and upmarket wharf conversions that now lined the river, belied the fact that in Victorian times huge iron furnaces belching out fire, smoke and steam once dominated the town; stories about which were now used by tour guides to illustrate the horror of those times to the schoolchildren who visited the nearby World Heritage site. It was also far enough away from his place of work to reduce the risk of accidently bumping into someone who knew him.

On one previous date he'd found himself sharing a bar snack with a woman called Jackie who had informed him in their initial exchange of emails that she had spent most of her life in Hollywood. Impressed that a woman with such a glamorous background could actually be interested in him, he readily agreed to meet her. It was only when he met her in the flesh – of which there was plenty – and hearing her accent, that he realised she had meant the Hollywood suburb of Birmingham. Such was her size that the woman could easily have been a body double for the matron in *Carry on Nurse* – but without the humour. He still had a mental picture of the awful moment she had leant forward very close as if to kiss him and was much relieved when instead the woman whispered loudly in her distinctive Brummie tones, "Are you goin' to leave those chips?"

What made the date all the more embarrassing was that, unbeknown to Dave, he'd chosen a pub in Wensbury that some of the guys from work frequented. He was spotted by them and ribbed about it for days afterwards. To avoid any further embarrassments of that sort, he kept his trysts well away from anywhere he was known.

Dave started on his second pint of bitter and began to relax, his initial feelings of anxiety laid to rest for the time being. But as he did so, different concerns came to mind. What if the evening progressed well and she was eager to get on with the physical side of things – would he be able to? She was definitely on the big side, though not as big as she appeared before the first of his two drinks. Dave felt 'voluptuous' would now be a more accurate description.

Then again, although he had tried hard not to notice the bulges accentuated by her overstretched leggings, inevitably he found his eyes being drawn back to them.

Concerned the mental picture would stay with him and have a dampening effect on his ardour, Dave wondered how best to counteract it. Her ample breasts stood out as the most obvious remedy. He discreetly surveyed the territory he could soon be roaming over. The contours of her green mohair jumper resembled two challenging lakeland peaks; conducting an intimate exploration of both summits should provide him with sufficient stimulation in the trouser department, he decided.

Having resolved that particular concern to his satisfaction, he suddenly became aware of the silence.

"Dave?"

"Er… sorry Penny, is it my turn to speak?"

"I have gone on a bit, haven't I?"

"No, no… I wouldn't say that exactly."

"You're being sarcastic again aren't you?" asked Penny. "I'm just getting used to your sense of humour now. You're very dry."

"No, not now – those two pints have just seen to that," replied Dave flashing a smile at her.

"Very good – and so quick with it too!"

"Now you're being sarcastic."

"Not me. Come on Dave, it's your turn to tell me some more about you. You've not said much so far."

"Really? Well, I don't know where to start."

Chapter 2

Dave took a moment to reflect on the events that had led up to the meeting with Penny. It had been a real eye-opener joining the internet dating service. He hadn't realised quite how many women of a similar age were available and vying for his attention – if the advertising blurb for the dating site was to be believed. It seemed they were mostly looking for the same thing: a tall, non-smoking, solvent, professional gentleman with a good sense of humour; he must like cats, country walks and scented candles – or something like that.

Penny had made the initial approach after reading his profile, sending a short message alerting Dave of her interest in him. Although he could not now recall much of the detail, the word 'bubbly' figured prominently in the description of her. He did remember, though, that she commented favourably on one of the lines in his profile; a line he had deliberately inserted in the hope of appealing to ladies of a sensuous nature.

Although not blessed with a particularly keen insight into the workings of the female psyche, Dave had learnt that by constructing a few well-chosen words and phrases he could project the image of a confident, outgoing man-about-town who knows his way around a woman's erogenous zones.

The phrase in question had come from a copy of *Take a Moment* magazine, which he happened to find on a train one day. Being without any other reading matter at the time, he'd leafed through it looking for the one feature common to all these types of publications – the problem page. Comparing his own personal circumstances with those of the featured correspondents helped him to keep his recent marital misfortune in perspective.

On the facing page, he'd noticed an article entitled 'The Art of Successful Seduction.' It immediately drew his attention. When he read the phrase, 'kissing an attractive lady on the nape of her neck,' he knew it had the right sensuous inference to attract a woman with certain needs, so copied it down with the intention of inserting it into his own online profile. These words were, he reckoned, infinitely more subtle than some of the phrases he'd seen used on the website to attract women. He'd exchanged several lively emails with the lady sat next to him, each one a little more suggestive than the last, so it appeared to work in Penny's case.

With no restrictions on the number of women he could correspond with, he'd exchanged similar missives with other ladies too, so sometimes had difficulty in recalling which details belonged to whom. He didn't want to risk another cock-up like the one he'd made earlier over her name. Dave was all too aware that these details easily slipped from his memory.

Noticing the expectant expression on Penny's face, Dave brought his mind back to the question in hand.

"Er… well, as you know Penny, I'm fifty-two, and I work as a train manager for Mercia Mainline. I've got a daughter aged twenty-six who lives with her current boyfriend in Nottingham. My wife and I separated twelve months ago, though the relationship was going downhill way before that. As a matter of fact, it pretty much followed the same route as my pension fund," he quipped.

"Yeah, I already know that, and you cracked the same joke in one of your emails," said Penny, showing some impatience with his reluctance to elaborate further. "What about your marriage? You never said anything about how it went wrong."

"Well, if you're interested – and if you're sure you really want to know…" answered Dave, taking a few seconds to gather his thoughts.

He still found it difficult to revisit the events that led to the break-up. Not that they were actual events as such, more a series of small cuts that gradually drew the lifeblood from his marriage, but where to begin the story was the difficulty. Dave decided to outline the bare facts and fill in with more detail if required.

His partner had a young daughter from a previous relationship, explained Dave, so becoming a husband to Jane also meant taking on the role of full-time parent to Emma – her biological father had abandoned his parental responsibilities to the girl some years previously.

It was not an easy co-existence to begin with, but through hard work and patience the relationship began to flourish, and by the time she reached adulthood he had come to regard her as his own flesh and blood – and, likewise, she him.

With Emma becoming an independent young lady, his wife decided the time was now right to restart her career – her current position working for a national charity was in her words, 'too boring'. He agreed to support her while she studied full-time at a local college to gain additional qualifications.

After successfully completing a two year course in business management, she began applying for positions previously out of her reach, eventually landing a lucrative job in the insurance industry. With a good salary, generous expenses and business trips away, Jane revelled in her newfound status.

It was shortly after completing her new company's probationary period that he first noticed the change in their relationship. Her attitude towards him became cooler and more critical, finding fault with him in any way she could. This invariably led to arguments between them, giving his wife the excuse to repeat her favourite mantra: 'this relationship isn't working any more,' a charge he found increasingly difficult to deny. It reached a point where his very presence seemed to antagonise her. His attempts to discuss the underlying cause of her discontent would only provoke her into throwing the blame back at him, but staying silent gained him no peace either.

With his patience wearing thin, trying not to react to her taunts became almost impossible. He came to realise her constant needling – and only a long-term partner knows the most effective way to goad their opposite number into a conflict – was a tactic to force him into making the decision to end the marriage.

Worn down by it all and with his patience finally exhausted, he reluctantly accepted the inevitable. Following a miserable last Christmas at home, he left the house hoping she would show some sign of regret for the step they were about to take, but to no avail and their marriage effectively ended that day.

Penny sympathised. "That's really sad."

"Yeah, well, it's obviously what she wanted, and I just came to accept it," said Dave, shrugging his shoulders. "Anyway, it's all in the past now.

"Once I'd moved out, I decided to make a completely fresh start, so applied for a transfer to our West Midlands depot in Wensbury. After that had been approved, I began looking around at properties and found a house I could just about afford in Bridforth. I didn't envisage having to make a new start at fifty-two, but now that it's happened, I just want to get on with my life and have some fun again – I reckon I deserve that. Look, I'm sure you've heard enough sob stories for today."

"No, no," said Penny, "I'm interested in hearing it. So what about your daughter – sorry, stepdaughter, how did she take it?"

"Oh, she was fine with it all. She could see what was happening, and to her great credit, she stayed impartial. She still lives with her partner in Nottingham – near her mother, in fact. She's busy with a life of her own, but we keep in touch."

"That's good then." Penny sat absorbing the information for a moment. Having filled in that particular gap of her knowledge, she decided to explore a different avenue.

"So what do you do in your spare time – you know, hobbies and the like?"

"My hobbies? Well... actually... now that you've asked, there is a project I have been working on for some time," replied Dave, relieved to be moving onto matters he had a better understanding of.

He did wonder whether he should bore her with the details of a new type of workbench he had been developing for the last two years. After all, talking about universal clamps and saw benches didn't exactly make for riveting conversation – certainly not on a first date when trying to impress the lady in question with your ranging, witty repartee. Then again, the workbench in question was truly multi-functional and streets ahead of its rivals. Having previously worked in an engineering role for a number of years, he still liked to tinker in his garage at home; this latest project was his pride and joy.

"Er... are you into DIY at all Penny?"

To Dave's surprise, Penny seemed to take quite an interest in his innovation and did not seem at all fazed about having the details described to her. Having delivered a fairly concise presentation for Penny's benefit, and then taken one or two questions from her on its finer points, she asked, "So what are you going to invent next?"

Emboldened by a third pint of Bathams, he decided to reveal his quest into territory of a more erotic nature. Taking a long gulp from his pint, Dave took the plunge.

"As a matter of fact, I've been thinking about vibrators."

"Vibrators!" a now laughing Penny exclaimed. "Well I should be an expert on them – I've been without a man for so long!"

Dave, while noting the admission, began to explain what he considered to be the technical failings of current models.

"So how come you know all about them then?"

"Well, having been married for several years, and like you do, you start talking about all those intimate things that you wouldn't talk about with anyone else... and well... the subject must have just come up!"

"I bet it did!" said Penny, laughing again. "I think you're a bit of a dark horse on the quiet."

Pleased with the impression Penny was now forming of him, Dave smiled and attempted to carry on, "Anyway, as I was saying – also I think I read somewhere – it was probably that *Take a Moment* magazine, women can find the effect that a vibrator produces is more of a tingle than actual stimulation. This is obviously not what was intended. No, I reckon what is needed is a proper thrusting action!"

"You took the words right out of my mouth," said Penny, giggling again.

Trying hard not to laugh himself, Dave continued, "Well, it seems that the feedback from those er... ladies who'd tried them was that most vibrators tend to be er... well... hard and unyielding."

"But isn't that supposed to be the idea?" she said, while trying to control her giggles.

"Look, you know what I mean. The real thing is well... more user-friendly. You know, it's more tactile, and er... feels warmer and more pleasant to the touch."

"Well Dave, I'll have to take your word for that. You seem to be the expert here," said Penny, laughing out loud and obviously enjoying the banter between them.

He hoped the sexual innuendo was also wearing down her inhibitions too. Those three pints had now loosened any reservations he had had about having gratuitous sex with her. She was becoming more desirable with every gulp from his glass. It seemed Penny had also overcome any lingering doubts she may have had about him – judging by the firm pressure being applied from her thigh to his own.

Dave was feeling pleased at how well it had gone after such an unpromising start. The sexual innuendo, once inserted into the conversation, never really left it, and by closing time even Dave, with his stunted emotional responses, had gained the distinct impression that the prospects for a satisfactory conclusion to the evening looked good. He had not planned to bring up the subject of vibrators, but Penny somehow seemed to have led him into that particular train of thought.

As they left the pub, Dave's offer to escort Penny back to her car was readily accepted. He took the opportunity to embrace her waist as he guided her through the door; the gesture was not unwelcome. Strolling over the bridge with its outline now illuminated against the darkness of the river below, they slowly made their way to the now-deserted car park on the other side. Conversation – like the river they had passed over – was still in full flow when they reached Penny's car.

"Would you like to sit in the car with me for a bit?" Penny casually inquired.

"For a bit of what?" asked Dave, testing the water.

"You'll just have to wait and find out, won't you?" she teased.

They both laughed at the implied meaning of their exchanges. Penny eased herself into the car and pulled her seat back. Dave followed suit. As soon as the interior light extinguished itself, Penny reached over towards him and locked herself onto his lips.

So as not to appear overly hasty, he watched out of the corner of his eye until the second hand on his luminous Mercia Mainline watch had reached the thirty second mark before sending his right hand on a mission to explore Penny's full to overflowing globes, working his fingers under her bra and over her hardening nipples.

Although they were in the darkest corner of the car park, the thrill of being in the public domain seemed to add a frisson of sexual urgency to his actions. Dave felt himself instantly stiffen in response to Penny's hand sliding up his leg.

"Ooh, what's hard and unyielding now!" she teased.

"Don't make me laugh, I might just lose it!"

"Surely not, anyway, let's see if it really is user-friendly!"

"Now *you're* being sarcastic, but do feel free to find out."

With a dexterity that could only have come from experience, Penny zipped open his trousers and hooked her hand down his Y-fronts.

"So, what have we here then?"

"I'm just pleased to see you, that's all."

"Obviously!" With that Penny began working on him with her fingers.

After such a long absence, he welcomed the return of a female hand to his member. Thinking it only polite to return the favour,

Dave slid his hand under the tight elastic of her leggings and headed south to determine the layout of the territory. Exploring each fold of flesh in turn, he eventually arrived at the correct destination.

Without prompting, Penny pushed off her shoes, moving the position of her legs to allow him better access. With his hand going numb due to the tightness of her waistband, he took the opportunity to ease the leggings from under Penny's bottom – pulling them down to her ankles in readiness for the act of penetration which he hoped would shortly follow. He completed his preparations by sliding the seat back to its last notch and undoing the fastening on his trousers. Penny then raised an unexpected query.

"We're not going to do it here are we?"

As far as Dave was concerned, a sudden change of venue was not on the agenda. He was keen not to lose either the moment – or his erection.

"Well why not? It's quiet, dark, and there's no one about to see us – anyway, I'll only be a couple of minutes!"

Penny flared her eyes at him.

"It's alright! I was only joking about the last bit."

"Have you got something then?" Penny asked.

"No, my last blood test was all clear," joked Dave.

"You idiot, I mean a condom!"

"Er... do I need one then?"

"Well... you know, just in case."

"Just in case of what?" inquired Dave, not quite sure whether her concern was becoming pregnant, being infected with something – or both.

Penny, becoming a little exasperated, asked again, "Look! Have you got one or not?"

"Yes, yes! There's one in my wallet somewhere – can you just wait a moment?" replied Dave, hoping his hard-on would wait too. He fiddled with the interior light switch a couple of times to throw some light into the car. Sorting through a wad of petrol receipts, he eventually located the one he'd placed in his wallet for just this eventuality some years previously. But when he pulled open the packet, Dave noticed that the thin rubber was now wrinkled and the oily surface had all but dried out. He realised it might well split without any lubricant on it, so thought for a moment. *Where was the WD40 when you needed it?*

Helped by a spot of lateral thinking, the solution came to him – grease! The mechanic at his garage would always smear a dollop of grease onto the door hinges as part of his car's annual service. Presumably, Penny's car would be serviced in a similar way. If he were to open the door a fraction, he could discreetly wipe some of the excess from her door hinges on to his condom without her noticing.

It was then he noticed Penny delving into her handbag. After rummaging for a moment, she handed him a small packet.

"Here, use this. I brought one along with me just in case; a good job too," she said, nodding in his direction, "I wouldn't want that pathetic looking thing inside me."

Dave assumed it was the withered condom she was referring to. He tried to let it slip from his fingers, but the thin latex clung to his hand. After eventually shaking it free, he took the fresh packet from her and ripped it open – a knobbly type that smelt of strawberries, he noticed – and unrolled it on himself.

The awkwardness of their relative positions now became apparent as he tried to align himself for entry between her legs. The position of the handbrake digging into his knee didn't help. Dave eased himself back slightly, but recoiled when he felt something probing him in the rear. He fumbled around in the darkness, pushing the gear lever one way, and then the other, in order to free himself from its intimate advances. When at last he was ready, in the dim light he struggled to make out the area to aim for, and without the offer of a guiding hand from Penny, he could only make an educated stab at the right entrance. The first time he tried, his aim was deflected by a rip in the car seat.

As he prepared himself for another attempt, a sudden tap on

the window stopped him in his tracks. Instinctively, he mouthed the words, "What the fuck..." Then, thinking it might be the police checking up on what was going on inside the car, he began preparing his apologies for their state of undress. He reached across over the top of Penny to shield her from view and wound down the window.

Chapter 3

The woolly hat worn by the person staring back at them through the gloom proved his first assumption wrong. Not at all impressed by a complete stranger interrupting things at such a critical moment, Dave was curt and to the point, "Yes? You got a problem mate?"

The man bent down towards the open car window, and blinked repeatedly from behind his glasses. "You're supposed to leave the light on, you know!" replied the stranger in a nasal monotone.

"You what?" replied Dave.

"Leaving the car light on; how can we watch if you don't leave it on?"

"What do you mean *watch?* And who's *we* anyway?" asked Dave peering out into the darkness, thoroughly mystified by the stranger's line of conversation.

"Me and my mate over there with the binoculars." He pointed behind him towards some trees. "We saw you give us the sign for us to come and watch, then you went and switched the light off. That's not allowed you know, the rules of dogging clearly state that..."

"*Dogging?*" interrupted Dave. "What the hell are you talking about?"

"That's what you're doing here, isn't it? As I was saying, the dogger's official code of conduct states that when the interior light of a car is flashed on and off twice, then the occupants will allow any interested person or persons present to watch the action taking place inside the vehicle."

"Like hell you will!" said Dave. "We're not doggers and have no intention of letting you two pervs watch anything!"

"Come on Dave, let's just get out of here, we can go somewhere else," said Penny, hurriedly pulling up her leggings. Dave, his penis now as limp as the stranger's excuse for disturbing them, very much resented the enforced coitus interruptus and was not as yet ready to comply with her request – after all, an important principle was at stake here.

"So, what makes you think you have the right to go round spying on respectable people trying to have sex in a public car park, eh? You're just a fuckin' weirdo – and that goes for your mate too!" he shouted out to the man's accomplice, whom he assumed to be within earshot nearby.

The woolly-hatted man visibly bridled at Dave's criticism of his activities, "I'll have you know that dogging is a perfectly legitimate pastime. This particular car park is listed on all the internet dogging sites, and as well as its excellent picnic facilities, is rated four stars for the quality and frequency of the dogging activity carried out – that is until you two turned up. If you didn't want us to watch you having sex, then you shouldn't be going giving us signs to the contrary!"

Dave unexpectedly found himself on the defensive, "Well, obviously I wouldn't have done if I'd known that would I? Hang on! So you're telling me that Ironridge, as well as being part of a famous World Heritage site – so called because it is generally acknowledged as being the birthplace of industrialisation in Great Britain and the rest of the world – is also in the top slot for dogging activity, is it?"

"Yes! That's about it."

"Funny, I've never seen this amenity mentioned on any of Tealford and Reakin District Council's information on local attractions. Maybe I missed the tourist information sign on the way into the car park. Do they have a leaflet on it at the tourist office?"

"Is everything okay Baz?" came a lone voice from out of the bushes, "I could do with being a bit closer if I'm going to get the action on camera."

23

"*On camera!*" shouted Dave, now incredulous at the thought of having their intimate encounter recorded in a movie clip. Seeing the outline of a man equipped with a camcorder advancing towards them, Dave issued a robust greeting to him, "And you can fuck off too!"

"I recognise that voice!" replied the man. As he got closer to the car, his face broke into a grin when he saw Dave's outline. "What are you doing here?" Seeing their half-naked bodies entwined together he quickly added, "Well I can see what you are doing, but I didn't know you were into dogging Dave?"

"Christ! I don't believe it, Duggie of all people. And no for the last time, I'm not a dogger. I'm just having a few quiet moments in the car with my... er... ladyfriend here. But what about you, I thought you were supposed to be working tonight?"

"Oh, they cancelled the last part of my job. There's been a major points failure at Mapeley Junction, so I managed to finish early. I often have a walk down here with the dog in the evening. We don't half see some sights you know. Sometimes the couples let us join in."

"Surely not with the dog as well?" asked Dave, now getting altogether more curious about the activity.

"Oh no, nothing like that, Nipper's only allowed to watch."

"Excuse me!" came a voice from beneath Dave, "What's going on Dave? Do you know this pervert?" demanded Penny, still trying to rectify her state of undress.

"Penny, it's alright it's only Duggie, he's one of the train crew from work... Oh Duggie, this is Penny by the way."

Duggie nodded to her through the open car window. "Pleased to meet yer Penny, er... everything okay?"

"Yeah, really great. Whad'you think?"

Pushing Dave roughly aside, she drew herself up into the seat and folded her arms tightly across her chest. Dave noticed her granite-faced expression, "Don't be like that, Penny," he pleaded. "Duggie's okay, he's..."

"I don't give a toss who he is," snapped Penny as she rummaged around under her jumper trying to adjust her breasts back into position. "I've had enough of all this, you can keep your dogging mates. Just get out of my car, I'm going home!"

"She's a bit touchy, your er... ladyfriend," ventured Baz.

"Can you just stay out of this, eh?" ordered Dave. "Look, Penny, be reasonable, none of this was my doing you know."

"Do you really expect me to believe that? You've set all this up so they could watch us. You're just as bad as these two pervy mates of yours."

"No, only Duggie's a perv... I mean, a mate of mine."

"I really don't care!" said Penny, "You can keep your weirdo friends and your crap jokes as well – and to think I was going to have sex with you."

"But you still can Penny – you still can."

"Just get out of my car will you!"

"Look, there's no need to be like this, I honestly didn't plan any of this, please believe me!"

"I said *out!*"

"Please Penny!"

" *Now!*"

Dave could see in the dim light from Baz's torch the intensity of purpose in her eyes. He quickly realised she was serious.

"Alright, alright, okay, I'm going!" He hastily zipped up his trousers and scrambled out of the car, failing to notice that the loose end of the condom was still hanging out through his trousers.

Dave decided to make one last effort to redeem the situation so held on to her door whilst explaining, once again, that he really had no idea this was a dogging site and honestly hadn't planned for them to have sex in front of an audience – nor for it to be recorded on camera.

Penny was having none of it, so Dave made one final plea, "Can I give you a ring in a day or two when you've calmed down a bit?"

"Fuck off!"

With that she slammed the car door to, and in so doing,

trapped the loose end of Dave's drooping condom. As she revved the engine and accelerated away, the rubber gripped his penis like a noose, yanking his foreskin through the trouser zip. Dave let out a mighty howl as the metal teeth bit into his exposed member. The rubber – instantly stretched beyond its critical failure point – then snapped and shot back to hit Dave in a double blow to his manhood. As he dropped to his knees, Baz, watching it all happen, winced and turned away.

"Christ my cock!" Dave wailed as the pain hit him. Cupping his crotch in his hands, he performed a rabid dance to try and relieve the agony.

"Jesus it hurts... I daren't look... Duggie, you take a look at it will you... is it still there? Is it all right?"

Borrowing Baz's torch to throw some light on the injured member, Duggie bent down to make an inspection.

"Well... it's not a pretty sight – but then I never saw what it was like before!"

"You're no fucking help, are you?" said Dave, still cursing. He staggered around, the pain lessening only slightly. Summoning up the courage to look for himself, he half expected his penis to be awash with blood. He was relieved to find very little – just some angry red weals where the metal zip had bitten into his penis, surrounded by a ring of ruptured rubber from the torn condom. His foreskin though was still caught between the teeth of his zip. After a few minutes of trying to free it, he gave it up as too painful a process. He was just wondering what to do next when the headlights of a car turning into the car park illuminated the grotesque scene.

Dave groaned out loud when he saw the blue strobe light on the roof flash several times as it slowed. The police car halted directly in front of them and two officers stepped out.

It was a moment before either of them spoke, both trying to make sense of the bizarre scene they were confronted with. Keeping both hands cupped over his injured penis, Dave decided to jump in first with a general inquiry.

"Er… evening gents, er… is there a problem at all?"

The first officer, with his eyes fixed firmly on Dave, and obviously wondering why his hands were shielding his groin area, answered.

"That's just what we're here to find out. There's been a report of loud screams coming from the area, so we were sent to investigate..." His gaze shifted to Dave's groin, "…to see what's going on."

He turned to take in the figures of Baz in a woolly hat, and Duggie in a long raincoat – his clumsy attempt to conceal the camcorder thwarted by the second officer who held it up to show his colleague. The first officer nodded his acknowledgement and turned back to Dave. Looking at the situation from the policeman's perspective, Dave could just imagine the sort of activities he suspected them of being engaged in, so felt at least some relief that Duggie had chosen not to bring his dog along. The officer asked the obvious question, "So what exactly is going on here then?"

Dave, his mouth now as dry as the Gobi Desert, and still in pain from being physically attached to his zip, felt utterly wretched. He could not believe how an evening which had promised so much could end in such embarrassing circumstances. But how could he explain to the policeman what had really happened? He could hardly believe it himself. Dave resigned himself to his fate. Honesty would have to be the best policy in this instance. "Well officer, it was like this…"

He was two thirds of the way through his explanation when the officer held up his hand and said, "Look, can I stop you there? I don't need – or necessarily want to know – all the detail; too much information as they say. What you three adult men get up to in private is your own business..."

Dave realised that the policeman had completely dismissed his tale of woe with the now-absent Penny.

"…What I am concerned about, is that whatever it was you were doing, you were doing it in a public car park. Judging by the screams, it must have been something very painful. God knows what pleasure you people get out of this sort of thing!"

The officer shook his head and sighed, as if all too weary of having to deal with some of the sordid situations he was called out to.

Dave tried desperately to explain once again the true circumstances of what had happened. At the end the officer still looked sceptical but said, "I'd better just take a look then."

Putting aside his embarrassment at having to once again present his manhood for inspection, Dave removed his hands to allow the policeman to look at his injury.

"Has it always been that shape?" the officer asked before calling his colleague over for a second opinion. Already feeling utterly humiliated by the experience, Dave stated in defence of his organ that apart from the immediate injury, he had never had any problems with its shape – and only a few minor complaints about its performance.

The officer's attitude noticeably softened when the state of Dave's penis bore out his story and he realised the discomfort Dave was in.

"Do you want me to call for an ambulance then?" he was asked.

"God no!" replied Dave, he just wanted to go home, providing that the officer would allow him to; he still wasn't sure whether he had committed any sort of arrestable offence. There was no way he was going to expose his predicament for the amusement of paramedics, doctors, nurses, porters, cleaners and any other non-essential workers who just happened to be passing by the treatment room. He'd endured enough humiliation for one night. He would sort himself out somehow when he got home.

"Okay then," said the officer, "I'll tell you what I'm prepared to do. We'll take your names and addresses and get you all checked out..."

He nodded to his colleague who started taking down the details, "...then providing you are all who you say you are, you'll be free to go..."

Breathing a sigh of relief, Dave was about to thank the officer.

"...All except *you,* that is!"

Dave began to protest. The policeman cut him off, "Look, we can't have you walking the streets in that state, can we? You could get yourself arrested!"

Yes, very funny, thought Dave – *very funny.*

"Just keep yourself covered up and we'll give you a lift to the taxi rank. Now then, what's your name?"

"The name's Bland, David Bland."

After receiving a stern lecture about the risks of having sex in public places, the officer dropped him off by a single waiting taxi with the warning, "Don't let me see you here again!"

The taxi driver quickly put away his newspaper, and after expressing surprise at seeing Dave's awkward crouched stance, was keen to find out the reason for his predicament. Dave, though, was not at all inclined to discuss the matter. This did not prevent the driver from speculating on the possible causes.

"Cos we get a few doggers around here you know, comin' n' goin'. Well they would be wouldn't they, eh?" He laughed several times on the strength of his own off-the-cuff wit.

"Yes I get a bit of business one way and another – a bit like doggin' really, eh? One way and then another!" The taxi driver laughed again.

"Mind, I've never had a fare holding onto his crotch like you – you've not been sticking it anywhere you shouldn't, 'ave you?"

The laughter erupted once more. Dave sighed loudly several times hoping that the driver would take the hint. He didn't know which was worse: the pain from his penis, or the pain from the taxi driver's inane comments, followed each time by an outburst of irritating laughter. Dave was determined not to be drawn into providing any explanation about his condition – he'd had enough probing for one evening.

It was with some relief when Dave arrived at his house. Paying his fare to the precise penny, he swung his feet out – and conscious of the driver watching his every move through his rear-view mirror – carefully extricated himself from the taxi. By taking very small steps up to his front door, Dave found he could alleviate most of the discomfort.

He'd already worked out a way to free himself. Inside the house, the first thing he required was some anaesthetic. Taking the whisky bottle from the kitchen cupboard, he poured himself a large measure and gulped it down quickly in several swallows, hoping to rapidly dull all feeling. With a bag of frozen peas, he fashioned a hole through the middle approximately the right diameter and carefully placed the punctured bag over his manhood. He reckoned the peas should still be edible afterwards, as long as they didn't thaw too much during the procedure.

As the numbness started to take hold, Dave considered the need for something to bite on to help endure the pain. He tried gripping the handle of a wooden spoon between his teeth, but realised it could easily splinter and cause as much pain as the injury he was trying to alleviate, so dismissed the gesture as being overly dramatic.

When his groin was as cold as he could tolerate, he grasped the zipper, closed his eyes and pulled down sharply – cursing out loud as the pain shot through him. He danced around the floor to try and ease it. Cradling his penis in his hand, he peered down at it to examine the damage. Apart from one or two drips of blood where the zipper had dug into his flesh, he was relieved to find that it all looked okay.

He now needed to dress the wound. Some kitchen towel secured in place with an elastic band would be ideal, but then he recalled that a similar method of constriction was used to dock animal's tails. To minimise any risk to his own appendage, he tested the elasticity of a few first; mainly ex-Royal Mail ones he'd retrieved off the driveway and saved for just such a situation.

Two were found to be just right, having enough tension to make the cocoon of tissue a snug fit around his manhood without restricting the blood flow to his organ. Dave tried a few tentative paces up and down the kitchen to test the cushioning effect of the kitchen towel. Satisfied that he was now as comfortable as he could make himself, he returned the thawing peas to the freezer. To alleviate any post-operative twinges later, he decided to treat himself to another slug of whiskey.

Feeling suddenly weary after the evening's extraordinary events, he decided to forego his planned viewing of the epic war film, *The Longest Day* just starting on TV; his own day had been long enough already. Taking it a step at a time, he made a slow ascent of the stairs, any feelings of discomfort being eased by the generous intake of alcohol.

It was while lying in bed a short time later that he began to feel pained – as he brought to mind all the derogatory comments made about his penis during the course of the evening.

Chapter 4

Dave had a fitful night's sleep once the effects of the whisky had worn off, waking up repeatedly from either the dull pain in his loins, or through reliving the calamitous events of the previous night. He gave up the struggle in the early morning and eased himself out of bed to make a cup of coffee and to take a much-needed pee. Sensing that his bladder ought to be given priority, he headed for the toilet whilst the kettle boiled, being careful to lift his penis very delicately over the top of his Y-fronts. Although still sore down below, he was optimistic there would be no permanent damage to his manhood.

Heading back to the kitchen, he made a mug of his favourite premium instant and turned on his computer, eager to see if there were any emails for him.

Dave had signed up with Dates for U on a special six month offer. In order to get his money's worth out of the dating service, Dave had spent many hours trawling through their database looking for suitable partners. To his great surprise, he found himself literally spoilt for choice.

Not quite knowing where to start, he had decided to adopt a logical approach and initially selected ladies whose requirements matched, as near as possible, his own. He then determined how far he was willing to travel for a date. What complicated the process for him was that he was entitled to free travel on Mercia Mainline's network. This meant he could range over areas of the country without it costing him a penny; an important consideration now that he was saddled with a hefty mortgage.

He realised he needed to be brutal so had narrowed the list

down to 120 or so, then considered how best to approach them. Composing individual emails to each of them seemed out of the question due to the amount of work involved. Instead, a standard missive expressing a general interest but without going into too much detail, seemed to offer the best solution.

After several attempts at trying to strike the right balance between friendly interest and cool nonchalance, he was eventually satisfied with the result. Adding the individual's client number to each one, he sent out his 'email shot' and waited.

The results were not quite what he had hoped for. Out of 131 actually sent, only twenty replied. Of these, he eventually arranged to meet fourteen, though only seven of them actually turned up at his favoured meeting place.

Apart from Penny, the only other person to show interest in him was Daphne, a druid from Dudley. Mistaking his polite patience for interest, she'd contacted him on several occasions during the past few weeks, each time revealing another interminably long episode of her life history. Her most recent call ended with the 'ultimate revelation' of how she believed herself to be the reincarnation of an Aztec god. Final confirmation that this was a person best avoided came when she asked if he was free to attend one of her group's sacrificial blood-letting ceremonies the following week.

Dave was disappointed that females of the more normal variety hadn't taken the initiative and approached him. He decided to take another look at his profile and the photograph he'd uploaded with it.

The problem with the one he'd used was that to remove his ex-wife from it, he'd been forced to cut the holiday snap down the middle and scan his half into the computer. Not only had it left him with virtually no right shoulder but had, unfortunately, left him with an extra hand resting on his hip – complete with handbag. It looked obvious to him that the hand belonged to the female formerly by his side, but with hindsight conceded it might look misleading to anybody taking a cursory glance and send out the wrong message about his inclinations.

Dave had thought it strange when in another email he'd received, the lady in question had asked about what skincare products he used, and then 'knowing it must be difficult for you,' as she put it, had offered to take him clothes shopping. Perhaps he should have taken her up on the offer if she was equally skilled at choosing men's clothing.

His clothes certainly needed updating. Dave remembered a derogatory comment his wife had made about him shortly before they'd parted. In withering tones she'd asked, 'Why do you buy such crap? Look at you! Shiny nylon trousers and a South Korean shirt too short to meet them! You're the original Primart Man.'

He assumed she meant the comment as an insult; as for being total crap, he had to disagree. Dave recalled how readily the synthetic fibres had burnt the day she made a bonfire of them on the lawn – it being her own idiosyncratic way of ending an argument.

Faced with the unexpected loss of these garments, he had been quite relieved at having paid so little for them in the first place, though the pyre of molten nylon did ruin the effects of the Growwell he'd applied to the lawn the previous day.

She may well have provided him with the answer he told himself. He needed to go upmarket – dress to impress as they say. Dave removed his glasses to clean off the smudges from the buttered toast he'd inadvertently smeared on them. As he rubbed, he reflected on how they too really needed replacing. The persistent green tinges of mould, now well-entrenched in the soft plastic and against which he'd fought many a battle to eliminate, had started to spread up into the frames, giving him a distinctly sickly look when viewed through the unforgiving eye of a camera lens.

Glasses, especially the varifocals he wore, were expensive items to replace. He did recall winning a temporary victory one day when he accidentally knocked them off his face into the toilet pan during his weekly house cleaning routine, and much to his surprise, cleaned up rather well after a rinse. A regular application of household bleach may just be the way to salvage them, he decided.

Dave realised he also needed to take another look at his profile.

Injecting a bit more humour into the content might improve his appeal. It was well known that ladies were attracted to men who made them laugh. Unfortunately, he was not one for remembering, or telling jokes as such; he could never seem to get the timing right. No, he considered himself to be witty rather than funny; the problem was getting the women he was interested in to think the same.

It might improve his chances if he were more outgoing – flamboyant even, like those arty types he'd read about in the pull-out section of the Sunday newspapers. They seemed to have no trouble attracting women. Being an author, poet or painter seemed to almost guarantee success with the female sex. Unfortunately, he never had much of an artistic bent: too much logic and too little imagination – according to his ex. Instead of presenting a vibrant and colourful image to the ladies, he was more the black and white still life that rarely gets noticed; the one found leaning against the wall at a party – and when did he last get invited to a party?

Still feeling tender, like John Wayne after a day in the saddle, Dave sensed that his nether regions were not up to the rigors of being jostled about on a swaying train for a day or two, so thought he'd better ring in and report sick. It was Mick Halliwell, the train crew manager, who answered.

"Yes Dave, what can I do you for?"

"I just want to report sick. I was supposed to be booking on at 14.30 today."

"Er… okay Dave, I'll get your job covered for you. Do you know how long you'll be off?"

"Just a couple of days hopefully; shouldn't be any longer than that I wouldn't have thought."

"No problem, so what's wrong with you then, if you don't mind me asking?"

"I'd rather not say."

"Okay then, I'll sort it m'cock."

"What did you say?"

"I said I'll sort it."

"No, you said I'll sort it *m'cock*." insisted Dave, now growing suspicious. "You've never used that expression before!"

"It's just something you say isn't it? Like mate, or pal. I jus' said m'cock instead."

Dave could now hear laughing in the background.

"He's told you, hasn't he?"

"Who's told me what?"

"You know what! That bastard Duggie's gone and told you, hasn't he?"

The laughing in the background became louder.

"Look Dave, you know I wouldn't listen to any *cock* and bull stories from Duggie. Mind I know he is a bit *fly*, you want to tell him to *zip* it!" Mick could contain himself no longer and erupted with laughter. "I tell you Dave, I've never heard anything so funny in my life!"

"Well I'm glad you all find it so fuckin' amusing! I'll murder that Duggie when I see him next." Not wishing to prolong his embarrassment, Dave cut the conversation short. "I'll phone you when I'm ready to come back to work!"

"From what I've heard Dave, you won't be in a fit state to *come*, for a good while yet!"

More peals of laughter resonated from the audience assembled around the phone at the other end. With an abrupt goodbye, he terminated the call.

Now irked by the further embarrassment of the whole depot knowing about the previous evening, he decided another cup of strong coffee was called for. Dave heard the post drop onto the mat as he headed for the kitchen, so diverted through the hall to take a look. Shuffling the envelopes, he noticed there was another mail shot from Sarga.

How did they get hold of my details, he wondered? As soon as he turned fifty, they'd bombarded him with junk mail; pushing everything from elasticated comfort-fit trousers to electric recliner chairs.

The rest of their product range conjured up a more depressing picture. It seemed that all he could look forward to with certainty in his advancing years was declining mobility, together with increasing incontinence. It made for a worrying combination with many an accident just waiting to happen. He was glad now that the house had both an upstairs and a downstairs toilet, especially as it seemed that Sarga's predictions appeared to be eerily prophetic. In the last couple of years, his need to urinate often interrupted the last hour or so of his sleep.

The next envelope was plain brown with no indication as to its contents. On opening it, to his surprise it contained a brochure advertising a varied selection of porn: everything from naughty nurses to Bangkok lady boys, all pixelated in the appropriate places. He had to think for a moment why he had received it. It must be as a result of him sending off to a traditional Dutch mail order company for some adult DVDs to keep him entertained during his evenings spent alone. He'd reasoned that *Hot Asian Babes* would not be a title available for hire at his local Blockbusters.

His details must have been added to the company's mailing list in order to solicit repeat sales. It suddenly struck him that Sarga were missing a trick here. There could be a potentially huge market in selling sex to the pre-pensioner population. By promoting quality porn in their mail shots, they could easily benefit from increased sales of other related products too.

Flicking through their brochure, Dave identified a few possibilities: the flexible wrist support with Velcro fasteners would certainly be in demand from the widower or single gentleman. For couples, the all-in-one unisex lycra/winceyette-mix body corset with magnetic inserts would be a real help in supporting an arthritic back in full thrust. And those suction-cap grab-handles, not only useful for getting in and out of the bath, but when fixed to the headboard of a bed, could provide valuable support in a wide range of sexual positions.

Dave briefly wondered whether he should send Sarga an email outlining his suggestions.

The last piece of post was one he recognised; he'd received the same reminder letter several times previously. Dave opened it:

'*Our records show...*' it announced. This time the TV license people were threatening to pay him a visit in person if he didn't buy a license – with the added threat of up to a £1000 fine. He screwed it up and threw it in the bin.

Having lived in the house for over a year, he'd received several of these, all similar in nature without ever receiving a knock at the door. Besides, he reasoned, how many of the burgeoning underclass – which he met all too frequently in his job – would bother to buy a TV license when they were unwilling to tax, insure, or even register their cars. No doubt other taxes dutifully paid by him and other good citizens to provide their benefit payments, were also avoided by these same people. With such a vast number of defaulters to choose from, he calculated that there would only be the remotest chance that the authorities would choose to pay him a call.

With the post now sorted and binned, Dave sat down at his computer again to deal with the business in hand. There were just three emails of any consequence: one from his estranged wife; another from Rob, an old friend who had stayed loyal despite all the slagging-off his ex had done at the time of their break-up; and one from Dates for U.

Eagerly opening the last one first, he was surprised to see that it originated in Russia; from one Galina Troski. Surely not a descendant of the famous – no it couldn't be. Anyway he'd voted UKIP at the last election, so didn't see himself having much in common with her if it was. He was sure the name was spelt differently too. The message was short and to the point:

Dear Dave,

> *Have looked at your photo and like it very much. In profile, you sound like a good, kind man. Maybe I could have feelings for such a person. I like England very much and have been told Englishman make good husbands. I had good husband once. But he is now dead. I was very sad for long time. I still keep his gun under my pillow as keepsake. Now some time has gone by, I want*

to make new life for myself, so I send you photo. Maybe you like me too also.

Your friend Galina

Dave clicked on the photo of Galina attached to the message. It showed a heavily made-up blonde leaning over the bonnet of a black Mercedes, her hands swathed in jewellery. Not unattractive, though, at all; she had an eighties look about her – sort of a late-model Bonnie Tyler.

As flattered as he was, he couldn't contemplate conducting a relationship with what appeared to be an ex-Russian Mafia gangster's widow. Although he realised Great Britain was the first choice for many a would-be immigrant seeking a better life, why had she picked on him? Perhaps she had adopted the same strategy as him and was sending the same message to every suitable Englishman on the website.

Nevertheless, rather than just ignore the message, he decided to let her down gently with a polite refusal.

Dear Galina,

Thank you for your email and your kind remarks. Your photo very nice too – he found himself lapsing into the same vernacular – *I have also been married, but my ex-wife still very much alive unfortunately, I feel the distance between us would be a major problem in conducting a relationship. I've checked my Collins World Atlas, and if we wanted to meet for a drink say, the halfway point would be Lodz, in Poland. The thing is, Redditch would normally be my limit of travel in your direction.*

I hope you understand, and I thank you once again for your interest.

Regards

Dave

Dave felt satisfied with the result. Not too blunt, but conveying a clear message that he was not interested. He clicked send. Reluctant as he was to read the contents of his ex's email, he felt he needed to know the worst.

Hi,

I took the car in for an MOT and service today. They said it needed a new Cambelt. Graham at work said they often need replacing at this sort of mileage. You'll have to send me some money towards it; I'm cleaned out after paying the balance on my holiday. Graham also says you really should be giving me an allowance each month – at least until we get the divorce finalised. He said something like £250. I didn't think that was unreasonable, do you?

I'm sure you wouldn't want me to take you to court over it!

Reply soonest.

Jane

More demands for money! And who was this bloody Graham? She'd never mentioned him before. And why was she still running a second car? He could barely afford to run one. Dave instantly dismissed the idea of sending her anything.

He turned to other matters of the day. Getting his car back from the car park in Ironridge was the first priority, so he checked the bus timetable for a convenient departure time.

Two hours later, he had the vehicle back on his driveway and was scrambling underneath to examine it. After poking at the exhaust with a screwdriver and receiving a face full of rust for his trouble, Dave decided to accept the inevitable and get the garage to replace it. He made the phone call to book it in.

The rest of the day was spent in his shed making a few minor alterations to his invention. The following Monday he would be delivering a presentation of the multi-purpose workbench to the

West Mercia Inventors Club. Meetings were only held once a month and he wanted to ensure that the demonstration would be of a sufficiently high standard to impress his peers.

For his evening meal, Dave had thawed out a plate of chilli, one of the dishes he prepared in large quantity before dividing up into daily portions – this particular one being allocated for Wednesday. He settled down with his meal to watch TV, trying out a new wine from KostKwik as he ate. It was described as 'Oak aged Rioja,' from their new gourmet range. He unscrewed the plastic cap, poured himself a glass, and took a gulp.

Scanning through the television guide, once he'd eliminated all the makeover, reality and TV talent shows, there was really nothing else that took his interest. He contemplated watching one of his adult DVDs just to check his reaction to stimulus was intact, but was wary of doing so in case the expected response should prove painful.

After another glass of KostKwik's finest, he decided to risk it anyway. He recalled seeing the preamble up to the point where the gardener, with his hose poised, catches the lone housewife sunbathing naked in her garden – then promptly fell asleep.

Awakened by loud banging at the door, Dave forced himself out of his seat and had the presence of mind to switch the TV over to a terrestrial channel before answering it. The episode that followed, he related later that evening in his email to Rob.

Rob

Well here's the email I promised you. I had rather an eventful time this evening. Had a visit from a man who stated he was from the TV licensing dept. As they did not have any record of me having a valid TV licence for this address, it seems I am committing an offence by watching the TV without one. So I had a rummage through my paperwork and found one from my previous address which the man closely inspected. He then declared, "This is last years and out of date."

So, quick as a flash I replied, 'So are most of the programmes.'

He did not appear to appreciate this vintage joke though, so I went to offer a range of excuses – as you do, very sorry and all that.

Anyway, the upshot of it was that to avoid any possible prosecution, I needed to purchase one there and then. Well what could I do? I had to give him my bank details. I suppose it beats queuing in the Post Office – and I'd got away with it for twelve months. I reckon I'll just make the one licence payment and then cancel the direct debit. I can always blame the bank for making a cock-up if there's any comeback. Honestly, out of all the people there must be without a licence, they had to come and pick on me.

Really, I don't know what the world is coming to when you cannot sit in the comfort of your own home enjoying some porn, without being disturbed by some little jobsworth demanding I pay an extortionate amount for a service I barely use. I told him this licence fee is a complete rip-off for people like me. When was the last time they showed some Bangkok Babe action on TV? So much for the BBC supposedly catering for all tastes and ethnic groups!

Then to cap it all, about half an hour later there was another knock at the door. I thought Christ, he's changed his mind and come back to nick me. So I tentatively opened it a bit, and it turns out to be two snotty little kids with their hands out demanding 'Trick or Treat.' I'd forgotten it was Halloween and I told them to sod off – the little scroats were getting nothing from me. They were obviously amateurs at this sort of extortion because when I checked my car later, they'd made no attempt to trash it.

Anyway Rob, that was my evening. Life seems a little fraught at the moment. Hopefully things will get better. I hope all is well for you and your family. We'll have to get together sometime soon for a drink. Just let me know when is convenient.

Regards

Dave

He went to bed, his mind again mulling over another extraordinary series of events.

The dream seemed so real. He was handcuffed to the bed and the woman standing over him was naked except for a Halloween mask. She had a strong Russian accent and was demanding to know where he had hidden the TV. The woman began to wave a piece of paper at him, threatening him with unspeakable treatment in the gulags if he did not confess. It was then that Dave woke up. Now hot and sweaty, his hands clutched his groin area. Damn! He needed to pee again.

Chapter 5

Two days later, and feeling a lot easier in the nether regions, Dave decided to return to work. All through the thirty minute journey into Wensbury, his thoughts were on the ribbing he was likely to receive from his workmates. They would be aware of all the circumstances by now, so he knew he was in for a hard time. He paused outside the door of the crew room to mentally prepare himself.

As predicted, he was bombarded by a barrage of lewd greetings as soon as he stepped through the doorway. Trying to make himself heard above the noise, he sought to play down the affair, insisting to anyone who would listen that the whole incident had been greatly exaggerated.

Inevitably, his mates wanted to know all the details. Dave knew he would get no peace if he refused so, to dispel some of the wilder claims being bandied about, he set about revealing what actually happened. He denied being arrested by the police, and attempted to correct the popular belief that it had been his penis and not the end of the condom caught in the car door. Despite all his denials, several of his colleagues were still insisting their more colourful version of events was the correct one; the ladies in the accounts office upstairs had heard the exact same thing, said one of them. The latest rumour being that Big Betty in the payroll section was willing to kiss it better for him if it was still painful. This new revelation sparked off a further round of taunts from his colleagues.

One of them, curious to know whether Big Betty's concerns were justified, suggested a simple way to find out. Dave though, was not the least bit inclined to allow an inspection of his injury, nor was he willing to test Big Betty's unique powers of healing – he'd suffered more than enough ridicule for one day.

Despite all the barracking, he could not help but be amused by some of the choice comments made about him. Dave realised he would just have to get used to his newly-acquired nickname of 'Twang' for a while. There was little he could do about it, and at least it had gone someway to disavow him of his 'Bland by name, Bland by nature,' persona.

The incident had, in a perverse sort of way, given his self-esteem a much needed fillip. Although aged fifty-two, he'd shown that he was still capable of some laddish behaviour – getting up to the sort of shenanigans a man half his age would be only too happy to admit to.

With all the barracking dying down, and with just fifteen minutes before his train was due to depart, Dave set about preparing his ticket machine and checking his float. Stepping out of the door in time for his train's departure, he was helped on his way by a final round of lewd taunts from his colleagues.

As he walked down the platform, the station announcer interrupted the permanent hiss from the tannoy with the message,

"Mercia Mainline would like to apologise for the delay to their 14.20 service to Manchester. This is due to stubborn geese on the line in the Tipton area."

The first part of his journey to Kenilworth went smoothly enough. With an average of only three minutes between stations, little time was left for checking and selling tickets.

Just before Birmingham International – the station for the NEC and Birmingham Airport – Dave was suddenly aware of the smell of cannabis smoke coming under the vestibule door. He regarded the taking of such a liberty on his train as a direct challenge to his authority, so moved swiftly to open the door through to the train in order to seek out the culprit, hoping that his well-tuned nose would lead him to the offender.

Unfortunately, there was now no indication of who had been

smoking it, and the smell was beginning to dissipate. Dave decided that discreet enquiries would have to be made in order to locate the perpetrator.

"Right, which drug-dependant cretin has been smoking a joint on *my* train?" he bellowed as he walked through the carriage. The passengers remained silent, their guarded faces giving nothing away as he walked up the aisle looking at each one in turn. There had to be witnesses. It would be impossible to light up a spliff on a busy non-smoking train without the people close by knowing about it, though he knew it was unlikely anybody would volunteer the information; the instinct of the public generally was not to get involved.

From experience, he knew he could probably dismiss anybody over forty, children – those up to the age of eleven anyway – and single females. His eyes focused on a youth aged about nineteen and his girlfriend. The shell-suited youth was engaged in whispering asides to her and laughing like an asthmatic hyena after each one. To Dave's prejudiced eye, he fitted the profile and behaviour of a typical cannabis smoker. He looked down at the youth's feet to see if there was any incriminating ash, as indeed there was.

"Can I see your ticket please?"

The youth ignored him. Dave patiently repeated the question, this time louder and a lot closer to his right ear.

"Alright! I can fuckin' 'ear you."

"Well where's your ticket then?"

He slowly turned towards Dave and pushed his matching cap to the back of his head.

"I ain't got one!"

"You'll have to buy one then. It's an offence to travel without a ticket."

"Got no money!" Turning back to his girlfriend, he laughed Mutley like in her direction.

Trying not to show his irritation Dave asked, "Where were you going to?"

"What's it to you?"

"Everything! This is my train, and I ask the questions. You'll have to get off if you refuse to buy one!"

"Fuck off! I'm going nowhere!"

"That's right, got it in one. We're leaving you on the platform at the next stop!"

"Ha! Ha! Just piss off, will yer. What a twat!" he said in another aside to his female companion.

Dave could feel his patience rapidly depleting.

"Now look here! You don't have a ticket, you're refusing to buy one, and you're being abusive to me in front of all these good people. I can tell you this train is going nowhere with you on it – and you can take your feet off the seat while you're at it!"

The youth erupted, "Why don't yer just fuck off and leave me alone eh? Or d'yer want yur fuckin' 'ead cavin' in!" He screwed his face up into a mask of aggression as he spat the words out.

At this juncture, Dave thought it worth taking a moment to assess the threat posed by him. Looking him up and down, he reassured himself that the youth was indeed as skinny and short as he appeared to be.

"Any other hobbies?"

"Yer what?"

"I said, what other activities do you enjoy besides cavin' peoples heads in? Filling in colour-by-number books perhaps, or trying to fit those different-shaped plastic blocks into their respective matching holes – always a tricky exercise, eh? Maybe that's a little too advanced for you!"

"You takin' the piss?"

"Nothing gets past you, does it?"

He wasn't looking for a fight, but experience had taught him that if a 'customer' was going to become violent, they would have done so by now. Having gained the psychological advantage over the youth, Dave was rather enjoying himself.

"Anyway, we ain't gettin' off," the youth reiterated, backing off from outright aggression and bringing the female sat next to him into the dispute.

"Fine, if you won't get off voluntarily, then I'll get the police to do it forcibly."

"Oh yeah! And where you suddenly goin' to find them from? You can't do fuck all an' you know it."

Now, what the youth said was normally true. When train crew did have problems with passengers and needed a swift response from the authorities, often as not it would be on some remote suburban line late at night with the nearest police unit often miles away. As a consequence, train managers often chose to ignore breaches of the regulations by troublesome passengers. But Dave was determined that this was not going to be one of those times.

When the train pulled into Birmingham International, Dave exited the cab and sought out one of the platform staff to make an urgent request. He returned to the train and proceeded to explain a few facts to the offender.

"Now, I'll just list the offences you've committed so far. You're travelling without a ticket and refuse to buy one. As well as using abusive language, you've been smoking illegal substances too. Last but not least, you've threatened me with unspeakable acts. We're at Birmingham International now. Because of the airport, armed police are constantly on patrol here. As security is so tight, very little happens in the way of petty crime so the police literally fall over themselves to help out when they get a call from someone like me, asking them to come and make an easy arrest of a scroat like you.

I'm sure they'll be able to find a nice cell for you to stew in whilst they process the charges and any others they can find, after you've been strip-searched and had the rubber glove treatment – understand?"

Nothing wrong with laying it on a bit thick, Dave thought. The youth looked at him blankly as if beyond his comprehension that he was going to be held responsible for his actions and behaviour. His girlfriend glared across at him and nudged his elbow. She wanted to get off the train now, if it wasn't too late.

Unfortunately for them, it was. At that moment, two armed

constables stepped into the carriage. Dave outlined the situation to them and repeated the charges against the youth. One officer asked some preliminary questions before cautioning him. Still protesting his innocence, the youth was led away, his girlfriend trailing lamely behind.

Allowing himself a smile of satisfaction, Dave ticked the air and murmured, "One to me, I think." He reported the delay to control and the reasons for it, before resuming his duties with renewed enthusiasm, promising to open another bottle of that KostKwik Rioja when he got home. Winning a rare victory in the battle against anti-social behaviour – perpetrated by foul-mouthed youths with annoying laughs – was a cause for celebration.

On reporting for work the following day, he expected the call asking him to report to his manager's office. Eric Vines was a short, officious man, who walked with a stiff gait due to circulation problems in his leg. Inevitably he was given the tag, 'Varicose Vines.'

"Yes, yes, I know all about the incident yesterday, I read your report and it seems to cover everything so well done, you handled the situation well. No, it's not about that, I've received a complaint actually."

Dave wondered what it could be about, he hadn't been abusive or threatened any passengers – well not recently, anyway. Neither had he hit anyone, even though he was sorely tempted to yesterday. His manager explained.

"What it is, two schoolteachers and three assistants were conducting a party of children around Curzon St Station yesterday – some sort of school field trip apparently. While crossing over from one platform to the other using the over-bridge, they – that is the children and adults – were watching a train come in and saw, I'll just quote from the report here, 'A man in the rear cab of the train pull down his trouser zip and expose his penis.'

Dave was conscious of the fact that his face had suddenly gone bright red. It could only have been him, but he wasn't flashing – well not deliberately, anyway.

It was at the very end of his shift. His Y-fronts had been chafing him all day, and he desperately needed to adjust himself before he made the long walk back up to the crew room. While it was to hand, so to speak, he decided to get it out and check on his injury. He knew that the cab windows were too high for him to be seen from the platform, but never imagined anyone would see him from the over-bridge. Of course! It had glass sides with a direct view over the tracks. How stupid of him, though it was a thousand to one chance that he would have been seen. The odds seemed to be stacked against him again. But what could he say? No one would believe his excuse.

"Now the complainants are quite certain that it was one of our trains, and we've narrowed it down to possibly three or four services. Having checked on the timings, it appears yours is one of them." Eric looked up from the report to give him an interrogative stare.

Dave quickly spotted a flaw. "How did they know this chap – whoever he is – was flashing his er... penis. They must have very good eyesight from where they were standing."

"Well, it seems one of the children had brought along a pair of toy binoculars so they were borrowed for a better look."
"The person could still have made a mistake," Dave suggested.

"Ah!" said Eric, checking the report again, "It seems all five of the ladies took turns with the binoculars and confirmed the details."

"Really! Did they give a description at all?"

"What do you want to know, a penis is a penis isn't it? Though not any great size by all accounts," replied Eric.

Dave blinked quickly a few times. "No Eric, I meant a description of the person."

"Yes of course. It's very vague though. Apparently he was looking down at the time, checking his watch. One detail they did recall is that he was going bald; they could see the reflection off the back of his head."

Dave had an urgent desire to scratch his, but Eric was again staring pointedly at him so he made a conscious effort to keep his hands still. It was looking bad for him; he could see he was going to have to bluff this one out.

"Well it could be anybody; every other person has a shaved head nowadays."

"Hmm, that may be so… look Dave, I know you've had a few problems recently, what with one thing or another."

"What do you mean?"

"Well you know, I understand your marriage has broken down, and I also heard about a little incident you and Duggie had a few days ago. Is there anything you want to tell me about?"

"Look, what happened the other night was all just a misunderstanding, that's all."

"I know, it's none of my business. To tell you the truth, I don't really want to know who the person was responsible for exposing themselves yesterday. For all I care, you can all walk round with your cocks hanging out – as long as you don't do it during the company's time! But I have to be seen to be doing something. For all I know, this person might have a perfectly innocent explanation for it."

"I ha... I'm sure they have."

Eric, seeming not to notice the comment, continued, "All I'm saying, Dave, is that this person – whoever it is – needs to get themselves straightened out, if you understand my drift?"

Eric gave him another long, penetrating stare.

"The railway industry gets a bad enough press as it is without a story like this leaking out. I don't know, the world seems to have gone sex-mad. I never had the time – or the energy – for any malarkey like this, what with having to bring up six kids."

His gaze became wistful and more distant, as if looking back to a time he had more understanding of.

"What we don't want is a repeat of the episode we had last year with Colin Philpot!"

Dave remembered the incident well. In fact, it was the talk of the depot for weeks. Colin was a driver, and his colleagues had started to notice that occasionally when passing him in the other direction, they were given a fleeting glimpse of what appeared to be someone in the cab with him – which was strictly against the regulations. This figure would appear at random, and then disappear just as mysteriously. His fellow drivers were intrigued and despite much ribbing and questioning, Colin refused to offer any sort of explanation.

Inevitably, word got back to his manager who, alarmed at the apparent breach of rules, lay in wait for him one day at a station on his route, and was taken aback to discover that it was in fact a blow-up doll sitting coyly in the other cab seat.

Colin, when made to account for his behaviour was quite unabashed. He explained that the doll was company for him as it got quite lonely driving a train for hour after hour. When told in no uncertain terms that he would have to forego the company of 'Katie,' as he called her, he refused to comply and said there was nothing in the rulebook which prevented him from continuing the arrangement. Furthermore, he requested that Katie be issued a company uniform so that 'Katie would not look out of place,' as he put it. The management – by this time it had gone to the human resources director – were nonplussed, and scoured the rulebook for a clause to discipline him with.

Carrying an unauthorized passenger in the cab was thrown out, as Katie was not a living person. Similarly, as Katie could neither walk nor talk, a case could not be made for the doll being a distraction to a driver's duties. In desperation, the company sent Colin for psychiatric assessment and, much to their disappointment, came back with the all-clear. It seemed the fact that the blow-up doll in his cab was real, and not imagined, meant Colin was deemed as being perfectly sane and fit to carry out his duties. The management team, feeling that the real issue here had somehow escaped the consulting psychiatrist, had to seek another means of resolving the problem. He was sent on sick leave for a couple of weeks whilst the company tried to find a way out of the impasse.

It was at this point that the tabloid press got hold of the story, announcing it to the world with headlines like, 'Train Driver Keeps on Track with Blow-up Babe.' The company became a laughing stock after the story was syndicated around the world; the management being castigated by all and sundry for their inept handling of the situation. Even the driver's trade union found it hard to defend their member from the tabloid onslaught.

Unable to sack him, and unable to reinstate him whilst he insisted on having 'Katie' with him, a compromise was eventually reached by offering him a job in the booking office of a quiet country station on the Welsh borders, while still retaining his driver's pay. As the only member of staff on duty there, he would be allowed to keep his 'companion' as long as she was out of sight of the customers. To everyone's relief Colin agreed the move.

All went well initially, but it seems the boredom of being in such a quiet location got to him after a while. Mercia Mainline started to receive complaints from passengers about the doll being displayed in full view of the public. Not only was 'Katie' being dressed in a variety of erotic costumes, but was also being displayed in very provocative poses. As one complainant put it, "I looked through the booking office window, and there it stood, bent over, its legs so far apart, I could see right up to the inflation valve."

The rubber doll was obviously very realistic, fooling more than one passenger. A retired army major wrote in to complain, "The little hussy seemed to be wearing less each day. By the Friday, I had to hide my state of excitement behind the Telegraph gardening supplement!"

Management had by now had enough and a dismissal notice was sent out. This obviously affected Colin badly as the very next day, after serving his customers in the morning rush hour, he left a carefully composed note in head office's pigeon hole. It was understood he then picked up 'Katie,' dressed more conservatively this time in a knee length black dress, stockings, and leather boots. Stepping onto the track clutching his companion, Colin waited for the 09.52 through express from Holyhead. By 10.13 it had still not arrived, so he went back into the booking office only to find out it had been cancelled due to a seagull attack on the driver at Machynlleth. This meant waiting for the 11.52. The delay had put him in a quandary as he was due to finish his shift at 11.30.

The solution was found in the last entry ever written on this mortal coil by ex-driver Colin Philpot. It was for the twenty-two minutes of overtime booked in lieu of his late arrival at the pearly gates, which was somehow fitting when bearing in mind his record of punctuality.

The funeral was well attended at the crematorium, and when his coffin had been consumed by the flames, more than one mourner remarked that there was a distinct smell of burning rubber.

"Yes indeed, another scandal like that we can well do without," reiterated Eric.

"So Dave, you've nothing more to add to what you have already told me then?"

"Er... no Eric, sorry I can't help you there."

"Very well then, I've got another three to interview, I don't really expect them to be any more forthcoming. Let's face it, no one is going to voluntarily own up to being a flasher are they?"

"Precisely," said Dave, blinking rapidly once again. As he got up and turned for the door, Eric imparted some final advice.

"Look Dave, you've got a good attendance and work record. Do yourself a favour and keep away from Duggie and his sordid nocturnal activities. Find a good woman to settle down with. Take it from me, it works. This is my fourth marriage and I've never been happier."

Chapter 6

After a week had passed with no new communications from the dating website, Dave toyed with the idea of ringing Penny again, hoping that in the meantime her attitude might have softened towards him; then thought better of it, when he recalled the venom with which she had delivered her parting shot to him.

'No good dwelling on failed relationships' Dave told himself, 'you must learn to move on' – to quote a common saying of his ex. But move on to what? For him, there was nothing but open sea on the relationship horizon.

The following Sunday was Remembrance Day. Rather than attend the local service in Bridforth, Dave decided to present himself at the war memorial in Ironridge now that he was more than familiar with its location.

Well before the eleventh hour, he joined the throng of people gathered outside ready to witness the ceremony of the wreath laying. As he waited, Dave found his gaze wandering once again up to the granite soldier's weathered face. The nod was again imperceptible, and this time, was it also accompanied by the faintest of winks? Perhaps the gesture was in relation to his assignation the previous week; a subtle inquiry into whether the evening was a success or not.

Dave found himself responding with the briefest shake of his head. He sensed the soldier would understand and commiserate with him. Suppressing their own physical urges would have been a necessary requirement for the men who lived and died in the trenches of the Great War. The soldiers' only chance of sexual relief being provided by the *'prostituées de la rue'* who proliferated in the local towns behind the front, readily available to satisfy a soldier's needs during their short periods of leave.

For many of the young Tommies, it was probably their one and only experience of being intimate with the female sex. A few, brief minutes spent experiencing the joy of lying in the arms of a lover – albeit a paid one – before being returned once more to the horrors of total war.

He recalled a visit he had made to the war museum in Ypres a few years back where one exhibit had featured thousands of photographs from the First World War. Collected from photographers' studios at the end of the war, the pictures showed a succession of uniformed soldiers posing proudly for the camera. These formal studies were popular mementoes at the time. Soldiers would send them to their loved ones back home in Blighty; a keepsake to be cherished until their safe return. The intended recipients were destined never to receive them. All of the Tommies featured in the photographs were killed in action shortly after having their image captured for posterity.

Dave always found Remembrance Sunday a poignant experience – a grandfather he never knew had been killed in the great conflict. But it was also therapeutic, in that it put his melancholy state of mind into perspective when he remembered the ultimate sacrifice made by these men.

A procession of dignitaries took Dave's attention as they marched down from the church and assembled in line facing the memorial. Proceedings commenced with the vicar voicing words of tribute to the fallen, as well as offering solace to those bereaved in more recent conflicts.

The ceremony of the wreath-laying followed, with representatives from both civil and military organisations waiting in turn to pay their respects, each one laying their symbolic arrangement of red and green at the feet of the unnamed soldier.

At the stroke of eleven, the bugler began to play the haunting notes of the Last Post. Men, women and children all stood in silence; their heads bowed for that brief moment each year when those lost in battles past and present were held foremost in people's minds.

The sounding of the reveille two minutes later broke the crowd's quiet contemplation. Lifting up their heads, the audience's gaze drifted towards the source of the shrill bugle call. As the last notes faded into the chill November air, the vicar stepped forward to offer a final prayer. He used the opportunity to reiterate the commonly-made appeal for mankind to resolve conflicts by peaceful means rather than with bloodshed. It drew from the crowd a collection of murmured "amens" at the end.

With the Remembrance service completed, the British Legion Band took their cue and started up a rousing version of 'It's a long way to Tipperary,' before leading off down the street – the dignitaries following in step behind, their cloaks and chains of office displaying their civic status.

Representatives from military and civic bodies followed suit with senior citizens, adults and children all marching as one, the diverseness of their uniforms adding colour to the retreating procession.

Once the last stragglers had passed by, the audience too began to drift away, their Sunday routines to resume once more. While most dispersed into the surrounding streets, a few people remained behind for a moment's quiet reflection. Dave too lingered, undecided about what to do. He would have all the rest of the day at home on his own.

Seeing several men wearing British Legion blazers adjourn to the pub across the road, he decided to follow suit. Indulging in some banter over a pint or two with other ex-forces personnel was just what he needed right now. Then later on, he resolved to try his luck on the dating site once again.

Chapter 7

Later that evening, Dave decided to treat himself to a takeaway before sitting down to a session on the computer. In a lethargic state the previous day, he'd sought the revitalising effects of food and eaten two of his pre-prepared main meals in a single session, leaving the supply left in the freezer out of kilter with the days of the week. A kebab from his local takeaway would correct the irregularity.

"How you goin' Dave! Been a while innit?" asked Yannis turning up the flame on the rotating meat after seeing Dave walk in.

"Is it? No, I don't think so."

Dave knew he made the same remark to all his customers, and assumed it was done to encourage them to call in even more frequently for a kebab.

"The usual Dave? So how you doin' with the ladies? You found anything you like yet? Chilli sauce?"

"Yes please – and no, nothing that stands out."

"Jus' like your cock then, eh Dave?"

"Sadly Yannis, that's very true at the moment."

"How about I find you nice Cypriot lady?"

"Only if she comes with her own kebab shop," he joked.

"No way, I first in queue for that. A woman is easy to find, but a good shop, well...

anything else Dave?"

"No, that's the right money I think you'll find."

"Hope to see you again very soon Dave!"

Dave smiled at the not-so-subtle message hidden in his

farewell. The banter, though, had been a welcome diversion, so he responded with an equally friendly goodbye. He picked up the warm package and gave Yannis a final wave before exiting the shop. Ten minutes later he was sitting in his computer chair eating the strips of spicy meat as he logged into the dating website.

Over the last couple of days he'd spent some time re-hashing his profile and uploading a new photo. He was disappointed therefore to see only one new message waiting for him. It was a reply from Galina. Dave wondered what she had to say.

Hi Dave,

> *I happy that you now reply. Yes, I would like to meet you for drink sometime in future. In Russia people like to drink very much, but I do not know you very well yet, I think I should get to know you better first, before we meet and have drink together. Redditch is very long way for me I guess. Is there airport there?*

> *You make jokes about your wife and this make me laugh. Like we make jokes about our governments. Is a joke also too? But I know you not make joke when you tell me your wife still alive unfortunately. I guess she hurt you bad eh? Is possible for this problem could be dealt with for you, yes?*

> *You not say much about yourself, maybe you have things to hide. I know some men not like to say a lot, especially Englishmen yes? So you reply soon.*

Your good friend Galina

Christ! He didn't remember saying anything that sinister about his ex. Dave clicked on his last email to Galina; the keys were sticky from the chilli sauce on his fingers. Yes, he could see his mistake now; it was where the word 'unfortunately' came in the sentence together with a missing comma that had caused the confusion. She'd also misunderstood the 'meeting for a drink' bit; taking him literally, when in reality he was just trying to fob her off.

Dave was shocked to read of his ex being described as 'a problem that could be dealt with' – why on earth had he not thought of it before? He began to think through one or two scenarios that would lead to her successful demise, but quickly dismissed the suggestion; he recalled his ex was a strong swimmer and the concrete weights would surely get traced back to him.

It was all simply a misunderstanding – of that he was sure. But just in case she was touting for a contract to put the way of one of her gangster friends, he would set the record straight immediately, and send her an email containing a very clear and concise message telling her he wasn't interested.

He pondered over the wording before starting his reply.

Dear Galina

> *Yes I agree it is all a bit soon. We know very little about one another, and we live so far apart. Alas, there is no airport in Redditch. Even if you were to visit England, where would you stay? My house has no curtains or even Sky TV.*
>
> *Furthermore, you have only seen my photograph, how do you know you would like me in the flesh?*
>
> *Regarding my ex, I couldn't possibly allow 'the problem to be dealt with,' as you put it. She owes me 3 payments for some furniture I bought and which she still has possession of, so I don't think your solution would be a good idea at the moment. But I hear what you are saying and thank you for the suggestion.*

Your good friend also.

Dave

The next morning, he readied himself for work. The sandwiches, which through repetition had become a favourite of his, were invariably the same: ham, cheese and tomato, with an apple and a banana to follow. He was loathe to pay upwards of two pounds for a sandwich in the shops near the station, and the savings he made helped to offset his KostKwik wine bill. Dave left the house, stopping off at the newsagents to pick up a copy of Private Eye. He overheard a pensioner in front of him explaining her problem to the assistant.

"I bought this get-well card a couple of weeks ago and... well I never got around to sending it. Do you mind if I swap it for a sympathy one instead? It's a lovely card mind... just a shame I don't know anyone else who's that ill."

The young assistant smiled and nodded her head, prompting the old lady to shuffle off down the shop in search of a suitable alternative. Dave promptly stepped forward, paid with some loose change, then set off to reach the station with just a few minutes to spare. After booking on, Dave checked the company notice board in the office. He spotted a recent addition.

To all Mercia Mainline employees

The company would like to remind all train crew to regularly check their state of dress, especially those in regular contact with the public. In a recent incident, a male member of staff was reported as exposing himself whilst in company uniform and on company premises.

Whether accidental or otherwise, this is clearly not an acceptable practice when on duty. If any further incidents of this sort are reported against our staff, then firm action will be taken against the offending member.

Arthur Robertson
Senior Train Crew Manager

Dave was aware of his face colouring up. He realised that this directive was a result of his interview with his line manager the other day. At least the word hadn't got out that he'd been one of the suspects, or he would have never heard the end of it – not after his recent dogging incident with Duggie. The management had obviously been unable to unearth any real evidence to identify the culprit, so instead had issued a general warning on the subject. As the notice signified the matter had now been brought to a close – Dave felt somewhat relieved.

Checking the diagram he'd just picked up, he saw that his day consisted of travelling as a passenger into Birmingham Curzon Street, two trips to Halesowen, one to Kenilworth, then finally a trip to Harborne.

Dave was on the return journey from Halesowen through to Birmingham, and knew from experience he would be picking up mostly OAPs as they were entitled to free travel after 9.30am. He had a few spare minutes to think about the email from Galina. There was no doubt she was an attractive woman, but was also a bit of a mystery. Could she really be mixed up with the Russian Mafia? It did seem rather unlikely.

Although it was all a bit premature, the lack of any other female interest in his life did make him wonder whether he should pursue the relationship; she might quite possibly bring some much-needed excitement into his life.

The almost-full train had now pulled into Southfield. As he exited the rear cab and released the doors for the passengers, a woman from the end carriage caught his attention.

"Excuse me, there's a dog on the train."

"Yes?" replied Dave, not quite knowing what she wanted him to do about it, though stopping himself from making the obvious quip of, "Does it have a ticket?"

"Well... it got on at the previous stop, and it's sitting in the seat by the door just over there – look!"

Dave peered around the passengers in the direction the lady was pointing, and saw a dog of mixed parentage perched on the seat.

With its wet nose pressed up against the window, the dog sat watching the passengers as they ebbed and flowed through the train doors while leaving behind a trail of mucus over the graffiti-etched glass.

"Is it on its own then?" inquired Dave.

"Well I didn't see any other dogs with it," the old lady replied. Dave shot the woman a sideways glance. She still wore a concerned expression.

"No, I meant was the dog with somebody? That is, its owner."

"Oh, I don't know about that. All I know is it just rushed past me when the doors opened and jumped onto the train. But I don't think its right that a dog should get a seat on busy trains, especially when I've had to stand up. I am pensioner you know, and I should be entitled to one!"

Irritated by her complaining tone, Dave couldn't help but react.

"Yes, well I'll just find out from the dog whether he's prepared to do the decent thing and give it up for you then."

"Really, there's no need to be sarcastic!"

"Look madam, the dog will have to be removed anyway. It can't remain on the train unaccompanied, so providing he comes quietly, you'll be able to have his seat."

Dave approached the dog cautiously, trying to gauge its temperament. He speculated for a moment on whether he was maybe a regular commuter, perhaps with a series of engagements in the city and had found from experience the train to be the most convenient mode of transport. Dave tried a tentative pat. The dog responded by jumping up and licking him. Reassured by his friendly nature, Dave slid his hands underneath the dog, lifted him up and carried him off the train over to the nearby booking office.

He explained the situation to the female booking office clerk and asked if she wouldn't mind keeping the dog until he could be put on the next train back to Langbridge. When released at the station, hopefully he would then find his own way back home. The young girl, her brow furrowed and still puzzling over why the dog should have got on the train in the first place, suddenly advanced a theory.

"It's not an escaped guide dog is it?" she asked

"Er... well... with all their training I wouldn't have thought a guide dog would actually have any desire to escape as you put it. But if it is, it's done a very good job, losing both its owner and its harness; there's only a collar and name tag on him."

"Well, we can't keep him here," she eventually decided. The customer assistant had been in the job long enough to know the importance of avoiding any complications to the working day. All unusual requests – of which she received more than a few in the course of a Saturday night – were by tradition met with a firm refusal.

"Look, can't you just hang on to him till the next train to Langbridge arrives? It'll only be for a few minutes!"

"No way. We're not insured for dogs. He might do a pee up the wall – and I'm not cleaning up no dog poo neither!" she added. "We have enough trouble with the pissheads on a Saturday night as it is! You don't know what we have to put up with. Only the other night, some bloke tried to shove his hotdog through my window, jus 'cos he'd missed his last train home. As if it's my fault! Left ketchup all over the ticket shute it did, and me 'atch stunk of fried onions for days!"

Dave, overwhelmed by such a graphic image was stuck for a reply, and could only respond with a 'Really?' before sighing and taking a glance at his watch. He'd been stuck here ten minutes already. With Mercia Mainline Control constantly monitoring the progress of their trains, they would soon want an explanation for the delay. Dave decided to take the animal with him on the train and then let management sort it out at Birmingham. Out of courtesy he thanked the booking office clerk anyway.

"S'alright," she replied, now reminded to again spray the offending hatch with a can of air freshener. She wrinkled her nose to test its effect.

Back out on the platform a Revenue Protection Inspector had appeared and was carrying out additional checks on passenger's tickets. He turned to Dave as he passed by. "You're not supposed to bring your pet to work you know," said the Inspector, half-joking.

Dave stopped to explain. "Well... er, he's not my dog, it was discovered on the train and I'm trying, though without much success, to return him to his rightful owner."

The official's eyes lit up. "Right, so you're telling me this dog is not being accompanied by its owner – that is, a fare-paying passenger?"

"Correct."

The inspector reached into his top pocket to take out his notebook.

Dave, now feeling the full weight of the dog in his arms, went to walk to the back of the train.

"Whoa! Hold your horses, that dog's going nowhere."

"A contradiction surely?"

"Pardon?"

"I said... oh never mind. Why ever not?" Dave asked.

The inspector raised himself to his full height. Now level with Dave's shoulder, he delivered his reason. "No valid ticket, that's why!"

"What? You know full well that a dog doesn't need a ticket to travel on one of our trains," countered Dave.

"Ah ah! I have to correct you there!" said the official. Eager to demonstrate his encyclopaedic knowledge of ticket regulations with regard to the carriage of animals, the man continued. "The dog can only travel free..." he paused for effect before reciting the critical sub-paragraph he was able to quote from memory, "...if 'accompanied by a fare paying passenger for the entire length of the journey,' which as you have just indicated, isn't the case here."

The inspector rocked triumphantly up and down on the heels of his highly-polished shoes.

"Don't be so ridiculous! All I'm trying to do is get the dog back to its rightful owner. It's what is known as customer service. Maybe you have heard of the expression?"

The inspector seized on the flaw in Dave's argument. "I must correct you again. The dog's owner, as far as we know, is not an actual customer, might not have been on a train for years. The dog will have to walk I'm afraid."

Dave, now exasperated by the inspector's attitude, made his feelings known to him. "Just how petty can you get? Look, this is my train, and I say who – or what – gets on it. I say he's coming in the back cab with me, alright?"

The dog appeared keen on this idea, as he started to lick Dave's chin.

"You can't do that, it's not allowed!" replied the inspector.

Dave held his tongue, turned and, dog in arms, started to walk away.

"I'm going to make out a report about you! Ignoring the terms and conditions for the carriage of animals indeed!" the inspector shouted after him.

"One more report won't make much difference!" Dave shouted back over his shoulder, muttering under his breath, "I might just get my dick out too, for good measure…"

"What was that?" he heard the inspector utter as they boarded the train. Dave ignored him, closed the cab door and gave the signal to the driver. The dog jumped onto the seat in time to emit a low growl as they slipped past the inspector on the platform, now scribbling away furiously in his notebook; the steadily increasing distance between them reducing him to a figure of insignificance.

The dog appeared to settle well in its new environment, being quite happy to watch the world pass by in a constantly changing montage. Dave made the radio call to control explaining away the delay, and requesting that his new-found friend be collected from him at Birmingham Curzon Street Station.

A new problem then became apparent. The dog liked being stroked, and whenever Dave stopped stroking him, he began to bark in protest. Though this was only a minor inconvenience, it did mean he was unable to carry out his duties in the train whilst the dog was in the cab.

At the next stop Dave tried his best to keep him inside, but as soon as the cab door was opened, the dog shot through his legs and promptly fell onto the track. Dave groaned; he now had to follow suit in order to retrieve him. After coaxing the dog out from under the train, Dave lifted him up, placed his front paws on the platform edge and gave a hefty shove to his rear end. The canine showed its enjoyment of this new game by wagging his tail in Dave's face, but refused point-blank to get into the cab. Dave paused for a moment to consider the options while he removed the last of the moulted dog hairs from his mouth. There was only one thing to do he decided: getting hold of the hound by the scruff of his neck, Dave dragged him forcibly into the confines of his cab and quickly closed the door.

The dog's response to being shut in was to bark loudly in protest, varying this occasionally with a long howl. Dave had only just managed to quieten the dog down again when there was a knock from the other side of the vestibule door. He cursed at having to now deal with a passenger as well as the dog. Didn't the public know he had better things to do? With one hand engaged in intensive stroking to keep the dog quiet, he could just about reach the vestibule door with the other and pushed it half-open. A face peered around it from the other side.

"Yes?" he asked curtly.

The woman standing there firstly apologised for having to bother him, and then asked if she could buy a ticket to Birmingham Curzon St. The booking office, she explained, had been shut at Kings Naunton.

"Yes well, I am actually fully-stretched at the moment, but if you could just give me a second." He was reluctant to take his hand away from the dog, but needed it to operate the ticket machine. The action provoked the onset of barking again.

"I didn't know you could bring your pets to work," she said above the noise.

"Actually, it's not my dog, it's a stray," Dave shouted back as he inputted the destination into his machine.

"What's it doing on the train then?"

"It got on by itself at Langbridge."

"Where's it trying to get to?"

"I don't know – Barking perhaps?"

Seeming not to have noticed his little joke, she inquired further, "Do you get many strays on trains then?"

Now more than a little irritated by the flurry of questions, Dave delivered his reply as he handed over the woman's ticket. "Well thereby hangs a *tail* you see. Dogs can only travel *fur* free if accompanied by a fare paying passenger, which I know from personal experience, can be a *bone* of contention. This one's on his own, so I think somebody's been *leading* him on, which is a pretty *paw* joke to play on a dog, if you ask me!"

"Right, yes I see now," she replied in all seriousness, and was still nodding her understanding as she backed away clutching her ticket.

It was when the train stopped three stations along at Sixways that the real trouble began. As the train was coming to a stand, the dog caught sight of a squirrel scavenging in the shrubbery at the rear of the platform. Not being quite as vigilant as when he'd first tried to escape, Dave could only watch helplessly as the dog launched himself through the gap in the door and shot off down the platform in pursuit of its quarry. The chase only lasted as far as one of the tall poplar trees that lined the rear of the platform. His charge was left barking and jumping up at the spot where the squirrel had climbed it just seconds before.

A woman standing close by, seeing a pet dog on the platform began to make a fuss of him. Although appreciative of the attention he was receiving, it also had the effect of altering the nature of the dog's excitement and directing it towards the lady now stroking him. To her great embarrassment, the dog jumped up and, with both paws clasped around her leg, began humping it.

The lady frantically shook her leg to free herself. When this didn't work, she gyrated one way and then the other in an effort to loosen the dog's grip. By now Dave had worked his way through the crowd and grabbed hold of the dog by the scruff of his neck. As he pulled one way and the lady pulled the other, she screamed at him. "Just get him off me! Get him off me!!"

"I'm trying my best, I really am." But then Dave just couldn't resist saying, "He does seem to like you madam!"

"Like me? Is that supposed to be funny? I take it this is your dog then?"

"Well not exa…"

"It shouldn't be let off its lead if it does things like this… it's disgusting. Of course it amounts to sexual harassment, you know that?"

"But it's just a dog!"

"That's no excuse. You should keep it under control. What sort of person brings a dog to work with them? It's a stupid thing to do."

Dave was getting more than a little tired of explaining. After all the trouble he'd caused, he now wished he'd never set eyes on the mutt.

"Look madam, this is not my dog, it's just a stray that happened to board the train. I am…" He decided not to go through the whole story again. "Look, I'm sorry for what it just did… but you know, dogs will be dogs, and unfortunately it chose you to be the victim of his er… affections as it were."

"Well I still call it sexual harassment… I could sue, you know. Look, it's laddered my tights and I've got saliva all over my leg. This is all your fault, I could claim compensation for this!"

"I can only apologise once again. If I'd had a lead to keep it on, I would have done so. If you want to take this further, you might want to contact the train company to make an official complaint."

"Yes, well I might just do that!" she said, dabbing at her leg with a tissue.

As he wended his way back to the cab door pulling the wayward dog with him, the woman realised she had omitted to ask an important detail and called after him. "Oi, you! A name! I'll need a name to make a proper complaint!"

Dave thought carefully for a moment. Turning over the dog's

metal tag he shouted, "It's Buster, madam!" He spelt it out for her. "B-u-s-t-e-r."

As the train neared Curzon Street station, Dave foresaw another problem. To make his announcement to the passengers as the train entered the station, he would need the use of both hands; one to hold the handset and the other to keep the PA button pressed while he spoke. Dave could see immediately what would happen when he did this – he would need to have words. Looking directly into the dog's very liquid eyes, he delivered a short lecture on what the dog must not, under any circumstance do, or he would be a very bad boy – a very bad boy indeed! Dave just hoped that the stray would understand him.

Unfortunately, as the train began to enter the station and Dave removed his hand from the dog to press the PA button and make his announcement, it was apparent that the dog hadn't understood at all. Throughout the whole train there came the sound of loud barking over the public address system – along with Dave vainly trying to make himself heard above the noise in his cab.

"Ladies and gentlemen, we will shortly be arriving at Birmingham Curzon Street where..."

"wruff, wruff... gr... wruff!"

"...Stop it!... This service will..."

"wrooff, wrooff, wrooff!"

"...Quiet boy!... terminate. Please remember to..."

"wruff, wruff... grrr... wruff!"

"...Look, I won't tell you again... take all your..."

"woof, woof, woof... woofff!"

"...Shut up will you!... personal belongings with you."

"ruff, ruff, ruff!"

"...when leaving the train!"

"grrrrr... ruff!"

"Thank you!"

It then occurred to Dave how funny all this must sound to the passengers in the train and began to laugh himself the more he thought about it. He put on hold the rest of the announcement while he attempted to compose himself, but kept getting the giggles every time he tried to speak, causing the dog to bark even louder. After several more unsuccessful attempts he gave up trying to finish the broadcast.

Once the train had come to a stand he stepped from the cab, this time taking extreme care to ensure that the dog remained behind. Several of the passengers were still chuckling as they stepped off the train and stopped to thank him for the quality of the entertainment provided on the journey. One gentleman said it was the funniest thing he'd heard for years. Feeling very much the all-round entertainer, he bowed and thanked his appreciative audience for their kind comments as they walked past.

With the crowd now thinning out, he spotted a member of the platform staff sloping towards him holding a length of rope, "Ah ha! Salvation at last," uttered Dave.

"No, me names Dwayne," said the young man.

"No, no, I meant... oh it doesn't matter, so you're here to collect my friend then?"

"Yeah, I got the shit job, gettin' stuck wiv a dog like."

"Don't worry, it's happened to me many a time!"

"Yer what mate?"

"Getting stuck with a... never mind, we all have to start at the bottom you know."

"I ain't touchin' 'im there, I'll jus' stroke 'is 'ead, 'e don't bite does 'e?"

"Not so far, even though I have made some very caustic comments about him. There you go, he's all yours now. He needs to get back to Langbridge by the way."

"Langbridge, yeah, right – 'e don't need a ticket does 'e?"

"Now don't you start!"

Chapter 8

The next day was a rest day from work. Dave had set aside most of it to work on the drawings for his multi-purpose workbench. His demonstration at the inventor's club the previous week had been well-received by the members, with several encouraging him to take his invention to the next level by applying for a UK patent. The drawings, together with a detailed description of the invention were needed to support his application. By about seven in the evening, Dave was in need of a break. He decided to check his emails; there was again a reply from Galina.

Dear Dave.

> *I am thanking you for reply, and you make me laugh again. I am understanding your British sense of humour now pretty well I think. I am sad you not have time for me, but you very bad man! Saying what I will think of you without your clothes on. But I can be bad like that too, unless we meet sometime, how can I tell if all okay when you in the flesh Yes? Ha ha!*
>
> *I tell you now I have to come to England soon for my work. I hope to make assignations in your country. If you are not okay with meeting sassy Russian woman then I will understand, but you have not said yes, and not said no. Is it your English way to not make simple decision?*

Your very good friend

Galina.

He now felt a complete prat. His attempt to let her down gently by subtly conveying his reluctance to meet with her, had again completely passed her by. Consequently she now regarded him as weak and indecisive – well, she was probably half right.

Dave was intrigued though by her reference to him naked. He realised that the 'in the flesh' reference had been misinterpreted – which perhaps he should have anticipated – but was encouraged that she had responded in kind with a risqué remark of her own. Maybe there could be something of a spark there after all, he thought.

He brought up her photograph on the screen for further examination. Maybe in the Urals or wherever she lived, long perms were still the height of fashion – or it could be just an old photograph she'd used. There was no doubting her attractiveness though. And if she was coming to England anyway, then what harm would there be in meeting her?

Emboldened by a combination of lustful longing and rare decisiveness, he took up the challenge and fired off an email of committal.

My dear Galina,

Why, did I not say? If you are already planning to come to England, of course I would be delighted to meet you. Just let me know the dates, and I will try my utmost to secure some free time to show you the sights. I could even meet you at the airport if you would like me to.

After his effusive beginning, Dave paused to think about her latest email in more detail. Just what sort of assignation was she referring to? In normal circumstances, he would take to mean a secret rendezvous with a lover, but she would hardly be telling him that if this was the case. He guessed something had again been lost in translation and she probably meant assignment, but what sort of assignment? Who for and involving what? It still gave him no further clue as to whether she could actually be a Russian hit woman, a high-class prostitute, or none of these. Despite her mystery – or maybe because of it – Dave felt a tingle of excitement at the prospect of meeting this intriguing woman and continued his email in the same purposeful vein.

You would also be most welcome to stay at my house for a few days; I do have a spare room available.

Dave felt that Galina might like to savour a little of Britain's industrial heritage when showing her around the local area.

We could do some sightseeing together; perhaps take a trip to the Victorian museum at Ironridge, or maybe a ride on the heritage Worfe Valley Railway with working steam engines.

He hoped she was familiar with some of the best-known tourist attractions in the area, so for good measure he added another.

There's also the Black Country Museum in Dudley we could visit too!"

Finally, as a concession to her gender,

Perhaps you would like to do some shopping at Primart in Tealford?

Kind regards

Dave

P.S. Just as a matter of interest, what sort of assignation are you coming here for? Perhaps I could help you with it.

Dave reread his message three times to ensure nothing could possibly be misconstrued before pressing the send key.

He signed off and got up from his computer to pour himself a fortifying glass of Rioja before deciding to settle down with a DVD. Having managed to acquire the original version of *The Italian Job*, including all the outtakes and extra scenes, he was looking forward to watching it. He reached down to switch on the DVD player, a simple enough procedure in theory, but a regular source of irritation in practice.

For some unfathomable reason, the manufacturers had felt it necessary to equip it with the smallest of on/off buttons. It only required pressing just a tiny amount, and with a slight tremble of the hand – which was often the case after a glass or two of KostKwik Rioja – it was easy to inadvertently switch it on and off again in the same movement.

The process was further complicated by a delay in the red power light illuminating, which forced him to stay crouched over it awaiting visual confirmation he had done it correctly. It was just the same when switching it off. What was wrong with having the positive action of a simple toggle switch? As would have been the case before the style gurus and ergonomics experts got hold of things.

It was just the same with the controls on his car stereo. Instead of one simple rotating knob to alter the volume up and down, it now had two separate buttons to do exactly the same thing. This required either one or the other to be held in to increase or decrease the volume, again complicating what was previously a simple method of adjustment. It all confirmed to him, as he reflected on his own deprived situation, that functional knobs of any kind were very much out of favour.

No criticism of style could be made about the film though. It starred some of the finest British actors of the time: Michael Caine at his Cockney best, brilliant cameos from Noel Coward and Benny Hill, a host of well-known supporting actors from the 1960's, as well as an excellent story line wittily scripted – the Mini car chase providing the grand finale.

To further his enjoyment, Dave judged that another glass of KostKwik's finest would be the perfect enhancement, and for the inevitable peckish moment later, that day's earmarked spaghetti bolognese meal.

Dave wondered whether Galina had seen the film and appreciated its perfect blend of humour, action and suspense. Maybe she thought of England as it had been in the 1960's: a society inhabited by suave, well-mannered gentlemen who drove around 'swinging London' in Mini-Coopers with a union jack emblazoned on the roof. He resolved to replay it for her when she came over.

It was two days later when Galina replied to his offer; her reply had been eagerly awaited. His excitement was tempered though, by another email from his ex. Dave decided to have the bad news first.

Dave,

> *I've still not heard anything from you about the money. I hope you're not ignoring me. I won't just go away, you know. Graham at work says you're being completely unreasonable in not replying. I told him this is just what you were like when we were together. You would always walk off whenever I needed to make you see my point. Graham said I may be able to divorce you by citing this very reason.*
>
> *According to Graham, denying a wife the right of reply could be considered unreasonable behaviour by a judge; but if it also included refusing her the last word, possible mental cruelty too.*

Jane

P.S. The outside of the house needs painting, I'll send you the estimates when I get them. Graham says the paintwork should be done every five years. I don't remember you doing it that often!

Dave sighed, more expense! And why was she telling this

Graham person all their personal business? It's Graham this, and Graham that. How did he get to be her confidant, all of a sudden? It can't just be advice he was giving her, surely!

Just sod off and leave me alone! was his instinctive reaction to her demands. As far as he was concerned, the quicker he got a divorce from her the better. The grounds used to obtain one were of no concern to him. He reached for the Rioja and poured himself a large measure before turning to Galina's reply.

Dear Dave

I thank you for your kind invitations to stay at your home and if you happy with me, I would be glad to accept.

You ask me if I visit your old buildings and railway with you, but in Russia many of us live in such old towns and streets and have railways like this.

I would look forward to visiting your other great British institution like Marts and Spender. Is Primart store in Tealford famous like Harrads in London? Then I would look forward to visiting it also.

You ask me question about why I have to come to England. I learn English some years ago and now in my new work, would like to earn contracts in your country.

You know many people in my country still think Englishmen are all gentlemen who drive around in their mini cars, but I have seen you English at football matches on TV. Men with shaved head and tattoos just like in our Gulags, but with earrings like pirates. They fight, they swear, and drink too much beer, then have relief in street. Why? Are there not toilets in England? I hope you are not like them and you are respectable man! You do seem like it is so in your emails. That is why I'm happy to meet you. I can arrange a flight for me to come to England. When is good time for me to stay?

Your good friend Galina

Dave was delighted that she had accepted, and would plan her visit accordingly – but what an indictment of his country. Unfortunately, it was mostly true; he saw the same behaviour for himself on a regular basis in his job. Dave sighed and wondered whether it was really a good idea to invite her over and have her fears confirmed. He would just have to keep her away from the worst areas – like any city centre on a Saturday evening.

Being none the wiser about her occupation, he mulled over what she meant by, 'earning contracts in this country.' Was there really a sinister meaning behind her use of the phrase? He thought back to her earlier email, where she had talked about solving the problem of his ex. She had not made any further mention of it since, or the likely fee for carrying it out, which would surely be a priority for any professional in that line of work. Then again, she wouldn't want to put anything incriminating in writing. Maybe she was just trying to hint that such an arrangement was possible, leaving the details to be sorted out when she arrived.

No, the more he thought about it the more he realised he was just being over-dramatic again. He was sure Galina would not turn out to be the cold-hearted killer eager to solve his 'wife' problem for him. Worryingly, he felt a tinge of disappointment.

Excited by the prospect of Galina's visit, Dave began to think through the social occasions he would be sharing with her. It was his belief that enjoying an intimate meal together offered the best opportunity to impress a lady like Galina. He reasoned that she would know little about quality British cuisine so it would be up to him to educate her. He conjured up a likely scenario.

Arriving at their restaurant, he would affect a light touch on Galina's waist as he guided her through the door. Welcomed with a deferential nod of recognition by the waiter, he'd wait for them to be shown to his favourite table, only sitting down himself once Galina had taken her seat. Such lost social graces, he was sure, would not go amiss with a woman like Galina.

In order to impress her with his knowledge of food and wine, he would make his personal recommendations from the menu and then entertain Galina with his witty repartee while they ate. At the end of the meal, he'd casually broach the subject of the bill; explaining that while it was now the custom in English society for couples to go Dutch, as Galina was his honoured guest, he ought to be allowed to pay.

Once he'd allowed her a moment or to protest, he would graciously give way and agree to her leaving the service charge – if that was all she could afford. The rest of the bill he would settle with some Withyspoons' vouchers he'd received by way of compensation after an incident on a previous visit to one of their restaurants.

It was back in the summer and he was on a rare third date with a woman from Middleminster. The lady, although rather forthright in her views, was nevertheless attractive and possessed of a dry wit. They were enjoying a meal together at her local Withyspoons when an altercation developed between the staff and some drunken diners on another table. The conflict very quickly escalated and the protagonists began using their main course as ammunition in their dispute with the management. Not being in the direct line of fire from the offending table, Dave was surprised therefore when he received the full impact of a Withyburger and fries to his chest, the melted cheese providing just enough adhesive grip for the burger to make a controlled descent down his shirt front before coming to a rest in his lap, having cooled sufficiently in flight to cause no injury to himself.

Unfortunately, his female dining companion received collateral damage in the form of the accompanying tomato relish. Not being one to make light of an incident of this nature, she demanded that he go over and remonstrate with the men. Dave had already noted the size of the three burly offenders and how the waiting staff, now nursing a variety of injuries, had backed off into the far corner and were now urgently calling for back-up from the door security staff over their two-way radios. No matter how much he apologised for having to trouble them, he quickly recognised that any approach from him with a view to seeking redress from the belligerent group would only have one outcome. He tried vainly to pass off her suicidal demand.

"I'm sure it was all just an accident, I'll just let things calm down a bit then have a word with the waiter. Look, the cheese has cooled down now, and the strands are coming off a lot easier. The stain I'm sure will come out in a hot wash."

Taking a few seconds to study his companion's soiled blouse, he advised her, "I think yours might need a soak in Vanish first."

His dining companion, though, did not take lightly to such indignities as having her Dorothy Parkins polyester blouse splattered with glutinous relish and seemed distinctly unimpressed with his advice on stain removal. Dave sensed she was expecting a more testosterone-fuelled response from him, confirming it when she stated that if he was any sort of man at all, then he should immediately go over and sort them out.

Her reaction had left him in a severe quandary over what to do to save face. He looked over towards the stand-off. The other diners, initially transfixed by the salvos of food being thrown, were now picking up their own partly-eaten meals and moving to a quieter sector of the restaurant.

Dave weighed up the odds. Although he and his ladyfriend had made significant progress in their relationship during previous dates, receiving a good kicking in order to achieve consummation was not a price he was prepared to pay. His overriding concern was not to inflame the situation in any way, although to placate the lady, he knew he had to be seen to be doing something.

He turned to his military training for a solution. 'Be bold' was always the motto. A measure of bluff too, might well work in this situation. Many a military commander had used the same principle to win victory against the odds.

Having hesitated for as long as he could, he raised himself from his seat and adopted a position somewhere between a crouch and a stoop. Then, in a display of bravado, he displayed his cheese, burger and tomato relish stained shirt to the aggressors. Yes, though he may be wounded as it were, he would not weaken. Stubborn defiance was what he would show them! He was just working out how much stubborn defiance to safely show should the situation escalate – when it did. Angry shouts of "Do you want some as well then?" were now being directed at him from across the room.

Dave felt his courage rapidly dissipating. It was at this point that his ladyfriend broke into his train of thought with a comment typical of her nature.

"So are you goin' to just stand there then?" she remarked helpfully.

He did indeed stand there, transfixed like a rabbit caught in a car's headlights desperately trying to think of a non-combative course of action that would salvage the situation. Further shouts of "Come on then you wanker!" only made the forced grin harder to maintain.

His prayers were answered by the appearance of three heavies in dark suits, followed somewhat incongruously, by one of the restaurant chefs from the kitchen brandishing an egg whisk in his hand. After a brief verbal confrontation, the suits quickly gained control of the situation and escorted the aggressors to the main exit. When certain that the men were safely out of the building, Dave made a cursory rude gesture in their direction and sat down.

"Well I think we've sorted the situation out to everyone's satisfaction," he ventured, trying to appear suitably smug at the conflict having been resolved.

"What do you mean, we?" was her withering response. "You never did a thing – it was those three bouncers who got it sorted."

This was perfectly true, but he wasn't about to admit it. "No... I was able to remain cool and keep the situation calm until as you say, the cavalry arrived."

"Oh you were cool alright – more like frozen to the spot!"

Dave winced, that hurt.

He tried his best to recover from such a mortal blow, but

realised he'd never convince her that his subtle use of psychology had indeed contained the situation.

She regarded his lack of courage in confronting the perpetrators as a turning point in their relationship, and her attitude towards him changed from one of positive interest to one of thinly-veiled contempt. Their relationship quickly died a death after that – which when Dave reflected on it, was a more satisfactory outcome than *him* suffering that fate.

It was some small consolation to him at the time that the manager waived the bill for their meal, and following a letter of complaint to Withyspoons' customer service department, Dave received with his reply, vouchers to the value of £30.

In what appeared to be a transcription error by someone in their Mumbai customer service department, the accompanying letter, as well as conveying the company's regret over the incident, also expressed the hope that he had enjoyed his recent dining experience at their Middleminster restaurant. Furthermore, it said, the staff looked forward to seeing him again in the near future.

There was no mention of the dry-cleaning bill for his ruined shirt.

Dave hoped his liaison with Galina might at last come to something after his catalogue of disasters. As long as meeting him 'in the flesh' didn't disappoint Galina, Dave felt he was in with a good chance. The new photo he'd posted on the website of himself was a fairly recent one – certainly not more than five years old – and taken in favourable light.

Then again, he asked himself, how recent was the photo Galina had posted? He clicked the icon to study it again. The Mercedes she was draped over looked to be an early nineties model, so the photo could be up to ten years old. That would also explain the perm. If that was the case, he just had to hope that like him, she too had aged well.

Chapter 9

Dave left his car in the short stay car park at Birmingham airport and walked briskly along the service road heading for the mass of airport buildings. Galina had informed him two weeks previously that she would be able to fly to the UK on this particular Thursday. He had suggested the date in order to coincide with the start of his long weekend which occurred every three weeks in his work rota. Adding on a couple of days of annual leave, he would now not have to be back at work until the following Friday evening, giving Galina seven whole days to spend with him. Not for the first time he worried that it might be too long a period. Could he keep her interest for that long? What if she got bored?

He had grounds for concern. Galina had inexplicably rejected his suggested visits to two well-known museums of industrial history in the West Midlands. Nor had she shown any enthusiasm for exploring the nation's rich steam railway heritage either. Other than shopping – an urge he was convinced was firmly imprinted on all women's genes – what else was she interested in? The one other activity that did spring to mind – even if she was willing – would take up just a few minutes of the night time hours. He would have to play it by ear and discover her other interests when she arrived.

Still pre-occupied with his concerns, Dave had reached the airport buildings when he realised he'd left the car park entry ticket behind in the car, forcing him to do an about-turn in order to retrieve it.

Several minutes later inside the arrivals terminal, Dave was scouring the panoply of signage for directions to the toilets. The full-size mirrors above the wash basins enabled him to carry out a final inspection before meeting up with Galina. He checked his nose once more for protruding hairs. He'd removed a few strays previously at home and wanted to check no more had sprung to life during the journey. The next task was to reposition a few strands of wayward hair back across the top of his head.

Although he felt it would be a gross exaggeration to draw a direct comparison with 1960's footballer Bobby Charlton's famed style of hair distribution, he was finding that combing his remaining hair to the side did help mask his increasing baldness – as well as giving him the secondary benefit of reducing the glare from florescent lighting. Dave checked his watch once again. Yes, there was just a little more time before Galina's plane was due to land.

Now beginning to feel nervous about meeting up with her, his bladder reacted in its customary manner. Although he guessed there would be little to expel, he would try anyway. Unfortunately, as he started to relieve himself, the faltering dribble of urine declined to go in the direction it was aimed, but instead took an altogether different trajectory: bouncing off the edge of the ceramic urinal and splashing the front of his new chinos. Dave cursed; they were the sort of cotton to clearly show splashes of this sort. Having experienced the same type of accident before, he knew the remedy was to stand on tiptoe with his nose squashed up against the wall whilst the hand dryer's hot air nozzle blasted his groin area for five minutes or so – which he knew from experience was too long for comfort. For some reason, boil in the bag dumplings came to mind as he carried out the procedure.

Dave rinsed his hands, this time bending forward almost double to keep well away from any splashes of water. Drying them quickly, he was at last satisfied that his ablutions were complete.

He returned to the concourse and searched for Galina's flight on the arrivals screen. More time had passed than Dave had anticipated, and her plane had landed slightly earlier than scheduled. Damn those jet streams! They were so unpredictable nowadays.

Having informed Galina that he would be carrying a newspaper to aid identification, he now urgently needed one. The newsagents he could see on the other side of the concourse would provide the missing accessory; he rushed inside and picked up a copy of his usual paper.

Not being entirely sure whether the passengers on the flight from Riga would yet be through baggage reclaim and immigration, he nevertheless moved swiftly towards the customs exit just in case the baggage handlers had been super-efficient in unloading the aircraft.

He was met by a throng of people exiting through the barriers. Although a Malaga flight had also recently landed, none of the passengers looked to be the typical British holidaymaker returning home with a recently acquired out-of-season suntan. To Dave's untrained ear, the snippets of conversation he could hear sounded enough like Russian for him to conclude that these passengers must indeed be from the Moscow flight. Using the photo he'd brought along of Galina, he anxiously scanned the arrivals hall to seek out likely-looking females.

After circulating for some minutes, he eventually located a woman with features similar to the one in the picture, busily engaged in conversation with a man. Dave checked the picture again. It certainly looked like Galina though her hair was not permed as in the photo, but straight and streaked with highlights. She looked curvier too – nicely so, in his opinion. The face was definitely a match: her expression more animated in real life, and as she talked a smile rarely left her face. It had to be her, but who could the man be? The stranger was dark like himself, a little taller maybe, but had a moustache. Of course it was possible Galina had arranged to meet a selection of suitors here at the airport. He took a quick look around just to make sure there were no others queuing up to make her acquaintance.

On observing the pair in more detail, Dave was again struck by the man's similarity to himself. Then as they talked he produced a folded newspaper to emphasise a point he was making. That was it! He realised Galina had unwittingly succumbed to a case of mistaken identity. Dave decided to advance a few steps towards them and listen to their conversation. What he was able to hear seemed to confirm his theory; the woman definitely had a foreign lilt to her voice.

Dave realised he would have to expose the imposter. Advancing a couple more paces, he broke into their conversation. "Er… excuse me, but would you by any chance be Galina Troski?" enquired Dave, ignoring the man.

The woman looked at Dave, then at the other man, then back to Dave before answering. "Why yers! Ernd so you murst be Dave?" asked the smiling woman, her eyes again flicking between the two of them.

"I certainly am!" he replied trying to sound confident, but feeling unnerved by the close presence of the other male, and by Galina's eyes darting back and forth as if making a direct comparison between them.

"…Thern I'm most pleased to meet you," announced Galina after a short pause. Dave shook the offered hand and enquired further.

"So how was your journey?"

"Very gourd… ernd your journey to aeroport too?" responded Galina.

"Yes, er… likewise."

An uneasy pause followed with all three remaining silent. Dave, anxious to find out who the man was, took the initiative.

"So, er… Galina, I don't think I've been introduced to your er… friend."

"Ah! Yers, thirs is Lawrence, we meet here at aeroport. He herv newspaper like you say, and he lurk so murch like you from photograph – now I can see he maybe a bit taller perhaps, ernd maybe a bit younger, ernd… he not eat so well as you I thirnk," she said with a little laugh.

"Really?" Dave forced a thin smile of his own. He turned to

Lawrence and nodded. "But I don't have a moustache!" Dave hissed as he turned back to Galina.

"You could herv grown one, merny Russian men herv moustaches!" she explained.

"But I would have told you if I had!"

"Is not important, I like mern without moustaches too, she said breezily. "Is easy mirstake to make. Your photograph is not so like you, I thirnk."

Dave begged to differ. He couldn't have changed that much in the five years since it was taken. Lawrence, taking advantage of the brief lull, edged forward between the two of them and cleared his throat.

"Well er... anyway, I must be on my way. It was nice meeting you Galina – if only briefly and you have my number if you do want to get in touch."

"Yers, okay Lawrence, thernk you, it wers very nice to meet you too."

Dave stood in silence and watched as Lawrence started to walk off. Dragging out his farewell, the man stopped after two or three paces and turned to give Galina another wave before exiting the concourse.

On resuming his conversation with Galina, Dave's tone was rather more accusing than he intended. "Well you must have made quite an impression on him!"

"Not really, he's jurst a nice mern who would help me if you not arrive like you say. Is not bad to do thert, yers?"

Dave realised he had allowed a tinge of jealousy to affect his attitude, and as a consequence had been rather abrupt in his manner. He accepted the fact that it had all been a misunderstanding, with Lawrence merely the unwitting party in it all.

"No, no, of course not. Sorry!"

Dave was pleased that he now had Galina's full attention, but what was that remark she made about Lawrence not eating as well as him – was she trying to say he was fat? Even his ex had failed to find too much to criticise about his weight, though he did recall her once saying his stomach bulged out like the plastic film on a gone-off pack of supermarket chicken. Yes, he would admit to having a problem with putrefying gasses now and again, but didn't all men?

Aware that Galina was looking at him with some expectation, Dave dismissed his concerns for the time being and threw out his arms in a gesture of welcome. "Well Galina, it is wonderful to see you at last, allow me to take your suitcase."

"Thernk you, I did not know if you were pleased to see me or not. Maybe you thirnk I had another mern yers?" teased Galina, smiling mischievously.

"No, no, not at all," he lied. "I'm sure your Lawrence is truly a very nice man, and I accept he was just being kind," said Dave, wanting to call a truce on the matter. He grasped the handle of her suitcase and took up the weight, then immediately dropped it back down on the floor.

"Christ! What have you got in here?"

"In the case? Is just my clothes enrd equipment thert I need to carry out my assasign... er, assignments here."

Her confusing answer suddenly brought to mind those early emails he'd exchanged with Galina and the ambiguity of her replies when he made enquiries about her profession. He had previously dismissed the notion that she could be a hit woman as a flight of fancy...

"Well, actually you never did say what your er, line of work was."

"Why, I werk as a plurmer!"

"Sorry, a what?"

"A plurmer!"

"A plurmer?" queried Dave.

"Yers, a plurmer! You know, I fix ernd make water pipes, yers?"

"Oh right! Yes, you mean a plumber!"

"Yers, thert is what I said, a plurmer, I herv my tools irn case."

"So why have you brought them with you to the UK?" asked Dave, now rather confused.

"I train as plurmer in Russia ernd now I come to UK to take examination in British plurming, so thert I may werk here. I wirl herv assignments to make, you understand?"

"Ah right! I see. Yes I do understand now. I was just a little puzzled, that's all. So when you qualify as a plur... plumber, you intend staying on here to try and find work, is that correct?"

"Yers, thert is correct."

Dave was surprised by the news and wondered just where she intended living. Her stay with him was supposed to be for just a few days, he really didn't want the arrangement to become open-ended. Then again, seeing Galina in the flesh did confirm to him the impression gained from her photograph, she really was attractive for her age. She had obviously taken care over the years to retain her looks – he only hoped that she came to the same conclusion about him.

Having completed the welcome formalities, Dave suggested that they make their way to his car. Once he realised that Galina's suitcase did in fact have wheels, he switched to pulling the laden weight behind him. Annoyingly, a serious flat on one of them caused an irritating ba-dum... ba-dum as he pulled it along. Above the noise of the damaged suitcase wheel, he attempted to make polite conversation as they traversed the arrivals hall heading towards the exit.

It suddenly struck him as being a bizarre situation. Here he was with a woman who had just flown 1500 miles to stay with him – and he knew almost next to nothing about her. Nor did he know on what sort of basis their relationship was to proceed – if at all. He just hoped Galina would find him as agreeable as he found her, though unfortunately they hadn't got off to the best of beginnings. It was no use fretting about such things, he told himself. He had plenty of time to create a better impression over the next few days. All he needed to do was to simply keep up the image of a self-assured, well-mannered English gentleman as depicted in his series of emails. They had just reached the car when Dave realised that he had forgotten to get his car park ticket cancelled inside the terminal building. He apologised to Galina for his oversight, and dashed back to put right the mistake.

Negotiating his way out of the airport, Dave nodded silently in response to Galina's pleasantries concerning the weather and English countryside. He was concentrating on the route he needed to take out of the airport – looking initially for the M42, before then heading north on the M6 towards Wensbury. It was getting dark, and the layout was tricky with a plethora of intersections and exits to confuse even the sharpest of motorists, so out of necessity, he tried to avoid all distractions until safely on the correct route.

Once on the familiar M6 motorway, he belatedly responded to Galina's subjects of conversation. The topics ranged from budget airline food to motorway service station toilets – which only came up when Dave needed to stop at one, blaming his weakness on the large coffee he had drunk earlier. Although he was curious to know more about her plans to live and work in the UK, Dave thought it best to leave the matter to a more opportune moment; he didn't want to appear to be interrogating her so soon after her arrival.

In just over an hour, they had reached the outskirts of Bridforth. Dave made the turn into his road and drew the car up onto the driveway in front of the house, giving Galina a view of her home for the next few days. She seemed to nod with approval when he said, "Well here we are Galina" before getting out of the car. He unlocked the front door and gestured her through into the hallway. As he heaved Galina's case over the threshold, Dave was relieved to find that the central heating had come on as programmed. It was an old system and was proving to be unreliable. He really needed to get the boiler looked at sometime. It made him wonder just how advanced Galina's plumbing skills were.

"Welcome to your home for the next seven days," he said, thinking it worthwhile to reiterate the length of her stay.

"Yers, is very nice Dave – ernd you joke wirth me, you do herv curtains!"

"I managed to acquire some especially for you." Dave flashed her a smile. While Galina viewed her surroundings, Dave took the opportunity to study his houseguest more closely. With her blonde hair now streaked, to mask the effects of aging he guessed, and her high cheek bones, she could be easily mistaken for a Scandinavian. He'd had a thing about blonde Swedish girls as a young man in the 1970's, when actresses like Britt Ekland and Ann Margret were the female celebs of the day. If he played his cards right, he just might be able to fulfil that teenage fantasy of his over the next few days.

His musing was interrupted when she turned and caught him ogling. Quickly averting his eyes, he suggested they move through into the lounge where they would be more comfortable. Dave thought to offer Galina some refreshment as they sat chatting and suggested coffee. He had some of KostKwik's finest Paraguayan blend in the cupboard, specially purchased for her visit, though the extra caffeine it contained was having an effect on him.

"So, is your plurming okay Dave?"

It's funny she should ask that just now, he thought. He did seem to be going a lot more frequently. Was it that noticeable?

"...because irt is not so warm in here, I thirnk."

Of course, yes. He wondered why Galina had kept her coat on. Dave agreed that it was a little on the cool side, but explained that the heating system was quite old and he was concerned that it might break down if he overburdened it by warming the house properly.

Galina looked at him for a moment as if not quite understanding. Dave joked that it was normal to feel cold in a British home; it was a long-standing tradition. He did have a fan heater though if it was a problem for her.

She decided not to question his reasoning. Her considered opinion was that despite the lack of warmth, it was a good thing to own your own house. Back in Russia, she had only a small rented flat – but it was well heated.

The boiler wasn't the only problem. The windows needed replacing too. It was a 1960's house, and although nicely situated near the river with a south-facing garden, it did need some updating. A neighbour had offered to supply him with some on the cheap only the week before, but due to lack of funds, he had been procrastinating in the hope of driving the price down.

The next couple of hours passed by with the two engaged in polite chit-chat mostly about their respective situations; the proceedings being conducted with a degree of formality until Dave brought up the subject of the emails they'd sent to one another. To Galina's amusement, he explained how he'd initially taken her for a gangster's ex-moll – either that or a hit-woman. He thought it prudent not to mention his other theory – that she might have been a prostitute looking to expand her business abroad.

Further laughter followed as they recalled the ambiguous content of their messages and the misunderstandings that ensued from them. More cups of coffee and slices of Battenberg cake kept the light-hearted nature of the banter going on into the early-evening.

With the conversation flagging and realising Galina might well be hungry, Dave suggested they go out for a meal. It was politely declined by Galina.

"If you do not mind Dave, I am very tired, I herd to get up very early today, so would like to go to my room now if I may."

"Er... okay," Dave tried to think of something she might need before retiring. "Would you like a drink? – A nightcap perhaps? I've got some vodka in specially."

"No, thernks Dave, thert is very kind – burt maybe tomorrow."

"Well okay, right then, I'll show you to your room. I expect you'll want to freshen up first and unpack your... er, tools and the like."

"Yers, I hope you don't mind Dave.

"No... no, of course not," he said hiding his disappointment. "I'll just drag your suitcase up the stairs and show you the way."

After a short pause on the landing to get his breath back, Dave manoeuvred the case through the doorway of Galina's room. Inside, he pointed out the fresh nylon sheets and a striped beach towel for her ablutions.

"Now the bathroom is next door, and if you need anything... anything at all, I'm in the room just across from you." It crossed his mind to give Galina a conspirital wink as he said it, but then thought better of it.

"I'm just going downstairs for a while. Have a good night's sleep and I'll look forward to seeing you in the morning!"

"Yers Dave, I'm sorry not to come and herv drink with you, but I erm very tired. In the morning I wirl be much better."

Chapter 10

Dave retired downstairs and helped himself to a glass of Rioja before switching on the TV. As he randomly flicked through the channels, his mind wandered back over the day, and in particular, their evening spent together. On balance, he judged it had gone as well as could be expected.

It would have been nice to spend a little more time in her company, maybe share a nightcap or two before retiring to bed. But in Galina's defence, she had endured a long flight and would naturally want to freshen up – perhaps have a shower before unpacking her clothes. She might want to check over those wrenches and spanners too before taking to her bed, which reminded him, he must have a word with her about that weeping joint on the lounge radiator – maybe she could just nip it up a bit tighter for him.

Having reflected on the day's events, the mixture of alcohol and fatigue were now beginning to tell on him. He could feel his eyes starting to close and his head beginning to droop forward. It made him realise he too was in need of sleep – if only he could just rouse himself.

He finally made the effort to get out of the chair and turn off the TV. As he climbed the stairs he paused for a moment outside Galina's room and was puzzled to hear the sound of metallic clanging coming from inside. *Had she brought some exercise weights with her too?* he wondered. The weight of her suitcase would certainly have justified that assumption.

Intrigued, he continued to listen but could not imagine what she was doing in there. The unfamiliar noises gave him the excuse to find out. Dave gently knocked on the centre panel of the door, then again a little louder as another metallic clang transmitted its sound through the bedroom door.

The sounds suddenly stopped. He heard Galina walk up to the door before opening it just enough to peer around.

"Er, sorry to bother you Galina, but I couldn't help wondering what it was you were doing. The noise sounded er... well... unfamiliar to me, is everything okay?"

Galina opened the door just wide enough for him to see her dressed in a long negligee, underneath which he could clearly see the outline of her – briefer than he would have expected – bra and knickers. Though he tried to keep his eyes uppermost, the item of clothing that most drew his attention was the sturdy leather tool belt tied around her waist – complete with an assortment of spanners and wrenches protruding out of individual pouches. Further adding to the incongruousness of her appearance were the thick cotton and leather gloves on her hands. Dave was finding Russian bedtime attire quite a revelation.

In answer to his obvious puzzlement over her nightwear and the unusual noises, Galina explained without prompting. "I hope you do not mind burt I was jurst testing my turls on your water pipes and heating stove – I curd see thert your cock is not upright..."

Dave automatically shot a look down to his groin.

"...ernd I make it upright using my wrenches, so I now know they all right size to fit! I am so pleased to know thirs. I hope you do not mirnd. I could not sleep urntil I knew for sure!"

It took Dave a second or two to work out that Galina was referring to the bedroom radiator and its associated pipes. She had just straightened up the thermostatic valve, which he did indeed recall being a little out of vertical, though he didn't expect Galina to be manipulating his pipework at such an early juncture.

Dave thought it best to humour her. Maybe a little eccentricity was normal for newly-qualified female Russian plumbers on assignments in England, who happened to be staying with a male internet friend with an unfamiliar central heating system.

"Yers... I mean yes, all our pipes and unions are now in metric sizes – just like in Russia; have been for years in fact and thank you for doing that."

"Yers, now all is okay. I erm herpy to go to sleep now."

"Right Galina, so there's nothing else you need then; a hot drink after your endeavours perhaps?"

He could have suggested that on such a chilly night as this, maybe she would like something warm inside her – but knew the double-meaning would be lost on her, as was the case with her 'upright cock' remark.

"Copious amounts of tea are the normal accompaniment to this type of manual work," he joked.

"Tea... Dave?"

"It's okay, just a little levity – it is of no consequence."

He was really just trying to extend the encounter in any way he could. As she stood close to him in the doorway, her perfume filled the air, arousing his senses. The bedside light in the room perfectly silhouetted her shapely body and full breasts, whilst soft glints of light danced off the set of chrome vanadium spanners as she moved. Dave found the whole scenario increasingly erotic. A sexual fantasy involving tight leather tool wraps suddenly took hold of his conscious thoughts, reaching within seconds an erotic conclusion. Her reply brought him back to reality.

"No, er... I don't thirnk so Dave. I erm very tired now, burt thank you for asking. Gourdnight!"

Dave gathered up his drooping bottom lip and stuttered a response.

"Yes... well... I'll be er, seeing you in the morning then."

Galina gave a little wave of her hand, before closing the bedroom door to him.

Dave retreated, and with a heavy heart crossed the landing to his own room. Once in bed, he picked up a book to try and take his mind off the encounter. As enthralling as Anthony Bevor's account of the siege of Stalingrad was, his consciousness kept drifting back to the arousing sight of Galina. His female visitor was still very much on his mind when he switched off the light and settled down to sleep.

The next morning, he woke up with a vague recollection in his head of a dream involving Galina, but struggled to remember any significant detail. The sound of the shower running in the bathroom prompted Dave to look at his watch. It was just after eight.

He recalled the exchange he'd had with Galina in the bedroom doorway about her radiator, and reached out of bed to feel his own. Dave was relieved to find that it was warm. At least she'd not attempted to meddle with the rest of the central heating system during the night. He hoped she would also leave the shower just as she had found it – at least until he'd had a chance to use it.

As soon as he heard Galina vacate the bathroom, Dave went in to quickly complete his own ablutions. He wanted to ensure he was ready in the kitchen for her when she came downstairs.

For breakfast he assembled several packets of cereals on the table, together with fruit juice and a pot of coffee. The toaster was already primed with slices of bread – the more expensive granary variety with seeds and hard bits. He imagined it to be more the sort of rustic bread eaten in Russia.

Dave extended a warm, but formal greeting to Galina when at last she appeared and was acknowledged politely in return. After inquiring how well she had slept, Dave couldn't resist teasing her about the toolbelt he'd caught her wearing. A now embarrassed Galina began to giggle as she realised how incongruous it must have looked underneath her flimsy negligee.

When asked if the spanners had not got in the way whenever she turned over in her sleep, Galina replied in all seriousness, "Oh no! I do not wear it irn bed!"

Dave tried hard to keep a straight face. He then enquired whether she'd carried out any other adjustments to the plumbing during the night.

Galina looked puzzled. Dave explained that he was certain the radiator in the kitchen had been in a different place before they went to bed last night. Galina looked at the radiator – then at Dave – then at the radiator again.

"Burt I do not urnderstand…"

"I just wondered whether you had decided to move it in the night," he explained, struggling to keep his face straight.

She shook her head. "I do not know what you mean Dave, I really don't."

Seeing the look of bewilderment on her face, he was unable to contain himself any longer and began to laugh. Galina was not at all amused and sat glowering at him. Dave wondered if he had gone too far, but before long she too began to laugh, wagging her finger at him in mock admonishment for his teasing. Dave was pleased to see that she was taking it all with good humour.

After apologising for his mischief-making, he explained that he couldn't resist the opportunity offered after last night's unusual encounter on the landing. The laughter though, led the conversation onto a more serious aspect of her work as a plumber: how she actually intended to embark on her new career in the UK. In between sips of coffee, Galina explained her strategy.

Having qualified as a plumber in her native Russia, she needed to familiarise herself with UK working practices and gain the necessary trade qualifications in order to work here – there just happened to be a college offering the course she needed in Wensbury, Galina informed him.

Luckily, she had a niece living in the West Midlands. Irina had been working in the UK for the last two years and had offered to accommodate her for the duration of the course. Although they'd been in regular contact by phone, for some reason her number was now unobtainable. It was probably just a temporary problem, explained Galina. She did have her address and intended to call in there sometime over the next few days.

Dave couldn't help but wonder after hearing all this whether it was all just a coincidence, or had he indeed been selected by her for his geographical location. He would keep the thought to himself for now.

While they were on the subject of plumbing, Dave thought it an opportune moment to tell Galina about his invention – his multi-purpose workbench. He quickly explained its many useful functions to her and offered to demonstrate it after breakfast – just the thing for an up-and-coming plumber, he advised her.

Once he'd piled up the dishes for washing later, Dave led Galina out to his garden workshop. He demonstrated how the workbench separated into two equally-sized sawhorses, how the adjustable jaws could hold a twenty-two millimetre copper pipe steady, and how the workbench doubled as a pair of steps, allowing a person to work up to ceiling height with ease.

Just as he'd expected, Galina was suitably impressed. As a woman of practical abilities herself, she obviously appreciated having several useful functions combined within one piece of equipment. Although still a prototype, Dave marked her down for a possible sale, if and when he got it into production.

With a common rapport established between them, the rest of the morning quickly passed by, helped along with further cups of coffee and custard cream biscuits.

Rain showers permitting, Dave suggested a walk down to his local KostKwik after lunch; he needed some essential supplies. The Rioja stocks were getting low and Galina had expressed a liking for herbal teas and pickled gherkins.

Dave had promised to take Galina to a traditional British curry house in the evening as a treat. With several in the town to choose from, he plumped for the one he was most familiar with – The Star Balti House. Due to the more sustained rain falling, Dave decided to drive to the venue, and was in luck when he found an available space almost opposite the restaurant.

On pushing open the door, they were assailed by the enticing aroma of exotic roasted spices. Vijay, one of the establishment's regular waiters, turned to welcome them.

"Mr Dave! It's good to see you again – and *ladyfriend*!"

He tried to ignore Vijay's look of surprise and his heavy

emphasis on the word 'ladyfriend'. Now feeling obliged to carry out an introduction he announced, "Yes, this is my friend Galina – she's Russian you know!"

Vijay nodded. "No problem, not too many in yet so we can serve you very quick Mr Dave."

Dave laughed, "No you misunderstand me – she is a Russian person in fact."

"Ah! I see! Your ladyfriend is from Russia! We are indeed highly honoured madam, and your first time at The Star Balti too. You sure you in no hurry Mr Dave? She has to make such a long journey home."

"No, no." Dave smiled again at the waiter's inability to comprehend what he was saying, "Galina is on a visit to this country. She is stopping with me at my house for a few days, so there is no rush."

"Really? At your house?" queried Vijay.

"Yes, my house!" repeated Dave, now getting rather irritated by Vijay's repeated expressions of disbelief. "Galina happens to be enjoying a short holiday in our country, so we have all evening to enjoy one of your most excellent curries." He paused. "Once we get to sit down at a table that is."

"Ah, yes of course! I give you the best table in the house."

"The one near the working radiator?"

"Indeed!"

It was Dave's considered opinion that the evening had passed most agreeably – in fact, rather better than that. During the meal, they had both been pleasantly surprised to learn that they had several things in common: a love of Beatles music, a period of service spent in their respective armed forces, and both of them had been married – though unlike him, Galina had been bereaved.

The chicken jalfrezi had gone down well with Dave, and Galina's tandoori chicken had been similarly well-received. With their ice cream desserts finished and the coffee cups drained, Dave suggested they make their way back home.

Tipping Vijay more generously than he would have done if he'd been alone – an act which precipitated the final raised eyebrow of the evening – Dave returned the effusive goodbyes of the staff as they made to leave. Remembering his manners, he held both the restaurant and car door open for Galina prior to undertaking the journey back to the house. There he hoped they could relax together with a glass or two of wine.

Dave dug out some of his Beatles CDs on their return, selecting 'Revolver' to play in the background while he waited for Galina to return from the toilet. Her face lit up when she entered the room and heard her favourite 60's group playing. After complimenting him on his choice of music, she began humming the current track, mouthing the words she could still remember.

His attention to detail was obviously working. Dave smiled and patted the cushion next to him. She took up his invitation, sinking deep into the low-density foam of his second-hand 1980's velour settee. As Galina attempted to get comfortable, Dave thought about their earlier conversations and realised there were still many things he didn't know about her. Two questions immediately came to mind: what made her leave Russia, and how did she come to speak English so well?

After using all of his spare cushions to even out the height difference, Galina explained how she became interested in learning English through immersing herself in western pop culture as a teenager. Finding herself with a gift for languages, she went on to take a degree in English at university after leaving school. At that time, graduates were obliged by the Soviet authorities to undertake some form of public service in return for their comprehensive state-funded education. Unsure as to what direction her life should take, and encouraged by her father who had enjoyed a long and distinguished military career himself, she made a decision to enlist in the army. Her language skills were much sought after by the military, and as a consequence, she obtained a coveted posting to the Intelligence Corps.

Seconded to East Germany for most of the time, the bulk of

her work consisted of listening to recordings of NATO radio traffic and translating the intercepted information. On hearing this, Dave wondered whether she had ever listened to his own radio transmissions during his time in the forces. He had been on exercise near the border with East Germany several times during that same period.

It was in the army where she had met her future husband, a captain in the same unit. While he was looking for advancement in the military, she was anxious to have the children she longed for. By pulling a few strings, she managed to obtain a transfer into a civilian role within the Defence Ministry, thereby removing the last obstacle in the way of starting a family. Unfortunately, events were to conspire against her in the implementation of these plans.

Following the removal of the Berlin Wall and the dismantling of the Soviet Bloc in the late 1980's, the Russian military authorities began scaling down their forces in response to the diminished threat. This meant fewer promotion opportunities for junior officers like her husband, so his decision to resign from the army made sense at the time. He could see better prospects for himself in the new Russian police force, now being kept increasingly busy by the rise of the crime mafias.

All went well in his new career until one day during the pursuit of a criminal gang, a shootout occurred and her husband was fatally wounded, leaving her a widow at only thirty six. His death was a tragic blow, and recovering from the trauma of it all proved a long and painful process, confessed Galina. Not only had she lost her husband, but also all hope of having the children she'd always wanted. Too distraught to carry on working, she gave up her job; then discovered that as a widow of a low-ranking policeman, the pension was barely enough to live on.

As she came to terms with her loss, her focus became getting her life back into order. Thinking some form of manual work might be therapeutic in exorcising her troubled state of mind, she decided to retrain as a plumber; her choice of trade partly influenced by having to correct problems in her own flat after the state-supplied service proved less than adequate. Studying at her local technical college equipped her with the necessary qualifications, but in the newly-formed Russian market economy, she struggled to find sufficient paying work.

Her private life fared little better with few places in her provincial town for a woman in her forties to socialise with eligible men. Having only her sister-in-law – Irina's mother – close by for company, she truly felt the enforced loneliness of her high-rise flat.

It was at this point, explained Galina, that she decided to take stock of her life. Weary of living in dreary post-Soviet Russia with its accumulation of sad memories, she made a life-changing decision – to seek out a new life for herself in the UK. With knowledge of its language and culture, and with a niece willing to accommodate her, Great Britain seemed the obvious candidate. Her plumbing skills, she reasoned, would also be transferable to her country of choice.

While using the internet to research the trade qualifications needed to work in the UK, she clicked on an ad for dating sites and decided to join. One of the profiles that came up was Dave's. The rest of the story he already knew.

Dave could only agree with the logic she had employed in making such difficult life decisions. He might well have taken a similar course of action himself had he been in her shoes, though he'd never had to undergo the experience of his partner being murdered. Thinking back to the problems with his own ex, he wondered once again how difficult it would be to arrange.

As the evening wore on, and the refills of wine took effect, Galina's mood deepened as she further reflected on her misfortunes. Dave, sensing her melancholic state of mind, recalled a quotation he felt appropriate to her situation. He recited it for her, "Only by making sense of the past, can one see back to the future."

Galina's face took on a puzzled look.

Her reaction made him wonder whether he had got the quotation right. He recited it again in his head then altered the words around a couple of times before dismissing it with the conclusion that it probably wasn't that appropriate anyway.

When late in the evening the flow of conversation finally began to ebb, Galina thanked him for being such a patient listener. Dave assured her that he had been more than happy to hear her life story, "In its entirety and in just one evening too!" he joked.

Galina gave a sort of laugh and apologised again for monopolising the conversation, admitting that since her husband had died there had been precious few others in her life to confide in, so thanked him once again for his indulgence. With that she kissed him on the cheek and declared her intention to retire to bed.

Dave didn't know what to say. He had done very little apart from sit and listen. But he could understand her situation. Here she was at a major crossroads in her life, embarking on a bold new enterprise in an alien country and, quite naturally, was experiencing all sorts of doubts and fears about how life would pan out for her. Having no one else to unburden these concerns to, she was understandably appreciative of someone like him having the time to listen. It just proved to him the importance of appearing attentive, but saying little, when in the company of a female in 'emotional' mode.

He was about to tell Galina that her expressions of gratitude were really not necessary when his eyes were drawn to Galina's nipples, now standing proud under her blouse. They hadn't been visible the last time he'd looked. Had the heating gone off early, he wondered? The room certainly felt cooler; he reminded himself to check the timer before going to bed.

Dave tried to steer his focus back to more altruistic concerns for Galina. He wanted to offer her some reassurance after her emotional outpouring. Putting his arm around her shoulder seemed an appropriate gesture of empathy. Unfortunately, by the time he'd reached out to her, she was already out of the chair and he was left with an arm hanging awkwardly in the air. Galina laughed when she caught sight of him. Pausing in the doorway, she waved back, saying, "I thirnk you are gourd mern Dave – funny – burt a gourd mern. I wirl lurk forward to seeing you irn the mourning!"

Dave noticed she still seemed amused about something.

He sat listening to her footsteps as she mounted the stairs and pondered on the words she had just spoken. Dave hoped she had meant funny in a 'ha ha' and not a 'peculiar' sense. But then why would she have cause to think that?

Sipping the last of his wine, he thought back over their conversation. The evening had proved to be quite a revelation. He could easily understand Galina feeling like she did after revisiting all she had been through. Hopefully a good night's sleep will see her spirits restored; further improved perhaps by a brisk walk in the fresh air after breakfast. He would suggest the idea to her in the morning. The remedy had proved its worth to him over the past few months.

Dave realised he was already becoming protective of her – he liked the feeling it gave him, the thought of caring about someone again. He almost dared not think it, but he could get used to all this. Having an intimate meal together, sinking into the sofa afterwards, discussing the meaning of life over a glass of wine whilst listening to their favourite music – it was all very appealing.

As he listened to the sounds of Galina moving around upstairs, it brought home to him the comfort derived from having another person in the house. Even without the exploratory clanging of her spanners on his pipes, her presence was giving new life to the place – becoming less the lonely tomb he had recently come to think of it.

Chapter 11

Dave lay in bed the following morning, waiting for his turn in the shower. He could hear the water running so knew that Galina had risen and beaten him to it yet again. The thought of her suddenly brought to mind his dream from the previous night.

It was a fantasy about Galina. She was standing in the shower, naked apart from the leather toolbelt strapped tightly around her waist. There appeared to be a problem with the shower head and she was reaching up to adjust the flow with a 22mm open-ended spanner. For some reason, he was in the shower with her. He stood behind Galina, his hands gripping her buttocks, lending a steadying hand while she tweaked the union. As she worked, little rivulets of water ran down her back into the narrow valley of her bottom.

Dave was aware of a stiffening sensation down below and could see from his horizontal position in bed what appeared to be the beginnings of a tent pole gradually being erected underneath the duvet.

Before he could recall properly the conclusion of his erotic dream, Dave was interrupted with an urgent message from a deeper place. His digestive system having had eight hours to fully process the previous night's curry was signalling to him that a call of nature was now urgently required. With Galina still in the bathroom, he realised he would have to relieve himself in the downstairs toilet.

Luckily, Galina was well away from the aftermath of an evacuation he predicted would be significant. By way of a brief respite, he expelled the build-up of wind while pulling the sheets up tightly around his neck in an effort to form a gas-tight barrier. Despite the precaution, within a minute the malodorous smell had reached his nostrils and permeated the bedroom.

He was just preparing himself to get out of bed and seek proper relief when Dave was startled to hear a faint tapping on his door, followed by the sound of Galina's voice.

"Gourd mourning Dave, can I curm in? I herv coffee for you."

Dave panicked. In normal circumstances, he would be delighted to have Galina enter his bedroom – but what should he do? This would be so embarrassing. The noxious smell was nearly making him gag.

"Er... wait a minute Galina." His mind was racing. "Look, why don't you just leave it by the door."

"Werl, okay Dave... if do you not want me to curm into your room – but I herv mersage fer you as well!"

What! Was she really saying she wanted to give him a massage? She would soon change her mind if she entered the bedroom in its present state. What on earth should he say to her? He had to clear the smell from the room – and quickly!

"Yes... yes of course!" he shouted through the door. He was out of bed now, frantically trying to open the window and rid the room of the fetid air. Now grabbing a bottle of aftershave in each hand, he sprayed long bursts around the room.

"Is thert yers of course I do wernt to herv mersage now – or yers of course I do not wernt to herv mersage now?"

Dave was still trying to open the window. The wood had obviously swelled in the recent wet weather. He was now cursing himself for not having those cut-price UPVC windows he was recently offered by a neighbour – before the man lost his job with Stayclear West Midlands when accounting irregularities were discovered.

"Yes! Yes! Of course I do!" he shouted back. Panic was now setting in as the window still refused to shift.

"Burt you still not say one way or other. You play games with me again I thirnk – I leave your coffee by the door."

Dave was now thumping the window frame with his shoe.

"No, no! Galina… I mean yes, yes! I do very much want to… I do!"

"There is furny smell on your corridor Dave, is your drain okay?" announced Galina, now with her plumber's hat.

Christ, thought Dave, *it must have been one of those stealth ones and crept out under the door.*

"No, not that I know to!" denied Dave. Administering a final heavy blow, the window suddenly gave way, along with the glass which cracked into several pieces, two of which fell from the casement and dropped the thirty feet to the ground below with an almighty crash. Dave winced.

Galina, having heard the noise through the still closed door, responded. "Dave! I do not know whert is wrong, burt I would not come into your room now, so there is no need to break window to escape!"

He heard an exasperated Galina stomp down the stairs.

Dave wanted to cry when he thought about what he had just missed out on. He now had two urgent missions to carry out. The original one was still keeping up the pressure, but also he desperately needed to explain his behaviour to Galina. Desperate to relieve the former, Dave shuffled off with the greatest of care to the vacant bathroom, locked the door and sat down to instantly commence proceedings.

Ignoring the collection of *Reader's Digests* stored in chronological order on top of the cistern – any one of which he would normally absorb himself in whilst engaged in this particular function – he set his mind to thinking through his approach to Galina. Thinking of a way to explain his reluctance to take up her offer of a massage was the problem; he couldn't believe she had just come out with it like that!

After giving it some thought, he decided that honesty would probably be the best policy, after all everybody breaks wind; it's just unfortunate that a very hot chicken jalfrezi eaten the night before does add somewhat to the potency of its bouquet. Dave remembered reading somewhere that certain members of the royal family were noted for their bottom burps and it never seemed to put their many distinguished guests off. He also recalled that in old Imperial Russia, breaking wind at the dinner table was seen as a compliment; an audible sign that you had enjoyed the food. He wondered if the sovereign's advisors had been advised of that particular custom before the Royal visit there a few years ago.

Having formulated an explanation he was satisfied with, Dave was finding his legs starting to go numb so reached for the toilet roll. It was then he realised that one of the tasks he had set himself the previous night, and had completely forgotten about after his evening with Galina, now manifested itself in the ultimate worst case scenario – there was just one sheet left on the roll!

As a single gentleman, he normally used kitchen roll in the toilet, it being stronger and larger on a sheet by sheet basis than conventional toilet roll, so giving greater coverage for less cost. With a woman in the house, he had realised it was not really suitable for a lady's more delicate requirements, so before Galina's arrival he'd substituted it for some of the soft quilted stuff, of which there was now none! Just what had she done with it all? Did she think the stuff grew on trees?

He cursed under his breath. What to do about it was the dilemma now facing him. Unfortunately, all the spare toilet rolls were in the downstairs toilet. Dave scanned around the bathroom in the hope of finding some suitable alternative material. He considered for a moment ripping some pages out of one of the *Reader's Digests*, but then dismissed the idea as the pages would be too small and the astringent nature of the residue would only take the print off the pages. Having the 'Laughter in uniform' section transferred onto his bottom would really be no laughing matter.

Remembering that he had a box of tissues in the bedroom, Dave calculated that if he were to leave his boxer shorts around his ankles, he could just about shuffle across the hall to retrieve them. It would only take a few seconds. He could do it whilst Galina was still safely downstairs.

Dave lifted himself off the toilet seat, carefully opened the door and peeked around it to check the coast was clear. By taking the very tiniest of steps and feeling very much like a Japanese Geisha at a demonstration of the tea ceremony, he shuffled out of the bathroom.

Pausing for a moment at the top of the stairs, he peered down for confirmation of a clear run across the landing. Unfortunately on picking up his step again, he inadvertently caught his foot in the leg of his shorts, causing him to come crashing – bottom down – on to the landing carpet. Dave cursed loudly. Before he had time to pick himself up, he heard a concerned Galina shout up to him, followed immediately by the sound of rapid footsteps up the stairs. Dave frantically tried to cover up his predicament before Galina reached the landing. Unfortunately, he wasn't quite quick enough.

Her face had a look of utter incomprehension as she stood staring at Dave sitting there with his bare bottom on the carpet, his underpants around his ankles and with his hands covering his vitals.

Dave was mortified, utterly lost for words. There was nothing he could think of to explain the situation. His embarrassment was absolute, total and without precedent.

Galina stood open-mouthed for what seemed like an eternity before she spoke. "I wers bringing new roll of paper – but you herv used carpet! I do not understand, I do not understand at all! Thirs irs not good Dave. My friends warn me thert Englishmen do weird thirngs sometimes. You know once I had dog thert did this – would drag ass along floor, but I did not know that a man curd do such a thing! Is not normal for a person to do this – I thinrk I should leave!"

"No, no, Galina, look I can explain!"

"Whert is there to explain? I see whert you do with my own eyes! I thirnk I should go!"

"Please don't Galina!"

"I go downstairs now!" she announced. With that Galina threw the toilet roll at him. It rebounded off his head, hit the banister and bounced down the stairs, closely following in Galina's footsteps.

Dave's misery was complete. He'd truly surpassed himself in achieving the most humiliating situation of all time – not quite how he'd intended to start a new day in Galina's company. Aside from his soiled bottom, there was the grievous damage done to the image he had been at pains to cultivate: that of the cultured, urbane, well-mannered Englishman. Not as now seen through her eyes – some pervert with an overriding interest in scatology acting out his sick fantasies on the landing.

It was at a moment like this that he could easily have given in to despair by taking himself into a quiet corner and banging his head hard against the wall several times. Much to his surprise, this was not how he felt on this occasion.

He found himself calm and reasoned. Dave liked Galina immensely. He wanted her to like him. Although his predicament was not easily explained away – it was not impossible. She was aware that the toilet roll had run out, so what was he to do? He would just tell it like it was, hoping she would understand. After all she was still a human being like him, with all the faults and foibles common to the species. She had helped to bring up her sister-in-law's three children, so was used to a soiled bottom or two – though maybe not one belonging to a fifty-two year old male friend perhaps. But like most women with experience of life, she would be acutely aware of man's failings. It was a well-known fact that the methodology employed by the male species when using the toilet for a no.2 was a complete mystery to members of the female sex.

Dave retrieved the toilet roll, tottered back to the bathroom and set about the task of cleaning himself up. He showered, shaved, put on some respectable clothes, then carefully checked his appearance in the full-length mirror before making a nervous descent down the stairs. Galina was sitting in the kitchen sipping coffee, staring intently at the wall as he walked in.

He took up a position on the other side of the table, leaning against the chair back for support. Galina refused to look at him as he nervously shifted his weight from one foot to the other. He cleared his throat in order to break the awkward silence.

"Look Galina please let me explain, what happened was..."

"...No Dave, I do not wernt to hear thirs. I really do not like to thirnk about whert you were doing jurst now!" interrupted Galina.

Dave broke his hangdog expression to flash Galina an apologetic smile when she briefly glanced at him. He seized the opportunity and launched into his explanation for the scenario she had just witnessed, desperately trying to portray himself a victim of his own bodily functions. Galina sat poker-faced with arms folded, nodding every now and again as he explained the catalogue of misfortunes – each one sending him deeper and deeper into the mire, as it were.

At the end of it all, he sensed that Galina was reassured at least to know that events had truly conspired against him and that he did not have some sort of bizarre toilet ritual – the origins of which a psychiatrist would undoubtedly have traced back to a traumatic incident during potty-training in his early childhood.

Now that he seemed to be making headway with Galina, he went on to emphasise once again that he really was quite normal – well in his toilet habits anyway, he quipped – when the chair which he had been leaning heavily against suddenly slipped backwards and Dave collapsed onto the floor.

Galina, watching it all happen, burst out laughing as Dave's pride took the full impact again. He grimaced but managed to force a smile as he pulled himself up off the floor.

"I'm sorry Dave, burt I couldn't help laughing, the way you jurst collapsed like thert."

"Well I'm glad you found it funny!"

"Sorry Dave, are you hurt?"

"Just my self-esteem – once again," he said, rubbing his back. Still feeling anxious about what had happened earlier, he asked, "I hope you now accept my explanation for the er, little accident on the landing Galina?"

"Why yers, I could see whert had herpened."

"You could?"

"Why yers!"

"So why did you not say? It would have saved me the ordeal of trying to explain it all to you."

"Because how you say, you 'tease' me so bad yesterday, so I thirnk I do same to you today, is fair yers?"

Dave recalled his jokes about her spanners, and yes, he had to admit he was fair game. She had certainly fooled him. He really had thought she was going to walk out. Now much relieved, Dave began to think about some form of compensation for what she had put him through. He recalled what Galina had said when she stood outside his bedroom door. A plan formulated in his head. As he went to sit down, Dave winced as if in pain. He rubbed his back for a moment before grabbing hold of the table, using it for support while he eased himself into the seat.

"Are you alright Dave?" asked Galina showing concern.

"I'm not sure, I think may have damaged something," said Dave, pulling what he thought was an appropriate expression of pain. "Look Galina, you said something about a massage earlier? Er... perhaps it would be a good idea if you could give me the massage now?"

"Yers of course!"

Dave just managed to prevent his grimace morphing into a grin.

"That's good. So er... I expect you'll want me to come upstairs with you then?"

Galina gave him with a puzzled look. "Why? Whert is wrong with me giving irt you here?"

"Well, I'll need to lie down won't I?"

Galina was more confused, "Why would you want to lie down? Irt is not bad news I have for you!"

It was Dave's turn to look perplexed. "What do you mean, not bad news?"

Showing her exasperation, Galina spoke very deliberately. "The... mersage... whert... I... have... been... talking... about! The mersage from your neighbour who called at door early thirs morning to say if you are still interested, he would take another fifty pounds off price of new windows!"

Realisation belatedly dawned on Dave. "Oh right! You mean a message – you had a message for me."

"Yers, mersage! That is whert I said! You sure you okay Dave, you not like you were yersterday. Maybe you herv too murch wine last night!" said Galina, amused by his series of lapses. "Or like my friends warn me, it's jurst because you are Ernglish! Is so, yers?" she teased.

Dave sat wearily with head in hands and agreed. "Yes, I think you must be right Galina – it's just because I'm Ernglish."

Chapter 12

Following their delayed breakfast and with a clear day forecast, Dave suggested a walk around the town to show Galina the sights.

The late morning sun was now high enough in the sky to melt the patches of overnight frost formed on the surface of the riverside walk they were following. A flotilla of ducks changed tack and steered a course in their direction when Dave and Galina stopped by the bridge to admire the misty scene. Anticipating an offering of food, the water birds made vocal their demands when it failed to materialise.

Amidst the cacophony of noise, Dave tried to explain some local history to Galina, though without being too specific due to his own lack of knowledge of the subject. He found it difficult to maintain a dignified appearance with his mind repeatedly slipping back to the episode on the landing. It was only by busily pointing hither and thither along the riverbank as he spoke that he was able to maintain an air of normality. At one point Galina started to giggle for no apparent reason, and when asked why, she had to admit that she kept reliving the image of him sitting bare-bottomed on the landing. He felt the blood flow to his facial cheeks at the very mention of his most embarrassing moment ever in his entire life – never to be equalled!

However, Dave was able to smile the more he thought about it. He was relieved that Galina could see that he truly was a victim of misfortune. Providing Galina would let him – and she had shown herself to have quite a mischievous sense of humour so far – Dave resolved to put the incident firmly behind him. He could, as it were, start again with a clean sheet.

They carried on walking and crossed over the bridge to make their way up to the town gardens – the highest point in Bridforth – telling Galina how it offered one of the finest views in the whole country. Dave stopped to point out a couple of well-known landmarks to Galina – the Worfe Valley Railway Station and Engine sheds, easily identifiable by the pall of smoke slowly rising from the engines under steam in the yard. He allowed Galina a few minutes to admire the rich scene before pushing on into the town.

A coffee shop drew their attention, its rich arabica aroma wafted to them on the breeze, enticing them inside. The young assistant at the counter rattled off the questions at a cracking pace.

"Small, medium or large?"

"Brazilian or Colombian blend?"

"Ordinary or decaff?"

"Latte, cappuccino, mocha or espresso?"

"To drink inside or take out?"

"Any toppings at all?"

Then finally the up-sell.

"And would you like a muffin with that?"

With all the questions answered – including a change of mind from Galina which necessitated starting the algorithm over again – Dave was presented with two steaming mugs together with a side order, which he carried over to a vacant table.

Between sips of latté and bites of blueberry muffin, Galina explained more about her plans to launch herself into the plumbing business. As well as working towards the gas qualification needed to maintain and repair central heating boilers, she also intended to pursue her ambition of setting up her own plumbing business, using her niece's house as a base.

"Well it sounds like you've got it all sorted then," said Dave. "When we get home, we can check it out on the internet and see whether we can't get you on this course of yours."

"Burt Dave, I wernt to get on thirs course, not for you to see if you cannot get me on it."

"No, no Galina, it's just a peculiar figure of speech. The

English language is littered with them. We will get you on the course, I'm sure of it!"

Dave's face broke into a smile. He was finding it a natural reaction wanting to please her.

"Thert's gourd Dave, you are most kind." Galina smiled back at him and with that Dave received his second kiss on the cheek.

With no demands on their time, they retraced their route back to the house at a leisurely pace. After making preliminary enquiries on Galina's behalf via the phone and through the college's own website, Dave was satisfied they could do no more for the time being.

For that evening's meal he'd promised to cook Galina a traditional British spaghetti bolognese, which for good measure he intended to lace with plenty of KostKwik Rioja. He was sure he had some tiramisu in the freezer for desserts.

Two days later they had cause for celebration: her Russian paperwork had caused something of an administrative delay, but after a bit of investigation work her plumbing qualifications were indeed found to be valid in the UK. With the issue satisfactorily resolved, Dave drove Galina into Wensbury where she enrolled on her chosen BTEC (gas fitting) course, starting in just a few weeks time. After completing all the formalities, Galina accepted Dave's offer to take her clothes shopping in Birmingham.

Compared to her provincial hometown in Russia, Galina found herself overwhelmed by the range of colours and styles on sale. After trying on a whole swathe of garments, she eventually chose a close-fitting pair of light blue overalls with extensive tool pockets, together with a matching pair of stout safety shoes from the workwear department of B & Cue.

Galina was thrilled with the purchases, and couldn't wait to get back to the house and try them on. Donning her new attire, she did a twirl in front of Dave seeking his approval.

"It looks great, but I still prefer you in what you wore when I came into your room on the first night!" Dave added a suggestive wink for good measure.

Galina giggled, "I thirnk you murst wait some time before you see thert again!"

With that Galina laughed, amused by her own teasing tone and its effect on Dave. He played along, aware that an evening at Withyspoons lay ahead of them and with sufficient wine, who knows what might happen. With this thought in mind, he decided to make sure the house was nicely warmed when they returned; a frost was again forecast, so he cranked up the central heating to maximum before they left the house.

On arrival at the restaurant, Dave played the generous host, insisting Galina choose anything off the menu, though she still insisted on checking with him before making her choice.

"Like I say it's my treat, so anything over six pounds is fine – after all, we are celebrating!"

The drink did indeed flow freely, together with copious amounts of laughter arising from their banter. Galina, now becoming familiar with the repressive traits in Dave's character, was becoming quite adept at identifying his sensitive areas and teasing him about them. During their main course, Galina asked quite out of the blue, "So whern did you start losing your hair Dave?"

"Er... well, when I found out you were coming over to see me. I had a full head 'til then!"

Galina feigned outrage and gave him a playful thump in his side. Dave played along by crying 'ouch!' Quite pleased that what was left of his hair still showed healthy growth, he added, "I think it will need cutting soon though."

"So which one is irt needs cutting Dave, I wirl do irt for you – wirl take only one second!"

It was Galina's turn to laugh. Dave shot her a look of indignation before replying.

"I'll have you know it's taken me years to grow this bald patch!"

The lively banter continued right through main course, helped more than a little by Dave's frequent refilling of their wine glasses.

After a pudding and an Irish coffee each, both were replete, agreeably inebriated and ready to depart homewards. Galina coughed as a swirl of cigarette smoke wafted into the doorway. She shivered, pulled up her collar and grabbed Dave's arm, leaning against him as they set off for the walk back – their arms closely entwined.

An unwelcome surprise greeted them when they stepped through the front door – the house felt bone-chillingly cold. Dave wondered what could have gone wrong. After his earlier adjustment of the thermostat, he had expected to find the house shimmering in a heat haze when they arrived home.

Dave soon identified the boiler as being the cause of the problem and judging by the freezer-like temperature, guessed it must have failed sometime during the early evening. He cursed at having his carefully-laid plans blown asunder like this.

Putting aside his disappointment for the moment, Dave set to work checking the components with previous form for this type of malfunction. The thermostat and timer appeared to be blameless so he removed the cover of the boiler, poking his head into the dark gloom of its interior for a more in-depth look at the problem. Thick layers of dust coated the components, but what was it he should check? With Galina standing there, still with her coat on, he needed to be doing something. But just as he set to work randomly fiddling with each knob in turn, Galina suddenly announced that she was going to bed.

What! Why did she have to go so soon? Couldn't she see he was doing his best to try and fix the problem? He'd already provided her with a hot water bottle. She was Russian for goodness sake, they were supposed to be used to the cold. Perhaps she would change her mind if he were to offer her the use of that fan heater.

He realised there may well be another reason. Having made his intentions all too clear during the course of the evening, she could be using the excuse to escape from his clutches, but what was he supposed to do? He was a man after all and men were programmed by nature to make obvious the subject that dominated their waking moments. And like most testosterone driven males, he adopted a simple but direct approach when trying to get a woman into bed. It seemed he'd been successful in achieving that. The only slight glitch being that he'd somehow failed to get the all-important invitation to join her. So he faced another lonesome night and now he had a boiler to try and fix in the morning.

Before giving up for the evening, he decided to give the ignition button a few more tries. He noticed from his crouching position that Galina's feet had moved and were now positioned directly by his side. Surely she was not going to stand and watch him? He hated anyone looking over his shoulder, especially when he didn't have a clue what he was doing. Could she not find something useful to do like make a hot drink? He shot her one of his disapproving looks, but Galina appeared not to notice. She seemed pre-occupied, wearing an expression of anxiety as if she had an awkward request to make but was afraid to ask. It's probably that fan heater, he thought; she's going to ask me for it after all, but where had he put the thing? It was more than likely in the garage, so now he would have to go and find it for her – as if he didn't have enough to do. Well, she'll just have to wait. It was typical of a female to want a man to do another thing before he'd had chance to do the previous thing. Why did women have to be so… so… womanlike?

Galina interrupted his train of complaint against the female gender with a request completely different to the one he was expecting. She bent down and quietly whispered in his ear the question, "Would you like to join me?"

Dave was so startled by her suggestion he caught his head on the lip of the boiler cover when he straightened up. *Would he like to join her?* Too right he would like to join her! But did he hear her right? Still rubbing his bruised head, Dave looked to her for confirmation. Galina gave him an almost imperceptible wink before turning away in the direction of the stairs. Dave reacted by screaming a silent, triumphant 'Yes!'

Before he followed her upstairs, he realised some pre-coital preparations were required. After promising to be there directly, Dave slipped into the downstairs toilet.

Pulling his coat well out of the way as he peed, Dave thought how easily Galina had succumbed to his charms. One boiler breakdown and it seemed she was his for the taking. *That's one seduction technique not covered by the relationship gurus in their problem pages,* thought Dave. Maybe he could send his unique story off to *Take a Moment* magazine and earn himself fifty quid for it. His tips might just help other would-be suitors with boiler problems achieve success in the bedroom.

He turned to admire his profile in the mirror. A loud belch suddenly erupted from his mouth – its seismic reverberations causing him to let loose a fart at almost the same time, sending it on its way with a shake of his trouser leg. He voiced his thoughts to the image facing him in the mirror, "So you haven't lost that magic touch after all, you smooth talking sod you!"

Feeling that the occasion warranted some enhancement of his aromatic ambience, Dave decided to apply a second coat of aftershave. He looked at the label on the bottle. It described the Lacompostè cologne as 'warm and earthy.' *How apt,* he thought, just like himself, and slapped on a liberal application.

Quickly rinsing his hands, he vacated the toilet, mounted the stairs, then stopped halfway up. A thought had just occurred to him. She did mean join her in *her* bed and not join her in going upstairs to *their* respective beds?

Due to linguistic difficulties he knew she might not have meant what he thought she meant, but reaching the top of the stairs, he saw that Galina's bedroom door was open – she normally kept it shut. He took this as a positive sign and advanced towards the doorway.

Illuminated by the light from her bedside lamp he could see Galina was sitting up in bed, her face almost totally obscured by the woollen scarf wrapped around her neck. As she turned towards him, Galina removed one of her gloves and made a come hither gesture with her finger. Satisfied that his interpretation was indeed correct, Dave launched himself into the room and began pulling his clothes off – but then lost his footing trying to remove his trousers and ended up falling almost directly on top of Galina. He quickly righted himself, tossed his one remaining sock onto the floor and leapt into bed, drawing the covers over them both.

Galina reached out to embrace him, in so doing chose to place her ice-cold hands on a part of his body normally well-insulated from such thermal shocks. She appeared highly amused by his screams of protest. But despite some shrinkage caused by the sudden cooling of his equipment, and with very little in the way of preamble, Dave proceeded to make enthusiastic love to her.

Feeling drowsy after their frantic bout of coupling, Galina succumbed to a post-coital nap, waking some minutes later to see Dave staring intently at the ceiling. Sensing that her new lover was in need of reassurance, Galina whispered some words she hoped would give him comfort.

"Don't woury Dave, the boiler probably jurst need a new thermo-coupler. I wirl lurk at irt for you in mourning, yers?" said Galina, kissing him gently on the cheek.

She was getting to know him too well; his mind had indeed regressed back to the problems with the boiler. Galina's offer of help highlighted a situation that he didn't feel entirely comfortable with. Although he was grateful for her offer – it avoided the expense of calling out a heating engineer – he felt inadequate in not having the plumbing skills to mend the boiler himself. He knew it was an old-fashioned attitude to take, but somehow it didn't seem right for Galina to have to take on the repair.

As he mulled over her proposal, Dave felt Galina's hand working its way down to his groin area; obviously her offers of help took many forms. He tried to shut his brain off from the problems with the central heating and concentrate on Galina's hand now stroking his manhood; she would be expecting an appropriate response.

It might take longer than she realised. Old and worn out, the whole thing really needed replacing – but could he afford the expense of a new boiler? A new thermo-coupler would be cheaper, providing he could get hold of one. He began to explain the potential difficulties to Galina when she interrupted him with a question completely unrelated to central heating.

"So can we do irt again thern Dave?"

"…Sorry?"

"Again, can we do irt again?"

"You mean make love? Again?"

"Why yers!"

"So once is not enough then?"

"Yers, burt two is better!"

"But was it okay for you, really?"

"Why of course!" adding after a pause… "maybe a little bit longer next time yers?"

Dave immediately felt a sense of guilt on realising he might have completed the act too quickly for Galina's needs. He was about to apologise for his haste, promising to pace himself a little better when a thought occurred to him. *Does she mean longer time-wise or longer length-wise?* His anxiety just increased.

If it was the latter, hanging weights off it was supposed to help, or he could buy one of those suction tube developer things – he'd seen some adverts for them in one of his magazines. As he lay there with his mind churning, Galina began to giggle. Was she now laughing at his performance too?

"What Galina? What is it?"

"Sorry… burt I make a little fun with you! Irt wers long enough really, I would jurst like to be lurved again – irt has been a long time for me, you know!"

"Really?"

"Rearly!"

"You rotter! Look, men are sensitive about these things… and you don't help either! You'll have to give me a few min… er… hours now!"

123

Dave did indeed rise to the challenge and their second bout of lovemaking was at various times both loving and tender, the after effects of which quickly sent them both into a deep, blissful sleep.

The next morning Galina set about diagnosing the problem with his boiler, though it wasn't the simple job she anticipated. Unfortunately, the pump needed replacing. Dave managed to source the part locally, but it took her the best part of a day to fit. The physical nature of the work demonstrated to Galina the need for regular refreshments, giving Dave the opportunity to introduce his new lover to her host country's tradition of supplying endless cups of tea and biscuits to workpeople in the home.

Galina was ecstatic when the system was eventually switched on and it all worked as it should. On a high after carrying out her first repair in her new country, she was keen to celebrate her success. Galina's new-found confidence only served to emphasise Dave's feelings of inadequacy in lacking such plumbing skills himself, but not wishing to appear churlish, he offered to take Galina out for a meal as a thank you for all her hard work.

She mulled the suggestion over for a moment. Then with a directness that he had not seen in her before, sidled up to him, pulled at his trouser belt and suggested that they should maybe go upstairs first. Without waiting for an answer, she grabbed his hand and led the way.

In bed some minutes later, Galina was attempting to console him.

"It's okay Dave, I don't mind. It's no problerm for me if you can't, really it's not!"

"That's kind of you, but it's a problem for me!"

"Please, do not worry, I thirnk it herpens to lot of mern at some time."

"But it's never happened to me before. I should be able to; it's what men are supposed to do!"

"Lurk Dave, irt really is no big deal. In my country, merny women are plurmers ernd mend boilers. Jurst because you're not

124

able to, does not mean you're less of a mern. You do lots of other clever things. Thert invention you show me I could not do – so why you worry? You're jurst being Ernglish again!"

Having attempted to allay his anxieties, Galina turned towards him, looked him in the eye and smiled mischievously. "So we make lurve now, yers?"

"Yes, you're right Galina," he conceded, "I know, I'm just being Ernglish again. Yes, of course we make love now!"

Two days later, Dave was facing a dilemma. It was fast approaching the time Galina was supposed to leave. This was not what he wanted to happen so had deliberately avoided making any mention of it, but he needed to know how Galina saw the situation. It could be she just regarded the past week as a bit of a diversion, a fling to pass a few days until she located her niece. Although he always knew Galina's intention had been to stay with Irina in the long-term, after going to the address and finding out her niece had not been there for several weeks and still unable to contact her by phone, Dave knew that Galina's options were now limited.

He was hoping that Galina would stay on because she wanted to continue the relationship and not because she had nowhere else to go. Even if that were the case, he wouldn't ask her to leave. She needed a secure base if she was going to start a plumbing business and complete a college course. With both a garage and a workshop, his home would be ideal for her needs.

Dave knew he was being premature in asking her how she felt about him; after all, it had only been six days since they first met. With everything else going on in her life she probably didn't even know herself how she saw her future, but he was anxious to hear her response nonetheless.

He decided to put his thoughts to her that evening. Trying to sound calm and reasoned, he broached the subject after serving up Galina's favourite – cottage pie. He explained how, from a business point of view, it made good sense for her to stay on – she needed a base and he had the space to accommodate her. With regard to the finance side of things, he was prepared to forego any contribution from her towards the household expenditure until she got her business properly established.

With the logic of his proposal out of the way, what he now wanted to do was tell her how he felt on an emotional level. He pushed his plate to one side and licked the smears of gravy from his fingers. Reaching out, he slid his moist hand over hers and looking directly into her eyes, explained how much he'd loved having her around over the last few days. He truly felt that she was the best thing that had ever happened to him and very much wanted her to stay here with him on a permanent basis.

Galina sat looking at him...

Dave wondered if he'd gone too far in stating his feelings. He was just about to apologise for his outpouring when a delighted Galina threw her arms around him and squealed that it was just what she wanted too! Dave was overjoyed to know that she felt the same. Dismissing all thoughts of the butterscotch flavour Angel Delight he'd left setting in the fridge for dessert, Dave suggested they adjourn to the bedroom and celebrate with a bottle of KostKwik cava.

They both quickly settled into their respective routines after that. While Dave went off to work, Galina would attend college working towards her BTEC qualification in gas fitting. On other days she would work at her plumbing business. The time they did get to spend together was always productive in making new discoveries about one another. Jokes made and shared, bits of personal history revealed.

As the weeks passed, they came to understand better each other's needs. Dave would, on occasion, come home to find the table set for an intimate romantic meal, after which Galina would disappear upstairs; only to reappear shortly afterwards in a flimsy see-through negligee, naked underneath except for the leather tool belt strapped around her waist. Dave knew what to expect. It invariably followed the same routine. Pushed onto the settee, his trousers would be lowered to his ankles whereupon Galina would immediately straddle him – her need as urgent as his own.

Above the jingle and rattle emanating from the spanners and wrenches housed within the pouches as they made love, Galina would, as the need took her, urge him on in her Russian tongue. The exact translation of the phrases was never made clear to him – though the meaning was pretty obvious.

The particular fetish was not without its hazards. During one vigorous session a long thin screwdriver slipped from its pouch and nearly impaled Dave's scrotum to the cushion. After that, all sharp implements were banned by mutual consent.

Occasionally, Dave would bear witness to Galina's deep-seated feelings of insecurity. It would always be after some minor personal setback where she would question again all the plans she had made. After the tragic death of her husband and the collapse of her earlier career, Galina's fears were that it could all go wrong again.

His remedy was to remind Galina of how much she'd achieved since arriving in the UK. With her business building up steadily and her gas fitting qualification almost in the bag, she really had nothing to worry about. Yes, she had to work hard to achieve her goals, but so did everybody who wanted to achieve something in life. They were a couple now and together shared all that life threw at them, so why worry? That, after all, was his prerogative.

The future was looking brighter in other ways too. After discovering that his ex and 'Graham' were indeed having a relationship and that he'd moved in with her, Dave was able to negotiate more favourable divorce terms with her. It had necessitated him keeping watch on her house to confirm his suspicions, but with proof of two incomes going into the house, all her demands for maintenance had stopped.

His application for a patent had gone into the patent office and was now being processed. He knew a search of their archives would take place in order to find out whether the multi-purpose workbench's features were indeed unique. Having carried out some research of his own, he was sure no other similar device existed and was hoping it was just a matter of time before the patent was granted.

Their only real concern now was for Galina's niece, Irina. Impulsive by nature, it was not unknown for her to go off without informing anyone, but nothing had been heard of her for several months. Dave knew that Wensbury, like any major city, could be a hostile place for an unwary Russian girl alone, so shared Galina's concern. His fears were increased when he eventually learnt that Irina worked in the 'entertainment' industry. Galina was untypically vague about which area of entertainment her niece actually worked in, but Dave knew the term covered a multitude of sins.

It was a few months later in the spring after Galina had successfully passed her BTEC course in gas fitting that, out of the blue, she received a telephone call from Irina. After a long and very animated conversation, Galina was able to relate the gist of it to Dave.

"Rina, she moved to Aberdeen last year – is a long way in Scotland, yers? She worked in a club for a while. Thern she had a problem and had to leave, er… she not say too murch about thert burt I'm very glad she's okay. Now she has moved back to Wensbury. So we can go to see her now?"

Dave readily agreed to take her, though he had the feeling that Galina wasn't quite telling him the whole story regarding Irina. He had a suspicion that the 'club work' in question was not entirely reputable. She was obviously relieved to know that Irina was alive and well, so he felt it better to let the matter rest for the moment.

After further phone calls, Irina was adamant that she would come over to Dave's house for a belated reunion with her Aunt. Although Dave had offered to pick her up, Irina had insisted on arriving by taxi.

An hour later than stated, Galina's niece appeared on the doorstep expressing her apologies and bearing a gift of flowers.

She greeted them both with kisses and fierce emotional hugs for her Aunt 'Lina.

On first meeting her, Dave thought Irina very attractive, but on closer study, realised that her beauty, enhanced by a carefully applied veneer of make-up, was more superficial than he originally appreciated. Irina's clothes, which were few, looked expensive and her strong perfume filled the hallway.

He took a step back as the pair continued their emotional greeting. On further reflection, he decided tarty would be a more accurate description. Not that he would hold that against her, she was still a delight to the male eye. He realised that the look seemed to be de rigueur for Russian women. Dave recalled Galina's photograph on the dating website – with the big perm, heavy earrings and leather look top.

After completing the welcoming, and knowing that they had much to tell one another, Dave left them to their own company. Having the rest of the day free he decided to go for a walk up to the station and treat himself to a pint or two at the Platelayer's Arms. He put his head around the door of the conservatory to inform the two of his decision, but such was the intensity of their conversation that he stood there open-mouthed for at least a minute, waiting for one or the other to draw breath before he could pass on his message. He departed the house with only the briefest of acknowledgements from them.

As he took a first sip from his second pint of Bathams, Dave received a text from Galina. They were setting off for a walk around the town and would be joining him for refreshments in about half an hour and would that be okay? Indeed it was. The news was most welcome – most welcome indeed.

On a warm summer's evening he and Galina would often take a stroll up to the station, bring a drink out onto the south-facing platform, settle into one of the benches and with the evening sun warming their faces, chat about the day; while in the background would be heard the hiss of escaping steam and the soft, muted chuff of a light engine carrying out shunting duties in the engine sheds behind. More pleasant surroundings would be hard to find, he had to say. It seemed that Galina was now about to introduce Irina to their shared pleasure.

It was actually forty-five minutes later when they walked into the bar. Galina's face lit up when she spotted him even though it had only been a short while since he'd left the house. He guessed that the reunion with her niece had served to elevate even further her happy disposition; no dour Russian this one. Her warm expressive nature was one of the things he loved about her. Whereas he noticed that Irina, although twenty-odd years younger, had a harder, more Slavic look about her. He guessed that more than a few troubles lurked behind that guarded expression she wore.

Dave extended a warm greeting to them both. Bathams-induced bonhomie was having its effect on him and he insisted that both ladies have large measures of their favourite tipple. He was eager to get to know Irina a little better; she had only spoken a few words in English since she arrived. They took a recently vacated table situated near the door leading to the platform. Dave noticed the many glances Irina's appearance was drawing as they settled in their seats. He too found it difficult keeping his eyes away from her short skirt and low-cut top.

Irina attempted to join in the conversation between Dave and Galina, though her English was more limited than her aunt's. During one lull Irina suddenly observed, "There irs merny mern here, do nert women come here?"

"Well, there is reason for that," Dave answered. "A lot of them are trainspotters."

Irina's face looked blank. Dave attempted to explain. "That is, they like to see and make photographs of trains... Yes?"

Irina's face still wore a blank expression.

Dave pointed to an engine standing in the platform, then in mime made as if to scribble something down and take its photo. Irina nodded her understanding.

"Ernd women, no?"

"Well they do not like trains so much, so no, not many women come in here – certainly not ones as attractive as you!" gushed Dave, casting a glance down Irina's top which had started to gape open.

Irina's face expressed a thin smile; Galina's face showed no smile at all.

Dave shot a look of contrition in Galina's direction, and resolved to make that his last drink. After another half an hour with Dave struggling to make intelligible conversation with Irina, Galina thought to remind her that she had a taxi booked for the trip back to Wensbury. Irina had refused the offer of a meal, together with a bed for the night, saying she had arranged to go out later.

Over the next few weeks Irina made regular visits to them, sometimes bringing a female friend, of which she seemed to have quite a few. All were either Russian or Eastern European and sometimes stopped over at their house for a day or two. It was company for Galina on the weeks that he worked his late shifts, when it would be past midnight by the time he returned home.

Due to the twenty-five year age gap and the rigours of her plumbing work, Galina had little interest in hitting the town at night; whereas Irina and whoever was accompanying her on the day would look forward to going up into the town in the evening. Dave had even seen them at the station pub looking rather incongruous amongst the bearded, paunchy, middle-aged, steam-loving fraternity. For some reason, Irina and her friends seemed to enjoy the attention they received there.

Chapter 13

The two steam railway volunteers sat in the corner of the snug after purchasing their first pints of the evening. Holding open the newspaper, the first volunteer pointed out the article to the second.

"Look, here it is, 'Worfe Valley Railway voted best heritage line in Britain.' Typical, bloody typical! Worfe Valley this an' Worfe Valley that. That's all we read and 'ere about nowadays. You'd think it were the only preserved heritage railway in the country."

"Too right Frank," agreed Eli. "And that's why they've got money to hire in best engines as well. We only lost Sir George Greatly to Worfe Valley 'cos it were able to outbid us. Now that would 'ave brought crowds in!"

"And we keep losin' our volunteers to 'em. *'Oh, we want to work on Britain's most scenic railway!'* I've 'eard 'em tell all poncey like. *'They've got trees an' hills an' a river on their railway!'* Well I say what's wrong wi' lookin' out carriage windows an' seein' a line of o' mill factories all converted for open-plan 'xecutive livin' eh? And them slag 'eaps look a picture too now they've been landscaped and turned into dry ski slopes by the council. D'you know, we've now got more municipal ski centres in Yorkshire than in whole of rest o' the country? Aye, and more ski lifts than in Shammy knee i'n't French Alps!"

"Yeah, but 'ave yer ever been on one?"

"No, but that's not the point Eli, this is Britain's industrial legacy this is, all ready to be passed down to future generations o' Yorkshire skiers. It's the same for our own heritage railway o' course. Mind, I don't know fer 'ow long though. It meks you wonder why we bother, the society bein' in such a mess an' all!"

Frank and Eli were both active members of the Postlethwaite Rail and Tramway Society. After attending the sad spectacle of their extraordinary general meeting, they had adjourned to the Fettlers Arms to better digest the bad news.

"I can't believe society's lost so much money. We're not gettin' anythin' like numbers we used to."

"Well you know why, don't you? Worfe bloody Valley's tekkin' it all. Sure, local folk still come to support us, but that in't enough to keep railway goin'. The problem's fewer and fewer visitors are comin' in from outside the area," stated Frank.

"But I still don't know what we can do about it. Committee said there's hardly enough money in the bank to keep us goin' till end of the season."

"Aye, well I fer' one am not goin' to see society go down – not after all the 'ard bloody work I've put in over the years. Layin' rails, clearin' vegetation and rebuildin' near on whole bloody station. No, I've put too much hard graft in to let that 'appen."

"But what can y'do that's not already been tried?"

"Well, it's obvious in't it? I tell you, fix that bloody Worfe Valley Railway fer a start!"

"How y'goin' to do that Frank?"

"Well I've bin 'avin a bit of a think, and I've got my lad workin' on summat that'll show them buggers down south a thing or two."

"Right – your Darren yer say?"

Frank gave a confirming nod before picking up his pint to take a sup.

"Er... 'as he finished his community service now?" asked Eli.

"Oh aye, that's all done n'dusted."

"Right... so what's 'e plannin' on doin' then?"

"Well I can't say too much, but y'know he's always bin' interested in pyrotechnics and the like?"

"I do, that's 'ow he got in trouble in the first place, y'know, when he set fire to the police station."

"Look! That's all bin' gone over a thousand times before. Suffice to say it were shut at time, and the lad were only tryin' to keep warm on a winter's evenin.' I'll 'ere no more on the subject," said Frank, angered at the very mention of his son's misdemeanour.

"Okay, okay – so what's the lad got in mind then?"

Giving Eli a searching look as if deciding whether he could be trusted or not, Frank announced in hushed tones, "Well Eli, between you' an' me..." He paused to take a quick look around the bar, "...and this is in the strictest confidence mind. 'E's bin on the internet and found out a thing or two about summat that might just wipe the smile off their bloody faces down at Worfe Valley – that's all I'm sayin'. Aye! With a bit o' luck their next steam weekend should go with a rite good bang! I can tell you that for nowt!"

"Well it all sounds a bit dodgy to me, I hope y'know what yer doin' Frank'!"

"Aye, that I do lad – that I do. You'll see!"

With that Frank picked up his glass, drained the contents in one go and banged it back down on the table. "'Avin' another?"

Chapter 14

It was just after 11 am on the following Saturday when Dave arrived for work at the station. As he entered the car park, Dave noticed a figure lying spread-eagled on the ground. Next to him, an array of discarded lager cans littered what appeared to be the only vacant bay. He decided to search for an alternative, but after completing a circuit and finding no other available space, Dave realised there was only one choice left open to him. Carefully, he edged his vehicle into the limited gap, crushing a number of the empty cans in the process.

Stepping out of the car and around the comatose man, his gaze fell on the drunk's lifeless hand which was still clutching a can of the same extra strong lager. Its contents had long since dribbled out, leaving just a wet pool on the tarmac and soaking the nylon leisurewear of its wearer.

With a weary sigh, Dave grabbed his workbag, locked the car and headed for the station concourse. The public address system was just broadcasting an announcement.

"Cambrian Railways would like to apologise for the late arrival of the 14.47 service to Birmingham. This was due to a pigeon strike near Aberystwyth."

His outward journey to Aldridge was an all-stopper service. On the way back the train was running semi-fast which meant only stopping at two intermediate stations, this gave Dave time to work his way through the train checking tickets.

Darren and his mate Kevin had boarded the service at West Bromwich, intending to leave the train at Smethwick West, and from there catch a train to their target destination of Middleminster. Kevin was nervous due to the nature of the mission they were undertaking and kept visiting the toilet to partake of a well-charged spliff. Darren, carrying the bag which he had carefully nursed all the way from Postlethwaite, was more confident. It was almost the last leg of the journey and a successful conclusion to their trip now seemed certain.

Settling into his seat, Darren gently pushed the bag underneath out of sight and opened his phone. His dad, Frank, had made it clear that he was to check in with him at every leg of the journey *'Just t'mek sure y'don't bloody well cock things up!'* as he put it. Darren scrolled down for the number, pressed the button and waited.

Brenda Bradshaw, on the seat directly behind him, was making her weekly journey into Birmingham. As was usual she had with her Sam, her third guide dog puppy, undergoing obedience training with her on behalf of the Association. Getting the dog accustomed to public transport she knew to be an important accomplishment required of all puppy walkers.

Her elderly mother also accompanied Brenda on these occasions. It was a welcome trip out in the company of her daughter as well as gaining assistance with her shopping. Busily engaged in conversation with her mother, Brenda failed to notice her charge sniffing eagerly around the carrier bag tucked conveniently under the seat just in front.

Drawn on by the powerful scent being emitted, he inched forward and knowing no better, started to chew the bottom of the bag, very quickly breaking through the thin fabric. Possessed of the voracious appetite common to many a young Labrador, Sam proceeded to lap up the contents now spilling onto the floor.

As well as engaging in chit chat with her mother, Brenda was blessed with the ability common to many of her sex, and was picking up snippets of the conversation Darren was having with his dad. She became increasingly alarmed by what she was hearing.

"I say Mother," Brenda whispered, "I'm sure the man in front is saying something about a bomb on his phone!"

"Yer what Brenda?"

Trying to keep her voice down, she leaned nearer to her mother.

"I said – I'm sure the man in front is saying something about a bomb on his phone!"

"Eeh! These mobiles, they can do everything nowadays can't they?"

"No, you don't understand, I'm sure he's telling somebody on the other end of the phone about a bomb he's brought onto the train!"

"A bomb you say? Well that's not right, I got told off for bringing a shopping trolley on once. The man said I was blocking the aisle with..."

"And I'm sure this man's saying something about going to Middleminster with it," said Brenda, cutting her mother short.

"What's that you say? We're goin' to Middleminster? They've never put us on the wrong train have they? You know, I knew it was a mistake to ask that Polish man on the platform. A lot of these immigrants never know the way home you know."

Her mother then thought for a moment. "I say, I've never been to Middleminster before, is there an Eldi there do you know Brenda? Only I always do my shoppin' at Eldi."

"Look mother, this is serious, he's definitely talking about a bomb in his bag."

Oblivious to her daughter's state of alarm, the woman suddenly had her attention diverted by something else. "I say Brenda, can you smell something? Is it your Sam? You've not been feeding him liver again have you? Your dad were just the same after he'd had liver. I notice he's gone very quiet down there – just like your dad used to whenever he…"

"Mother! No I haven't and before you ask, it's not me either! Sam, what are you up to down there?"

Brenda could see his tail sticking out so reached underneath, grabbed Sam by his harness and pulled him brusquely back to her side of the seat. She noticed he was chewing something, and there was powdery stuff all over the floor. This, Brenda presumed, was where the smell was coming from. Her mother once again broke into her thoughts.

"Anyway our Brenda, I'll have to go me'self now, which way is it, do you know?"

"Er, I'm not sure mum, er…" she replied hesitantly as she looked up and down the carriage. "The end of the train's that way, so it must be the other way I think." Brenda, still pre-occupied with her concerns, gestured vaguely in the direction her mother should follow.

"Yes, well don't worry about me, I'm sure I'll find it eventually," said her mother when she realised that the expected assistance would be unforthcoming. "I just hope nobody's been smoking that skunk in there like last time. Made me feel proper queer it did. Do you know, I ate two packets of munchies afterwards out of the multi-pack I'd bought – and I've never done that before!"

"No motherrr…" Brenda was more concerned with whatever was going on underneath the seat and had no time for trite conversation. She just wished her mother would get on with going. When she at last tottered off, Brenda discreetly peered under the seat and saw a well-chewed shopping bag, and two loose wires hanging down from it. She realised at once that if all this talk of a bomb from the man in front was true, then Sam, due to his insatiable appetite, had probably just eaten the main components.

Brenda was panicking, just what was it that her dog had eaten? If it was a bomb then the substance could well kill him, but it certainly didn't look or smell like she thought explosive ought to. Whenever she'd seen news items about homemade bombs, it would be in the form of a chemical white powder. This was dark brown and judging by the smell being given off, it was more like an animal by-product.

Riven by doubts over her interpretation of the conversation she had just overheard, but at the same time anxious to find out the true contents of the bag should Sam become ill, Brenda nervously made her approach to the owner – though not entirely sure how to phrase the question she wanted to ask.

"Er... sorry to bother you, but are you the gentleman with the... er, bag on the floor? Only I think my dog may have damaged it. He... thought it was something to eat – look, I feel so stupid asking this, but... it's not a bomb is it?"

Distracted by the conversation he was having with his dad, Darren took a moment to take in what was being said to him. Suddenly understanding, he threw the phone down on the seat cushion and began frantically feeling for the bag under his seat. He felt the two loose wires trailing across the floor of the train.

"What... what 'ave yer done?" shrieked Darren, looking at the chewed bag with its contents strewn about the floor. "I... I don't believe it! I only…"

"What don't you believe?" asked Dave as he arrived at the seat occupied by the youth. He'd been busy checking tickets down the other end of the carriage when he heard the raised voices so had come to investigate. Not being quite sure what the problem could be, he stood looking at Darren waiting for an answer. Dave's nostrils now picked up the odour from the bag's contents. "Crikey, what's that awful stink?" he asked.

Darren, still shocked at how rapidly it had all gone so disastrously wrong, just shook his head in disbelief, "That bloody dog, it's just eaten the... er ... me bag like. It were alreet a minute ago!"

Now certain her suspicions were correct, Brenda could contain herself no longer. Turning to Dave the words spilled out. "He was telling somebody on the phone about a bomb – I'm sure he said that. Look there's wires coming out of the bag – and I'm worried my dog may have eaten it!"

Dave, trying to take in such an unlikely scenario, was puzzled rather than alarmed and went to pick up the bag to take a closer look. Darren quickly snatched it away from him, and clutching it tightly to his chest shouted, "Stay back!"

He reached into the bag and pulled out a device with two wires attached to it.

"Stay back! Else… else… I'll blow us all up!"

As he backed away, Darren began to look around the carriage desperately searching for an escape route.

Although surprised by the young man's extreme reaction to him taking a look in his bag, Dave was accustomed to people making bizarre claims – they were an occupational hazard in his job. Public transport seemed to attract fantasists of one sort or another; he assumed it was because they liked to have an audience to play to. Having a box or a bag about their person that held a special secret was a common trait. He'd found it best to just humour the person concerned and then, on some pretence or other, quietly slip away. Dave assumed that the substance spilling out was also the source of the smell. Whatever the dark brown powder was, the dog was straining at his harness to eat it. As far as Dave could recall, bomb-making material did not normally double up as a tasty treat for dogs so he felt very sceptical about taking the man's claim seriously, but because the person concerned seemed to be causing alarm to another passenger, he thought he'd better investigate further.

"Look, this is all ridiculous," he told him, "Let me have a look in that bag."

Darren turned away to shield his possession and repeated his threat.

"Get away! Get away! or… I'll blow us all up, I really will!"

At that moment Darren's mate Kevin returned from the toilet feeling a lot calmer, that is until he took in the situation confronting his accomplice. Kevin looked at the ripped bag incredulous.

"What 'appened?"

"Never mind."

With that Darren threw him the bag; without hesitating, Kevin passed it back to him.

"I don't want it, this were your idea don't forget!"

The top of the bag fell open to reveal some of the contents.

"It's a thermos!" said Dave derisively.

"No, there's a bomb in there as well!" Darren insisted.

"And are those sandwiches I can see in that tupperware box underneath?" added Dave.

"Yeah, me mum always... no, the bomb's underneath but you can't see it... really, it is a bomb."

"Look," said Dave trying to resolve the bizarre situation, "I think this charade has gone far enough, I don't belie..." The nauseous smell was getting to him now and Dave could feel himself wanting to gag, so asked the question that he'd wanted answering since he first arrived on the scene.

"Just what is it giving off that awful stink?"

"Ah! I'm glad yer asked that," said Darren, a thin smile now spreading across his face. "Per'aps you'll believe me now, yer see this is a fertiliser bomb."

"A fertiliser bomb?" repeated Dave, with disbelief. "Tell me, just what type of fertiliser have you used in this so-called bomb of yours?"

"Dried blood and fishmeal," came the confident reply.

"Dried blood and fishmeal?" Crikey, this really has to be a joke! Do you really expect the ingredients of a fishy black pudding to explode? Even with my very limited knowledge of bomb-making, I know you've used the wrong type of fertiliser. The smell will kill us before the bomb ever does. Whose bright idea was all this then?"

After some shuffling of feet, Kevin nodded to Darren. "It were your idea."

"Yeah, and who built it – you did!" said Darren accusingly. Turning on his accomplice he added, "I told yer it couldn't be right, smelling like that!"

"How was I to know it weren't right type o' fertiliser?"

"Well, yer could 'ave tested it first!"

"What, an' blow myself up in't process!"

"At least we'd have known it worked!"

"Well thanks a lot!"

"Yeah, well if…"

"Look, when you two have quite finished bickering, we have an issue to resolve here," interrupted Dave.

Just then the train came to a shuddering halt. The two would-be bombers looked at each other in alarm. Dave didn't know why it had stopped, they weren't at a station. For the time being he would have to leave it to the driver to sort out. Within a few seconds, Dave heard the corridor door being opened. He turned around to see Jim, the driver, standing in the doorway.

"Someone's pulled the Passcom in the toilet Dave, I jus... 'ello, what's goin' on here then?"

"Wait a minute Jim."

Dave took the startled driver to one side and quickly brought him up to speed on the events so far. Jim, like Dave, had been in the job long enough to treat with scepticism the claims of such people, though he agreed it was unusual for one to claim that they had a bomb in their bag. Darren renewed his threat for the driver's benefit.

"Yeah, if yer don't let us off now, we'll blow train up."

Dave resumed his sarcasm. "What, with a bag of manure?"

"It's a bomb I tell you."

"No it's not a bomb."

"Yes it is!"

"It... is... not... a... bomb! A bomb is made of explosive!"

"Yes it is a bomb, there's other stuff in here as well. Look there's wires, and this here is the switch to detonate it. I'm keeping it in me 'and in case you try any funny business like, so stay back!"

Dave instantly recognised the handheld switch.

"You know, if you hadn't told me that what you were holding was a crucial component of your so-called bomb, I would have said it looked very much like a Scalextric hand throttle."

"So what if it is? Me brother never plays with... look, it's just a switch right? That's all yer need! I've wired it to bomb with wire. All I have to do is press this once and it'll go..."

"What? brrrmm brrrmm!" interrupted Dave.

"Look I'm warning you. Don't push me!"

"I thought maybe you were stalling." Dave allowed himself a little chuckle at that one.

"Steady on Dave," Jim was having concerns about Dave's goading. "The lad's getting agitated. Just back off a bit in case he does have something dodgy in that bag. Look, it's not our job to sort out a situation like this, let's leave it to the proper authorities, eh?"

"Okay Jim, have it your way, but I still think they're just a pair of jokers. I'll get onto control and let them know what's happening."

"Yeah Dave, let them sort it out, it's not our job to. Mind, I don't fancy being stuck here for too long, I've got a darts match on tonight, and my missus will be wondering where I've got to, I've normally got the tea on well before *Emmerdale* starts!"

"Yes, I don't think these so-called 'bombers' are fully aware of the serious repercussions that might result from their actions. If this goes on into the evening, you could well miss *Corrie'* as well!"

"All right Dave, there's no need to be sarcastic, we're all feeling a bit tense right now. You get onto control and I'll keep a watch on things here."

"Okay... this could prove interesting."

As he wended his way to the cab at the rear of the train, he noted the anxious looks on the faces of the passengers. He realised he needed to offer some explanation for the delay. One lady actually grabbed him by the arm to express her anxiety at the length of time they'd been held there. She was worried about her little Pekinese. He didn't like being left too long and was worried about what she might find when she got home as he had a tendency to eat draught excluders which then made him very constipated. Dave tried to reassure her by saying that everything was being done to overcome a minor operational problem and that they would be on their way as soon as possible. He suggested a possible remedy would be to move the draught excluders out of the way whenever she left the dog for long periods.

Brenda's mother tottered back into the carriage. Failing to notice the stand-off in the corner, she immediately addressed her daughter.

"Eeeh, that ruddy driver! Do you know, I'd only just finished and when I pulled the handle to flush it, he went and stopped the train dead – just like that! Nearly went arse over tip I did – he wouldn't be foreign the driver, do you know?"

Brenda went to speak. "Moth..."

"And another thing our Brenda, they've been smoking that stuff in there again, I feel proper queer I do. I say, you wouldn't have a Mars bar in your shopping, er... a large one by any chance? I just fancy one now. I ought to sit down, you know my heads gone all fuzzy."

As she went to take her seat she noticed Darren with his bag.

"Why's he standing there with a Scalextric? Seems a funny thing to bring on a train."

"It's a long story Mother – just sit down will you!"

On reaching the cab, Dave's first action was to issue a carefully-worded message over the public address system in order to placate the rest of the passengers. The broadcast could have come straight out of the Mercia Mainline's own training manual. It was a masterpiece of well worked industry clichés containing almost no factual information at all. He hoped it would be enough to prevent a multitude of individual requests for information when he next walked back through the train. Dave then considered for a moment how best to explain the situation to his control.

He inputted the number, put the handset to his ear, and above the noise of the crackling static, made his call for help.

Chapter 15

"Hello, this ..**zzz**.. Train Manager Dave Bland working ..**zzzz**.. two Charlie two four, Ald ..**zzz**.. idge to Birmingham service, we ..**zzzzz**..ve a problem."

"Hello, control here, you're very difficult, but yes, I can see on the screen that you've been stationary for sixteen minutes, so what's wrong?"

"We've got two male passenge..**zzz**.. threat..**zzzz**..ing to b..**zzz**..mb the train! ..**zzzz**.."

"Say again two Charlie two four, we're getting a lot of interference this end!"

"I said, we've got two men on ..**zzz**.. the train threat..**zzzz**..ing to b..**zzz**..mb u..**zzz**.."

"Still difficult two Charlie two four, I think I may have missed some of it, but I read that last message as, 'We've got two men on the train threatening to bum us,' which doesn't sound right to me. Surely you mean, 'offering?'

"No! I'll... say... it... slowly... this... time... so... that... you... can... understand... me... We've... got... two... men... on... the... train... threatening... us... with... a... *bomb!*"

"Oh right, two Charlie two four, yes I can read you more clearly now, Dale on the next desk has just turned his razor off. So you're saying you have two bombers on the train threatening to blow you all up? Blimey! Is that correct, please confirm?"

"That is more or less correct, yes," said Dave. He decided not to quibble over control's slightly overstating the threat. Believing them to be in imminent danger of being blown to pieces, would hopefully result in a quicker than normal response from them, and as far as Jim was concerned, certainly before *Emmerdale* started.

"Look, sorry about all the misunderstanding, the reception was very bad. We weren't sure if we'd heard you right Dave. This obviously is an emergency situation, so we're going to connect you to the police; they're obviously the right people to deal with a situation such as this. Just hold for a minute will you... I say we've never had to deal with a bomb threat before; everybody here's listening in eagerly. It's quite exciting isn't it?"

"No, not for us it isn't, but I'm glad it's keeping you all amused though!"

"Yeah, sorry... no, I suppose it wouldn't be for you. Right, you're through now!"

"Hello!"

"Hi, this is the Mercia Transport Police; my name is Duncan, so how can I help you today?"

Dave hesitated initially, thinking the cheesy call centre response was a wind-up. What ever happened to the brusque manner of an old-fashioned PC in the days when PC meant Police Constable and not politically correct.

He began by repeating the details of what had happened whilst trying not to get irritated by the listener saying 'really?' every time he finished a sentence.

"How awful for you Dave! Hmm... so, just to get the important details right – these bombers, they wouldn't be gay then?"

Dave sighed. "How should I know? And what does it matter anyway? I could always go back and ask them if they go to all the Erasure concerts if you like – that should confirm it one way or the other.

"What about transsexual then?"

"What?"

"Transsexual? Do you think either of them could be transsexual Dave?"

"Look, what's the point of all this?"

"Hmm, maybe they're cross-dressers then, any signs of it at all? You know... shirt buttons on the wrong side... kitten heels... a touch of blusher perhaps."

"What the hell! Look, never mind about all this diversity clap-trap, when are you going to start doing something about resolving the situation here?"

"Now Dave – you don't mind if I call you Dave, do you? I can tell you're stressing here; just try to stay calm. It's just that to comply with new police procedures, a person's sexuality is one of the factors we are required to take into account when trying to establish a dialogue with them – that's all, Dave."

"How would that work if they were gay then? Appeal to their feminine side first of all by having a little chat about quiche recipes to put them at ease, before asking them why they want to blow up a train full of people?"

"There's no need to be sarcastic Dave – you're still sounding stressed to me. And I have to take issue with those stereotypical homophobic remarks you're making!"

"No… look, I don't care whether they're gay or not. I've just had enough of all of the crap. I am trying – though with great difficulty – to make you aware of the situation we're in here. The simple facts are we have two jokers on the train who claim to have a bomb – that is if their claims are to be believed. They are threatening to blow up the train – and us with it!"

"Yes, I know it must be awful for you Dave. But picking up on something, you said 'if their claims are to be believed.' Do you think these boys might not be serious after all about their threat to blow up the train then Dave?"

"From what I've seen of them, *'these boys'* as you choose to call them, appear to be a couple of amateurs who haven't a clue about bomb-making – but what do I know? I could be wrong!"

"The thing is Dave, due to limited police resources we have to prioritise our response so in order to categorise the urgency of your call, I need to probe a little deeper Dave – do *you* think it could be a fake bomb then?"

"It certainly didn't look real to me."

"Hmm, so did they threaten you with any type of weapon at all Dave?"

"Such as what?"

"Well, you know Dave, a gun or a knife – something like that."

"No, not that I noticed."

"That's a pity Dave."

"What do you mean, that's a pity?"

"Well, those are classed as offensive weapons you see, so your call would get a higher priority. Never mind Dave, I'll have a look at bombs and incendiary devices in a minute. I just need to enter your details first. So you're saying that this Darren threatened you with a bomb in the second carriage, is that correct?

"...as opposed to Colonel Mustard with the lead pipe in the library you mean?

"Sorry?"

"Well, you're the one making all this sound like a game of Cluedo."

"There's no need to be sarcastic Dave. It's just that bombs aren't actually listed here. My guess is that it'll come under another menu. Let me just go into the next screen Dave, and hopefully I'll be able to find out for you."

"Well if it's not too much trouble – no rush like!"

"No trouble at all Dave, I'm clicking on it now Dave, shouldn't take a minute."

"Whatever..."

"It's thinking about it... seems to be taking a bit longer than normal... er, is there anything else I can help you with today Dave?'

"No!"

"O... K... I reckon it's this new computer program Dave, we've had problems with it before. Hello... no, sorry, it's still loading. So... been away anywhere nice this year Dave?"

"What!"

"Ah ah! Got it at last. Hmm, that's funny Dave, it doesn't seem to be listed in any of the menus. I'll have to put you on hold for a minute while I ask a colleague – you'll find the techno-chamber music very calming though."

"I really don't believe this! Look I'll tell you what, I'll carry out a bit of 'prioritising' of my own here and get the hammer out of the train's emergency cupboard and hit one of the little twats round the head with it! Maybe that'll galvanise you jokers into action – and another thing, stop calling me Dave all the time!"

"There's no need to get all shirty with me Da... I can see you're showing your aggressive side again – and anyway that would be taking the law into your own hands. I'd like to remind you that this is the police service and we have the right not to respond to threatening behaviour. If you continue in the same aggressive tone, I shall have no option but to terminate the call – I really will!"

Dave now channelled his seething anger into delivering a suitable response.

"Fine, you do that and when the powers that be want to know – as they will, why the police failed to respond when bombers threatened to blow up a passenger train with a couple of hundred or so people on board, I can tell them it was all because the operator had a hissy fit and put the phone down on me! What was your name again by the way?"

There was a long pause before Duncan came back with the terse message, "I'm handing you over to a colleague."

"Yes you do that – Duncan!"

Chapter 16

After a further pause, the radio once again crackled into life.

"Hello Mr Brand, Sgt Edwards here, I've caught the gist of what's happened. So first of all two things; firstly my apologies for the previous response you received. It certainly was not up to the standard laid down in the Police Service Charter and I can understand your frustration at not having your concerns addressed. Secondly, you will be pleased to hear that we are giving your call top priority and that all paperwork currently pending has been put on hold whilst we assess the situation. Thirdly, once we've carefully assessed all the issues involved, we'll be formulating an action plan to resolve the situation very soon."

"Great!"

"I thought you'd be pleased!"

"No, I was being ironic! Yes I've heard all what you have just said, but what exactly are you going to do after you've done all this assessing and formulating? And how long is all this going to take? I mean, I'm sure these so-called bombers are not for real. They're a nuisance more than anything. All it really needs is for a couple of your boys to meet the train and arrest them before their threats alarm the rest of the passengers."

"Believe me, you cannot be too careful in tricky situations like this Mr Blond, we can't just go in there mob-handed you know. You leave it to us! We'll be getting the meeting under way in just a few minutes; then we can start to look at all the issues involved. I'm sure...

"A meeting?" interrupted Dave. "But why do you need to have a meeting?"

"Well, with incidents like this one, there could well be serious implications for police officers and er, their pensions, should things go awry and the Police Complaints Authority subsequently becomes involved. That is why we need to get our heads of department together to discuss all the possible risks, and then seek ways to reduce that risk – together with any blame and responsibility. Working through a set of procedures and protocols, we carry out a thorough risk assessment and when we've identified all the factors..."

"Can you not just get the Bomb Squad to come and sort this out?"

"Who, sorry?"

"The Bomb Squad!"

"...Do you know, I knew there were some other people I should... yes, thank you for that. I'll get onto them straight away. Look, I've just been handed an urgent sandwich, let me pass you onto one of the other members of the team, and then I'll get back to you a.s.a.p Mr Blund. Thank you!"

Dave didn't reply, he was left feeling numb. Any residual anger had been dissipated in the long struggle to have the situation promptly resolved and he suddenly felt weary of it all. He just wanted to get it all over with and go home. Why did the misguided idiots have to go and spoil his day like this – and the hijackers were just as bad.

A female voice sounding almost normal broke through the static in his ear.

"Hello Mr Bland this is WPC Heather Mitchell. I've just taken over from Sgt Edwards... and yes, well... I've been fully briefed on the situation and I've spoken to your control. As you are probably aware, everything is backing up behind you so a decision has been made to allow you to proceed to Birmingham – but no further!"

"Well that's something I suppose. So no back up or anything? You know, police helicopters, armed response teams or anything like that?"

"No sorry. Look off the record, I think they're trying to keep it all low-key until they've made a decision about how to handle it. They don't want to be seen to be going over the top with rescue missions and the like if they are just a few misfits with nothing but a grudge in their carrier bag. On the other hand, if they do have serious intentions then we need to react accordingly. Perhaps you could try and find out what it is they want?

"If I can I will, but why is it all taking so long?"

"I understand how you must be feeling about all this, but just bear with us. Hopefully, as our inside man so-to-speak, the information you supply will enable us to respond appropriately – and swiftly!"

At last he had a promise of some sort of action. Accepting the logic of her reply, he said he would do what he could and replaced the radio handset. Now deep in thought, Dave started to make his way through the train. A good twenty minutes had passed since he had first made the call, and the passengers were now clamouring for information. Previously he had laid the blame for the delay on a lineside equipment failure – very much a catch-all-excuse used throughout the industry, usually when the train crew has yet to discover why the train has come to a sudden grinding halt.

Dave considered revealing to the passengers the real predicament they were in, before eventually deciding on a compromise. He entered each of the three carriages in turn and announced to the passengers that the delay had been due to some difficulties with a couple of passengers, but hoped to be getting underway very shortly and added a fulsome apology on behalf of his company.

From previous experience, Dave had learnt that a personal approach in explaining operational problems to passengers often worked better in these situations – that is providing it was during normal working hours when the majority of the passengers were likely to be sober and therefore less prone to belligerence. He thought it prudent not to make any mention of a bomb.

"Fuck me! You took your time didn't you? So what's happening then?" Jim demanded to know on his return. The stand-off was still taking place at the front of the train; the hijackers, now huddled in a corner, were busily whispering to one another.

"Well, it's a long story, I won't bore you with all the details, but basically we've got the okay to proceed into Curzon Street station; what happens after that, I just don't know."

"Great! I've had a piece of good news too Dave, I got through to the missus on the phone and she's recorded *Emmerdale* for me, and if we're goin' into Curzon St now, I can get off home, have my tea and still make the darts match…"

"Well I'm glad you've got everything sorted to your satisfaction. That still leaves me here firmly in the kak though!"

"Sorry Dave, but you know how it is. The missus gets really funny if I don't get home on time, she'll never believe all this lot." Jim gestured in the general direction of the hijackers. "Audrey will think I've been up to something; she's always been the same!"

Dave eyed him sceptically. Jim looked to be about sixty, though he could have been younger. He was almost bald and several stones overweight. The large beer gut and florid face were, he guessed, due to years of drinking. It was hard to imagine why his wife should believe that there were women just waiting to entice him into an elicit liaison.

Turning his attention back to Darren and his accomplice in the corner looking sullenly back at him, Dave guessed they were waiting for news of some kind. He went over to them.

"The police want to know what your demands are!" he announced.

"Demands?" repeated Darren.

Kevin and Darren looked at each other. Kevin responded with a shrug of his shoulders. As far as he was concerned, they had never planned for being in a situation where demands were expected from them.

"Demands… well… er… look, can yer just give us a minute?"

"Yeah, sure, why not? Just take as long as you like; we've got all the time in the world. Well I have anyway, Jim here will probably tell you something different."

Jim shot Dave a reproachful look.

153

The two huddled close conferring with each other. Jim stood tapping his fingers on the window, giving an occasional glance at his watch.

After a minute, Darren announced, "Yeah, we've decided, just take us in to Middleminster will yer."

"Middleminster? We can't take you to Middleminster. This is the wrong line, you'll have to go into Curzon Street first." Dave informed him.

Kevin and Darren looked at one another before Darren said, "Okay, then, Curzon Street'll do! Just get this thing goin' will yer!"

"That it? No holdall of money in used notes, a waiting BMW or anything?" enquired Dave.

"Steady with the sarcasm Dave," advised Jim. "You'll be putting ideas into his head else. Let's just keep things simple, and we might get this wrapped up a bit quicker." Jim looked at his watch again. "Curzon Street, eh? We can be there in 10 minutes!"

"'Ang on! Yeah, well seein' as 'ow yur askin', a cup o' tea and a biscuit or summat, would be nice," requested Darren.

Kevin nodded, "Yeah, some crisps an' a can o' coke as well," he added.

"What did I tell you," sighed Jim.

"Er... sorry lads, this is only a local service, we don't have a buffet car. There is though, a wide range of such refreshments available at Curzon Street – should circumstances permit of course."

Dave allowed himself a wry smile, knowing they would have to make do with whatever refreshments the police canteen stocked.

"Anyway, Curzon Street was where we were going until you stopped the train!" said Dave.

"It weren't me that stopped train like. I thought it were you!" said Kevin.

"No, I didn't!" replied Dave

"Well somebody pulled the Passcom," said Jim, "That's why I left my cab! We'd have been there thirty minutes ago else." he added, checking his watch once more.

"Er, sorry to interrupt," began Brenda who had been following the conversation. She leaned over across the seat, then in a hushed tone said to Dave, "I think it may have been my mother when she went to the toilet. She's done it before, the handles are close together and she gets, well... confused."

"Okay, it's not a problem," answered Dave, "I'll just go and reset the emergency handle; we can be on our way then."

Vaguely aware of the continuing delay and her daughter's involvement in it, Brenda's mother asked, "What's goin' on our Brenda? Is it them two in the corner with the Scalextric causin' the hold-up?"

"It's alright mother, don't worry, they've got it all sorted out now, we should be on our way very soon."

"About time too, your Sam's already started sniffin' 'round this haddock – it won't stay frozen much longer you know!"

"That's a good sign for Sam then!" Brenda replied cheerily.

Dave made his way to the back cab, glad to be on the move at last. As Jim powered the train up, Dave's mobile buzzed into life.

"Hi, WPC Mitchell here, just getting back to you about the situation; any news on their demands?"

"Well, they seemed quite surprised by the request. I don't think they had intended to make any demands. They have though, agreed to be taken into Curzon Street. They did want to go to Middleminster, but I explained it wasn't possible."

"Middleminster eh, I wonder what the significance of that is?"

"They had tickets for there, so I guess that was going to be their final destination all along."

"So it's possible that Middleminster was the intended destination for their 'bomb' then."

"It could well be, they've brought it all the way from Yorkshire, so it would seem like it. What about your end, anything been decided yet?"

"Well, they've just had a plate of ham sandwiches sent in, so that's one less decision to make, apart from that, nothing as yet. Just between me and you, my gut feeling is that an attempt to resolve this situation will be made at Curzon Street station. There's a well-equipped canteen there and they're bringing in extra bodies as preparation."

Just then, Dave felt a sudden surge of braking, so broke off the conversation and leaned over to his cab window. A hazard light was illuminated on the second carriage. Dave wondered whether the old lady had pulled the Passcom handle again by mistake. His main fear was that the plotters would try to escape from the train at some point by using the emergency release handle on one of the external doors. In either case, an automatic full brake application would occur to bring the train to a halt.

He kept a watch out of the cab window. Yes, a door was open. The one called Kevin had jumped down and was running off, Darren was now following him. They had picked the ideal place. The train had just entered the long tunnel that leads into Yew Street station. The huge expanse of shops was directly above. They could easily reach it by climbing over the lineside fence and be lost in the crowds of shoppers. There was no CCTV in the tunnel or any way of observing from the air. It was quite a clever move – which from his own observations of the two, surprised him. Dave went to update WPC Mitchell on the situation.

All they could do now was continue on into Curzon Street station and wait for the police to arrive. Dave worked his way through the carriages issuing a further update, fielding the inevitable questions from passengers as best he could. When he reached the front of the stationary train, Jim came out from his cab to meet him.

"Well, what a pair of pricks! I suppose we'll have to wait for the police to come to take statements and all that," complained Jim as he stood looking at the open carriage door. "I should have decked them both as soon as soon as they started all this, we could be home by now."

"Really Jim?" responded Dave, sounding distinctly sceptical.

"Anyway, let's just get this train into the station; we've had enough delays for today – I'll be getting another phone call from Audrey else." He began walking back to his cab.

Mrs Bradshaw looked over to catch Dave's eye as he walked back through the train. He stopped and bent down to stroke Sam's head. The dog reciprocated in kind with a lick or two to Dave's face. Brenda raised her fears over the substances that Sam had eaten.

"Well he looks okay to me," said Dave by way of reassurance. "You could get him checked over by a vet, but I don't think there was any explosive contained in what he ate. My one word of caution would be, if he does happen to get a touch of wind later – don't let him anywhere near an open fire!"

After all the tension of the hijacking, Brenda surprised herself by laughing heartily at Dave's quip.

That evening Dave couldn't wait to relate the day's events for Galina's benefit. He saw the look on her face change from surprise to concern as he recounted the details. She gasped with shock when he told her how the two hijackers had threatened to detonate a bomb; he decided not to mention that it was an obvious fake.

Although impressed by Dave's bravery in standing up to the hijackers, Galina chided him for taking such a risk with his life. She wanted to know why he had not simply shot them both at the outset. This would have certainly been the case in her country, she went on to explain.

Well, yes, he would concede having a weapon about his person might have helped to resolve the situation a lot sooner. He could also see how being armed would make his job of keeping order on a train a lot easier. Pressing a 9mm automatic pistol against a fare dodger's temple would certainly be an effective way of extracting the ticket money from them. But this being England, a country noted for the restrained behaviour of its public servants, that was not how things were done, he explained. In fact, only the police were allowed to shoot people dead on trains.

The next morning Dave was sitting in his manager's office being congratulated by Eric Vines on a job well done.

"Yes, I don't think the incident could have been handled any better. God! It would have been a disaster if the bomb was genuine and the train had been blown up – they cost about five million pounds apiece, you know. Then there's all the negative publicity that goes with it, drop in revenues, etc, etc."

"Not forgetting the small matter of us and the passengers getting killed or maimed!" added Dave.

"Quite so, Dave, quite so. It was very fortunate that this er..." Eric scanned the piece of paper in front of him, "...Mrs Bradshaw had her dog with her. It makes quite a story really. I've already got onto the editor of the company magazine and given him all the details. They're going to send down a photographer. I'm sure they'll want you in it as well. It wouldn't do for management to get all the credit, would it now?

"Anyway that's by the by, I dare say the local press will be on to the story soon enough too. But don't trouble yourself over that score either, I know you're the quiet sort and you won't want to be bothered with all the fuss and such like – not after what you've just been through, so I'll look after that side of things for you."

"Yes well, that's very good of you Eric, kindness itself I'm sure. Funny though, how people not even involved manage to manoeuvre themselves into the limelight."

Not that it really bothered him. Senior Mercia Mainline management had given him a week off, along with Jim the driver to help them get over the ordeal. Eric, missing the irony in Dave's reply, carried on.

"Just one of the many onerous duties of management I'm afraid, yes indeed! But time marches on as they say; things to do and all that. WPC Mitchell is here waiting to take a statement from you so I'll send her in now. We'll see you in a week's time then Dave and well done once again!"

Eric picked up his papers and headed for the door, leaving it ajar for the female police officer. Dave turned towards her as she entered the room.

"Good morning Mr Bland, now I can put a face to the voice."

"Not too much of a shock I hope!"

"I've seen worse – as you do in my job. So how are you after yesterday?"

"Well, I've had duller days I must admit, but okay thank you – any news yet on the two would-be bombers?"

"Obviously enquiries are ongoing, there's a lot of information to collate and leads to follow up. We know absolutely nothing about these two at the moment, but we're hoping that will change. The first thing we need to do is to get a statement from you as you were one of the central characters in all of this."

★

Frank and Eli were once again sat in the snug of The Fettlers Arms, this time conducting an inquest into the debacle of Frank's son's bomb attempt on the Worfe Valley Railway.

"'E were just unlucky that's all. 'Ow could yer reckon on some bloody woman's dog goin' an eatin' the bomb afore he even got to the place? Must be a million to one chance that!" stated Frank.

"Aye, funny thing fer a dog to eat though."

"Darren told me it were 'cos 'e coated it in dried blood an' fishmcal – to fool any sniffer dogs like."

"It worked alright, fooled 'em so well, dog went an' 'et it!"

"Look! That dog were obviously no explosives expert then was it? Otherwise it would never 'ave scoffed it. I tell yer, my lad were just unlucky that's all; could 'ave 'appened to anyone. Anyway, they both got home alright wi'out gettin' caught – that's the main thing. It's all water under the past now so I'll 'ear no more about it!"

Eli knew when to drop the subject. "So what yer goin' to do now then Frank?"

"I've been 'avin a word with a few of the other lads about all this. They're as concerned as us over precarious state of Postlethwaite Railway, so I made a little suggestion – that we all pay the Worfe Valley a visit sometime soon, after things 'ave quietened down a bit like. I've noticed they're 'avin a special steam weekend down there in a few weeks time, where they run trains all

159

thru' night. Be an ideal opportunity to cause a bit o' mayhem down there, don't y' reckon?"

"What, you mean a bit o' sabotage and the like?"

"That's about it yeah, so are you with us then Eli?"

"Is your Darren goin' as well?"

"You can count on it! I've told 'im."

"And 'is mate?"

"Oh aye, I dare say he'll be there"

"Well I don't know, I'm sure the wife 'as got somethin' arranged for that weekend. I'll jus…"

"Look! We need all the 'elp we can get this time, the future of our railway 'angs on us wreckin' theirs. It's as simple as that! Anyway, Ernie Blowfield wants to see us on the very same subject."

"Not Ernie Blowfield the scrap metal magnet? Look, I never wanted to get involved in this, now we've got Ernie Blowfield wantin' to see us. It don't bode well Frank, it really don't. Did 'e say what 'e wanted to see us about?"

"Well all I know is that 'e's got an interest in our scheme to sabotage Worfe Valley Railway."

"'E would 'ave, wouldn't 'e? He's 'onorary secretary o' Postlethwaite Rail and Tramway Society, an' we all know he's got big ambitions for'it. And we also know what 'appens to anybody that gets in the way of 'is plans."

"Them stories about 'im givin' the blokes that owned that land 'e wanted a shove into his crusher are just rumours. Nothin' was ever proved. The police couldn't find any evidence."

"No, and they couldn't find the bodies neither, probably inside a mangled cube o' car somewhere."

"Look, it's no good tryin' to bottle out, 'e wants to see us and that's that!"

Frank picked up his glass, drained the last half pint from it, banged it back down on the table and said to Eli, "Your round I believe!"

★

A few days later, Dave received a call from WPC Mitchell seeking clarification on some aspects of the incident. He took the opportunity to quiz her on any developments.

"Well, I can't tell you everything, but what I can say is that, first of all, it was not a bomb as such. You were right about the ingredients, it would never have exploded. Secondly, as you noticed, they had combined train tickets for their journey to Middleminster and the Worfe Valley Railway. So we can only still speculate on whether for some reason, this was their intended target."

"But why? The Worfe Valley Railway is probably the most popular preserved railway in the whole of Britain, why would anyone want to cause it disruption with a bomb – even a fake one?"

"That, unfortunately, we do not know as yet."

"Any clues as to their identity?"

"Nothing so far. We're pretty certain that they originated from Yorkshire. CCTV footage is still being checked at stations en route, it's a long job though."

Dave mulled over the information for a moment. "Well, if for some reason their target was the Worfe Valley Railway, I'll keep my eyes peeled. I'm a regular visitor there. I also know one or two people who are volunteers, so I'll mention it to them too. You never know, they might unearth something."

"Yes, good idea, we'll obviously be getting in touch with the Worfe Valley ourselves to see if they have any ideas on who might have a motive for carrying out such an attack. Well, I think that just about wraps it up for now, I'm sure we'll be in touch again Mr Bland."

Chapter 17

Sgt. Edwards arrived for duty at the South Mercia British Transport Police HQ shortly before 8.00 am, meeting up with the night duty sergeant who was waiting to brief him before going off shift.

"Just the usual Sarge: a few drunks, one assault, one criminal damage – oh, and a prostitute for soliciting."

"Right," said Sgt Edwards casting his eye casually over the log.

"Yeah, a bit unusual the last one, apparently she'd been seen loitering around the station a couple of times recently and been warned off, so this time it was decided to nick her."

"She must have been a bit desperate, after being warned off twice."

"Yeah, seems she's Russian," he checked the book, "a... Ms Irina Troski. Very attractive, not your ordinary scrubber; speaks very little English though – or so she says. Wouldn't give us an address, but when she was searched, found one scribbled on a piece of paper, out in Bridforth it is. Again a bit more upmarket than usual – that is if it turns out to be her address. Anyway she's been charged, bailed, and was released a couple of hours ago. DC Wilson was the arresting officer."

"Bridforth you say?"

"Yeah, does that mean anything?"

"Hmm, it might do."

"How come?"

"Well, you remember that gang of Venezuelan ladyboys we caught touting for trade from a hot dog van in Kings Heath station car park? Well, she could be part of an Eastern European vice ring operating in a similar way; you know, a quiet suburban street in a quiet suburban town – that's where this sort of thing happens!"

"You think?"

"Middle England is becoming rife with it now according to a confidential intelligence report I was privileged to see recently – Daily Mail readers all of them, probably. So you never know; needs looking into anyway."

"Yeah, er… well, I'll leave it with you then."

"So, Russian you say?"

"Yes – and attractive!"

"Hmm… I'll be going over that way later myself. I'll take D.C. Wilson with me. We've had a bit of intelligence about those hoax bombers on the Worfe Valley Railway. With Heather on annual leave, it's been passed onto my desk. I'll see what's going on at this address too while I'm over there. What's the name of the owner by the way?"

"The house is registered in the name of a Mr Dave Bland."

"Dave Bland?"

"Yes, you heard of him?"

"I'm sure I have. I never forget a name... Dave Brand, eh."

Rostered on afternoon shifts all that week, Dave was making his sandwiches ready for work when he heard a knock at the door. He opened it to see two unfamiliar faces, introduced by a name he did recognise.

"Ah yes, Sgt Edwards, of course, I believe we spoke on the phone one time during the bomb hoax incident."

"I knew your name was familiar to me! Never forget, you know. It's all up here!" he announced tapping his head.

Recalling the sergeant's inept handling of the situation, Dave had a somewhat different opinion. He decided to humour him, "Of course, so any further developments then?"

"Actually, we're here about another matter."

"Really?" Dave struggled to think what that could be; certainly no intentional criminal acts had been committed by him as far as he could recall. He had a valid TV license; his car was now legal too. Surely it couldn't be about that dogging incident – it was ages ago.

"Yes, can you confirm that a..." Sgt Edwards referred to his notebook. "...Ms Trorsky lives at this address?"

"Er... a Ms Troski does live here," corrected Dave. "She's not in at the moment, but if it's about her working in this country, I can..."

"All will be revealed in the goodness of time Mr. Blend. Can we come in? We just need to ask a few questions that's all."

"Er…yes of course." Dave led the way into the lounge whilst racking his brain over what the police would want with Galina. He was sure all her paperwork was in order. Standing in the lounge the sergeant continued.

"So, this Ms Trotsky is not at home then?"

"No, I just said she's out."

"So you did Mr. Brand, so you did. Would she by any chance be out 'working' as it were?"

"Yes, I said that as well – no law against it is there?"

"It so happens that's just what we're here to find out. What time do you expect her home?"

"Well, she left the house at about eight this morning; I expect she'll be tied up for most of the day."

"Gets tied up eh? Put that down Wilson. A busy woman then, this Ms Troska?"

"Er… yes, she has quite a few clients now."

"I bet she has."

"Look, just what is all this about?"

"Are you familiar with the phrase 'living off immoral earnings?'"

"Immoral earnings? But that's ridiculous, there's nothing immoral about what she does, in fact her rates are more than reasonable, and she always agrees a price with the customer first."

"Very commendable, I'm sure," said the sergeant.

"So what would her normal price be, would you say?" asked a curious DC Wilson.

"Well, it all very much depends on what the customer wants doing, but if it's just a small job, she'll charge her standard hourly rate. For anything bigger, she generally takes a few measurements before working out a price."

The sergeant looked astonished. "That's certainly a new one on me Mr Blond, charging punters by the size of their... er, uses a tape measure, does she?"

"Yes... of course she does," said Dave, still trying to work out what it was he was missing here. "The thing is she's new to the game, and is just trying to build up her business, so she takes on as much work as she can in order to gain the experience. She keeps records and everything so it's all above board."

Dave was anxious to allay any suspicions they may have about Galina's business activities in case further enquiries ensued. Dave had been hoping to keep the authorities in the dark about Galina's income for a year or two to avoid her having to pay any income tax that may be due. But if all this was about her immigration status, although not strictly the province of the police, details of her income could well find their way to the Inland Revenue if they had any suspicions she was living here illegally.

"I think we'd best be the judge of that Mr Brant. Does she work alone?"

"Yes generally, but if something comes up that's too big for her to take on, she does have one or two colleagues she can call on for help. Like I say to her, you don't want to struggle on your own; it's only money after all."

"Yes Mr Blund, very considerate of you – sounds very accommodating, your Ms Trotsa."

"And flexible as well!" added D.C. Wilson.

"Yes, that too. So she does work with others in the 'trade' then?" pressed the sergeant.

"Yes, though as I say, it depends on the circumstances."

"What did I tell you Tomkins," he muttered to his assistant, "there is a gang involved – just like those Venezuelan ladyboys."

"Sorry?"

"Nothing, Mr Blond, nothing. I'm impressed though. Seriously! Yes, it's obviously a very well organised operation you're running here with Ms Trotski, I'm surprised you're so up front about it."

Still not understanding the reason for all the cryptic questions, but not liking some of the inferences, Dave went on the offensive.

"Look, I still don't know what all this is leading up to sergeant, but there's nothing immoral about honest manual work!"

"I'd say more like dirty work," sneered the sergeant.

"And how do you mean that exactly?"

"Well, you know, coming home 'soiled' from plying her 'trade' as it were. Doesn't it bother you?"

"Well... yes, but she always cleans herself up well with Swarfeger afterwards," explained Dave.

"Swarfeger?" exclaimed both policemen.

"It's a bit extreme, don't you think – using something as strong as that," suggested Sgt Edwards.

"Not if her hand's been up a customer's wastepipe, it isn't."

"Yes, I can imagine Mr. Brand – I can imagine. Look, as much as I appreciate your candid revelations, I really don't think we need to know all the sordid details." He exchanged a confirming nod with his subordinate. "We've pretty much got the picture by now."

"Now wait a minute," said Dave. "I've just about had enough of all these insinuations you keep making. You obviously believe there's something sleazy about what she does. But you have got completely the wrong idea. I think I'd better ask her to call in so we can clear all this up. She's up at the doctor's surgery this morning. I can give her a call to see if she's finished."

"Getting herself checked out is she? A wise precaution I'm sure."

"I strongly resent that remark sergeant! If you must know she's actually fitting a new sink."

"Oh, come now Mr Brand! A new sink indeed! Please don't play the innocent with me, you've already admitted everything. It seems even the medical profession is not safe from your sordid activities – looks like we'll need to get the Vice Squad in on this one, Wilson."

Dave was incredulous. "Vice squad? Just what..."

"Don't play games with us, you've already admitted that this Ms Trotstik of yours provides sexual services – and with such an ingenious way of charging the punters too! I'm intrigued, tell me Mr Brand, when she prices up her 'bigger' clients, does she charge them by the inch – or has the vice trade now gone metric?"

Ignoring Dave's look of total astonishment, Sgt. Edwards continued. "If further proof were needed, then I have to tell you that at 01.30 hours this morning a Ms Trostky was arrested outside Wensbury Railway Station and charged with soliciting for sexual purposes! Furthermore Mr Blend, I allege that you are the pimp running the whole show. Perhaps you would care to reveal exactly how many other girls you have working for you?"

"This is all ridiculous!" stated Dave, now realising the full extent of their calamitous error. "You've obviously got the wrong person, because Galina – or Ms Trosky, was actually in bed next to me at 1.30 this morning, and I strongly resent the accusation that she works as a prostitute – she actually is a qualified plumber!"

"So that's what you call it now, do you?"

"No, that's not what I call it. That's what she actually is, believe it or not. It's what I've been talking about all along. Her clients are the people she's done plumbing work for. Look! Here's one of her cards and I've got some of her headed notepaper on the desk. She has her business chequebook and accounts upstairs as well if you want to see them."

Sgt. Edwards looked crestfallen after closely examining them. Thinking quickly, he ventured an impromptu theory. "She could be doing it on the side – a part-time job like."

"No she couldn't, she'd be too tired. She's normally too tired to even have... anyway, never mind about that. How do you explain away the fact that she was in bed with me all night?"

"You could be lying in order to protect her," suggested the sergeant, still trying to shore up his collapsing case.

Dave had a thought. "Now wait a minute... something has just occurred to me. You didn't say what her first name was?

"Er, I've got it here somewhere," replied the detective constable, leafing back through the pages of his notebook. "Yes, it's Irina."

"And how old is this Irina Trotski supposed to be?" enquired Dave.

"Oh, about twenty-five – and very attractive!" the D.C. added.

"Well, it can't be my Galina then can it? Not that she isn't attractive you understand, it's just that she's almost fifty, and even with her great beauty, would not pass for twenty-five," then in a dig at his accuser, "even to you Sergeant Edwards."

The insult had passed him by. Still deep in thought, and not about to give up hope just yet, the sergeant suddenly advanced another theory. "It could be her daughter!"

"No, she doesn't have one."

"Well there can't be two women in the area with the surname of Tortsky, surely!"

He suddenly remembered a further piece of evidence. "So how did she come to have this address on her then, eh? Tell me that!"

Dave decided to volunteer no information in response to that particular question, although he could have told him, as he had by now worked out how all this had come to pass. His initial assessment of Irina had been right all along: she was working as a prostitute and for some reason, which he had yet to find out, had given this address as her own when she had been caught doing it.

He was not best pleased at this turn of events – not best pleased at all, but he wasn't about to reveal to the police the connection between them. Galina he was sure would not want it to become common knowledge either. Dave accepted that the police would only be satisfied when they actually interviewed her. He wanted to speak to Galina himself before that took place. Luckily the two policemen were placated enough to allow a respite for the time being when he showed them Galina's passport and DC Wilson confirmed that it was not the woman he had arrested the previous day.

As they left the house Sgt. Edwards half turned to promulgate his final theory. "You sure she's not got a younger sister?"

"Absolutely certain!" confirmed Dave.

"Well, we will be interviewing this Ms Troyska, that's for sure!" Then, giving Dave one final look up and down, Sgt Edwards delivered his parting comment. "We'll get to the bottom of all this eventually Mr Brand! Mark my words we will!"

Chapter 18

Dave waited until he had returned home from work that evening before relating the drama of the police visit earlier in the day. As the story unfolded, Galina became silent. Her face, which initially had been a mixture of curiosity and anticipation, now took on a sombre appearance. He stuck to the facts, omitting any opinions of his own about her niece's activities. When he had finished, Galina, as if gathering her thoughts, took a few moments before speaking.

"I herv to tell you something which I could not tell you before."

Dave guessed what was coming, "Yes Galina?"

"It is about 'Rina, she is werking as... a..." Galina was finding it hard to say the word. Dave helped her out.

"A prostitute?" ventured Dave.

"No! werl... not exactly... She... er, entertains men. Is different."

"How is it different?"

"Well, she entertains."

"What do you mean, entertains? Does she perform a little song and dance routine for them in the bedroom, eh? Maybe tell 'em a few jokes as well? How is she with card tricks?"

"No! Thert is not whert I meant. You are making fun, but irs not furny. I worry for her!"

Dave could see the concern in her face and immediately regretted his remarks. He took hold of her hand, apologised and said, "Look, if you are worried about her, then so am I. Please tell me about it."

Galina's face registered relief when she realised that Dave's initial anger at her niece's troubles finding their way into their home had given way to genuine concern for her and Irina. She squeezed his hand in recognition of this. Slowly, and sometimes haltingly, she revealed the full extent of her niece's involvement in prostitution.

Irina had been working in the 'entertainment' industry for several years, graduating from lap dancing in men's clubs to eventual involvement in servicing all their needs. Over the last twelve months, she'd found it an increasingly difficult occupation to work in due to the many other girls – especially ones from Eastern Europe – competing for the same business.

Whereas at one time she would have considered herself a 'high class hooker' with lucrative liaisons in expensive hotels, she now had to be increasingly content with the lower end of the market. This meant several appointments a day in a shabby room with the type of client she would normally go to great lengths to avoid if encountered socially. Irina's increasingly seedy existence meant that occasional violence and non-payment for services became an occupational hazard in her daily life – a lifestyle she was very anxious to escape from.

Her soliciting outside the railway station had merely been a vain effort to entice a different type of client. Dave wondered if she had been trying the same tactic on her visits to The Worfe Valley Station in town.

Having learned the facts, Dave now understood why she had decamped to Scotland like she had. Irina had been trying to accumulate some extra money before Galina moved in with her. Aberdeen was the centre of the off-shore oil industry, and there were rich pickings for women looking for a good time – though in recent years the industry had been undergoing a decline in fortune due to the depleting oil reserves. Presumably that's why she had resorted to picking up her old life back in Wensbury and why she'd got caught at the station. Irina would be unaware that the transport police clamped down heavily on this sort of activity on their home ground. Local girls knew this and so avoided railway stations.

"So what can be done then?" asked Dave finally.

"Werl, I wourd not ask you thirs unless it wers very serious, burt I ask thert you let her come to stay wirth us. It werl only be for a short time," Galina quickly added. "She is not happy where she is living, it is a dump ernd it is not safe – burt she cannot afford anything better! Please let her stay, Dave! I know she werl be no trouble."

Dave noted the plaintive expression on her face. He was reluctant to agree to such an arrangement, after all, he knew next to nothing about her. Galina said only for a short while, but how long would it be in reality? What about if she started to go out picking up men again while she was living with them? What would happen then?

There was a lot for Dave to think about. He was also concerned about how it would affect his own relationship with Galina. The mutual affection they shared was exactly how he'd always imagined a relationship ought to be – and how he wanted it to stay. He had a secure job with all manner of incidents to make his life interesting, but always the highlight of his day was coming home to Galina.

Now she was working hard to build up her business, he accepted that their once raunchy and regular sex life would suffer to some extent – it still had its moments though. He was sure a good holiday with plenty of time to relax was all they needed to rekindle their physical passion. Dave feared that having another female living in the house – even an attractive one like Irina – could have unforeseen consequences and should any tensions arise from such an arrangement, it could just alter the balance of their own equitable relationship.

Dave decided to do what he always did when making a decision like this. He would pay a visit to the Platelayer's Arms to mull the problem over. The twenty minute walk gave him time to consider all of the factors in the equation.

Nodding to a few of the regulars at the bar, Dave took himself off to a seat in the corner. After the third pint and contrary to accepted wisdom, things began to appear a lot clearer – though he realised that he had arrived at a preliminary decision during the walk up there.

Yes, he would agree to take her in and see how things worked out. Unlike the fractured family life that was all too common in Britain, he understood that family loyalties still held sway in Russian culture and that it was a duty to help out a relative in times of difficulty. It was really a no-brainer. He could do no other than support the woman he loved by agreeing to take in her niece.

Dave recalled the time his marriage began falling apart and the disappointment he had felt when support from people he considered friends had never materialised. It was almost as if they regarded his marriage break-up as a sort of disease; themselves fearful of catching it if they got too close. Excuses for not offering – nor accepting – a social invitation were many: too far, too busy, too tired. He'd heard them all. Even a long-standing mate of his was now reluctant to meet him for a drink, the man's domineering wife preventing her weaker-willed husband from having contact with him. He knew that he was better off without such fair-weather friends, but that did not prevent him from becoming maudlin at times about their loss.

Rousing himself out his introspection, he quickly finished off his drink. He was eager to return home and inform Galina of his decision.

"I'm so happy, I know thert 'Rina too will be happy thert you make this decision, she werl be very grateful!"

Dave smiled, "Just how grateful do you mean?"

"She wirl try to pleas you irn every way, I know."

He started to laugh. "In every way?"

Galina looked puzzled for a moment, not quite understanding what Dave was inferring with his question. Although she now had a better appreciation of the subtleties of the English language, there were still some nuances that escaped her immediate understanding.

Galina then realised and started to laugh too. "You're very bad mern! No, you murst nert do thert with her!" With that she threw her arms around him, hugged him and said, "You are my mern now!" With that, she moved her hand down between his legs, took hold of him through his trousers and in a villainous voice said, "Do you understand Mr Blarnd?"

A giggling Dave immediately submitted. "Yes, yes… No please don't, I understand! I understand!" Once his laughter had subsided, a sly grin began to spread across his face. "I was just thinking… while you've got your hand down there…"

Irina moved in two days later. Galina was indeed correct about her. She was grateful to the point of subservience. Nothing was too much trouble. She cleaned, polished, hoovered and dusted; the work being completed with the utmost diligence by Irina. Dave did casually ask Galina at the end of the first week if Irina ought to be wearing suitable clothing for carrying out these chores – like perhaps a skimpy French maids outfit.

The suggestion was not well received. Although it was meant in fun, Galina had taken the suggestion rather more seriously. He realised that she really was on her guard to prevent anything untoward happening, especially if Galina was at work and Dave was at home with Irina alone. During these periods he noticed that she would phone more frequently, and then call in at odd times on the pretence that she had forgotten something.

Not that Dave in any way made advances on Irina, or vice versa. But what added to Galina's concern was that Irina had become accustomed to wearing very little around the house. This, at times, allowed Dave some unexpected viewing pleasure. The tension was further heightened by one other unanticipated consequence of Irina's sexual abstinence: her very audible masturbating sessions; the noises from which could be heard very easily through the bedroom walls.

Although Galina had asked her to try and be more discreet, on one occasion when Dave had brought his elderly mother over to stay for a few days, he had to pretend that the waves of groaning noises coming from the next bedroom were just Galina's niece having a work-out on her multi-gym. And when Irina inadvertently left her vibrator in the bathroom, his mother had mistaken it for a roll-on deodorant, telling Dave how she'd spent several minutes trying to get the top off before bringing it to him to undo. She blamed her own lack of strength on an arthritic wrist.

It was therefore not surprising that an air of sexual tension hung heavy in the house. Being confronted on a frequent basis with Irina's provocative behaviour and having the normal responses of any red-blooded male, Dave seemed to be in a constant state of arousal at home. In a reversal of the norm, it was somewhat of a relief to go to work.

Galina was well aware of the situation and constantly chided Irina for her behaviour, but she seemed to be oblivious of the effect she was having on them both. For her, it was a normal way to behave. It did have one positive side effect though: the sexually charged atmosphere at home seemed to increase Galina's libido too.

Physically, she needed Dave far more frequently now, and the particular aspect Dave found most strange was that Galina had suddenly become much more vocal during their lovemaking, as if in some way in competition with her niece. So much so that during another visit by his mother, she enquired the following morning, "Have you got that multi-gym thingy in your bedroom now?"

Irina was becoming increasingly frustrated in a different sense. She had been unable to find suitable alternative work; mainly due to her lack of UK-recognised qualifications and her limited spoken English. She had little money – certainly a lot less than she was used to – and little to do either, though she still kept in touch with her friends in the 'trade.' Dave would drop Irina off in Wensbury from time to time so she could visit them, coming home later on to re-tell their tales of woe. Both Galina and Dave felt that it was only the depressed state of the business that kept Irina from returning to her old vocation.

It was about this time that Irina heard officially from the police that no further action would be taken over the soliciting charges. Having made a few discreet enquires of his own at the station's security office, he had found out that the CCTV had not picked her up on that particular night. With no footage to use against her as evidence, the police had decided the case was not strong enough for a successful prosecution.

Although the news came as some relief, existing tensions at home were still causing problems. Galina decided that a meeting between the three of them was needed to discuss the situation. It was Irina who first broached what all three knew was the solution to the problem.

"I wurd leave, burt herv no morney, no jorb, norwhere to go. If I herv morney thern I cern do rest. I know I murst go herv sex fer merney again – there's no orther way!"

Galina spoke out at her straight away, and after some lively dialogue with Irina, she said to Dave, "I cannot persuade her, she says she wants to go back working again. If she find another town, maybe things werl be better – but I don't thirnk so."

Neither did Dave. Galina had offered her some of her own money if she was really desperate, but the amount Irina was thinking of to set herself up for the future was far more than Galina could afford. Dave had been letting her live at the house virtually rent-free and due to his protracted divorce proceedings, had very little in the way of savings.

Concluding the discussion, Galina revealed Irina's thoughts on the matter. "What 'Rina told me she would like – ernd this is in ideal world you see – is to find mern with money thert do not get their sex. 'Rina does not mind if they're, fat, bald, ugly or boring, as long as they pay her ernd do not harm her – ernd thert they don't steal from her afterwards. Where could she find such mern as this Dave? It is impossible I thirnk!"

Chapter 19

Dave drove to work the following day still thinking over Galina's words from the previous evening. He knew that, typical of her race, Galina took a fatalistic approach to life; accepting that if her niece wanted to work in the sex industry – though she may not approve, nor able to dissuade her – then she would try to do all she could to help her do it safely.

For himself, he had no moral objections to prostitution. He had seen for himself how it worked in countries that had made it legal. The Reeperbahn in Hamburg housed one of the most well-known examples of legalised brothels. Planned, executed and controlled with typical German thoroughness, the girls working there were free to ply their trade within that specific area of the city. The place had even become a tourist attraction with many visitors each year taking a stroll through its colourful streets.

In the UK, the situation was typical of the country's ambivalent attitude towards sexual matters – keeping prostitution suppressed and pretending it doesn't exist. Only making the news when the likes of a high court judge or a senior politician is caught making use of their services, thus exposing the double standards of those elected to sit in high office.

He turned into a space in the Mercia Mainline car park and found himself looking on as a man urinated against the wall of the nearby station building. Observing him for a moment, he calculated that if he aimed the stream just a little higher, it might wash off the dried vomit that had been deposited there by some inebriate the previous Saturday night.

Alas, it appeared that the man was very drunk himself, one of his arms being positioned like a prop against the wall, preventing him from falling into the stream of liquid he'd just produced.

Trying to put out of his mind why so many of the nation's social problems were exhibited at railway stations, Dave picked up his bag and made his way to the cabin. He noticed one of the people inside having a meal break was Duggie. It had been some time since he'd last seen him, so he asked his friend how the dogging activities were going.

Putting down his newspaper, Duggie described how it had not been a very good season – his viewings were well down on the same time last year. He reckoned this was due to the unseasonal cold weather, though he was hoping things would pick up as the weather improved.

Dave hadn't realised the activity was seasonal, but could understand how the parties involved would be less likely to cavort naked in the back of a car on a chilly winter's evening.

Taking his enquiry as a sign of renewed interest in the pastime, Duggie offered to give Dave a tour of the best sites, 'to get him started,' as he put it. The offer was politely declined by Dave, who explained that the hobby would not find favour with his new partner.

Mindful of the time, Dave now had just a few minutes to catch his train. He said his goodbyes and, grabbing his bag, set off down the platform to board his Lytham bound express.

Forty-five minutes later, his four-car train pulled into platform six at Crewe North. Stepping out of his cab, Dave noticed a throng of trainspotters grouped together looking out to the north end of the platform. With a few minutes to go before his train's departure time, Dave walked across and asked the one nearest to him what was happening.

"There's a Castle coming through on the fast in the next few minutes," the spotter replied, keeping the reply brief, his tripod-mounted camera facing down the platform in readiness for the awaited moment. Dave nodded and idly cast his gaze over the assembled throng.

Predominantly middle-aged, beards and paunches seemed to be the dominant characteristics. They were clearly not short of money as many were equipped with expensive cameras and camcorders to capture the scene. Although he would always deny being a spotter if anyone were to ask, he had to admit that a steam loco racing through a mainline station at speed assaulted the senses of even the most detached of observers, although he did find it difficult to understand the appeal of modern electrics and diesels.

Identical in every respect apart from their unit number, he could see little point in taking photographs of each one. He could only reason that the personality of a trainspotter was one where repetition and attention to inconsequential detail became major factors in their lives. Not a trait that seemed to have particular appeal for women, he would imagine.

There was a general perception that morris dancing and trainspotting were about equal as subjects least likely to engage a woman's interest. He wondered how many of them had a wife or girlfriend, and of those who did not, how many of them were forced to suppress their sexual urges. Surely they looked at more than just pictures of locos whenever these train spotters surfed the internet. And if they did find themselves clicking on images of a more erotic nature from time to time, what did they do to relieve themselves of their resulting frustration?

He suddenly had a brainwave – a very good one, the more he thought about it. Just suppose that a discreet sexual service was available, aimed specifically at the trainspotter, using ladies who were aware of their idiosyncrasies and able to cater for their specific needs. There could be quite a demand; yes, quite a demand indeed. That was it! He had the answer!

Once they were underway again, he phoned Galina straightaway.

"Hi sweetheart, you know what you were saying yesterday about finding some suitable customers for 'Rina, well I've just found the perfect solution. Yes! Really! I'll tell you all about it when I get home."

When not working the train checking and selling tickets, Dave spent the rest of the journey making notes and formulating a plan. On arriving back at Curzon Street, he went straight to one of the company's internet terminals and downloaded the information he needed.

Later that evening after he'd sat all three of them down with a drink to hand, he explained. "Nobody, as far as I know, has ever attempted to exploit what is potentially a huge market for the type of service that people like 'Rina can offer. No, honestly! Galina, when you said yesterday that 'Rina's perfect customer would be men who get little or no sex, but have money, and who won't be violent, and they can be young, old, fat or thin – well, when I went through Crewe today, there in the station the answer was quite simply staring me in the face!"

Dave waited for a reaction. All he got were two blank looks staring him in the face. Maybe it was his choice of phrase.

"Trainspotters, of course!" he announced. He knew that Galina could translate to Irina afterwards the detail of what he was about to explain, so carried on putting his case.

"Okay, they may be a bit odd in some ways with their fascination for taking down numbers and talking in railway terminology. And yes, okay they dress a bit differently with their unwashed anoraks, and personal grooming is not a high priority for them I know, but as a group of people they are generally well balanced and harmless, so in all respects they fulfil exactly the requirements you spoke about yesterday.

"Look, I've been doing a bit of research and there's a big steam festival coming up in a few weeks on the Worfe Valley Railway here in Bridforth. From Saturday to Sunday evening they'll be running trains non-stop throughout the day and night. Literally thousands of spotters and steam fans will be there. It goes without saying there'll be few wives or girlfriends in attendance – even if they had one to bring. And what wife or girlfriend is going to want to stop up all night watching steam trains? Exactly! There's where Irina comes in to the picture. If she can work the trains the way I propose, she'll find plenty of punters willing to pay for an individual sexual service. How's this for a slogan?

"'If you thought riding behind a prairie tank was exciting! Just wait till you ride behind randy 'Rina!' was... er... I thought, quite good. She is okay with it doggy style, isn't she?" Dave asked in a whispered aside to Galina.

He looked at both of them for a reaction. Irina still looked totally blank, Galina just looked thoughtful. Dave carried on. "Okay, never mind, we'll come back to the marketing side later. I reckon 'Rina's going to be a very busy lady. In fact if my estimates are correct, we're going to need several girls in total to cope with the demand. So I was thinking that Irina could recruit some of her friends in the trade, you know, a few of the better ones – no scrubbers like."

Pausing to take breath he asked, "Well, what do you think?"

Irina and Galina both looked at each other. Irina, not understanding very much of what Dave had said, asked questions of Galina which she did her best to answer, confirming the details with Dave from time to time. He noticed Irina had started to smile. He wondered whether Galina had just translated his amusing slogan – well, he thought it was witty anyway. Finally, Irina started to nod her head as if at last understanding the full picture. She turned to Dave, smiled and nodded her head.

"Yers, I know mern you say of, I thirnk they okay!"

"That's great! Look, we've only got three weeks and there's a lot to organise. To assess the market and get some advance bookings, I was thinking of putting an advert in the *Steam Railway Weekly* along the lines of: 'Young attractive Russian lady attending Worfe Valley Steam Weekend would like to be instructed in special working arrangements; very interested in all forms of reciprocating motion.' Then just include a telephone number – what do you think?"

Galina, who understood a good deal more about implied meanings in her adopted language now, replied, "Yers, is very clever, I understand you not quite say what you mean, burt you hope people wirl know what you mean. Is the English way, is irt not?"

"Yes my dear Galina, it is the English way." Dave stood, smiling at her. Now with a mission to fulfil, he was experiencing a rush of euphoria. He moved in closer to his partner and noted her radiant face. Dave remembered she'd been servicing gas boilers all afternoon which accounted for the healthy glow in her cheeks.

Now feeling distinctly frisky, he held her face lightly between his hands, kissed her gently on the lips, and said, "It is also the English way to have their way – if you know what I mean." He then whispered discreetly in her ear, "Therefore I propose to make passionate lurve to you tonight."

"Certainly not!" replied Galina, affecting an indignant tone. "It is certainly not the Ernglish way to make passionate lurv, burt I know you are exception to rule – werl so far anyway!"

Galina would often tease him with this remark – Dave being the one and only Englishmen she had slept with – so far. When she wanted to expand on her mischief, Galina would speculate on whether Laurence – the man she had met at the airport – would have been a capable lover, affecting to mourn with a regretful sigh, "If only I herd been allowed to find out!"

Dave normally replied with the claim that any man sporting such a thick moustache must surely be gay. If he wasn't, then the facial hair would tickle her mercilessly.

Galina came to her decision, "Very werl Mr Blarnd, it seems thert I must submit to your demands. Now if you wirl excuse me, I shall retire upstairs to take my bath ernd wirl await your presence irn the bedroom."

Dave started laughing. One of Galina's great passions he had discovered, were period dramas. Consequently, he had bought her a boxed set of DVDs featuring all the great classics to help pass the time when he was on a late shift. As a result, Galina had picked up the habit of using the classical phrases and language she had heard in them.

He immediately adopted his Mr Darcy role. Taking hold of Galina's proffered hand, he kissed it lightly with his lips. Then, taking a step back, he bowed, and with a sweeping flourish of his arm, announced, "Fear not my dear, I shall without further ado, be up forthwith!"

Having heard most of Dave's collection of double-entendres and innuendos several times over, Galina started giggling and said, "Werl, thert was the idea, wasn't it?"

With both of them now collapsing in fits of giggles, even Irina started to laugh, though she understood very little of what had been played out before her.

Chapter 20

The next morning Dave set about planning his campaign to bring sexual relief to the needy – *or should that be the nerdy,* he wondered? No, on balance he judged the description to be unfair; after all, some of them were his friends and work colleagues. He would though, plan the operation like a military campaign. If his twelve years in the Territorial Army had taught him anything, it was that planning and preparation were everything.

He recalled another important military adage, 'Time spent on reconnaissance is seldom wasted.' With this in mind, Dave set to work on his computer. It was a weekday and Galina was at work so he could carry out his research without interruption. Not that he minded an interruption from Galina. In fact, he reminded himself to ring her later about an item he had asked her to buy.

His mind wandered back to the previous evening. He realised that Galina had given him something that he believed did not exist, except in those gossipy women's magazines he used to find on the train: an overpowering love for a woman – his Galina!

Dave was utterly committed to ensuring her happiness. Now she had settled into her new life, Galina's only real concern was for the welfare of her niece. Whereas Irina simply saw it as her destiny to work in the vice trade, Galina inevitably took a different view. But as Irina could not be persuaded to give up her way of life, it was his duty to do all he could to ensure the girl's wellbeing.

He typed an appropriate heading into his search engine, looking for information on the attendance figures for last year's Worfe Valley steam special. Then, as if to impress an invisible overseer by his attention to detail, he checked the weather experienced over that weekend the previous year, against the weather forecast for the same weekend this year. No rain but a degree or two colder was the long range prediction, which led Dave to the not-unreasonable conclusion that similar attendance figures would be achieved for this year.

So, out of all the thousands attending the weekend, how many of them could be persuaded to avail themselves of the service being provided – that was the difficult question. There was no way of knowing. Such a distinct group of people had never been targeted in this way before, so the success rate was difficult to predict.

To form a basis for some sort of calculation, he worked on the principle that there were six stations on the route including the end termini, and remembering that the girls liked to work in pairs, calculated that he would need at least fourteen girls for the weekend, and possibly another two held in reserve.

The next consideration was a suitable location for the encounters to take place. During the quieter nighttime hours, he was certain that there would be sufficient empty compartments on the train where these liaisons could be conducted. For other times of day, he would need to find somewhere more private. A mobile home would be ideal, situated at a convenient location somewhere along the route. The Worfe Valley was a popular tourist area with several of these sites. Something secluded would be preferable, well away from prying eyes and ears. He would check suitable ones out on the internet first of all and then carry out some ground reconnaissance to confirm the best locations.

The advert for the *Steam Railway Weekly* classified ads needed to be uploaded as soon as possible in order to solicit some advance bookings. He just hoped the form of words would pass scrutiny. But before he could do that, he needed to make a call to Galina. Having asked her to make a cash purchase of a pay-as-you-go phone, he needed the number to insert in the advert. In this way, should there be any comebacks, the phone could not be traced back to them.

The time passed by quickly that day, lunch came and went. Galina called in briefly for a sandwich and to drop off the phone she'd purchased that morning. Eventually, armed with several sheets of downloaded print-outs and a local Landranger map, Dave set off in the afternoon for a detailed 'recce' of the more promising mobile home locations. He eventually picked out two. One was ideal, within walking distance from one of the stations. His second choice was unavailable, so picked out an alternative which was free on the dates he required.

Over dinner that evening, the three discussed their progress so far. Irina had made contact with several of her colleagues, and so far had recruited ten, left messages for others and was confident that she could easily find another six. Galina, as well as purchasing the phone, had also sourced and collected several other items needed for the weekend. Lastly, Dave reported on the progress he'd made, together with his intentions for the next day. A first bottle of wine was very quickly consumed, and they were well into a second before all the various items had been fully discussed.

Dave realised he needed to undertake an intelligence mission on the Worfe Valley Railway itself, so the following day took himself up to the station, purchased a return ticket, settled into one of the carriages and waited for the 11.15am to depart. Being a midweek day, he expected it to be a fairly quiet train. He was not disappointed, and once underway, he ventured out of his compartment to make his way along the slowly swaying corridors as the train climbed the gradient.

It was a composite train with different carriage types, so he needed to discreetly check each variant in turn. Finding his first empty compartment, he took out the tape measure from his pocket and a small notepad. Working from his list, Dave confirmed that the blinds fitted to the windows on both sides of the compartment worked correctly. He then opened and closed the sliding compartment door several times to check the action, made a few notes and took measurements. With his camera, he took a series of shots for reference purposes. Satisfied with his observations, Dave moved onto the next carriage type.

At journey's end in Middleminster, Dave gave particular thought to where the girls could entertain their clients. It was the largest station and thus likely to be the busiest, so proper arrangements needed to be put in place. He was struck with the thought that mobile brothels – like a Portakabin but with a bed in situ – ought to be available for occasional hire to cater for such events. It would be a valuable add-on for the mobile lavatory hire companies.

Filing the idea away for some future time when the moral climate had changed sufficiently to allow them, he continued to think through the problem in his head. Then it came to him, a motor home! Park it on the car park just outside the station, and it's just a short walk each time a girl has a client wanting to do business with her. Perfect! Now, if his memory served him correctly, there was a caravan and motor home business just a few streets away from the station. He checked his watch. There was a couple of hours to spare, so he still had time to go and check out what was available before returning to the station where hopefully he would have time for a quick pint in the station pub.

Luck was on his side. Being near the end of season, a four berth was free on the weekend required, and at what he considered to be a reasonable price. Although out on hire and unavailable for viewing, Dave booked it without hesitation. He could collect it on the Saturday morning.

Dave was pleased to find that his advertisement was accepted without a hitch, then again, why would a publication like The Steam Railway Weekly require a vetting procedure? It would not be an obvious choice in to advertise dubious products and services.

Following publication Galina, who had agreed to fence the calls on the girls' behalf, found that some of the callers had taken the advert at face value and genuinely wanted to meet up and explain the relative merits of different reciprocating motions and special train workings to the advertiser. Dave had not anticipated this. He put the problem down not to the couched terms used, but to the nature of the people he was dealing with, in that they took a very literal interpretation of the written word.

Galina did get a steady trickle of more interpretive callers, but then had a problem when the caller asked for details of individual sex acts and the cost. She was unable to openly discuss such matters if the call came while she was in a customer's house with the householder around. The problem was eventually solved by transferring the phone to one of the girls recruited for the weekend who spoke relatively good English, and who was able to talk 'shop' without interruption or embarrassment.

The weekend before the event Dave called everybody together at his house for a briefing. Sixteen girls had now been recruited, an assortment of Eastern Europeans which included Estonians, Lithuanians, Latvians, another Russian, together with a couple of Polish girls. Arriving in dribs and drabs over a two hour period, Irina greeted each one of them in turn, then made the introductions to both Dave and Galina. Dave noticed their standard of English varied somewhat, but Galina was on hand to translate when needed.

He mingled amongst them offering drinks and nibbles. Distracted in his duties by the girls' scanty clothing, it was not surprising that on occasion a cheesy Watnot would roll off the platter he was holding and become lodged in a girl's exposed cleavage. He dismissed all thought of personally retrieving them due to Galina's all-seeing gaze from across the room.

When he judged his guests to be suitably refreshed, Dave called them all through to the conservatory for the briefing. In the centre of the room, he had laid out a wallpaper pasting table. Borrowing houses and hotels from a Monopoly set, and with the aid of a model train, he had constructed a three-dimensional model for demonstration purposes.

"Right, if everybody would like to spread themselves around

the table, I'll begin." he instructed. As they shuffled along, Dave rapped his pointer stick on the table leg to gain their attention.

"Okay ladies, first of all I'd like to welcome you all to what will effectively be our mission headquarters next weekend. I'll begin first of all with a brief explanation of the mission and then your role in it. A role for which…" he stopped mid-sentence and deliberately cast his gaze along the line of girls, catching the eye of every one in turn before continuing, "…you have *all* been specially selected!"

The girls nodded and turned to look at one another. Dave paused for a moment.

"Our mission then is…" he allowed a further pause, "…to give sexual relief to the nerd, er… needy!"

Dave repeated the mission statement for effect. "In carrying out this mission, may I remind you ladies that a high price may well have to be paid." He adopted his most serious expression at this point before delivering the punch line. "…The price being whatever you feel you can get away with charging!"

Dave smiled and allowed himself a little chuckle at his pre-rehearsed quip. There were reassuring murmurs of approval from the girls too. "Okay, quiet down… right then, execution!"

Suddenly there were looks of alarm and raised voices amongst the girls.

"No, no! Don't worry, this isn't a Bond film, you're not expected to kill anyone – well not intentionally anyway. It's just a military expression. All it means is how the operation is executed, or carried out."

There were sighs of relief from the girls, except for one hard-faced Estonian, who now looked disappointed.

"As you can see looking at the table, I have made representations of the target stations using model houses, here… here…. here… here… here… and here!" Dave pointed to each one in turn with his stick.

"I've divided you into eight teams of two, the make-up of which will be decided later by drawing lots – it being the only fair way. Right, Team Alpha will be assigned to Middleminster, Team Bravo – Bawdley, Team Charlie – Apsley, Team Delta – Harley, Team Echo – Hempton, Team Foxtrot – Bridforth. Team Golf will be held as a mobile reserve to mop up any sudden surge in business. Right! Any questions so far?"

One or two of the girls coughed, while others nervously shuffled their feet; the seriousness of what they were about to embark on was obviously sinking in. He was sure a good few of them would at this point have lit cigarettes if smoking had been allowed in the house.

"Okay, I'll carry on then – equipment! For Team Alpha, we've arranged for a camper van to be sited in the car park at Middleminster station. For other teams, we have hired two mobile homes at convenient locations… here and er… here." Dave pointed to them both with his stick. "I'll give you the exact position later. Of course, I'm expecting a lot of the action to take place on the trains themselves during the nighttime hours. We will be making arrangements so that some compartments are kept free for this very purpose. Now over to Galina, who will brief you on the special equipment you will need to carry with you."

Carrying a clipboard and dressed in a smart white chemist's coat, Galina stepped forward. "Okay, ladies, could I ask thert you please pay attention while I carry out thirs demonstration. Whern you herv a customer and herv found a compartment, and you want to make sure you wirl not get interrupted…" Galina held up her hand to show the girls the device she was about to demonstrate, "…jurst place this clermp on the door like so!"

Dave had made a mock-up of the door handle arrangement of a MK I BR standard coach and developed a clamp in his workshop that would lock the doors together from the inside. Galina put the clamp in place over the two handles, and demonstrated how this prevented them from being pulled apart.

"Thirs wirl ensure thert not one person wirl be able to open the door from the outside! You all see – yers? Good! Now moving along, these wedges you use to reserve ermpty compartment for whern you herv a customer later. Whern in place, they prevent doors being opened by other passengers! You simply place between the door and floor whern you find an ermpty compartment – burt always pull blinds down inside first. Other passengers wirl thern think people are inside and do not want to be disturbed and so wirl go to another compartment. Okay yers?"

Galina looked up to see a line of faces nodding their understanding. She also noticed Dave in a position just behind and to the side of a pretty Polish girl in a low-cut top, staring intently at the girl's ample bosom. Galina immediately took him to task, "Do pay attention Mr Blarnd!"

Dave instantly diverted his focus back to the table.

"Communications! We wirl all exchange mobile phone numbers so thert we can all contact one another whern needed. Please add yours to thirs list." Galina passed over the clipboard then looked around the room inviting reactions. "Wirl, if there are no questions, I wirl hand you back to Dave."

He stepped forward and took up from where Galina left off, "Okay then, now ladies, we've come up with one or two special items to help stimulate interest – as it were – in you ladies. I've produced a pamphlet entitled *The Railway Girls,* which I'm hoping will appeal to the mindset of your customers. I'll describe the thinking behind it.

"In understanding the mind of a trainspotter we have to remember that their fascination for collecting numbers is a compulsive addiction, one that dominates all their actions. This though can be used to our advantage. If you look inside the booklets that Galina is handing out, you can see that we have listed each of you ladies in turn, together with a number and details – quite fictitious of course – about you. So if you look at girl 6010 Natasha – the tenth girl on the list by the way. Natasha, you can see that we have described you in the following way, '6010, Natasha. Originally from Smolensk, worked local services in the Ukraine, before transferring to express work over the Moscow – St Petersburg route.'

"Something similar has been written about all of you, as you'll notice. We recommend that you hand out these leaflets to your customers whenever you have the opportunity. Due to the compulsive nature of the trainspotter, we anticipate that once he learns there are sixteen of you in the class, he will want to arrange liaisons with as many as possible. This will of course generate extra business and revenue for you ladies. Rather a clever ploy we thought."

There were nods and murmurs of approval from the assembled girls.

"To aid you further in this strategy, we have reproduced your own individual number in the form of a T shirt and a henna tattoo which I'm asking you to transfer onto your body next weekend – somewhere in the upper thigh area. Your customer will then be able to gain the satisfaction of crossing your number off in his book prior to engaging in the er, act.

"You will also be issued with cards containing some phrases that you might find useful when making an approach to a potential customer, phrases such as 'Does this engine have a Kylchap exhaust chimney arrangement?' or 'How many engines in this class would have had smoke deflectors?' and so on. Once you've opened up a conversation, I'm sure we can rely on you to use your feminine wiles to achieve a satisfactory conclusion.

"Finally, your cover story. I've worked out a very simple one in case any officials start asking you questions, so please listen and memorise: you are all train attendants from your own state railways on an exchange visit to England. One of the highlights of your trip being a visit to Britain's premier preserved steam railway, i.e. The Worfe Valley. Remember these details ladies! You may be asked questions about it later. Right then, I think that just about wraps things up, any final questions at all?"

The next hour or so was spent dealing with a range of queries, which Galina and Dave did their best to answer. When eventually the ladies began to drift out of the conservatory, Dave reminded them, "Remember girls, we meet here at 11am on Saturday! See you all then!"

For some days Dave had been struggling with a dilemma over Duggie, who in his spare time worked as a volunteer ticket examiner on the Worfe Valley Railway. To help ensure the success of the operation, Dave realised it would be useful to have him on the team. He would, in effect, be like an inside man able to forewarn them if any of the Worfe Valley management – or indeed the police – became aware of their activities during the weekend. The dilemma for Dave was that Duggie just couldn't keep his mouth shut. If he showed his normal discretion, then the operation would become public knowledge very quickly – and knowing his prurient interest in all matters sexual, he was sure to want to get involved too.

Dave decided he would take him into his confidence – but only at the very last possible moment. That way there would be less chance of any leakage of secrets. The price to be paid for his silence would, he was certain, be a free 'go' with one of the girls. It would though, be a price worth paying to ensure the smooth running of the operation.

Dave reflected on just how big an operation it had become. From a simple idea of helping Galina's niece to find some safer and more lucrative 'trade,' it had now evolved into an awesome logistical exercise involving the cream of the West Midlands' call girls, covering a twenty mile stretch of railway at six different locations.

With all this responsibility resting on his shoulders, Dave was now beginning to worry about how successful the weekend was likely to be. Both he and Galina had invested a tidy sum in preparing for it, and he was just hoping they would get it all back, hopefully with a nice profit at the end. He could do no more, Dave told himself. They'd planned, plotted and organised as far as they could for every situation and eventuality; it was now all down to the girls.

★

At the appointed hour, Eli and Frank presented themselves at the barbed wired gates of the scrapyard and were ushered in by one of the attendant heavies. Eli noted the brass plate fixed to the gate,

Ernest S. Blowfield Ltd. Metal Recyclers.
Scrap cars and all types of roof lead bought for cash.
'Working towards a greener Yorkshire'

Eli and Frank jostled to be last as they ascended the stairway leading to the Portakabin situated 30ft above the scrapyard, their progress closely monitored by the heavies down below. Not wishing to startle the much feared man inside, Frank gave the door only a tentative knock when he reached the entrance.

It was immediately opened by another goon who, after looking the two up and down, gestured them inside. The great man himself was sitting in a large executive chair behind a desk which consisted of a large oak plinth, supported underneath by a cube of crushed car at each end. Pride of place amongst the scattered pens and other office flotsam on the desktop was an ashtray in the form of a chrome-plated car crusher. Along the back wall were a series of TV monitors, each one displaying a live view of one of his many scrap yards. Eli counted twenty-two in total.

The thought instantly crossed Eli's mind that within the two crushed cars supporting the desk could be the bodies of those two landowners who mysteriously disappeared. He shuddered at the thought. The pair remained standing in the doorway and waited for the man to speak. He slowly looked up from his copy of *Scrap Metal Monthly* and gestured to them, "C'mon in boys n'sit yerself down. I've bin expectin' yer."

The chunky gold rings on his fingers glinted under the harsh florescent lights as he directed the pair to their seats. It was only then that Eli noticed the ferret nestled in the crook of the man's left arm, the animal's fur blending into the background of Ernie's collarless white tunic – itself a close colour match to the short cropped hair atop the man's weather hardened face. The animal –

fronted by a pink nose that twitched as it took in the new scents – was of the purest white. It appeared unconcerned by the presence of the two strangers, but instead had its eyes focused firmly on a cage to the side which contained several mice scurrying about inside. The ferret's eyes followed the rodents' every move.

Eli and Frank sat stiffly on the office furniture. The two converted car seats were mounted low on the floor directly in front of Ernie's desk. Straining their necks upwards, they listened in rapt attention as Ernie addressed them.

"Rite lads, we have a bit of a problem I understand. Worfe Valley's tekkin' our business, and we need to do summat about it. I've 'eard all about yer efforts so far, and I 'ave to say, I'm none too impressed – I've a gorilla downstairs that could 'ave done better."

Eli had only noticed a Rottweiler in the yard.

"As you know, I 'ave 'onour o' bein' 'onorary secretary of our railway society, and 'avin' put a tidy sum int' coffers over the years, I'll not see it go down neither." He paused to give his ferret a few calming strokes of his hand. "So what I propose is a campaign of polite persuasion – if I can put it like that – to persuade visitors to stop visitin' Worfe Valley Railway. Me bein' somethin' of an expert in the art of polite persuasion, I reckon it shouldn't be too difficult to carry out – even fer you lot!

"Just to mek sure though – as I 'ave such an obligin' nature – I'll be sendin' a couple o' my lads along to 'elp yer in task, startin' with this special steam weekend they've got comin' up on the Worfe Valley. My boys'll give you the details."

He paused once more to calm the ferret, now getting restless at the sight of its natural prey in such close proximity. When he turned back, his genial expression had changed to one of dark malevolence.

"Now a word of warnin' to yer. What I don't want to 'ear of is any more cock-ups! What I do want to see, in the next *Steam Railway Weekly* fer example, is what a disaster this special steam weekend at Worfe Valley turned out to be. I don't think I need point out to you two, the consequences should that not be the case."

With that he reached into the cage holding the mice, picked one up by its tail and dangled it just above the ferret's nose. In an instant the ferret snatched it from his hand, despatching it with just one bite.

"Need I say more lads?"

Eli, his mouth now totally devoid of saliva, swallowed hard and turned to look at Frank who looked equally aghast. Leaving the ferret to devour his prey, Ernie calmly returned to his reading matter. From behind the page, he issued a curt, "Well, goodbye lads."

Frank and Eli instantly stood up and holding their caps to their chests, responded in unison, "Yes... goodbye er... Mr Blowfield, and er... thank you Mr Blowfield!"

As Eli and Frank backed out towards the doorway, the heavy stood aside and pulled open the door allowing the pair to exit the cabin. The fresh air came as a relief after the oppressive atmosphere of the Portakabin. The two quickly scurried down the steps.

When safely out of earshot, Eli screamed at Frank, "Just what 'ave yer got us into Frank? It'll be us proppin' up that desk of his if it all goes wrong, and I'm not at all optimistic about our chances either Frank, that I can tell you!"

Still ashen-faced, Frank tried to make the best of it. "Well, we're committed now Eli, can't change what's 'appened. We've just got to mek sure it does all go accordin' to plan. Anyway, he's giving us two of 'is goons, so if they make a balls-up Ernie can 'ardly blame us, now can 'e?"

"I s'pose not, but for both our sakes just make sure they don't!"

Chapter 21

On the Saturday morning, Dave had been delayed in his preparations for the weekend by an official-looking envelope landing on his doormat. From the logo on the outside he could see it was from the UK Patent Office, so it was with some trepidation that he slit open the envelope. As he pulled out the single sheet of A4 paper, an embossed certificate came out with it and fell onto the floor. It was when he bent down to pick it up that he noticed his full name, 'David Stanley Bland' printed prominently at the top of it. He quickly scanned the accompanying letter for confirmation. Yes! He'd been granted a patent for his multi-purpose workbench. He recited the number, 'GB2417458,' a couple of times in his head.

Dave was overjoyed by the news and dashed into the kitchen to show Galina. She was thrilled for him, but while not wanting to dampen his mood of celebration, she needed to remind him that he still had to collect the motor home from the hirers, drive it to the station car park and position it close to the station building before returning home!

He agreed that time was now pressing on their tight schedule, but saw his news as a good omen for the future success of their mission. He put the letter safely away in the bureau. With his brain now a whirling mass of competing thoughts, he set off to pick up the motor home, completing the task just two hours later. It was only when he dropped his car keys down on the hall table that Dave realised he had made a major omission – condoms!

It was something that Galina had mentioned to him, but had then completely forgotten while pre-occupied with all else that was going on. The girls would be starting to arrive soon and they needed to be issued with sufficient quantities to last the weekend. Dave got back into his car. Although he would have preferred to source them from somewhere out of town, due to time constraints he decided to visit the local chemist just a few minutes drive away instead.

Parking as close as he could to the shop, he hurriedly made his way inside. It was a busy lunchtime and peering around the throng of people waiting to be served, he noticed the condoms were on the counter directly in front of the leading customer.

Two members of staff were serving, one male and one female. Dave manoeuvred himself into the loosely formed queue favouring the male assistant. As he waited, Dave noticed the other queue going down quicker than his own, and there was now a danger he could be served by the female. He hung back in order to gain his assistant of choice.

Within a few minutes, he was at the counter being confronted by a range of condoms considerably more numerous than when he was a young man in need of such items. In those days, he recalled it was a simple case of deciding which of the three standard Durex types to choose, more often than not from a coin-operated machine only found in the gents toilets.

His hesitancy was not helped by the embarrassment of asking for items of a sexual nature in public – a throwback, he imagined, to when he faced the same scenario in his self-conscious, teenage years. Dave struggled to find the necessary words. Luckily, the male member of staff waiting expectantly behind the counter had the experience to sense a customer's unease.

"Good afternoon sir, er..." The assistant gave a conspiratorial glance both left and right before leaning towards him and in hushed tones enquired, "Was it, er… something for the weekend you wanted?"

"Yes, that's right!" Dave replied truthfully.

"A packet of three would it be sir? This one is our most popular brand." The assistant's hand hovered over the packet.

"Well er..." Dave was still working though the maths. He rechecked it again in his head for good measure, "Three hundred actually," replied Dave.

"Three hundred!" the assistant repeated out loud before lowering his head and adopting his previous hushed tone. *"For a weekend?"* he hissed.

The whole shop had now turned to look at the would-be purchaser. A woman standing close by, slowly looked Dave up and down before turning to mutter something to her friend, at the end of which they both began sniggering.

Dave could feel a slight rosy glow now emanating from his cheeks. He felt that some sort of explanation was expected from him and was, for once, ready with one. Dave opened his mouth as if to speak, but before doing so aped the man's actions and glanced both left and right before leaning across the counter towards the middle-aged assistant. The man, hardly able to contain his curiosity, followed suit, their foreheads almost touching.

"It's these pills the wife's on," Dave whispered loudly. "They were supposed to do something about her low sex drive, only I reckon she's taking too many. Now she can't get enough... all ways... all positions... all hours of the day. I've had to warn my neighbour about her for when I'm out at work. He's on his own all day you see! He said not to worry, he'd keep his door locked just in case she tried to get in."

"No! Really?"

"Oh yes!"

The assistant looked stunned for a moment, then a thought came to him. "So... er, what are these pills called then? Just in case we get asked for them, you understand."

"Oh, it's something complicated; I can't remember the name right now."

Trying to affect an air of only mild interest, he pursued the matter, "Perhaps you could er... find out for me and let me know? Work on all women do they?"

"I believe so, yes. Have you got three hundred?"

The man, still trying to take in all he'd just been told, stuttered a reply. "What? Er... yes... I think... er... I may have... I'll have to go in the stockroom and er... check. They may not be all the same type though."

"That's okay, anything, er... the same size is fine!" Dave shouted after the assistant.

He was aware of receiving further staring looks from customers. Dave resolutely maintained his straight ahead gaze, which just happened to fall on the embarrassing itching remedies lining the back shelf. Eventually, after what seemed like an age, the man came back with a box, placed it on the counter and just in case he'd simply imagined their previous conversation, confirmed once again the quantity with him.

Apparently satisfied, the assistant began to ring up the quantities of each brand on the till and in an almost apologetic tone, announced the combined total. Dave paid him in cash. The assistant methodically counted out Dave's change while cogitating on the effects of all that physical activity. A thought occurred to him as Dave was about to exit the shop. He called out to get his attention before pointing to the chilled drinks cabinet. "Oh, I just wondered sir, need any energy drinks at all?"

Dave glanced over to the line of bottles, "Er... no thanks, I get mine delivered direct – by tanker!"

"Oh... er... right!"

Dave had hardly got out of the shop before he burst out laughing. The comic episode was just what he needed to ease the tension. Back at the house, Dave related the events to Galina, who also roared with laughter when he retold the story.

Less than an hour later, the girls began to arrive in their ones and twos. A Ukrainian girl had been forced to drop out due to injuries received from one of her clients the previous day. Luckily, Irina had been able to recruit a young Thai girl to take her place instead.

In the conservatory, equipment for the mission lay on the pasting table. The girls' individually-numbered T shirts, together with supplies of condoms, lubricating jelly, vibrators and handcuffs, all needing to be issued and signed for. Dave and Galina worked through the waiting girls, checking their equipment with them, while reminding each one once again of their cover story.

Dave had concerns that Sammi the Thai girl, being a last-minute replacement and unfamiliar with the detail of the operation, could be the weakest link in the chain, but was reassured by her pledge to not let the side down.

The group was given a final pep-talk by Dave and reminded of the importance of the task that lay ahead of them. At the end, Dave and Galina spoke to each girl individually before offering them a very British, but somehow inadequate, 'Good Luck!'

With all the girls now assembled in the conservatory wearing their T shirts and with personal equipment stowed away in hand bags, the atmosphere became more subdued. Tension hung heavy in the air as they whiled away the time before departure. A few sat in armchairs reading newspapers; one Polish girl had brought an English language book to study. Another girl paced nervously up and down as she rechecked her equipment. Others went outside to sit in deckchairs and enjoy the September sunshine while they smoked their cigarettes. Dave, going over all the details in his head for the umpteenth time, sat with his mobile phone on the table waiting to receive the agreed signal.

Galina suddenly shouted through from the kitchen. Everybody in the room immediately turned and looked anxiously in her direction. "Tea's ready!" she announced brightly, as she walked through with a loaded tray.

A short time later, following three false alarms, Dave received a phone call from Duggie giving him the all-clear. The operation could now begin!

The girls gathered up their handbags and made ready to set out on their journey to the railway station. Dave led off, the girls following behind. As they ambled along in their small groups, he was pleased to hear laughing and joking breaking out amongst them. He took their high spirits to be a sign of good morale for the coming operation.

From the town, they climbed the hill up to the Worfe Valley Railway Station. Dave noticed that Sammi was particularly chatty. He just hoped that she wouldn't open her mouth at the wrong time and let something slip. This operation needed to be kept a tight secret from the authorities; he knew keeping it like that for the whole of the two days would take some doing.

Twenty minutes after setting off, they arrived at the booking hall. It was early-afternoon and just as he had hoped, there were large numbers of people already there.

As predicted, the crowd were predominantly male, middle-aged spotters and railway enthusiasts, all heavily laden with cameras, camcorders and notebooks. Perfect conditions for a successful weekend, he concluded. The girls were already getting some interested looks from the men. This he expected, though he'd requested that the girls not dress too provocatively – he didn't want their intentions to be so obvious.

Dave joined the queue in the booking hall and began thinking once more about Duggie. When he'd revealed the operation to him two days ago, his friend had immediately asked to be let in on the action. Dave decided to strike a deal with him. He could have a session with one of the girls providing he helped ensure the success of the operation and did not compromise it in any way.

There was a problem though. The girls wanted sight of the man before any of them would sanction the arrangement. Duggie, who would admit himself that he had been dealt a very bad hand in the looks department, understood their concerns and agreed to submit to the girls' scrutiny. It was during this discussion that he admitted dogging was the nearest he had ever got to intimacy with the opposite sex.

Dave was sympathetic to his plight, and suggested a way of putting right the deficiency would be for him to speak to the girls about the crucial nature of Duggie's role in the coming operation. Having put them in a more receptive frame of mind, he'd show them Duggie's photo and ask for a volunteer willing to take him on.

He readily agreed to the proposal, but it presented Dave with a problem. Even though he tried numerous camera angles and lighting modes, he was not able to much improve on the man's appearance. He eventually resorted to some digital trickery from his photo-imaging program to tone down the man's bulging eyes and drooling wet mouth. Despite his best efforts, the girls' reaction was not altogether a surprise. After some head shaking, they would only agree if lots were drawn to choose the unlucky candidate. Dave decided the decision would be best delayed until after the weekend.

Knowing that Duggie should be somewhere in the vicinity, Dave scanned the crowds hoping to locate him. He was anxious to discover the whereabouts of one of the Worfe Valley ticket inspectors who was known to be particularly zealous in his duties.

When his group reached the head of the queue at the booking office, Dave asked the elderly booking office clerk on the other side of the screen for sixteen two day rover tickets.

"What you got a football team with you or something then?" the man asked in jest.

"Yeah, something like that," Dave absently replied, trying to keep the conversation brief.

Actually, when he thought about it, with the girls wearing their numbered shirts, as a cover story it was a believably simple one and one that he just might stick with. Dave paid the man and handed out the tickets to the girls who remained in the booking hall chatting. He went to have a look for Duggie out on the platform.

Lord Lovernock, the patron of the Worfe Valley Railway, was on a visit to the station. After a leisurely lunch in the VIP dining car, the peer, accompanied by the railway's general manager Norman Watkins, made an appearance in the booking hall to meet some of the public. While circulating amongst the swelling body of railway enthusiasts, Lord Lovernock spotted the glamorous gaggle of girls, and purposely worked his way towards the group, greeting them with a particularly warm welcome.

"Well, it's certainly a pleasure to see all you females here today, especially ones so attractive. May I ask where you are from?" he asked, singling out Sammi the oriental one.

"I from Thai-land Sir."

"Really? Old Siam eh! How interesting! I say, I can't help noticing that you're all wearing numbered shirts, so what are you, part of a football team or something?"

"A huk-ker yes?"

"Oh Right! Yes! A ladies rugby team eh! I see now. You're a girl after my own heart you know. I used to play a bit myself in my university days. Jolly useful I was too... Well it's delightful to see you all here... A hooker eh! I suppose, being small, you can just slip between your opponent's legs what?"

"Well... no, nor-m-lay oth-er ray-wound!"

"Is that so? You prefer a position on the front then?"

"On fro-nt, on back, en-ee pos-i-shon for-me ok-ay!"

"Pretty versatile eh, jolly good! What about the rest of the team?"

"Oh, they ly-ke an-ee pos-i-shon too!"

"That's excellent. Well done! I can see you're all very enthusiastic about the game... You know it's been years since I had a ball in my hand."

"Ha-ve balls in mai ha-nd ver-ee soon I ho-pe!"

"Really! So you intend to have a bit of a practice session on the journey, eh? I like your spirit! Though a word of caution here, do be careful on the train with those balls, no tossing across the aisle please – we don't want to be hitting any of the other passengers now do we? Health and safety and all that, you understand."

"Yeah, no pra-b-lem, I cat-ch-it-all-in-tis-sue!"

"Sorry? Yes... er... quite... Well, we must be moving on, other stations to visit and all that. It was delightful to meet you and the rest of the team. I hope we bump into each other again over the course of the weekend."

"Be ha-pee for-yu to bu-mp mee en-ee time…"

Just at that moment Dave arrived back and taking in the scene, immediately interrupted her, "Sammi! We really have to be going now!"

He'd just returned after a fruitless search for Duggie. Catching the tail end of Sammi's conversation, he'd been thoroughly alarmed by her indiscretion. Dave tapped his watch at her to gain her prompt compliance. Luckily Sammi took the hint and after waving an enthusiastic goodbye to the peer, Dave was able to steer her away for a quiet word, explaining that while his position and status were not apparent to Sammi, by making her intentions so obvious, she was putting the security of the whole operation in danger.

As they walked to their waiting train, Lord Lovernock voiced his thoughts to the manager, "What charming ladies! It's so exciting to know that as a result of all the hard work carried out by our teams of volunteers on the railway, we are able to draw in such delightful girls from overseas and awaken their interest in Britain's great industrial heritage. We must keep it up Watkins, we really must!"

On the opposite platform, a group of Yorkshiremen had just stepped off the train recently arrived from Middleminster. They were part of the larger mob that had travelled down earlier in the day from Postlethwaite, intent on their assignment to cause as much trouble as possible to the Worfe Valley Railway. With half of them remaining at Middleminster to disrupt the railway's operations there, the ones at Bridforth were now advancing up the platform, heading for the Platelayer's Arms in order to slake their thirst and acquire the Dutch courage for the task in hand.

Having overseen the departure of the ladies to their various destinations, Dave was now feeling the pressure of their undertaking – his disposition made worse by Sammi nearly giving the whole game away in the first few minutes. He decided he needed a drink to steady his nerves.

The Platelayer was a lot busier than normal due to the influx of visitors. He ordered a drink and took it to one of the quiet corner seats where he could think through what else still needed to be done. After a few minutes, Dave became aware of some trouble being caused by a group of men at the bar. He got the distinct impression from their behaviour that they seemed to be out to deliberately cause annoyance, which he thought unusual in a place like The Platelayer's Arms.

Dave placed them by their accents to be visitors from Yorkshire. What had caused them to be so belligerent, he wondered? They were souring the whole ambience of the pub. Like the other customers enjoying a quiet drink, Dave was relieved when they were finally asked to leave by the bar staff, which they only did after abusive protests, promising retaliation as they stormed out.

He got back to the business of implementing the day's plan. Now that the girls had departed to their separate locations, he would act as forward observer, monitoring their success in attracting customers. From their phone calls and texts, he would be able to build up a picture of how the operation was going through the day.

The girls using the rented caravan had experienced a minor problem in getting rid of an overly-friendly couple from next door. Having come down for the weekend from their home in Selly Oak and noticing their new neighbours, the retired pair were keen to impart their extensive knowledge of park homes to the girls, and had brought round several back issues of *Mobile Home Monthly,* for them to look through. 'Just in case they were thinking of buying one,' the man explained

The camper van parked at Middleminster was being kept busy. Dave needed to take extra supplies of food, drink and bed linen. Using their initiative, the girls had already brought in some early business by offering to refill the thermos flasks of likely-looking customers. It was proving to be a good conversation opener.

Back at the house, Galina was working the plot. Each girl was represented by a marker placed on the map table, together with a tally of confirmed engagements so far. Should punters be massing in one particular location – due to, perhaps, a good photo shoot opportunity of a loco – Galina would vector available girls onto that area.

It had started off pretty much as he had expected: fairly quiet initially, but formations of trainspotters were now gradually building up in the targeted areas. The girls had been briefed to try and pick up any stragglers first before getting in amongst the main body of spotters. This tactic was proving successful as it allowed the girls some discretion in setting about their task while maintaining the security of the mission.

Due to the compulsive nature of their clients, some of the girls had found it necessary to introduce a booking system – making appointments for times that did not clash with the arrival or departure of trains at their particular location. More than one client had 'uncoupled' himself halfway through the proceedings to go and photograph a guest engine he would otherwise have missed. This enforced delay in completing the act did not go down well with the girls involved.

Dave was expecting the nighttime hours to be the busiest. The girls would be able to operate more freely under cover of darkness. With fewer people about, and more importantly, less train staff in attendance, they would be able to select and pick off clients at will.

He'd discovered that some of the trainspotters chose to sleep on the train during these all-night specials rather than book into a hotel. This would make them even easier pickings for the girls, especially if they'd had a drink or two. There was nothing like a drop of alcohol to loosen a person's inhibitions and with a buffet car on every train, he could foresee trainspotters' wallets offering little resistance to the predatory girls. For cash was certainly king for these ladies of the night; the ubiquitous credit card not being welcome quite everywhere.

Chapter 22

Nadya was encouraging the man she had just picked up to engage in some foreplay with her. As the nervous data entry clerk from Cleethorpes tentatively explored Nadya using her own vibrator, the compartment door was suddenly tugged from the other side. They both froze, their eyes now fixed on the clamp that Nadya had fixed to the door, ensuring it stayed in place. After a short pause and some muffled conversation from the other side, the door was jerked abruptly back in the opposite direction, causing the clamp to loosen and drop onto the floor. They both immediately sprung apart; the clerk having just enough time to pull Nadya's skirt down and place both hands over his lap to hide his obvious state of excitement. The door, now free from obstruction, was slid fully open and a middle-aged woman looked in on them.

"It's alright Ronald, it was just stiff; all it needed was a firm hand. C'mon, there are some spare seats in here," she said addressing the husband trailing just behind her.

"I'll sit by the window, if you don't mind. You will be careful putting the picnic hamper on the luggage rack won't you? I've packed some Marts & Spender's vol-au-vents, and unfortunately, they are not the most robust of travellers. You know, I don't often complain Ronald, but if I do have one criticism of their finger food, it is that their flaky pastry can be well... a little too flaky. I did mention it once in an email to them, but of course to no avail. That's it, now you sit there."

"Yes Marjorie."

Marjorie nodded politely at the two established occupants before turning her attention back to her husband. "Now don't go chattering away to me now will you Ronald?"

"No dear..."

"Because I would like to study this Worfe Valley Railway dining experience leaflet without interruption if you don't mind. Just be patient for a few minutes, and I'll inform you when I've finished."

"Yes dear."

After about a minute and several peevish looks in her husband's direction, she asked, "Tell me, is that a mint imperial you're eating Ronald? The noise is very distracting you know – can you suck it a bit quieter?"

"Yes Marjorie."

"Thank you."

After another couple of minutes, Marjorie became aware of a further disturbance affecting her concentration. Turning her head one way, then the other, she eventually satisfied herself with having correctly identified its source. Marjorie leaned over towards Nadya and touched her elbow.

"I believe your phone is ringing my dear. You must have it on silent – but I can definitely feel the seat vibrating."

Nadya looked askance at Marjorie. "Irs nert my phone!" she informed her curtly.

"Are you sure?"

"Yers!"

"Well it's certainly not mine dear," replied Marjorie. "It has an exclusive Mozart ringtone, and to my certain knowledge not a single note of his *Divertimento* has been heard by me for at least two hours. Ronald, my husband, does not have – nor does he require – a phone of his own. I would suggest you check yours. I think you'll find I'm correct." Having given the woman the benefit of her advice, Marjorie leant back in her seat.

Nadya spoke again, more emphatically this time, "Irs nert my phone!"

Marjorie turned to give Ronald her raised eyebrow look. From behind her hand she whispered, "I think she must be foreign – probably Polish!"

Nadya continued, "No, irs nert my phone.... irs thirs!" With that she extracted the still active vibrator from under her skirt, and with an exaggerated action, switched it off.

The data entry clerk, who up to that point had been paying very close attention to the line of hedgerows passing by the window during the exchange, now started whistling tunelessly, whilst the dormant mint imperial lying half sucked in Ronald's mouth, was propelled instantly to the back of his throat, instigating a severe choking fit in him.

Above the noise from all the whistling and choking, Marjorie's voice resonated through the compartment, "Well, *really* madam! There's a time and a place for everything you know – it's not even teatime! This is a first class railway compartment – not a back-street knocking shop! If I'd wanted to view acts of pornography, then I could have stayed at home and rummaged around in Ronald's potting shed until I found those magazines of his."

Just as Marjorie's husband had managed to calm the severe disturbance affecting his throat, on hearing his secret revealed to all, it instantly flared up again.

"Ronald! Stop all your spluttering and reach up for the hamper will you! I'm sure there must be some spare seats in another compartment – trust you to pick one with a live Anne Summers demonstration taking place within its confines!"

"But.... but it was you who..."

"I don't wish to stand here quibbling with you Ronald, just get hold of that hamper will you and follow me. And to think, this trip was specifically recommended to me by Mrs Brownlow. Wait till I see her in church on Sunday... mind, her husband is a gynaecologist you know."

Taking the opportunity to give the pair a final withering look of disdain, Marjorie slid open the compartment door and hurried her husband along with a hefty shove in his back, "C'mon Ronald, get a move on! Yes... yes... I've known for a long time. Just make sure those magazines stay in the garden shed where such filth belongs."

Leaving the train at the very next station, Marjorie strode

purposefully into the deserted booking office, leaving Ronald trailing behind with the weighty hamper. She peered through the ticket window to catch the clerk with her steely gaze. Although a broadsheet newspaper was spread out over the wooden counter, the man did not appear to be reading it, but was looking into the middle distance with his eyes half closed. On noticing Marjorie standing there he became flustered and shuffled the newspaper around as if trying to conceal something.

Unaware of his discomfiture, Marjorie launched into her narrative, "Far be it for me to make a complaint young man, but I really must bring your attention to some of the shenanigans taking place on the train Ronald and I have jus..."

"Oooh, a bit slower please," the man muttered under his breath.

"Er, very well, if you insist – though I do not normally have a problem with people understanding my spoken word. In fact, some of the ladies at our WI meetings have commented very favourably on the clarity of my enunciation – and indeed the volume too; but if as you say, I am not making myself clear to you, I will endeavour to speak a little slower."

"No, not you... ah, that's it!" the man's eyes glazed over once more, and resumed its vacant stare into the middle distance.

"Who, then and what specifically is it?" Marjorie enquired, now quite perplexed by the man's obtuse response. She looked around the booking hall. There was no other person in sight that he could be referring to apart from her husband. As Marjorie's gaze fell on him, he pursed his lips as if to speak, "Not now Ronald! There appears to be something of a communication problem here; not a situation I commonly experience as you well know, but I fully intend to persevere."

Turning back to the counter she began again, "Tell me young man, can you..."

"Ahhh... nearly there now!" he uttered in a strained voice.

Marjorie shook her head in exasperation. "And where exactly might 'there' be? As far as I'm concerned you're neither here nor there!" she replied sharply.

The clerk was now leaning fully back in his chair, his eyes almost closed. "Yes, yes..."

The realisation suddenly dawned on Marjorie. She recognised the look on the young man's face; remembering it from some years back when her Ronald was about to achieve orgasm. Now peering intently through the glass, Marjorie tried to see underneath the newspaper the man was holding over the counter. She caught a glimpse of the back of a woman in a kneeling position on the floor. The man's trousers were around his ankles and her head was moving rhythmically up and down beneath the part of the newspaper covering the man's lap. Marjorie gasped and turned smartly on her heels.

Leading Ronald outside, she expressed her disgust to him, "Well really! I would never have believed it! I've never seen such debauchery! The whole place is like Sodom and Gomorrah," complained Marjorie as she described the scene to her husband. "There's nothing but sex everywhere you look! And to think we were going to visit the tearooms here. After what we've witnessed today, I'd be loathe to even step over the threshold!"

Whilst nodding agreement with her feelings of outrage, Ronald took a rather different view regarding the refreshment facilities, "But Marjorie, while I agree with you making a stand, I am really gasping for a cup of tea. Now that we're here at the station, can we not just pop into the tearooms for one? Please?"

"What! And risk exposing us to further acts of fornication?"

"Don't you think you might be overreacting a bit? It's only a cup of tea after all and perhaps a cream cake – *if I'm allowed it,*" he muttered under his breath.

"I don't know so much Ronald. I would want to be absolutely certain that the hand dispensing my cup of lapsang souchon was unsullied by contact with another person's unmentionables!"

"I can't imagine any such goings-on taking place in a humble tearoom, surely Marjorie?"

"Hmm... maybe you're right. I must admit some liquid refreshment would be welcome right now... Oh alright then, call me an old softie if you like, but I suppose a cup of tea should be safe enough. I for one, though, won't be allowing anything solid to pass my lips. A freshly-prepared salad sandwich would have been the perfect accompaniment with our tea, but having seen all the goings-on around here, I dread to think where the cucumber might have been first!"

Marjorie led the way into the premises, choosing a table near the window while she waited for Ronald to bring over the refreshments. Marjorie took the opportunity to make a close inspection of the room. Her eyebrows went skywards when she scrutinised the nearby sweet trolley.

"Just look at the state of it Ronald!" she whispered loudly as he returned with the loaded tray. "I mean, all the cream's gone from the top of the sherry trifle, the cheesecake's got some suspiciously-shaped indentations in it, and just what is that drizzled over the Bakewell tart? I've never seen fondant icing that runny before! No, it doesn't take a genius to guess what sort of activities that sweet trolley's been an unwitting party to – in fact, I'm surprised to see it still on its castors! I'm afraid you can dismiss all thought of eating that jam and clotted cream scone you've just purchased Ronald – it's time to take our leave of this place."

"But... but... Marjorie..."

"C'mon Ronald, no arguing, just finish up your tea. We'll catch the very next train back to Bridforth, I believe there's a very nice National Trust property we can visit near there. Just check in the guide book before we set off, Ronald, and make sure there's not – as appears to be the case here – a Roman orgy themed weekend currently taking place!"

"Very well Marjorie."

In an almost deserted third class saloon further along the train, Sammi, well practised in recognising an individual receptive to her approaches, had just negotiated a mutually agreeable price with a large rotund man. Being of very slight build, Sammi suggested she mount herself on top of him rather than the other way round;

reassuring him that nobody was around to see anything, and that if someone did pass by, her long sari type skirt would be sufficient to cover both their lower bodies.

Her paying partner readily agreed to the arrangement. After taking up position, Sammi lowered herself onto him and steadily built up the momentum; the sturdy springing in the old British Rail seats helping to maintain her rhythm in the open saloon coach. As she rose and fell in the seat, two travelling VIP's further down the carriage caught sight of her bobbing head.

"I say Watkins, there's that delightful Thai girl again. It's obviously her first time on a train. She's so excited by the thrill of the journey, she's jumping up and down in her seat!"

Lord Lovernock enunciated loudly down the train, "Hi there, delightful to see you once again – enjoying the ride I see!"

Sammi raised and turned her head slightly to identify the source of the voice. On her next upward bounce, she was able to just see over the top of the seat. Recognising the peer, she gave him a smile and waved her free hand at him before sinking down again.

"May I suggest if you're going all the way, perhaps you would like to take some refreshment with us when you get off?" enquired the peer, timing his question to coincide with her next upward bounce.

"Okay, wu-rd ly-ke tha-rt ver-ee much!" she shouted on the cusp of her next descent. Looking down, she noted her partners arched body, closed eyes and salivating open mouth. "Shud-nart-be-tu-long-nau!" shouted Sammi, and reached down to give the man a further squeeze of encouragement.

Chapter 23

Aboard a different train en route to Bridforth, a lone Yorkshireman elbowed his way to the front of the small bar.

"A bottle of bitter... Aye, that's the one!" he said abruptly, as the barman pointed to a row of bottles on display. Ignoring the glass placed alongside it, the man took a long gulp of the contents then slammed the bottle back down on the bar.

"Tastes like piss this does!"

"I'm sorry?" said the barman.

"I said, it tastes like piss!"

"Well, you've got me there. I feel less than qualified to make such a comparison."

"Yer what?"

"I said unlike you, I am unable to make a considered judgment on the matter as I have never had the occasion to compare both liquids."

The man took a moment to digest the reply before staring hard at the person now drying the washed glasses, "Are you sayin' I drink piss like?"

The barman played him a little longer, "Well, you were making the comparison, so the assumption would be that you had actually sampled both in order to recognise the similarity."

"Think yer clever don't yer dick'ead? Well let me tell yer, this beer – like this furkin' railway o' yours – is just shite!"

"Well there again, I bow to your superior knowledge in these matters. Tell me, do you make these judgments in a professional capacity, or is it just a hobby of yours?"

The Yorkshireman immediately lunged over the bar counter

and attempted to grab the barman by the throat, but was thwarted by the man's quicker reactions as he deftly stepped back out of his reach. Frustrated at being made to look foolish, the Yorkshireman launched a tirade of abuse at him, causing other passengers cloistered around the bar to begin edging away as his ranting continued.

Just at that moment Duggie entered the carriage and witnessed the man in full vitriolic flow. He immediately confronted him, "Oi you! Watch your language! There's women and young families on this train you know!"

"You can furk off, an 'all!"

"You what?"

"Yer furkin' deaf or summat?"

"I can see you're going to have to leave this train," announced Duggie.

"Am I 'eck as like!" He turned to the barman. "Give us another drink – a proper one this time."

"You won't be served any more drink, and you're leaving this train at the next stop," stated Duggie. He moved to stand directly in front of the Yorkshireman.

"Furk off, I ain't movin'."

"You'll have to."

"I'm not!"

Duggie begged to differ. He seized hold of a Porter's trolley from behind the bar, forced the lip under the man's legs and levered him up. Before he had a chance to protest, Duggie had transported him to the carriage door, opened it and deposited him onto the lineside which, luckily for his victim, was slipping by at just a few miles an hour due to the 5mph speed restriction at that point.

Mr Etherington, the senior ticket inspector and company instructor who had been urgently summoned by the alarmed staff, entered the carriage just in time to see Duggie slamming the passenger door shut. Mr Etherington marched over to look through the door's window and watched with fascination as the ejected passenger rolled down the gentle gradient towards the river below.

He turned to Duggie for a moment. "Mr Walters! I don't believe we trained you to respond in quite that way when dealing with a difficult customer. Diplomacy and tact were my two golden rules if you recall. Exhaust all other avenues of persuasion before resorting to more punitive measures..." He paused to once again observe the figure now gathering speed down the steepening gradient, "...though I'm not entirely sure your choice of punitive measure was what the company had in mind whe..."

The ticket inspector stopped mid-sentence and watched as the rolling man reached the bottom of the slope, teetered momentarily on the river's edge, before dropping into the shallow muddy water.

"...Perfectly executed, though, I must say. He's almost entirely covered from head to toe in mud! I think a well done is in order Mr Walters."

"Thank you Mr Etherington."

"Well, carry on."

"Yes Mr Etherington!"

"By the way, just to let you know, we've already had a bit of bother with some other people like him on this service, they might be connected to one you have just er... ejected."

"What sort of bother, Mr Etherington?"

"Well, we don't expect people with any sense of propriety to put their feet up on seats recently re-covered in best heavy-duty dralon, especially if they're wearing studded boots, as was the case earlier. When Geoff the guard asked them politely to take their feet off, all he got was a mouthful of insults for his trouble. Then to cap it all they deliberately stuffed crisps and Nobber's Nuts down between the seat cushions – in blatant defiance of Geoff's request that they act with a bit more decorum. He was fuming, never seen him so angry. I wouldn't be surprised if we had more trouble from this lot before the day is out – you mark my words!"

"I'll bear that in mind Mr Etherington."

The Estonian girl was entertaining a client privately in another carriage. Having spent some considerable time on him, she was beginning to wonder if he would ever achieve climax. Elena looked at her watch again then shifted her position, hoping to heighten the sensation for him.

A few minutes later and with aching thighs, she decided to ask.

"Er... nerly there yert uh?"

The man looked blank for a moment. He reached over and eased back the blind slightly, "No, it looks like we're only just pulling into Harley, so another couple of stops yet!"

"No... I meanrt you, you nearly come now, or nert, whirch?"

"Oh... sorry, I thought you meant... how silly of me, er... could we change position? It might be better."

"Okay, burt I herv to..."

Just then the door burst open and several contorted faces appeared through the doorway. They immediately began hurling crude comments at the couple before one of them addressed the pair in person.

"So, what's goin' on 'ere then? You two are up t'no good, I'can see that... an' on a train as well! She must be a rite slag. Mind, she looks like a cheap whore. Oi mate! I 'ope she's not overchargin' yer."

Elena immediately pushed the man off her and sat up. She took great exception to the comments. Having to endure crap of this sort from men who paid her for the privilege was just about tolerable, taking the same from those who didn't – was not!

With her face barely able to conceal her contempt, she looked the group up and down. She noted all were similar in their appearance with their shaved heads and cheap shell suits. Elena guessed they shared the same Neanderthal-like mentality too; one that thought being grossly overweight and displaying multiple tattoos projected an image of toughness. Like the ones that came to her as clients, in reality they were just fat, uncultured dolts!

Far from being intimidated, she had nothing but contempt for their kind. With two degrees gained at university in her native homeland, and with considerable competence in the martial arts, she felt both intellectually and physically superior to those now casting insults at her.

Her startled client had by now readjusted his clothing, muttered the excuse that he did not normally do this sort of thing and scuttled out of the compartment. This was of no concern to Elena, having already been paid for her services.

Initially, she held herself in check and tried to ignore the abuse, refusing to be drawn into a verbal exchange with them. Eventually, tiring of it all, Elena got up from her seat and sauntered over to the one who was the loudest in making the insulting comments.

"So big boy, you wourd like sorm too, yers?"

"What, wi'a slag like you? An' pay fer'it an 'all? Not bloody likely!"

"Oh you do herv to pay you know – you do herv to pay, I cern guarantee thert!"

The man hesitated before laughing nervously at her unexpectedly cryptic response.

"Yeah, sure, piss off yer slag," he replied.

As she approached him the others backed off, unsettled by the strange malevolent look in her eye and the detached measured tone of her voice. Only the one who had just sworn at her was left standing in the doorway.

He was still leering when she stopped just a few inches away from his face. The next second he was doubled up in pain as Elena's knee delivered a decisive blow to his groin. Before he had time to react, she pulled the sliding doors to, crushing his neck between them.

She noted with some satisfaction that his face now wore a completely different expression.

Chapter 24

Dave had spent most of the afternoon on administration duties, ensuring that the girls were fed, watered and situated in the best places for trade. By the early evening he was also in need of some refreshment, so journeyed back to The Platelayer at Bridforth station. Stepping from the train, he noticed a small group of men loitering on the platform. He recognised them as being the same ones ejected from the pub a few hours before and could see that they were still behaving in the same loutish manner.

Of immediate concern to Dave was that one of his girls was being hassled by them. Although he expected females in their particular line of work to be experienced in dealing with difficult situations like this, he still felt-duty bound to intercede on her behalf, hopefully without inflaming the situation. Dave had a ploy at the ready.

He strode over to the group of men now being given a wide berth by the other visitors to the station. With arms outstretched, he called out in a loud voice, "Natasha! I've been looking all over for you. C'mon, we have a train to catch!"

Without hesitating, he purposefully broke through the encirclement, took hold of her hand and pulled her towards him. "Where have you been? We only have a few minutes before it goes!" he loudly reminded her.

Before the group of men had time to react, Dave thanked them for looking after 'his daughter' and apologised for troubling them. With a "Good day to you all," he marched the much relieved Natasha away to safety.

In her broken English, Natasha thanked him profusely for his actions. The situation had come about just as he guessed. Seeing a likely group of males, she had approached one of them thinking he might be interested in doing some business, but within seconds the mob had her surrounded. They then began to taunt and harass her; her escape being blocked each time she tried to get away. Dave was perturbed that there were such people behaving like this at the event, it really was most unusual.

He was even more alarmed when Natasha told him about the conversation she had overheard. They were bragging amongst themselves about what they intended doing to the engine sheds behind the station; the gist of their conversation, as she understood it, being that as soon as reinforcements arrived from Middleminster, they intended to wreck equipment vital to the running of the railway – the water and coaling facilities. Judging by their behaviour so far, Dave believed it was not just an idle boast.

After dispatching Natasha to a safer location, Dave thought about what he ought to do. He really needed to alert whoever was in charge at the station. As if on cue, Duggie came ambling down the platform. Dave guessed from his timely arrival that he must have been working the service recently arrived from Middleminster. He was just the man to have on your side in the event of trouble. Well over 6ft tall and built like the proverbial brick outhouse, he also had the strength to match. Dave shouted over to him. A big grin spread over the man's face when he saw Dave and immediately altered course in his direction.

Making obvious the subject now dominating his waking moments, Duggie made the shape of an orifice using his thumb and forefinger and slid the index finger on his other hand in and out of it several times; following it up with exaggerated winks for good measure. Did Duggie know what being discreet meant he wondered?

He took him to one side, and before Duggie could ask him yet again if he knew which one of the girls he would be losing his cherry with, Dave told him of the incidents involving the gang of Yorkshiremen and their threat to sabotage railway equipment.

Duggie was also alarmed by the news and agreed with Dave that they must be stopped by whatever means. Not being blessed with a gift for anything complicated such as coming up with a plan himself, he would go along with whatever Dave suggested; his only thought being that as a Worfe Valley volunteer, he should pass on the information to someone in authority. Mr Etherington, the senior ticket inspector would know what to do for the best.

"Good idea, you do that, and I'll get on to the police, forewarn them like. Hopefully, they'll have somebody available in the local area."

Just a short while later from his position on the overbridge connecting the platform to the coaling yard and engine workshops, Dave watched the Yorkshiremen with increasing concern; they were becoming more aggressive by the minute. If it really was their intention to disrupt the weekend – one of the most popular and profitable in the Worfe Valley Railway's calendar – then help was urgently needed. He anxiously awaited the return of Duggie with reinforcements.

In the meantime, Dave had taken the precaution of forewarning some of the regular Worfe Valley volunteers already ensconced on the overbridge – it being one of the best vantage points for photographing train movements. He explained about the mob's threats to deliberately wreck the infrastructure and asked for volunteers willing to help defend it.

Their positive response was almost unanimous, which in the absence of anybody else encouraged him in his initiative to mount some sort of defence of the station. He was grateful for their assistance, which was in direct contrast to the reaction of the Mercia Transport Police when he'd made a similar appeal to them for help a few minutes earlier. It just so happened that the duty sergeant was the ubiquitous Sgt Edwards.

"Ah, Mr Brand! It seems our paths are destined to cross once again. Well I'm afraid we're particularly short-staffed at the moment, and of course, this being a Saturday, things will certainly get worse during the course of the evening. You can hardly expect me to divert valuable officers to Bridforth station just because you believe there's a conspiracy amongst a mysterious group of Yorkshiremen, who you seem to think are out to sabotage the Worfe Valley Railway. It all sounds rather unlikely don't you think, Mr Blond?"

"Well, I believe it to be true. Remember those two hoax bombers?"

"Look, nothing was ever proven there, and without firm evidence, I'm afraid there's little we can do about this new 'conspiracy' theory of yours. We'll be busy enough here in Wensbury coping with the evening's drunks and brawlers without diluting our resources sending officers to Bawdley."

"It's Bridforth."

"Pardon?"

"Bridforth, I said Bridforth not Bawdley."

"So you did Mr Blund, so you did. I suggest you call your local police if anything does actually happen, I'm sure it won't though. By the way, how is your ladyfriend – Mrs Trotsky isn't it? Still doing her 'plumbing' is she?"

"Yes, Ms Troski is very well thank you, and yes, she is still carrying out her plumbing work; why, did you need something doing?"

"I hardly think so Mr Brand, just curious that's all."

Realising he was getting nowhere in his plea for help, Dave promptly terminated the conversation with a curt thank you and goodbye.

Sgt Edwards put down his phone and allowed himself a smile of self-satisfaction. *Yes, nice try Mr Blond – very nice try. I know what your little game is; trying to get my officers sent over to Bridforth Railway Station on a wild goose chase while he pursues his pimping activities elsewhere. Well, I'm not going to fall for that one!*

He'd received good intelligence that this Bland character was planning something big this weekend and was fully intending to act on it. When making further enquiries into the man following the interview at his house, he'd spoken to a neighbour. The lady, Mrs Battersly, had noticed a curious thing the previous week as she tidied the net curtains in her front window. More than a dozen young females had gone into the house on one particular afternoon and then left about three hours later. As they were coming out, by sheer coincidence she was also outside sweeping the front doorstep, so was in a good position to hear what was being said and she definitely heard them talking about all meeting up there again the following weekend.

That was it! The one bit of information needed to complete the picture! It all confirmed the theory that Bland – despite his earlier denials – was running a vice den from his house, and that there was going to be some sort of sex-fest taking place this very weekend.

On the strength of this intelligence, he had decided to keep a watch on the house during the next two evenings. The call from his suspect requesting police assistance in order to keep his officers at a location well away from the activities about to take place at his house, merely confirmed the correctness of his suspicions.

So you think you're being clever do you Mr Brand, well I'm afraid Sgt Brian Edwards is one step ahead of you this time. Oh yes!

At the railway station, through the deepening gloom of the evening, Dave continued to watch and wait from his position on the bridge. Another service from Middleminster had just pulled in and the passengers were beginning to disembark.

A group of six men immediately stood out. Unlike the other passengers they had a purpose about them as they set off down the platform. They quickly met up with the others who appeared to be awaiting their arrival. Greeting one another like old friends, Dave feared the worst as they joked and traded insults with each other.

After a huddled discussion, he saw the ringleader of the combined mob issue what looked like a call to action. As if on cue, several of them pulled out bats and other assorted weaponry hidden under their clothing. En masse, they began to stride purposefully towards the bridge he was now standing on. This is it he thought; he only had a few moments. Acting as their impromptu leader, Dave turned to rally his troops.

"Men, having completed twelve years military service in the not-too-distant past, I regard myself as having fulfilled my obligation to uphold those principles we hold so dear in this country. Now, several years later, I find those skills being called upon once more in order to defend a principle no less important; that is, the right to operate a volunteer steam railway without interference, coercion or intimidation. A right now under threat from the mob you see advancing towards us.

"To all you fellows of stout heart lending support to this most worthy of causes, all I ask is that you keep a steady nerve and stay resolute in the coming battle – and remember the oath you have all just sworn here today!" He shouted it out once more for their benefit. "They shall not pass over!"

Dave raised his arm aloft. The defenders with one voice repeated it back. "They shall not pass over!"

"Now take up your positions!"

The volunteers quickly slotted into their previously rehearsed places and unfurled their weapons. The first row of three crouched down across the width of the footbridge, upended their camera tripods, pointed the legs in the direction of the enemy and made ready to jab out at close quarter. A second line of volunteers stood shoulder to shoulder armed with thermos flasks held aloft, whilst the remainder behind improvised with any suitable weapon to hand.

One resourceful spotter had removed the heavy HP2 batteries from his mini voice recorder and wrapped them inside the multi-striped scarf knitted for him by an indulgent aunt. He practised his technique by swinging it around his head.

Remembering a tactic from the film *Zulu,* Dave ordered his men to take hold of their tupperware lunchboxes – a favourite with mums for keeping a trainspotter son's sandwiches fresh – and beat their weapons against them. He hoped the resulting cacophony of sound would help to intimidate the approaching enemy. In reality, the effect proved disappointing. Then he recalled it didn't help the Zulus much either.

The leader of the mob was now at the steps and mounted them two at a time. He did a double-take on seeing the reception committee all neatly formed up, their weapons at the ready. The man hesitated as his alcohol-induced bravado suddenly deserted him. Stepping deftly to one side, he urged the others past him while continuing to bark instructions at them.

"C'mon lads, we can tek 'em, we're not goin to let a few spotters stop us are we? That's it get stuck in... I'm... I'm, er... right behind yer."

Aye, and right behind yer is where I'm stayin, he thought to himself when he saw the first three combatants drop to the floor after receiving a vicious series of jabs to their knees.

The next wave fared no better; the defender's thermos flasks rang like church bells when struck against the attacker's heads, whilst the 'thwack' of muffled batteries hitting soft tissue served to discourage a couple of them probing on the defender's periphery.

After receiving such a mauling, the mob broke off contact and withdrew to a safe distance. A different tactic was then tried. The back of the mob let fly a volley of coal at the defenders.

Dave, who had been keeping the enemy under close observation, had anticipated the tactic after seeing them fill their pockets moments before the attack. On the shout of "Incoming!" his troops, like a well-trained Roman Legion, closed into tight ranks and raised their tupperware lunchboxes above their heads. Shielded under a close formation of impact-resistant polypropylene, the missiles bounced harmlessly off onto the ground and platform below.

Realising little damage had been inflicted on the defenders, there appeared to be some indecision by the mob about what to do next. When eventually they did step forward to take up the fight again, the Yorkshiremen fared no better than the first time, even though the front line of defenders were struggling to maintain their weaponry in the face of repeated assaults.

Several of the camera tripod legs were now bent and buckled. Locking screws had broken on others, causing the loosened legs to flail about in the air. A few of the thermos flasks had been lost over the side of the bridge and the nephew had seen both batteries fly off into the distance after rupturing the seam of his scarf. Lumps of coal retrieved from the recent volley were quickly substituted instead.

Some further half-hearted probing was tried by the mob, but when Duggie turned up with reinforcements in the form of two fitters from the engine shed armed with heavy spanners, the attack rapidly petered out again. The Yorkshiremen backed off to the far end of the bridge to lick their wounds. This led to a euphoric student of ancient history proclaiming in an aside to Duggie, "This is ace! It's just like beating the Persians at Thermopylae."

"Is it? I was never any good at board games – I did like snakes and ladders though."

Signs of dissent amongst the mob were now apparent as arguments broke out amongst them over the best course of action. Dave, looking on, judged this to be a critical moment in the conflict where the battle could now either be won or lost. The outcome rested entirely in his hands. He considered what his military heroes would have done at this point. Even without thinking he knew – attack!

As he led the advance, a young lad in their rear rank suddenly shouted out and pointed to the side of the bridge. Dave leant over the rail and saw one of the Yorkshiremen clinging to the outside trying to edge past them in order to attack from the rear. Dave was just wondering what to do about this new threat when an engine – uncoupled and in the process of running around – came to a stand directly underneath the bridge. The driver watching from his cab waited until the man had inched along into a position directly above the engine, then sounded the whistle. This resulted in a blast of scalding steam exhausting vertically and engulfing the man's nether regions. Screaming out in pain from his scalding, the man quickly scrambled back the way he came. If further discouragement were needed to any more forays of this sort, then it was provided by the fireman atop the engine's tender who was now randomly jabbing a red-hot fire iron at the attackers through the bridge's railings.

This was the last straw for the bruised and battered rabble reeling from all the injuries inflicted upon them. A cloud of defeatism very quickly took hold. Despite their leader in the rear urging them onto the offensive, they were in no mood to take further punishment.

One man suddenly articulated exactly what everyone else was thinking, "Bugger this fer a game of soldiers, I've 'ad enough, who's t'follow?"

He stood out in another way too: the man was almost entirely covered from head to toe in dried mud. Raising a pick-axe handle as his standard for the others to follow, he led the descent back down the steps of the bridge.

The police were now beginning to arrive at the station; their sirens could be heard on the approach road. Following the lead taken by their colleague, the threat of arrest quickly motivated all the other Yorkshiremen to follow suit.

Their flight presented the new leader with a problem – how best to escape the clutches of the police. On foot and without local knowledge, he realised they would easily be picked up in such a small town. As he stood desperately looking around for an alternative escape route, the Yorkshireman spotted an engineering train sitting by the starting signal ready to depart. Comprising a diesel shunting engine, open truck, and guards van, he realised it would easily accommodate them all if they were to commandeer it. The man turned to the others as they clattered down the last few steps and came to a halt puffing and panting alongside him. He quickly outlined his plan before asking the important question, "Does anybody know how to drive it?

He looked about the serried ranks of men. A voice piped up from the back. It was their deposed former leader. In between pants, he answered. "I do... aye... piece o' piss... they are... I've worked one... many a time."

Although he knew the bullshit factor was in the upper scale when it came to their former leader's accomplishments, the muddied Yorkshireman found himself with no choice but to accept his word.

"Okay then, there's only one o' them on the engine at moment. Looks like he's got token and road, so we can get goin' straight away. All we need t'do is chuck him off; then when we get to the end of the line at Middleminster, we can all leg it like!"

He glanced across at the car park where he could see the blue pulsing lights of the police vehicles screeching to a halt.

"Reet, we've not a moment to lose, everybody follow me."

Crunching over the ballast, he led the assault on the train.

The driver had been expecting the other members of the Worfe Valley Railway engineering gang, not the bunch of ruffians he was suddenly confronted with. Taken by surprise the old boy protested vainly as they forcibly removed him from the cab and dumped him on the lineside. Given a few kicks for his defiant non-compliance, the driver was left groaning on the lineside.

Their volunteer driver took his place at the controls and looked ponderously about the cab. It was not quite as he remembered it, unfortunately. He struggled to recall the start-up procedures. The man caked in mud leant out of the cab door to check on their pursuers. Several of the police were now out on the platform and heading in their direction. He knew they had to get moving fast.

"C'mon, do y'know 'ow to drive this, or not eh?"

"I can't quite... now let me see... er..."

"Oh fer fuck's sake!"

"Ang on... rite, I think I've got it."

With that, he put the engine into forward drive and released the brake handle. As the air vented and released the brakes, the train began to roll forward. Looking back out of the cab, the driver saw several policemen running towards them down the end slope of the platform. He opened up the power handle and the lightly loaded train surged forward. Taking a second look back down the line, a smile came to his lips when he saw the police give up their now futile chase. Accelerating past the line speed of 25mph, he eased off at 40mph when the ride began to get too uncomfortable.

Eli and Frank sat licking their wounds as they bounced along in the open truck.

"Well Frank, what a disaster that were. I reckon they'd bin tipped off y'know. They were waitin' fer us on that bridge!"

Frank, sitting on top of a toolbox just grunted.

"All I 'ope is that when Ernie gets to 'ear about it, 'e don't blame us fer the cock-up... Mind, I knew this would 'appen I did. I wished now I'd never got involved in this 'air-brained scheme o' yours Frank!"

"Oh, stop yer moanin', we got away didn't we?" he said eventually.

"Yeah, but for 'ow long? The police'll be after us soon. What 'appens when we get to the end of the line eh?"

"Stop witterin' on. We'll sort summat out."

"That's what you say! I'm not so sure. We need to have a plan, see. The trouble is nobody seems to know what they're doin'. I reckon we ought to split up when we get the other end; merge into background like, afore mekkin' our own way 'ome. We'll attract too much attention if we all stick together."

"That might not be a bad idea Eli. I'll need to speak to me lad though an' let 'im know what we're plannin'."

"Well I'm glad you agree with me fer a change, so what's 'appenin' with him then?"

"Darren? Well I left 'im at Hempton. I thought it best if 'im and 'is mate cause a bit o' trouble over there, well out o' 'arms way over 'ere like."

"So 'ave you 'eard anything from him?"

"'E phoned me earlier to let me know that 'e'd come up with summat 'e said would stop this Worfe Valley lot in their tracks."

"Well it sounds good. Did 'e say what it were exactly?"

"No, 'e didn't want to tell me. The lad wanted to make sure it all went off okay before 'e took credit for it. 'E said I'd be pleased though."

"It does sound like 'e's thinkin' things thru' a bit more, afore 'e buggers somethin' up."

"Aye, about bloody time an' all, I never thought e'd ever learn to use that brain in his 'ead."

"Look Frank! I can see the lights of that West Mercia safari park comin' up on the left, we must be gettin' near to Hempton... I say, talking o' your lad, isn't that Darren an' 'is mate just up ahead on the lineside. Can yer see 'im? Looks to me like e's got one o' them big spanners in 'is hands, y'know the sort you use to undo fishplate bolts that hold rails together."

"What? Where? Let me see!" Frank peered out into the darkness trying to locate his son. Suddenly he spotted him and knew immediately what he'd done, *"Oh no!"*

The severe jolt as the train parted company with the rails, took away his power of speech, save for one supreme effort as the derailed train veered off down the embankment and passed within feet of his now smirking son.

He leant over the side to address him. "You wanker! I'll fuckin' kil..." the bucking train stopped him in mid-sentence as it threw him violently over to the other side of the truck.

On hearing his dad's voice shouting out from inside the lurching train, Darren's face dropped as suddenly as the fishplate spanner he let slip from his grasp. He began to shout back after him as he followed in the wake of the derailed train, while his mate Kevin, nursing several injured toes, attempted a pain relieving dance with his good foot.

After their earlier lack of concern, Dave was extremely relieved to see the police arrive and take on the role he and his volunteers had been forced to assume. With all the ongoing commotion, he could now slip unobtrusively away and resume his duties.

He was anxious to find out how the girls were faring, in particular whether their activities were being affected by the behaviour of any other Yorkshiremen travelling on Worfe Valley's trains. Duggie immediately offered to accompany him. Still in the back of his mind was the reward promised to him by Dave. Anything that would enhance his chances in that regard, Duggie was prepared to do. They boarded the very next service leaving the station.

Chapter 25

Still gaining speed, the loco and its two trucks lurched violently from side to side as the train descended the grassy embankment. Cries of pain filled the air as the occupants were tossed back and forth, thwarting all attempts by those inside the cab to grasp hold of the brake lever and bring the train to a halt.

The outer perimeter wire mesh fence of the safari park loomed up directly in the path of the engine. A huge section of it was torn down as the train smashed through, causing a herd of startled wildebeest to scatter in all directions. The monkey house was next. Screeching chimps clambered up into the high tree branches as the structure was comprehensively ripped apart. By contrast, the lions looked on with barely concealed boredom as the clanking, swaying collection of vehicles cut a swathe through their reinforced metal fence. Now slowing, the train's momentum was finally exhausted breaching the concrete wall of the bear enclosure before toppling into the bear pit enclosed by it.

Darren set off in the wake of the runaway train. Ahead of him in the distance, he could hear the crash of demolition taking place. Meanwhile, the roaring and snorting of disturbed animals began to fill the night air with a cacophony of noise. Darren stopped to catch his breath. Unnerved by the thought of all the wild animals on the loose, he peered out into the darkness straining to see if any were in the near vicinity. His fear was that some beast would suddenly come charging at him out of the gloom.

With his senses on full alert, Darren moved as stealthily as he could. As he approached the wrecked perimeter fence, Darren had a sense of being followed. He turned around thinking it might be his mate Kevin trying to catch him up, but could see nothing in the darkness.

As he continued to make his way, a growing sense of unease took hold of him, as if there really was something out there stalking him. He turned around again – more quickly this time. In the distance, low on the ground, he could see what looked like two pinpricks of light. It took him a moment to work out that it was actually two glistening eyes being reflected back at him in the moonlight.

Unable to make out which animal it was, but frightened by the thought of what it could be, he began to walk faster, then broke into a run as panic took hold of him. Each time he glanced behind, the eyes were there keeping pace with him.

Darren was desperate to stay ahead of whatever was tracking him, but now tiring, he began stumbling on the rough tufts of vegetation. Within seconds, a pothole lying unseen in the darkness had taken his foot from under him and sent him sprawling into the long grass. He tried to scramble back onto his feet, but a sudden violent blow from behind sent him tumbling for a second time. Winded, he lay there pinned to the ground by the weight of his pursuer. Its huge jaws were now only inches away from his face; he could feel its warm animal breath exhaling against his skin. Shaking with fear, he cried out; his screams carrying for some distance in the cool evening air.

Kevin, limping along some way behind, immediately dropped to the ground when he heard the terrified scream of his friend. As he lay there listening, too frightened to move and hardly daring to breathe, he could only guess at the horror befallen by his mate. Suddenly, a bellowing roar filled the night air and the screams were no more.

Once the locomotive engine died and the huge cloud of dust had settled, two curious bears came up close to investigate, tentatively scraping at the cab door with their paws and sniffing the blend of human scents emanating from within it. They both quickly backed away when groans and curses from the bruised and battered crew broke the silence inside.

In what was left of the chimps' enclosure Bobo, one of the young adults, scampered down from the high branches of his perch and viewed the scene with interest. In captivity, he'd spent many an hour watching the steaming, smoking, railway engines come and go on the tracks that passed by the outer fence of the safari park. His amused keepers, having noticed the chimp's keen interest, had indulged him from time to time with railway DVDs played on the TV screen specifically provided for the chimps' entertainment in their enclosure.

Now presented with the opportunity to exploit his particular fascination, Bobo excitedly set off on his mission. He moved tentatively at first, barely comprehending that he was able to roam freely over ground only ever seen from the inside of his cage. As he moved closer to the shredded wire fence he became more wary, looking out for the animal keepers he feared would foil his escape. One last obstacle remained between himself and freedom. Although his instinct was to make one final dash for the wire, before moving off again, he closely surveyed the scene. When satisfied that it was safe, he launched himself through the gaping hole and bounded off in the direction of a stationary passenger train he could see in the distance.

The train was waiting to depart in the opposite direction to the one that had just crashed through the animals' enclosure. Aboard the engine, its driver and fireman as yet had no knowledge of the maintenance train's derailment. Their own train was some distance away from the incident on the other running line. The driver, Malcolm Forbes, was still waiting patiently for the maintenance train to pass by from the other direction. Only then would his train be able to proceed out of the loop onto the single line, using the token given up by the driver of the other train.

He checked his watch and tutted out loud. The maintenance train was now fifteen minutes late by his reckoning. Where has it got to, he wondered? Malcolm blamed the frenetic pace of modern life as the reason for such tardy attitudes to timekeeping. People nowadays didn't have time to be punctual; even fellow train crew were affected by the malaise it seemed.

After several more minutes, Malcolm checked his watch a second time. He decided to take the short walk back to the signalbox as required by the rulebook and find out what was holding it up. It could be that the overdue train had failed on the single section of track, in which case they wouldn't be going anywhere in a hurry.

Malcolm wiped his hands on his regulation piece of rag and informed the fireman of his decision. Resting his shovel for a moment, Derek nodded him an acknowledgement. Being stationary a while longer would give him the chance to climb up on the tender and shovel some of the larger lumps of coal closer to the front. Smoke was now swirling around in the cab after building up the fire in anticipation of the climb ahead; still more coal would be needed before journey's end at Bridforth. As Malcolm climbed down off the footplate, Derek clambered up on the tender and started work.

Bobo the chimpanzee reached the railway's boundary fence. He limbered over it and scampered up close to the simmering giant. Eyes wide with wonder, he sat on his haunches and took in the scene. His unblinking eyes watched in fascination as wisps of steam hissed gently from different parts of the running gear, while droplets of condensed water dripped from the steam chest and splashed down onto the rail. Bobo caught sight of the man standing on the tender breaking up lumps of coal and eyed him cautiously.

Unable to contain himself any longer, Bobo reached up to the grab-rail and hoisted himself effortlessly into the cab. Looking around, the controls were all familiar to him; his knowledge gained from watching the DVDs provided by his keepers, as well as the countless hours he'd spent mimicking the driver's actions in the confines of his enclosure.

He leapt onto the driver's seat and waited for the signal arm to be raised. When nothing happened, Bobo vented his frustration with a screech. From the back of the tender amidst the swirling smoke came a voice, "Is that you Malcolm, I have to say you're making some funny noises; anything to report then?"

The two escaped bears had taken it upon themselves to follow the chimp after the wrecking of the train. Several lions were now roaming freely, and the bears' instinct was to find somewhere secure to go to ground. Although bewildered and wary of the huge steaming engine – different again from the diesel locomotive that had invaded their bear pit – they were unable to resist the lure of the restaurant car three carriages down, from which a plethora of irresistible aromas were being wafted through the still evening air. Their investigative noses sought out every avenue of entry without success until, due to the enforced delay, one of the chefs happened to open a door to let in a little more air into the steam-filled kitchen.

Down at the signalbox, Malcolm was being informed of the cause of the delay. Details of the hijacking and subsequent derailment were still sketchy – the signalman had only just been informed of the incident himself, but he assured Malcolm that the police were on their way to the scene, and fitters had been despatched from Bridforth to put back the missing section of rail on the other running line.

Meanwhile, there was still a service to run. As the section of loop on which Malcolm train's stood was unaffected by the derailment, the signalman had been authorised to issue a replacement token for the one lost in the crashed train. This would give Malcolm the authority to proceed onto the single line towards Bridforth. He cleared the signal, allowing Malcolm to depart as soon as he returned to the train. Satisfied that events had now been returned to some sort of order, Malcolm thanked the signaller, and set off down the steps.

Loose ballast crunched comfortingly underfoot as he walked the length of the eight carriage train. Arriving at the tender he paused for a moment, using it to lean against while he filled his pipe in readiness for the onward journey. As he tamped down the moist tobacco, Malcolm took an admiring look along the line of his train now glistening majestically in the dim moonlight.

The sight of a streamlined A4 pacific never failed to impress him, no matter how many times he had occasion to gaze upon its distinctive outline. Specially designed air-smoothed casings provided the engine with its unique profile; an appearance enhanced by the lined-out green paintwork applied to each of the panels. Powered by superheated steam and delivered to the huge driving wheels through the pistons and sturdy forgings of its drive motion, the vintage engine still looked at the peak of its powers. A rake of eight teak-bodied coaches, only recently restored, sat coupled up to the tender, the fresh varnish highlighting the gold lettering on each one of the carriages.

As the engine simmered in the cool evening air, its power waiting to be unleashed, a blast from the engine's whistle interrupted Malcolm's musing. It must be Derek letting him know that the signal had cleared and they could now proceed, thought Malcolm.

Quite unexpectedly, the train jerked forward, causing Malcolm to almost fell over. *What on earth…?* He quickly recovered and shouted out in the direction of the engine. A blast of exhausted steam barking out from the chimney gave a very audible signal that the train had been deliberately set in motion. The first exhaust beat was soon followed by another. As the train picked up speed, Malcolm began running after it, repeatedly shouting at whoever was driving it to stop. He couldn't understand why it was being driven without him. Derek he knew would never do such a thing on his own initiative.

Bobo, having watched the semaphore signal arm rise to an

angle of forty-five degrees, had emitted a screech of excitement at the prospect of now actually working the controls of the train. He'd immediately set about his task, jumping down from the seat to select forward motion, giving a blast on the whistle before releasing the break and easing the regulator open. With only a small jolt and with a single exhaust beat, the engine had drawn forward, tightening the couplings and setting the whole train in motion.

"Whoa! Malcolm... 'ang on a minute, I'm still up on the tender, I very nearly... what on earth!"

Clambering down from the newly shovelled mound of coal, the night air coming into the cab suddenly cleared the pervading smoke, and Derek was astonished to see a chimpanzee sitting where Malcolm should have been. Aware of a human presence close by, Bobo turned towards him and pulled back his lips to expose his teeth in a half smile. He greeted Derek with a squeal.

"What the hell! Where have you come from? And where's Malcolm?" The questions though rhetorical, begged serious explanation. Derek was astonished by the sight of the ape and astounded that he was working the controls. Unsure as to what had happened to his driver, Derek leaned out each side of the cab in turn looking for him. He soon spotted Malcolm some distance behind frantically waving his arms, his shouts lost in the noise from the engine's barking exhaust. Derek waved and shouted back. Satisfied that at least Malcolm was safe, Derek turned his attention back to the chimpanzee.

After his initial shock at seeing him, there came the realisation that he was actually driving the train. No time to wonder how he'd managed it, Derek had to stop him before a disaster happened. Although he was confident with most animals, he knew that a full-grown chimpanzee was a powerful beast and could be aggressive if provoked. One wrong move might provoke a violent reaction from him.

He inched forward a step at a time. When within reach of the controls, he attempted to take hold of the regulator. Bobo turned towards him and bared his teeth. Was that a warning? He would soon find out. He tried to take hold of the regulator again. This time Bobo screamed and went to bite Derek's arm. He quickly snatched it back out of the way.

Though his overriding concern was regaining control of the train, Derek realised he would need to first gain the animal's confidence in order to obtain his cooperation. He closely watched the ape's actions for a moment. The chimp was proving surprisingly adept at the controls. Derek drew comfort from his apparent competence, as if he had been actually trained in the art. He knew chimpanzees were intelligent, but he'd never heard of one being able to drive a train. The crucial thing was did he know how to stop it? He certainly couldn't risk leaving him in control; he had to make a start in winning the chimpanzee over.

"Now, young er..." he glanced down at the chimpanzee's groin area.

"Now then young man, there's no need to be like that. I'm hoping we can be friends, you do want to be friends don't you?"

Bobo, still looking at the road ahead, ignored him. They were slowing on a rising gradient, so Bobo opened the regulator a touch more to compensate. As a passed fireman capable of driving the train himself, Derek felt well qualified to comment.

"That's right, well done er... lad, just keep it steady at that. So... where could you have come from then, I wonder? I know you can't tell me, but we do need to know so we can get you home again, someone will be worried about you!"

Derek hoped his concern for the chimp's welfare was being recognised. It felt to Derek like being the finder of a lost child who, although having a personality as well as a level of intelligence, was unable to communicate anything useful.

Bobo pushed out his bottom jaw, pulled his lips back, and shot him a brief toothy grimace. Derek beamed a big smile back at him. He recalled that facial expressions were an important means of communication for chimps, so endeavoured to maintain the forced maniacal grin.

Derek then had an idea. As well as his sandwiches, he also had some fruit in his lunchbox. Maybe he could gain his friendship with a gift of it. Derek moved over to the locker and removed the tin container. Bobo repeatedly flicked his eyes sideways, keeping a watch on Derek's actions, then held out his hand when the fruit was revealed. He moved the banana nearer to Bobo who immediately snatched it from him. In one deft movement, he had peeled and eaten it.

"That's right young man, wasn't that nice eh? Look I've got something else for you." he said holding up an apple. Derek had noticed that they were now picking up speed on the falling gradient. Unfortunately, Bobo wasn't reacting. He really needed to close the regulator and apply some braking. Derek edged a little closer.

"Look, I'm just going to help you a little bit, I'll just put my hand over yours, and then we'll move this lever, okay?" Derek slowly edged his hand closer to the chimp. Bobo just grunted. Taking this as a positive sign, Derek very slowly took hold of the chimp's hairy hand, paused for a few seconds, then gently tugged at the regulator to close it.

"See how easy that was? Very good... very good! Now we just need to do one more thing, and then you can have the apple."

Bobo started shrieking and screeching, before reaching out to grab it from Derek's hand. Derek quickly pulled it out of the way, "No! No! We have to put the brake on first. Yes, oh yes!"

With Bobo's begrudging cooperation, Derek managed to slow the train, but was roughly pushed away by the screeching chimp when he held the brake on in an attempt to stop it. "Okay, okay! You can drive it a bit longer then," he conceded.

Derek wondered what the hell he was going to do. The chimp was adamant that he would drive the train and would only let him help so much. It looked like stopping it was out of the question at the moment. He couldn't keep bribing him with food, as he was fast running out. Derek realised it was time to inform higher authority of his predicament. While maintaining a watchful eye on the gauges, Derek took out his phone and dialled the manager's office.

Chapter 26

Marjorie and Ronald, having boarded the train for the return journey, had walked almost the entire length before finding a vacant first class compartment. Directing her husband to his seat, Marjorie occupied her preferred position next to the window. She extracted a newly purchased copy of *Woman at Home* from her handbag and began leafing through its pages.

Her exasperated sighs and mutterings soon disturbed the quiet calm of the carriage. After one final utterance, she took off her glasses and turned to her husband, "You know Ronald, I despair, I really do! It seems the last bastion of middle-England womanhood has finally succumbed."

Belatedly looking up from his own magazine, Ronald replied, "Sorry, what was that Marjorie?"

"I said – that once healthy tome of morality and tradition for ladies of a certain age has finally been afflicted by the insidious disease sweeping this nation of ours."

"What disease is that?" he asked out of curiosity.

"I'm talking about sex of course!"

A startled Ronald immediately put down his own gardening magazine. *"Sex?"*

"Yes, sex! I could always guarantee that having purchased a copy of *Woman at Home,* I would enjoy a variety of interesting articles, i.e. nourishing supper recipes from the likes of Delia Smith for example, or Alan Titchmarsh's gardening section with useful tips for ladies on how to trim our shrubbery. Not forgetting travel reporting from someone of the calibre of Judith Chalmers enjoying a fling around the Maldives or some other far flung location.

"And instead what do I find when I buy this latest issue? Well, for a start, the cover's had what they nowadays call a 'makeover.' That set the alarm bells ringing straightaway, I can tell you. So I was not a bit surprised when I opened the cover to find the format inside had been completely changed. For instance, instead of 'Your very good health,' we now have something called 'Sexercise in your 60's' – I ask you!

"They've ousted the very discreet 'Our ladies questions answered' and substituted it with – and I quote, 'Sex advice from Harriet Tweed, Britain's best loved bisexual granny.' Then to cap it all, starting in this month's issue, we have 'A six part Sarga guide to sex toys.' Honestly Ronald, it is truly appalling!

"And I've yet to discover the fate of that popular evergreen 'Crosstitch Corner,' they've probably changed it to 'Crossdressers' Corner,' or some other such tawdry title. It's beyond belief, it really is!"

"It seems to be a sign of the times, Marjorie."

"Yes, the goings-on we've seen today certainly prove that. Sex seems to have become the national pastime, it truly has."

"Not for me unfortunately," sighed Ronald under his breath.

"What was that?"

"I... said I er... want to pee unfortunately!"

"Well you know where it is, you don't need my permission now do you?"

Ronald begged to differ, though he let it pass. "Actually, I was waiting till we got underway," replied Ronald testily. "Now that we are, I shall!" He got up to leave the compartment then hesitated as if about to say something.

Marjorie looked up at him. "Yes?"

"Oh... oh, nothing." and let himself out into the corridor.

Now devoid of any suitable reading material, Marjorie picked up Ronald's gardening magazine and opened it at a random page. A bold title declared, 'The amazing sex life of the honey bee!'

"I don't believe it!" exclaimed Marjorie as she threw down the magazine. Folding her arms tightly across her chest, she looked around the compartment for something else to occupy her.

In considerably less time than he normally took to perform such a function, Ronald was hurriedly letting himself back into the compartment.

"Whatever's wrong Ronald, you look quite startled?"

"There... there's a bear... in the lavatory!"

Marjorie's face took on a distinctly sceptical look.

"A bare what? Bare bottom?"

Ronald was about to reply.

"...It would hardly be surprising would it? After all it is a lavatory, though it does concern me that you are bursting in on people in a state of undress. Was the person female by any chance? Because I don't want any more of that peeping tomfoolery we had with you last year. I haven't forgotten you know; when you suddenly found an interest in astronomy and you bought that telescope to install in your shed and I found it focussed directly on the bedroom window of that divorced woman at No. 22. Yes, it certainly wasn't the night sky's heavenly bodies you were interested in!"

"No, no, just listen for a minute woman, I mean an animal – a real live bear!"

"There's no need to be rude, Ronald. Anyway, don't be preposterous. What would a bear be doing on our train? This is a passenger service for people and certainly not for the conveyance of animals."

"Look! I'm telling you there's a bear on the train, if you don't believe me come and see for yourself."

"I most certainly will; this is all quite ridiculous! You just lead the way Ronald and we'll soon settle the matter."

Cautiously, he led Marjorie down the corridor. At the end of the carriage he pointed to the half open lavatory door ahead of them. Ronald edged forward and peered around it. Sadly, it was now empty.

"It was in there, I swear it!" said Ronald.

"Look, you can drop the hushed David Attenborough tone of voice now, there's obviously no bear there now. I suppose it was a circus bear was it, specially trained to use the toilet facilities?"

"You know Marjorie, I'm getting rather fed up with your attitude towards me. All you ever do is critis..."

Just at that moment, Ronald saw the animal come bounding down the corridor towards them. Marjorie, with her back to it, was unaware of the danger.

"Quick Marjorie, it's coming back!" As she turned round to look, Ronald grabbed hold of his wife and pushed her forcibly through the compartment door; sliding it shut just before the bear lumbered past trailing a long link of sausages from its mouth. Both looked on in astonishment. Still holding on to his wife he asked, "Now do you believe me?"

Marjorie looked shocked by the occurrence. "Yes... I'm sorry Ronald, I... I just thought that you..."

"Well perhaps you think too much sometimes, I am capable of thinking, and acting, for myself. I'm not a child you know! You always have to..." He stopped himself short. "Anyway... enough said eh? Are you okay?"

"Yes... yes I think so Ronald," she said, now recovering from her close call. "...I wonder where it could have come from; it must have escaped from somewhere."

"Perhaps they were transporting it on behalf of a circus," suggested Ronald with just a hint of sarcasm. "We should be safe enough in here though."

Marjorie was still thinking over Ronald's criticism. "Look, I'm sorry for doubting you. I appreciate what you did Ronald, taking charge like that, you were... quite masterful."

"Oh it was nothing really, just the actions of a caring husband."

"Yes... well, I hadn't realised you did still care in that way. It was quite... quite like old times." Marjorie, a wistful look on her face, turned her head towards him. Ronald realised he was still holding his wife in a protective embrace. He pulled her in tighter.

"I've always cared Marjorie – though I have to say, there have been few opportunities recently to show it."

Marjorie looked away for a moment reflecting on his words.

"Yes, I know... I..." Finding a spoken response difficult, Marjorie instead pressed her head into his shoulder.

Ronald savoured the moment. His nostrils took in the smell of her perfume, 'Harrogate Nights' if he recalled the fragrance correctly. The unaccustomed physical closeness combined with her contrite demeanour initiated a stirring within him. Ronald's testosterone, having been suppressed for several years, once more started to course through his veins. Marjorie, in making no effort to break free from his embrace, only seemed to encourage him in his desire.

Recklessly he took the initiative and pressed his lips onto hers. Weak protests expressed her surprise, but were soon quelled by the intensity of his passion. She began to succumb, her lips responding to Ronald's ardour in a way she had not done for years. He gripped her tighter using one hand to caress the outline of her ample rear. His manhood responded and now began to press against her.

She sighed, "Oh, Ronald!" and pushed herself into him.

He perceived in her a compliance; a willingness to give herself to him. Marjorie's arousal was dramatically confirmed when her handbag – normally held in a vice-like grip – suddenly dropped to the floor. Ronald sensed the time was now right to exploit Marjorie's weakened state.

No resistance was offered as his hands roamed over her body. Only the substantial fabric of her Marts & Spender matching skirt and jacket, recently purchased from their 'Golden Hues' autumn range, prevented Ronald from carrying out a more intimate exploration.

Judging the moment right, Ronald reached down to sweep Marjorie's legs from under her and lay her down on the rough moquette seating. He leaned over to pull down the blinds on the outside window before doing the same to the ones facing the corridor.

Marjorie, regaining her sense of propriety during the lull, went to protest. "Ronald," she said in a hushed tone, "This is public transport, we can't just... just... someone might walk in!"

Not about to relinquish his mastery of the situation, Ronald, with a roguish smile now spreading across his face, had a solution at the ready.

"No they won't my dear!" and proceeded to turn over the page that carried the beaming full face photo of Harriet Tweed, before wedging the magazine tightly into the door runner. Turning his attention back to Marjorie, he drew his face up close to hers and in a deep low voice declared, "It just makes it all the more exciting my dear! Darling, while we're still able, let's live a little dangerously. What do you say?"

"Oh Ronald!" Marjorie then giggled in that girlish way Ronald remembered from their courting days, taking him right back to the time when they had enjoyed many a passionate encounter in the back of his Wolseley 16/60.

He paused for moment to gaze at her face, now soft and youthful-looking under the diffused ex-British Rail coaching stock lighting. Her complexion looked flushed from her unexpected sexual awakening. It all served to make his need for her that much more urgent. He voiced his longing to her, "Marjorie my dear, I want you and I want you now!"

It was sometime later when they heard the cries of the guard as he walked the length of the train, explaining to passengers clamouring for details that it was now safe to leave their compartments. The bear, he explained, had boarded the train undetected at an earlier stop after escaping from the nearby safari park. He offered the reassurance that the animal had now been rounded up and was locked securely in the guard's van.

Ronald went to look at his watch. He couldn't believe how much time had elapsed whilst they'd been in the throws of passion. Marjorie was relieved in another way to hear of the bear's recapture, an urgent call of nature beckoned.

Leaving Ronald to finish adjusting his clothing, she slid back the door – only to be confronted by the leering face of a man. As Marjorie recoiled back into the compartment, the Yorkshireman stuck his head through the doorway and caught sight of Ronald doing up his buttons.

"Yes, can I help you?" inquired an equally startled Ronald.

The Yorkshireman turned to take a second look at Marjorie. Drawing his conclusions from the scene, he turned back to Ronald. "I say, you drew the short straw endin' up wi' 'er didn't yer?" he asked, nodding in Marjorie's direction.

"I beg your pardon?" replied Ronald indignantly.

"Well, at least all the other tarts doin' business on 'ere are young and reasonable lookin' like."

"Now wait a minute, look…"

"I hope you're not insinuating what I think you're insinuating?" interrupted Marjorie.

"You 'eard me right."

"How dare you! Not that it is any business of yours, but I'll have you know that Ronald and I have been happily married for many years, and if we choose to enjoy the benefits that such an institution confers on us in the privacy of our first class compartment, then that is a matter for ourselves and nobody else. Isn't that so Ronald?

"Absolutely Marjorie!"

"Yes, so kindly remove yourself from our compartment and scuttle off back to where you came from… Strictly third class would, I'm sure, be the most appropriate carriage for someone of your ilk!"

"Hark at you yer' stuck up old cow, well y'know what you can go and do…"

"Just stop there!" demanded Marjorie, cutting him off in mid-sentence. "Ronald! Pass me my handbag!"

The man began to smirk. "What yer goin' to do luv, give 'im a refund?"

Marjorie's eyes burned ever deeper into her tormentor as she held out her arm for Ronald to load. He knew what was coming. Lifting it off the floor, Ronald placed the weighty accessory into his wife's hand. He almost felt a pang of sympathy for its intended victim.

Before the Yorkshireman had a chance to read her intentions, Marjorie had drawn back her arm and swung the bag with full force into the man's face. Ronald winced as the metal buckles made hard contact with the man's cheek. A fierce cry of pain filled the air. Before Marjorie could draw back her arm for a second blow, the man had staggered back out of the doorway and was fleeing down the corridor.

"Well I think that's just resolved the issue, don't you Ronald?"

"I couldn't agree more Marjorie. I thought you handled the situation superbly well."

"Oh it was nothing Ronald, just the actions of a... caring wife!" teased Marjorie, her lips displaying just the merest hint of a smile.

Ronald laughed, "Oh, touché Marjorie, touché indeed!"

Chapter 27

In the office above the station building at Bridforth, Norman Watkins, the railway's general manager, was suffering from crisis overload. Since being called back to the office earlier in the evening, all his time had been taken up dealing with one urgent matter after another. The latest being to sort out with his head of track maintenance the repairing of the line and the re-railing of the maintenance train

Prior to that, he'd spent some considerable time giving details of the hijacking and the sabotage attempt on the railway's facilities to officers from the Mercia Transport Police. In addition, he'd also received several phone calls from concerned railway staff alerting him to the aggressive behaviour of a group of men travelling on one of their trains; the nature of their activities leading Norman to the firm conclusion that they were part of the same group of Yorkshiremen who'd caused the earlier disruption.

His most painful exchange though was with the Head of the West Mercia Safari Park. Assuming poor track maintenance by the Worfe Valley Railway to be the cause of the train derailment, the manager had given Norman a severe ear-bashing over the trail of devastation left behind. Despite assurances from Norman that it was an act of deliberate sabotage carried out by a group of malcontents and that the railway was just as much a victim in this as the safari park, the manager persisted in holding the Worfe Valley Railway directly responsible.

All the railway manager could do was apologise repeatedly as the details of each act of destruction were described to him over the phone. When eventually able to get a word in edgeways,

Norman attempted to calm the man by offering assistance from Worfe Valley's own band of volunteers to help carry out emergency repair work at the safari park.

While the offer was welcomed by his opposite number, he regarded the rounding up of the escaped animals as being his top priority, pointing out to Norman on several occasions during the course of his tirade that some of the animals on the loose were dangerous predators and could pose a major threat to the general public if not promptly recaptured.

He'd already instructed his safari park wardens to scour the area with tranquiliser guns. Once help arrived in the form of a specialist team from the RSPCA and the police armed with night-sights, he was hoping to have all the animals rounded up by the morning.

The other issue concerning him were the financial implications. He stated in his typically brusque manner that he expected the Worfe Valley Railway to pick up the bill for all the damage. So far, this would include repairing the safari park's cages and fencing, all expenses incurred in re-capturing the animals, and an additional amount to cover loss of business while the repairs were carried out.

Norman finally managed to placate the park manager with an assurance that the railway was fully covered for incidents such as this and promised to get on with making a claim right away; though when he checked the insurance schedule afterwards, the particular clause he had in mind only mentioned, *'injury to, or loss of a member of the public's pet.'* Norman would have to check with the underwriters whether the cover extended to lions, gibbons and gnus.

After all the frenetic activity he could feel a headache coming on, so searched his desk to find some tablets. He now needed a drink to take them with. As if on cue, his senior ticket inspector Mr Etherington stepped into the room with a cup of tea. *Perfect timing,* thought Norman. He thanked him for bringing him some refreshment – rather than presenting him with another problem to sort out, he said only half-jokingly.

The man failed to reply. His light hearted remark had obviously passed him by. Noticing Etherington's pained expression, Norman wondered if there was indeed a problem of some sort. He watched as his subordinate set down the tray and methodically transferred the teacup, plate and other items onto his desk. After completing the familiar ritual, the man stepped back, his balance wavering slightly as he performed a military style one-two shuffle with his feet.

With the formality of a man well-versed in military procedures, the old soldier brought himself to attention, fixed his gaze on a spot just above Norman's head, and solemnly announced to the wall that there was a matter of some urgency he needed to speak to him about.

Norman groaned, *this looks ominous, what was it now?* he wondered. He was familiar with Etherington's habit of talking-up the trivial. If it was his ticket machine running low on ink again, he would just have to wait. He had far more important matters to consider at the moment.

Norman eyed up the plate of accompanying biscuits. Wavering between a jammy dodger and a custard cream, he rejected both in favour of a third contender. He took a bite of the biscuit and leaned back in his chair, "So what exactly is this matter of vital importance then Etherington?"

Before the man could answer, the telephone rang. Norman reached out to pick up the receiver. The call was from Malcolm in the signal box. He had some urgent news to impart – someone had hijacked his train.

"Hijacked!" repeated Norman, nearly choking on his chocolate hobnob.

No! No, he thought as Malcolm began outlining the facts. *This can't be happening surely? Not after everything else! The weekend had started off so well. Just what on earth was going on? This is a quiet, volunteer run, heritage railway, so why are these Yorkshiremen bent on its destruction? And why hijack another one of our trains? It makes no sense, no sense at all.*

Norman sat trying to fathom it all out and only half-listened to Malcolm relating every single detail of what had taken place. Having early-on gleaned the gist of his narrative, Norman was anxious to get a clearer picture of the situation from the fireman still on the train, so became increasingly impatient with Malcolm when he reiterated the salient points for a third time.

When finally able to put down the phone, it immediately rang again. Norman sat looking at it with sense of foreboding. What other bad news could be on its way to him? As he reached out for the receiver, Norman noticed that his hand had developed a tremor.

'Please, let there be no more disasters,' he prayed as he picked up the handset and went to answer. He struggled to find his voice.

"...Hello... Worfe Valley Railway, Mr Wa... Watkins sp... speaking."

"Hi Norman, it's Derek... Derek Carter here. Look, this is urgent!"

"Ah Derek! Yes, it's good to hear from you. I hope you're okay, I was just going to phone you." It was a relief to hear the fireman's voice. He tried for Derek's benefit to sound upbeat about his predicament. "We've just heard the news about your train; sorry you've got caught up in it... The police are already onto it I understand... We'll soon have you out of this... It's good that you're able to talk – so are you alright?"

"Yes, I'm fine thanks, so you know all the details then?"

"Well... yes, your driver Malcolm has just phoned me from the signal box. We're just trying to make sense of it all at the moment."

Norman had come to the realisation that there could only be one reason why these Yorkshiremen should carry out such an act, so asked Derek the question which would confirm his suspicions. "Have there been any demands yet?"

His train was obviously the Yorkshireman's real target. All the other stuff was just a diversion, he realised. He wondered what the hijackers wanted. They had certainly seized the main prize here. Having taken over the A4 pacific – a guest engine on hire just for that weekend; unique and totally irreplaceable – together with the eight coach set coupled to it, the repercussions didn't bear thinking about if it was wrecked.

"'Ang on a minute!" answered Derek.

He might as well know the worst. It could be a huge ransom they were after, together with flights to Beunos Aires, or some other such far-off place. The sky's the limit with such a valuable national treasure. The police would be arriving soon; they had trained negotiators for just these situations and would try to talk them down to something reasonable.

Norman heard Derek pick up his phone again, "So Derek, tell me the worst."

"Well... a decent sized bunch of bananas would do for a start!"

There was a delayed reaction from Mr Watkins. "Sorry... I thought you just said a bunch of bananas!"

"Yes that's right, and er... any other fruit you have, he'll eat anything like that."

"So let me get this right, you are talking about fruit... It's not a coded word for something else?"

"No, that's right – any sort of soft fruit will do... and plenty of it!"

Norman had trouble getting his head around it. Having hijacked their most valuable train, this Yorkshireman – one of several currently wreaking havoc on their heritage railway – demands as a ransom a bunch of bananas! He's having a joke, playing games with us. What were they really after?

Perplexed by the strange request, he asked if Derek was able to tell him more about their situation.

"Well we're stationary at the moment. I've managed to get him to bring the train to a stand in the platform at Harley, but he's cost me my last orange – and my cottage cheese and watercress sandwiches. I can't get him out the driver's seat though."

This is one peculiar hijacker, thought Norman. He knew Derek was a health food addict, but who'd ever heard of a Yorkshireman eating cottage cheese and watercress sandwiches? The man must have an eating disorder.

"Derek… if it's okay for you to tell me, what's he doing now?" asked Mr Watkins.

"No it's fine, you mean right at this minute?"

"Yes."

"Well he's picking fleas out of his hair and crunching them between his teeth."

"*What?*"

"It's just part of their grooming process isn't it; they do it all time."

It only confirmed to Mr Watkins his already established prejudices about Yorkshiremen and their unsavoury habits.

"How very uncouth, obviously personal hygiene is not a high priority with him then?"

"Well at least he's stopped making a display of playing with his genitals."

"*What!* Are you telling me he's been masturbating on the engine – and in full view of the public as well? I can't believe it! That is truly disgusting; what an insult to one of our greatest ever railway engine designers!"

"It's just something they do isn't it?" said Derek quite nonchalantly. "They don't have inhibitions like we do."

"Obviously not, I was brought up to confine that sort of activity to the privacy of your own bedroom whilst leafing through a well-thumbed copy of *Fiesta* with your other hand, secreted under the mattress for just such occasions. But then I was given a decent upbringing, unlike these shameless Yorkshiremen it seems."

"Sorry – what Yorkshiremen?"

"The Yorkshiremen who hijacked and derailed the maintenance train and now taken over yours."

"No! One of our trains has been derailed has it? I hadn't heard about that. Anyway, it's not a Yorkshireman, is it?"

"What do you mean?" queried Norman.

"Well, chimpanzees come from Africa don't they?

Mr Watkins was not following this at all. "That may be so Derek, I bow to your superior knowledge on the subject, but why would a chimpanzee have anything to do with hijacking your train?"

"Precisely! That's what I'd like to know too!"

It occurred to Norman that he must have somehow missed part of the conversation; though it could well be that Derek was the one not making sense. The stress of being held hostage was obviously getting to him. He tried a different tack.

"Look, I'm a bit confused here Derek. Tell you what, just describe the hijacker for me, it may help the police when they arrive!"

"Yes, its okay, he's busy tapping the gauges at the moment. Well, he's like any other chimpanzee really; you know, hairy, agile, long-limbed and shrieks a lot."

"Sorry, you've lost me again Derek. It must be a bad line; I'm asking for a description of the hijacker, not your all-time favourite primate."

"That's what I've been trying to tell you for the past ten minutes – it's a chimpanzee!"

Mr Watkins sighed and shook his head. Derek had really cracked up now banging on about this chimpanzee; he's obviously getting delusional and seeing things. He reminded himself to leave a note for the company doctor in Derek's medical file once all this was over.

"Look Derek, just calm down and think about it for a moment. How could a chimpanzee possibly hijack a train?"

"I don't know, but it has, and it is driving the train! I repeat – a chimpanzee is driving the train! Look, I thought you already knew this?"

There was a pause as realisation set in. "Are you serious? A *monkey* is in the driving seat?" an incredulous Mr Watkins shouted down the phone.

"Well he's an ape actually, but yes, I thought you said you knew all this, didn't you? Didn't you Norman? Are you still there? Mr Watkins!"

The manager had started to go into shock. His tone of voice

became more distant, "No… no… we didn't know that. We don't know anything… obviously… Malcolm never said…" He dropped the phone. Staring into the middle distance, he slowly repeated back the information to himself, "A chimpanzee… is driving A4 Pacific… Sir George Greatly…" Mr Watkins slumped back in his seat too stunned to speak anymore.

Mr Etherington came over to him.

"Are you all right Mr Watkins? Mr Watkins! You've gone very pale? Do you want a glass of water?"

The manager didn't hear him. Still struggling to comprehend the information, he began to slowly murmur, "A4 Pacific Sir George Greatly… one of the most prestigious steam engines in the world… Its class of engine the holder of the world speed record of 126mph for steam traction… on loan to us at very great expense… and it's being driven by a *chimp!* They'll blame me you know! I'll be held responsible for this fiasco! I'll be a laughing stock when this gets out! And to think I had a good steady job in the accounts department at Rail House… This was to be the pinnacle of my career…" He began to sob.

"Now don't go blaming yourself Mr Watkins, it's not your fault all this has happened."

"You don't understand Etherington! Once the rail regulator and the health and safety executive get hold of this, I'll be drummed out of office!" he sobbed. "I'll never work in the railway industry again! I'm a ruined man!"

Mr Etherington could hear Derek still shouting "Hello, hello!" down the discarded phone. He walked around the office desk and picked up the receiver to answer him.

"Is Mr Watkins still there?" asked Derek. Mr Etherington looked at the whimpering figure, slumped over his desk, repeatedly banging his head against the polished walnut surface.

"Well… yes… er… no, he's er… indisposed you could say at the moment; all the strain y'know. Can I pass on a message?"

"Yes, good news, tell him the chimp has just left the cab."

"Right, just hang on a minute!" Mr Etherington held the

phone to one side. "It's good news Mr Watkins, Derek says the chimpanzee has left the train!"

The manager slowly raised his head, and spluttered in between sobs, "Really? You're not just saying that are you?"

"No, no, it is true Mr Watkins... It is true."

"As... ask... Derek how he managed it," instructed Norman, dabbing his eyes with a handkerchief.

Mr Etherington went back on the phone. "Mr Watkins wants to know how you got him out of the cab."

"Well, I think the bear frightened him off."

"Bear, what bear?"

"Look, I thought you knew all about this; the... bear... that... got... on... the... train... the... same... time... as... the... chimp... after... escaping... from... the... safari... park!" stated Derek very deliberately.

"So you're saying there's a bear on the train now!" Mr Etherington looked directly at Mr Watkins as he spoke. The manager's face froze a second time before going deathly pale again. He let out a long howl of anguish before slumping onto the desk to resume his wailing.

"Please God, don't tell me there's a bear now driving the train! Please... for mercy's sake no!" wailed the manager as he thumped his blotter repeatedly.

"Now, now, Mr Watkins don't go distressing yourself again, bears can't drive trains now can they?"

He paused between sobs to look directly at him. "No, how stupid of me Etherington! Of course bears can't drive trains – just like chimps can't either I suppose!" he screamed.

Mr Etherington thought for a moment. "Er... yes, good point Mr Watkins... good point. I'll just check should I? Best to be on the safe side eh?" He put the question to Derek.

"No, don't be daft, bears' can't drive trains, anyway he's not in the cab now. The guard and two of the chefs chased him into the guard's van. That's what scared the chimp off I reckon. I'm sure the bear wouldn't harm anyone, he's scoffed all the food in the dining car though."

Chapter 28

Marjorie's dander was now well and truly up. Having dealt out her own brand of swift justice to one of the ruffians, she was now looking to see action taken against the rest of the mob.

"We need to summon the on-board staff Ronald and request that the riff-raff be ejected from the train."

"Actually Marjorie, I don't think you can just *'summon'* a person nowadays. It would, I'm sure, be considered too demeaning in today's egalitarian society – equality and employment laws being what they are and all that. I would be most surprised if 'being summoned by a member of the public' featured anywhere in the train staffs' job description."

"That may well be so Ronald, but we can't just let these oafs go around intimidating decent fare-paying passengers; some of these good people are Sarga members too you know. We'll have to go and find the train guard and see what can be done about it."

"Are you sure this is wise?"

"Yes, we have to Ronald! Such behaviour on a preserved heritage railway like this one really needs to be nipped in the bud. Before you know it, they'll be smoking in the toilets next!"

Marjorie slid back the door, poked her head around it, and looked up and down the corridor; her handbag held at the ready just in case.

"Right!" announced Marjorie, "The coast's clear, let's make our way to the refreshment bar, I'm sure there'll be some staff there we can make our representations to."

"Very well Marjorie, but I must insist on leading the way – just in case we do meet some opposition en route. You are in possession of our very own secret weapon as it were. It's a well known military doctrine to keep your assets well to the rear – which is exactly where yours are my dear," he sniggered.

His innuendo was followed up by a squeeze of her ample rump as he eased past her into the corridor. Unaccustomed to such familiarity from her husband, Marjorie took him to task, "Ronald! Behave yourself! We're in a public place now. There seems to be no stopping you, you old goat."

"You don't know what you've unleashed Marjorie, you really don't. But more time for that later eh? We have a mission to fulfil first. Just follow me – and keep that handbag handy!"

Ronald led the way with as much stealth as he could muster, though the combination of age and two arthritic knees did affect the fluidity of his movement as he advanced along the swaying train. On reaching the end of each corridor, he dramatically flattened himself against the carriage wall before cautiously peering around it to see if the way through to the next one was clear. After six carriages Marjorie sighed wearily.

"Ronald, is all this Johnny English stuff absolutely necessary?"

"Look Marjorie, you never know where those Yorkshiremen might appear next – nor that bear either. Both could turn up again at any time. Just stay close to me…" He reached behind him to pat her rump again. "…There's a good girl!"

Marjorie bridled. He was now pushing his patronising luck – but thought it prudent to hold herself in check for the time being.

Ronald looked through the connecting door and could see that they had finally reached the buffet car. Several of what he took to be the same group of Yorkshiremen were gathered around the bar area involved in an altercation with two men, the bigger one of the two dressed in the Worfe Valley Railway company uniform.

After their confrontation with the Yorkshiremen on the railway bridge, Dave and Duggie had been checking out the other trains working services between Middleminster and Bridforth; their concern being for the safety of any girls on board. While waiting for the train at Hempton, they heard from one of the platform staff that the service was running late due to a number of on-board incidents. Although surprised to hear that an escaped chimpanzee and bear had somehow boarded the train, Dave and Duggie nodded knowingly to each other when told there was now trouble being caused by a group of drunken male passengers on board.

When the A4 Pacific and eight coaches eventually pulled into the platform, the two men – now more than familiar with the Yorkshiremen's modus operandi – headed straight for the buffet car. Their arrival was timely. The barman, seeing the familiar face of Duggie, began frantically gesturing to him. The situation needed little in the way of explanation. The yobs, as well as helping themselves to free drinks from the ransacked bar, were now chanting crude rugby songs while enacting scenes referred to in the lines of their ditty.

In an effort to restore some sort of order, Duggie issued a firm but polite request that they all quieten down – and pull up their trousers. This only resulted in more braying from the mob. He demanded to see their tickets. Each one of them claimed to have 'lost' it. If that was the case he said, they would all have to buy another one – or leave the train at the next stop. Laughter erupted again when one of them reminded Duggie that the next stop was the end of the line and *all* the passengers would have to leave the train there.

Duggie was left fuming with frustration. Dave could only stand on the sidelines and sympathise with his predicament. Having no official role on the heritage railway, he could do little to help. But when one of them sought to goad Duggie further by going up to the man and sarcastically thanking him for the free ride, Dave couldn't stop himself from interceding on Duggie's behalf, coming back with a riposte he'd used when faced with a similar situation on Mercia Mainline's trains.

"That's okay. The company always allow free travel for twats, morons and arseholes on a Saturday night. You'll be pleased to know you lot qualify in all three categories!"

The other passengers in the carriage, previously cowed into sullen silence by the mob's behaviour, immediately burst out laughing at the humiliating put-down. This infuriated the Yorkshiremen, whose previous rowdy tone changed to one considerably more menacing.

As the mob made ever more threatening gestures, the other passengers began to edge away from the scene. Then Dave spotted Elena the Estonian girl working her way towards the front. She winked and gave him the thumbs up. Nice gesture, thought Dave, but they needed a bit more than that in the way of help.

His prayers were answered when a group of four men stepped forward to volunteer their services. Dave noticed their sweatshirts bore the emblem of the North Yorkshire Fire and Rescue Service.

The leading fireman explained how they'd had their own run-in with them earlier in the journey when the yobs had mocked the Wensleydale badges on their shirts, shouting out 'more cheese Gromit!' every time one of them walked by. The louts were tarnishing the good name of Britain's premier county and needed a lesson on how to behave in polite society, said the man.

Dave was more than grateful for the offer. After his earlier battle with the Yorkshiremen on the station bridge, he was wondering just how much two men could do against such a belligerent enemy. With another four on their side, they now had a better than even chance of a successful outcome if it came to a fight.

The aggressors appeared reluctant to be drawn into an outright confrontation now that the odds were more evenly stacked. Undecided over what to do next, they began arguing amongst themselves over the best course of action. This encouraged some of the braver passengers to begin jeering them for their lack of courage. The Yorkshiremens' predictable response was another round of abuse. Their bluster only increased the bystanders' goading until, in a desperate attempt to save face, the mob began to lash out at them.

Ronald, observing from the safety of the carriage vestibule, took in the developing situation on the other side of the door. He stood back against the wall of the corridor and whispered the details into Marjorie's nearest ear. The situation as described to her prompted Marjorie to take a look for herself.

When she recognised one of the men as being the person who'd accosted her earlier, her determination to even the score was redoubled. Realising that back-up might well be needed should the situation escalate, Marjorie made herself ready for combat by applying a touch of lipstick and reversing her hat to protect its flourish of silk flowers. With a steely glint in her eye, she issued her decisive words of command, "C'mon Ronald, let's confront these ruffians and leave them in no doubt that their behaviour will not be tolerated by the civilised majority!"

"Are you really sure this is wise Marjorie?" an increasingly apprehensive Ronald asked once again. "We certainly won't have the element of surprise like in our previous brief encounter you know!"

"Yes, but now is not the time to shy away from a fight, nor as you know, is it in my nature too either. This is a matter of principle after all Ronald!"

"Okay, have it your way, but just stay calm and let me do the talking. I want to give them a chance to apologise first."

"If they don't – then what?"

"Er... let's just wait and see shall we?"

A hesitant Ronald entered the carriage pretty much unnoticed, just in time to see the situation take a turn for the worse.

One of the Yorkshireman had begun physically shoving bystanders out of the away and in the process barged into Elena who had been observing the scene with increasing frustration at the lack of action. Pushed back over one of the seats, his actions gave her the excuse she needed and instantly came back with a running kick aimed at the man's groin. He just managed to sidestep this, but in the process, careered into Marjorie as she entered the buffet car.

With no word of apology offered, his lack of manners was all the excuse she needed to whack him with her handbag in retaliation. He in turn made a grab for her. This then stirred Ronald into action, attempting to rescue his wife with a series of chops to the man's upper arms, though seemingly without effect.

Elena suddenly leapt into the air again, delivering a hefty kick to the man's jaw with her feet. Dazed by the force of the blow, he staggered backwards into the counter of the bar, grabbing at the rail for support. One of the other girls seized the opportunity handed to her and produced from her bag a set of furry handcuffs. Quickly snapping one over his wrist, she locked the other cuff onto the rail of the bar, leaving him to struggle impotently on the sidelines.

Duggie was fully engaged in warding off blows from two others who'd been trying to attack Elena; while the barman, in a manner belying his advancing years, danced about the floor using the stick from a green flag to sharply rap the knuckles of any fist that came near him.

In fear of serious harm being done to his wife, Ronald tried to hustle her away from the escalating conflagration. Her handbag was already scuffed and the clasp broken from several blows she had delivered to would-be assailants.

Suddenly, a hand reached out and grabbed Ronald by the throat. The attacker forced his head down hard onto one of the formica-topped tables, and then again a second time.

Powerless against the superior strength of his attacker, a dazed Ronald was just bracing himself for a third impact with the hard surface when, out of the corner of his eye, he spotted what looked like two miniature guided missiles, heading in tandem towards the man with two heads who had just assaulted him. His vision cleared in time to see the rounded end of the black rubber strike his assailant right between the eyes. He wavered for a moment before slumping pole-axed over the table Ronald had just levered himself up from.

He looked in the direction of the aimer and saw that the dildo had been thrown with unerring accuracy by the valiant Elena. She winked and high-fived him. Ronald replied in similar fashion, though not entirely sure whether he'd got the hand gesture right.

Having lost the weighty accessory amongst the scuffling bodies, Elena delved into her handbag for a suitable replacement. She pulled out a butt-plug, one with sufficient girth and length to make its use against any would-be assailant a very painful experience – should she need to use it as a cosh.

With his vision returning to normal, Ronald's first thought was to get Marjorie and himself out of the carriage before further violence was inflicted on them. He pushed through the fighting towards the vestibule, skirting around a fierce contest of fists raging in the corner between one of the firefighters and a Yorkshireman of similar size.

As she reached the door, Marjorie suddenly recoiled. There was something pawing at it from the other side. Ronald, seeing the bear at the same moment quickly pulled her back towards him.

"Unless there are two of them, it must have escaped again. Damn! Don't worry I'll clear a way for us... somehow." His mind raced. "What we need is something to distract him with whilst we make good our escape. Look, go and get behind the bar where you'll be safe, then throw me over some of those packets of nuts and crisps, bears are always looking for food."

"But what about the bear, he might go for you."

"Look, just do as I say will you – there's a good girl!"

Marjorie again found herself complying without questioning. In a way not experienced before, she found herself quite in thrall to Ronald's decisive words of command.

Her husband studied the bear for a moment through the glass door. He looked to be little more than an adolescent and guessed that having been born and raised in the safari park, it would be used to human contact. With the aid of something edible to tempt the bear, he was pretty sure the plan he had hastily formulated would work without any harm to himself. Ronald hoped the Yorkshiremen would have an altogether different reaction when they witnessed the spectacle of a hungry bear amongst them.

He could see that the offenders were not proving easy to defeat. With a bit of luck, he may just be able to tip the balance. He looked over to Marjorie now madly gesticulating to him with the packets of nuts. Holding up his hands, she threw several over to him.

Ronald ripped the first one open and poured a small pile onto the floor. He pulled back the sliding door and backed away. The bear sniffed the air a few times before ambling through to snaffle up the tempting bait. Ronald began laying a trail for the bear to follow, matching his own pace with the bear's until he reached the heels of the leading protagonist. The rest of the Yorkshiremen had by now all stopped in mid-blow to stare at the unexpected sight of a live bear advancing towards them.

The man with his back to the animal was unaware of its presence, but sensed from the looks on other people's faces, that something unusual was taking place behind him. He broke off from trying to wrestle Duggie to the ground and turned around.

This was Ronald's chance. He threw an almost full packet of nuts straight at the Yorkshireman, showering both him and the surrounding floor with food. The man froze as the animal bounded forward to consume the extra bounty. Nervously, he watched the bear as it ate from around his feet.

Suddenly, the animal reared up on its hind legs to pick off the nuts held in the folds of the man's clothing. It was only when the Yorkshireman felt the bear's warm and nutty smelling breath inches from his face that his courage finally failed him. Emitting an anguished cry, he broke free from the bear's foraging muzzle and ran from the carriage. The rest of the yobs looked at one another, then at the bear, then at one another again, before they too reached a similar decision and fled through the same vestibule door.

Ronald, observing the rout was jubilant, and began high-fiving the others gathered together behind the protective barrier of the bar. The ursine interloper showed no interest in the bystanders, he was still busily engaged in hoovering up the remaining nuts scattered across the floor of the carriage.

Marjorie, while keeping an eye firmly on her husband's new

friend, summoned up the courage to leave her position and sidle up to him.

"Well done Ronald – or should I say Grizzly Adams! Yes, I must say I was most impressed with your performing bear act. Is that a smirk of self-satisfaction I can detect on your face?"

"Oh... it was nothing really Marjorie. I just seem to have this rapport with animals you know. Their behaviour is all governed by food. Once I had those peanuts, I had him eating out of my hand – well not literally of course, but I could have done you know Marjorie, I could have done!"

"If you say so Ronald, if you say so. I would though prefer to keep a bit more of a distance between myself and a hungry bear. Yes, all-in-all, I thought we came out of that rather well, though I notice one gentleman has acquired a right shiner."

"Yes, he was the unfortunate victim of a friendly fire incident!"

"Really? From whom?"

"I hate to tell you this, but it was you Marjorie!"

"Me? But I wouldn't have hit him; I knew he was on our side!"

"Yes, but it was when you drew your arm back one time to wallop that big Yorkshireman, you inadvertently hit the man on the backward swing!"

"Really? That's awful of me! I must go over and apologise to the poor man."

"Well I would be quick about it, we should be arriving at Bridforth very soon. I would have thought after all this trouble, the police will be there ready to make a few arrests. I suppose they'll also be wanting to take my new friend back to his home too!" said Ronald out loud, ruffling the hair on the bear's neck as it ambled back along the peanut trail, searching for any missed along the way.

"You're just a softy really, aren't you?" Ronald called out after him. As he spoke, Ronald noticed the train slowing on its approach.

He looked out of the window as the train pulled into the station and saw that the police were indeed in attendance, peering through the window of each carriage as it entered the platform.

When it came to a stop, Ronald heard shouting coming from the rear of the train. He looked out again and saw several of the men they'd just battled with fleeing in the direction of the station exit. The train guard was gesticulating wildly to the policemen who very quickly took up the chase. Marjorie chose that moment to extend a further compliment to her husband, "I have to say I was very taken by your authority... er, over that bear I mean, Ronald. As you say, you certainly seemed to have a way with the animal."

Flushed with confidence at his no small victory, he edged up closer to his wife and whispered, "That's nothing compared to this animal waiting to have his way with you again once we get home Marjorie!"

Marjorie's cheeks immediately coloured up. "Ronald, stop it! You're making me blush." Her imagination, now infused with the thought of what he might have in store for her, caused a shiver of excitement to run through her body. It prompted a question.

"So... er... in your estimation, how long will it be before we do actually arrive home?"

Dave, his eye still smarting, was trying to prise Duggie away from Elena. He was aware of the police working their way through the train and wanted to get away before their arrival at the buffet car.

Following Duggie's battle of fists with the two Yorkshiremen, Elena had cast several admiring glances in his direction as they sat recounting the blows together. When her advances went unnoticed she tried a less subtle approach, throwing Duggie a playful punch to the chest before asking if he was interested in some 'sport.' Duggie's eyes lit up. No woman had ever been willing to take him on before, so he eagerly accepted Elena's challenge of an arm wrestle.

Dave insisted there was simply no time for such games; they had to be going now! Elena looked disappointed but agreed to release her grip on him. Banging her fist into his, she blew him a kiss; then, as they parted, tucked a business card into his top pocket.

Well, at least that solves the problem of finding a girl prepared to volunteer their services for him, thought Dave.

With Duggie still waving an effusive goodbye to his new-found ladyfriend, they slipped anonymously onto the platform and headed for the nearest pub to partake of a much-needed pint or three. A barman about to take their order took one look at Dave and said, "Blimey, you've been in the wars haven't you mate! You want to put a bit of steak on that!"

"Yes… well, I don't know about steak," replied Dave, "but I've got some frozen peas back home. They did work very well before in a similar situation."

Chapter 29

Sgt Edwards was becoming increasingly impatient with the lack of activity within the Bland household. He'd been here for over three hours now and there had not been so much as a twitch of the curtains. With several cars parked in the driveway, he was sure something must be going on inside, but as to what exactly, he was none the wiser. He'd played all the games on his phone twice over, read his newspaper from cover to cover, and had just tried for the third time to complete the sudoku puzzle.

After first dismissing the thought, just minutes later he found himself rummaging around in the glovebox looking for the vehicle's instruction manual. Thinking it might be quite useful to know the strength of anti-freeze required for a Canadian winter, he began to leaf through the pages relating to Arctic conditions. He was just working his way down the list of possible causes should the engine fail to start in a temperature of 30 degrees below, when he was startled by a knock on his window. Turning towards the figure standing there, he recognised the woman as Mrs Battersly, the Bland's next door neighbour. Lowering the window, he nodded a perfunctory greeting to her.

"'Scuse me for interrupting you Sergeant, I just happened to be dusting the pelmet in the front room when I noticed you sitting here. So I thought, if you're waiting to see that Mr Bland, then you're out of luck, because he went off hours ago with those ladies – well, if you could call them that. I was just wiping the condensation off the windows at the time when I saw them all walk by."

Sgt Edwards looked startled by the news. "Really! So he's not in the house then?"

"No, as I say, he went out hours ago."

"And with some ladies you say?"

"Yes, they looked like a bunch of tarts if I'm honest."

"Really? Do you happen to know where they were going?"

"No, unfortunately I couldn't quite hear what they were saying, although I did have the window open – just to help the condensation dry out you understand – we haven't got double glazing; I think it cuts out too much sound. Anyway, like I say, I couldn't make out what they were saying. Not that I was tryin' to be nosey you understand, it's not in my nature to spy on folk."

"Yes Mrs Battersee, I can see that... Hmm, it's a pity I didn't know earlier."

"Why, is he in some sort of trouble then? 'Cos you know he's got a Russian woman living with him, don't you? And she comes and goes at all sorts of funny times of the day. Mind he does the same, what with him workin' on the railway. It's a job sometimes to work out whether they're in or not!"

He realised he needn't have bothered keeping a close watch on the Bland house himself, this Mrs Battersly would have been quite capable of doing the job for him.

"No, we're just pursuing a few lines of enquiry that's all Mrs Buttersly, nothing for you to be concerned about."

After further reassurances that he could manage perfectly well without her help, she returned inside, though her silhouette could still be seen lurking behind the net curtains.

This was further proof that this Bland character was running a vice ring from his house. Why else would he be in the company of such a group of women? But where would he have been taking them; to work the local streets? Surely not, there was a Marts & Spender only just down the road. He really needed to follow up this latest development and find out just what sort of operation this Dave Bland was running.

Just then his phone burst into life. Sgt Edwards answered and was thoroughly alarmed by what he heard, asking WPC Mitchell a series of questions – some more than once. Satisfied that he had understood all the details, the sergeant ended the call and raced off to the scene.

In the early hours of the following morning, PCs Wilson and Mitchell together with Sgt Edwards were waiting to be called through into the boss's office at the Mercia Transport Police HQ in Wensbury. The evening had been an extremely eventful one, with all three becoming involved in the later stages of apprehending the Yorkshiremen fleeing from justice. After much discussion between themselves beforehand, the three detectives had handed in their carefully compiled reports to the DI's office. They had a very compelling reason for ensuring their version of events contained no obvious inconsistencies.

To pass the time while they anxiously awaited the post-incident interview with their detective inspector, WPC Mitchell began filling in some of the detail of what had taken place earlier in the evening for the benefit of Sgt Edwards who had been late on the scene.

"Yes, it seems some of the train crew and members of a ladies rugby team who also happened to be on board all helped in apprehending them. Oh, and a recent acquaintance of ours, Dave Bland; he led a very successful defence of the station earlier in the evening by all accounts."

Instantly seizing on the name, Sgt Edwards snapped, "Dave Brand! What was he doing there?"

"Well, he lives in Bridforth and he works in the railway industry, so I guess he was there because he was interested in the events taking place over the weekend," she explained.

"I bet he was, any prostitutes involved by any chance?" he sneered, still trying to make a connection with his own line of enquiry.

"No, not that I'm aware of, why?"

"Oh… nothing – but a ladies rugby team you say?"

"Yes, an East European one apparently."

That was it! So he was right all along. It all fell into place now.

Damn and damn again! It seems he was in the wrong place at the wrong time. Never mind, people like Bland think they're too clever to make mistakes, but by God, he would get him on his next foray at the station!

The next moment the DI put his head round the door and called them through into his office. He'd been recalled back to the station due to the serious nature of the evening's events. Having read through their individual reports, he now needed clarification on certain points, so addressed his questions to all three detectives assembled in front of him.

"Right first of all, what's the news on the escaped animals; have they all been rounded up yet?"

"Yes we believe so; we're just awaiting final confirmation of numbers from the safari park," replied WPC Mitchell.

"So no problems there then?"

"Well, a member of the public was accidently tranquilised during the recapturing.

"Good grief, how did that happen?"

"It seems that a young couple were having a 'liaison' as it were in the local park. One of the search team heard grunting noises coming from some bushes and well… assumed it to be one of the animals."

"Is the person alright?"

"Yes, apparently the after effects are like a massive hangover and it could be a day or two before the gentleman can sit down. The safari park might have a compensation claim to deal with though."

"Okay then, next question. Were the Yorkshiremen who took the train that was derailed all picked up? It doesn't exactly say here."

No one spoke. The Detective Inspector looked up to study their faces. Sergeant Edwards shot a sideways glance at the other two before reluctantly offering himself up as their spokesman. "Er, all except er… one, actually chief."

"The one who got away eh?" joked the DI as he looked up from the page. He noticed his jocular tone out of kilter with the sombre expressions worn by his junior colleagues. What was wrong with them he wondered? Despite one of the villains still being at large, they'd had a good result here.

"Well... not exactly got away as such... we think we know where... er... he is!" replied an increasingly uneasy Sgt Edwards.

"If that's the case, why have you not arrested him then?" The DI looked at all three in turn. Again, no one spoke. The DI tapped his fingers on the desk and waited for an answer.

"C'mon then, somebody say something!"

"Well... er, because we have a problem." said the sergeant, shifting his stance once again.

The Detective Inspector, puzzled by their reluctance to elaborate, looked from one to the other then back again. "So then, c'mon what's the problem? He's not died on us has he?" The DI laughed at the implausibility of it.

Sgt Edwards shifted his stance. "Well... it's funny you should say that. The thing is...well, er... unfortunately... it appears one of the escaped lions got to him before we did, and er... well, we believe he's... well... been eaten!"

"*Eaten!* You are joking aren't you?"

All three stayed ominously silent.

"Come on, this has got to be a wind up! Hasn't it?"

All three gave an almost imperceptible shake of their heads.

"No! Seriously? You're saying the missing Yorkshireman has been *eaten* by one of the escaped lions?"

The trio nodded in unison.

"This is incredible! I'm stunned... I've never heard anything like it!"

"We have got the perpetrator though boss," DC Wilson quickly added... Well, we reckon we know the lion that did it. The victim... er Darren Pickersgill as was, apparently, his mate was on the scene soon afterwards, and is sure he could pick the offender out of a line-up; he had a sort of a light-coloured streak on his mane."

"Is this a joke?"

"No, straight up boss!"

I'm sure knowing the identity of the perpetrator will be a big comfort for the victim's family! What am I supposed to say to them eh? Sorry madam, your son's been eaten by a lion – but it's not all bad news. We do have a witness, and once we hold an identity parade, we're certain he'll be able to pick out the one that devoured your lad."

"Not here at the station obviously. We'd have to take the witness to the lion pen and do it there," the DC was quick to point out.

"I was being sarcastic! Do you seriously think for one minute that I would actually contemplate bringing a herd of man-eating lions into the station and hold an identity parade with them?" asked the incredulous DI.

"No, I s'pose not boss. Sorry, silly saying it really," conceded the DC.

"It's a pride actually," said WPC Mitchell.

"What's a pride?" snapped the DI.

"A group of lions is called a pride," she explained.

"Is it? Well I'm sure I'm a lot better off for knowing that. Look, this is a serious matter – that is if it turns out to be true. Despite your so-called witness, I'm still not entirely convinced. I mean who's ever heard of a lion kept in captivity eating somebody? Don't they feed them in that safari park? How do you know he's not simply done a runner from the scene?"

"Well..." said WPC Mitchell, "We found a watch, and a shoe that had teeth marks in it. That apparently was all that was left of him. The animal keeper said if we waited a day or so, we could have the droppings to get scientifically examined for definite confirmation."

"I don't believe I'm hearing this! Are you seriously telling me all we'll have to present to the family in respect of their dear departed son will be a laboratory-examined lion's turd, forensically proven to contain the last remains of their loved one? I'm sure the family will really appreciate that little memento of their son. Think how nice it'll look sat in a casket on the mantelpiece!"

While the three detectives made a close study of the floor, the DI sat digesting the information. "You know if it does all turn out to be as you say, the single most important question everyone will ask, is why we didn't prevent it. There'll be an investigation of course. All sorts of questions will be asked about our conduct. You'd all better be able to account for your actions at the time and can justify what you did – or rather what you didn't do yesterday. Unfortunately, as seems to be the way of things nowadays, the responsibility for saving people from the consequences of their own stupidity will be put down to us.

"God knows what the press are going to make of it all when they find out. You can just imagine the headlines. They'll have a field day over this; going over our actions piece by piece trying to pick the whole thing apart. Just make sure there's nothing for them to unravel! Got it?"

All three nodded.

"Have the family been informed?"

"I understand the West Yorkshire force is sending an officer round," replied WPC Mitchell.

"You know I'm still stunned… I can't imagine what the super's going to make of it all. He sat back in his chair and studied the ceiling while he gathered his thoughts.

"So Sgt Edwards, what were you doing while all this was going on?"

"Me chief? Well, er… I was well, ensuring that no further casualties occurred."

"And how exactly did you achieve that then?"

"Er… by keeping a safe distance from the danger in question."

"Yes that would do it! Keep well away from the crime scene, so a lion can go and eat chummy undisturbed."

"It wasn't quite like that!"

"So how was it then? Do tell me!"

"Well unfortunately I was late on the scene due to a surveillance operation I was conducting…"

"Yes I've heard about that. Apparently, you seem to have been under the impression that the very same Dave Bland who helped defend the station at Bridforth, is running a vice ring in the town. So with absolutely no evidence to back up your theory, you spend over three hours sat outside his house waiting for this group orgy to commence – if only my own house were to see that sort of action on a Saturday night! Meanwhile, not a million miles away this man Darren Pickersgill gets to be the evening special for an escaped lion!"

"But to be fair boss, there would have been very little I could have done to save him. Well… not without putting myself and my colleagues in considerable danger. I took the view that I should stay focused on ensuring the success of the operation."

"But it wasn't, was it?"

"Wasn't what?"

"A success I mean. A man was eaten for God's sake!"

"Well… yes… granted, but it's not like it was our fault, was it? After all he was the one who derailed the train that smashed through the lion's compound, so in a way you could say he got his just desserts!"

"Or rather the lion did… along with his main course too!" quipped the DI.

The three detectives exchanged looks with one other. Had the boss really intended to make a joke out of such human tragedy? Their answer came when the detective inspector started to giggle, quietly at first, then becoming increasingly louder. Soon he was rocking backwards and forwards in his chair helpless with laughter. The three detectives, stuck for an appropriate response, looked on in bewilderment.

Sgt Edwards, seeing a chance to ingratiate himself with his boss, took the initiative. "Ha ha… yes, very good… sir," and began chuckling along with him. The other two eventually resorted to doing the same, their forced laughter closely matching the affected mirth of their sergeant.

Chapter 30

Later that same morning, Norman Watkins was standing nervously in the outer office of the Worfe Valley Railway HQ at Bridforth waiting to be called in to address the hastily convened emergency board meeting. His face displayed the expression of a desperately worried man, as did his actions; repeatedly pacing up and down the lino covered floor as he waited to be called through.

The general manager had found little sleep during the night even though his wife had laced his nightly Bournvita with a good measure of brandy. Every time he did manage to succumb, the phone would soon wake him with a call from one or other of the different agencies involved in the continuing recovery operations; the responsibility of overseeing it all just adding to his already high stress levels.

It was the repercussions that followed from the events of the previous day and evening that now weighed most heavily on his mind. More than once he reflected on why he had allowed himself to take on a job with such onerous responsibilities. He should have taken his wife's advice at the time and stuck to his previous accounting position. As she said when he applied for the Worfe Valley Railway General Manager's position, 'Now don't go getting ideas above your station Norman, you're fifty-six now, with a good steady job at Railway Control HQ and with a nice pension at the end of it. You don't want to give all that up do you? In all the thirty-eight years there, you've never once mentioned changing your job, so where have you suddenly found all this ambition from?'

He was unable to supply her with a ready answer at the time; he didn't really know himself the reasons why. It may have been that he was looking for a measure of excitement in his advancing years; double-entry bookkeeping just didn't seem to have the irresistible lure it once held for him. Despite his wife's advice to the contrary, he found himself completing the application form and sidling down to the end of the road to post it.

Pleasantly surprised to hear that he had been selected for an interview, Norman was taken aback on the day to be actually offered the position; so flattered, in fact, that he didn't feel able to refuse it. Now he found himself wishing that he had, rather than ignoring his wife's dictum of 'Stick to what you know Norman.' If he had stuck to what he knew, then he wouldn't be in the fix he was in now.

Norman had risen early, having given up on any further hope of sleep; he was an eight and a half hours a day man normally. With no appetite for breakfast, half his morning had been spent dealing with the continuing inquiries from colleagues and the various authorities involved.

It had all happened too late the previous evening for the national newspapers to report the story, but as he discovered, local TV and radio were both leading with the colourful drama. Inevitably, it was the incident with the train-driving chimpanzee that featured prominently. It would, he reasoned, also be the one to cause the most problems for the Worfe Valley Railway and ultimately himself, as the overall man in charge.

Allowing an unqualified ape to drive a passenger-carrying train would undoubtedly be considered a grave safety of the line offence in the eyes of the rail regulators, (Light Railways Dept.) and the health and safety executive. Although, having scoured the rulebook during the early hours of the morning when sleep was proving impossible, he could find no clause that specifically forbade it.

If he was to still have a job tomorrow, he knew he needed to give a good account of his actions today, so had taken the precaution of preparing some arguments to counter the difficult questions he would surely be asked.

With the time for his appointment with the board drawing near, he had made his preparations to leave the house. Feeling like the condemned man about to take his final walk, he stood on the doorstep and kissed his wife goodbye. Breaking from his thirty-eight year routine, he gave her an additional second kiss on the cheek for good measure.

This signalled the point at which his wife handed over his sandwich box containing by tradition, two cheese sandwiches, a scotch egg, an apple, and on this particular day, an extra large slice of Bakewell tart.

"I thought you just might need a bit of extra fuel to keep you going," his wife had explained, seeking to lend a gesture of support to her beleaguered husband.

Still pre-occupied with what lay in store for him, he only absently returned her wave as he set off in his car to the office.

Suddenly, the door opened, framing their patron in the doorway. Lord Lovernock immediately locked eyes on him. *This is it,* thought Norman. *Brace yourself, give as good as you get, the inquisition is about to begin.*

The peer said not a word as he advanced towards him. Stopping a few feet short, he fixed the manager with his steely gaze. The intensity of his stare only increased Norman's discomfort, causing little beads of sweat to form on his brow. He sought refuge in a study of his feet, using the brief respite to go through once more in his head, the fulsome apology he was about to make. Norman heard the patron give a little cough. The peer would be unaccustomed to being kept waiting; he could delay no longer.

But on looking up again, he could barely contain his surprise at the change in the man. Now beaming from ear to ear and with his arms held out in a welcoming gesture, the peer looked as if he was about to greet a long-lost friend. Given the pickle he was in, this was not quite the reaction he'd had expected. He glanced round to see if there was someone else standing behind him before wiping his sweat-stained palm down the side of his trousers. A formal handshake now seemed a distinct possibility.

Lord Lovernock closed in on Norman, greeting him with a hearty slap on the back before grabbing hold of his tentatively proffered hand.

"Good morning Watkins, it's good to see you again. Yes, very good indeed. I'm glad you could make it so soon. I dare say you've not had a lot of sleep eh Watki... er... it's Norman, isn't it Watkins?"

The station manager was still reeling from the effusive greeting. "Yes, er... well... it is you too, and no I haven't really... and er, yes it is... er, thank you," said Norman, trying to remember each snippet of question and respond appropriately to each one; though not necessarily in the right order he realised afterwards.

"So let me say first of all well done! Praise is most certainly well deserved in your case, so well done indeed... er, Norman."

Following the lead taken by their official patron, the rest of the board members followed suit, coming through from the boardroom to enthusiastically shake his hand. Many added their own words of praise, along with some hefty pats on the back.

Norman was stunned, what on earth had happened to make him the recipient of such unexpected bonhomie?

A now bemused Norman followed the board members back into the room. By way of an answer to his question, Lord Lovernock rose to officially convene the meeting and address the assembled members.

"Gentlemen, before we get down to business, I'm sure you would all like to join me in officially congratulating Wat... er... Norman here, on his brilliant handling of what must have been a very difficult situation he was faced with yesterday. On behalf of the Worfe Valley Railway Board, I'd just like to say a very big thank you once again. Now before I reveal the full detail of Norman's role in it all, I'd just like to briefly recap on the days events.

"Yesterday afternoon the Worfe Valley Railway – our railway – was targeted by what I can only describe as a gang of thugs from Yorkshire. Hell-bent on causing trouble, they targeted our passengers, rolling stock and infrastructure with a view to causing as much damage and disruption as possible to all three. Their motive you ask? Well, it appears these persons are themselves members of the Postlethwaite Rail and Tramway Society, a little known heritage railway based in Postlethwaite, Yorkshire.

"It seems that P.R.A.T.S – if I may use the highly appropriate acronym – is suffering severe financial difficulties due to a dwindling number of visitors and for some reason, these members felt that the blame rests with us. As we all know, our railway is the premier preserved steam railway in Great Britain and the numbers of visitors we attract reflects that, together with a proportionate amount of public and media interest.

"Their perception it seems, was that we were drawing in visitors that might otherwise have patronised their preserved railway. How they came to this conclusion is not really understood. But even if that were true, how that could then justify their deliberate attempt to sabotage our railway is yet to be explained. I understand that we have recently enlisted some volunteers who were former members of P.R.A.T.S, and this may have exacerbated the situation.

"So gentlemen, that explains the motive behind the attacks. Regarding the attacks themselves, fortunately they did not cause the widespread disruption the perpetrators intended. As well as our own staff, we have to thank a certain Mr Dave Bland, along with several stout-hearted members of the public, for their sterling efforts in defending this station during a prolonged assault on its facilities. Some members of a visiting East European ladies rugby team also gave assistance too I understand. Individually, these ladies made a good account in themselves fending off the unwarranted attentions of these thugs. They also helped to disable and capture a number of them during a major confrontation in the buffet car of the 'Shropshire Flyer,' pulled by our guest engine, Sir George Greatly.

"One unfortunate casualty was our maintenance train, derailed after being hijacked by them in an attempt to escape from the police. The thugs, it seems, were unaware that two of their own had removed a section of the track ahead of them. This resulted in the train leaving the rails at a point adjacent to the West Mercia Safari Park and crashing through various pens and compounds within the site.

"Unfortunately, this in turn caused the release of a number of wild animals, some dangerous, some less so. The latest information I have is that nearly all have now, thankfully, been recaptured. The rail was reconnected almost immediately after the derailment and the train will be recovered in due course once the heavy lifting equipment is in place after the weekend.

"Now we come to the reason for our hearty thanks to our General Manager, Norman Watkins. As well as dealing with all the disruption caused by the mob of Yorkshiremen, he was also faced with a situation where one of the escaped chimpanzees from the safari park had climbed into the cab of Sir George Greatly whilst the booked driver was being detained at the signal box. This could have caused the Worfe Valley severe problems with the regulatory authorities if the chimp – Bobo, I think his name is – had taken over the train, and actually driven it. Yes... a ridiculous notion I know gentlemen, but apparently this particular chimp has a keen interest in trains, and it seems this was the reason why the chimpanzee had climbed aboard the engine.

"So it was truly an inspired idea of Norman's – that is the only way I can describe it – with his cunning plan to convince the paying public that Bobo was indeed driving the locomotive! It is surely testimony indeed to Norman's quick thinking and promotional flair to turn what could have been a catastrophe into a fantastic coup for the railway! In fact it would be no exaggeration to say that Norman here has pulled off the publicity stunt of the year!

"I don't think I need to remind everybody what a disastrous weekend it would have been had these thugs succeeded in their sabotage attempts. By the brilliant use of Bobo in diverting the public's attention away from the disruption caused to our services,

Norman has not only maintained visitor numbers for the weekend, but has vastly increased them. If you would all care to look out of the window you will see exactly what I mean."

The assembled men promptly left their seats and gathered round as their patron drew up the blinds and threw open the boardroom window. They were instantly met by a cacophony of sound coming from the crowd of people down below. Men, women and children of all ages were calling out a variety of chants, shouts, and calls... and all directed towards the now famous chimpanzee, "We want Bobo! – When do we want him? – Now! Now! Now!" The slogan being repeated over and over again. Banners and placards too, all boldly made the same demand.

The ranks of adults and children were further swelled by hastily despatched teams of TV crews and reporters passing amongst them recording soundbites from individuals in the crowd. The board all agreed that it was an incredible sight; nothing like it had been seen before.

"As you can see gentlemen, the reaction to Norman's inspired wheeze has been phenomenal. The spectacle of a chimpanzee driving – or more accurately appearing to drive a train – has really caught the public's imagination. The Worfe Valley Railway has never seen so many people all at one time. We've had to close the car park and direct the waiting visitors to other sites in the town."

Lord Lovernock stood in silence as the assembled board took in the scene for a few more minutes.

"So gentlemen, if we can retake our places, I think it's time to hear a few words from the man himself."

The peer stretched out an arm in Norman's direction as he sat down, prompting a hearty round of applause from around the table. The general manager stood up feeling utterly lost for words. He had been flabbergasted at the unexpected turn of events and was quite unprepared for this moment. He'd arrived at the meeting prepared to be condemned, not congratulated. Though the actual events were not quite as described, he certainly didn't want to disavow the board of their impression of his actions the previous day. A modest speech of acceptance seemed the most appropriate form of words he decided.

"Well er... gentlemen... it was nothing really, anybody else would have done the same, I'm sure…"

Norman paused for a moment to take in the beaming faces looking back at him. In all his thirty-eight years at Railway Control HQ he'd never been praised once. He found himself revelling in the attention being shown to him and wanted to savour the moment for as long as he could. As he stood basking in their admiration, the manager was unable to resist playing up his role in the previous day's events.

"…though on reflection yes, I suppose it was an inspired move on my part to turn the situation with the chimpanzee to our advantage and so create a big publicity coup for the railway. But then the ability to keep cool in a crisis has always been a particular forte of mine, oh yes! Long years spent in a challenging accounts department role does teach you a thing or two about the need to take swift, decisive action in order to resolve critical situations. Of course there were a few around me panicking about what to do for the best – no names mind! But I could see with absolute clarity the course of action I needed to take... oh yes. Yes... er, indeed!"

He paused to reflect for a moment. A further round of applause from the board members filled the silence. Now suddenly embarrassed by the appreciation shown to him after his heavily gilded address, Norman's modest nature began to reassert itself.

"So… er... gentlemen, thank you for your very kind words... I'm glad it worked out so well in the end... I'll just er... carry on as normal then?"

As Norman sat down, Lord Lovernock stood up to lead the final applause before answering. "Thank you Norman, yes please do carry on as normal. It's what you do so well!" He waited for their hand-clapping to die down before continuing.

"So gentlemen, we can see that having a chimpanzee acting out the role of driver on a real steam train has really caught people's imagination. If we think back to how successful the PG Tips chimpanzee adverts on TV were some years ago, we should not really be surprised. The railway has literally been inundated with requests for information about the incident. The phone has not stopped ringing all morning. I have had to ask Miss Pelling our receptionist to come in today specifically to take the calls – and we still can't cope with the volume!

"The publicity alone is worth millions as well as promoting a wealth of goodwill towards us, with the public both sympathetic due to the damage and disruption caused, and amused at the thought of a chimp driving a steam train. We therefore fully expect visitor numbers to keep on rising for some time to come.

"As you can imagine, the marketing opportunities are endless, Bobo books, Bobo tee shirts, mugs, stickers, etc. Already this morning, the idea has been mooted that we produce our own DVD with him as the central character in a series of adventures, along with a Johnny Morris type commentary. If we look at how successful the Thomas the Tank engine brand is in all its different media guises, we get an idea of what is possible in exploiting the opportunity presented to us. We have though, just one problem in all of this…"

He paused, the faces of the board members all turned expectantly towards their Patron. "…Without regular appearances from an actual chimpanzee on the footplate, people will feel cheated, interest will quickly tail off and we'll be left back where we started. Therefore, I propose that we contact the safari park in question and begin urgent negotiations with a view to 'leasing' Bobo as it were, for regular public appearances. I understand that he is well used to human contact, and also has a genuine fascination for steam trains. If you are all in agreement with this proposal then I'm sure that we can leave the matter in the capable hands of Norman here to push through such a deal, eh Norman?"

An open-mouthed Norman just managed to stutter a response. "Er… yes… of course… Er… would he be employed on the normal hourly rate for a driver? Or maybe you were thinking of the equivalent in bananas – or some other type of fruit perhaps?"

"We'll just leave you to sort out the detail Norman. You've proved yourself more than capable."

"Yes... er... Sir... quite; if you say so."

Chapter 31

That same morning Dave and Galina were sat at home listening intently to their local radio station. After the drama of their own exploits the previous day on the Worfe Valley Railway, both were eager to learn the full story behind the other dramatic events occurring over the weekend.

As expected, the latest news bulletin led with the astonishing story of a man being devoured by a lion, linking the victim with the gang of Yorkshiremen who were suspected of carrying out the malicious attacks on the railway. The gruesome nature of the man's demise – one unprecedented in the UK – led to a scramble by the media to cover every conceivable aspect of the story.

Over on TV, airtime was given to a special documentary on lions, covering its habits and normal diet of prey. A discussion in the studio followed, with an expert on lion behaviour invited on to speculate why, and under what circumstances, this type of predator would be likely to attack and eat a human being. The guest went on to quote figures for the number of such attacks and described recent examples.

He ended the discussion with a warning to the public that a fully-grown lion was an extremely dangerous animal and should never be approached in the wild. A touch over-dramatic, thought Dave. If there were any feral lions roaming over the sweeping savannah lands of the West Midlands, he'd yet to see one.

The police had inevitably sought statements from everybody involved in the series of events that led up to the fatal incident. Dave, thinking that to refuse might attract undue suspicion, duly obliged them, though the attention was something he and Galina would prefer to have done without.

Luckily Galina had been primed to give a very convincing performance as the 'manager' of the Eastern European ladies rugby team. With the girls feigning ignorance of anything but basic knowledge of the English language, it enabled Galina to act out her role as the girls' interpreter.

Naturally the answers translated by her for the interviewing officer tied in nicely with their concocted cover story. Unfortunately, over-confidence got the better of her one time, and in her desire to convince the police of their subterfuge, she challenged the assembled officers to put together a team of WPC's for her girls to play against. Luckily all were non-committal apart from one very well-built WPC who promised to find out if her mates were 'up for it!' Excuses would have to be made if anything further came of it.

Financially, the weekend had turned out to be a modest success. The ladies were showing a healthy profit, and his cut from each of the girls more than covered his expenses, leaving a tidy sum left over to use as working capital next time.

Taking an overall view of things, he realised that rather than just a one-off, the enterprise could be repeated next year, and maybe at other suitable heritage railway sites too. And if at some point a more liberal political climate were to allow the legalisation of prostitution, then he could see a wealth of marketing opportunities opening up – a combined gift package for instance.

Paying just one fee, the recipient of the gift card would be entitled to a ride on the Worfe Valley Railway followed by a session with one of the girls. Not so much a 'Red Letter Day' – more a 'French Letter Day', he decided in a moment of whimsy.

There were a few things he needed to tweak first. He'd already written out several pages of notes, one of the most important being to modify the special clamps for holding the compartment doors shut. There had been several close calls with passengers defeating the current design. A more robust Mark two version was definitely required!

By mid-afternoon, with the steam weekend drawing to a close, the mission was virtually complete and the ladies began arriving back in their ones and twos. Bacon and eggs were being prepared in readiness for them, together with a glass or two of champagne. In a reckless moment, Dave had bought several bottles in anticipation of the operation proving a success.

After a quick debrief of each girl in order to record their individual tallies, Dave had envisaged a quiet evening for himself and Galina after all the excitement. What he had not expected was Galina's suggestion – seized on enthusiastically by 'Rina – that they hold an impromptu party.

The rest of the girls were equally as keen to celebrate with their new-found work colleagues. As if out of nowhere, bottles of vodka appeared, whilst from the kitchen came pickles and other nibbles of a distinctly Russian flavour, stockpiled by Galina for just such an occasion.

Soon the party was in full swing with latecomers joining in as they arrived back. The volume of the conversation, fed by a steady stream of vodka, gradually got louder, with shrieks of laughter piercing the air at regular intervals. Dave, curious about the cause of such amusement, gleaned from the girls' gesticulations that the male sex organ featured prominently in many instances, or perhaps not so prominently if the little finger gestures that accompanied the raucous laughter were anything to go by.

Next door, Mrs Battersly was taking a keen interest in her neighbour's party. She had observed the return of the girls to the house and committed the details to her mental log. The noise, music, and shrieks of laughter filtering through her conveniently-opened windows, were all duly noted too. Inconveniently though, no line of sight into the Bland household was available from her viewing point. She took her Windoclene and dusters upstairs, but that proved no better for the purposes of confirming her growing suspicions.

Thinking the front bedroom window might afford her a better view, she took herself in there – just in time to see an expensive-looking car pull up outside her neighbour's house. A tall languid man stepped out from it holding a bouquet of flowers. He looked down at a piece of paper and checked it against the number on the wall of the house.

Apparently satisfied, the stranger rang the doorbell twice before being answered by a scantily-clad girl, who seemed more than pleased to see the man judging by the way she greeted him. Mrs Battersly had seen enough. She came back downstairs, reached for the telephone, and dialled the number.

"Hello, could I speak to Sgt Edwards please?"

The extension number rang for some time before activating a remote answerphone message. Mrs Battersly held herself in check for the duration.

"Hello! Yes... well, you asked me to give you a ring if I was to see anything suspicious going on next door. Well there is... Sorry, I didn't leave my name did I? It's Mrs Battersly here from No. 21 Richmond Street, Bridforth.

"Yes, it looks to me like some sort of orgy going on next door. There must be at least a dozen girls in there cavorting about. You should hear all the shrieking and carrying on. Then just a few minutes ago a man turned up at the door, all chauffeur-driven and posh-like. One of the floozies lets him in straightaway – I reckon he was a 'customer' if you know what I mean. Lord knows what they're up to in there now, but the cat's just been put out of the backdoor and that's never happened this early in the evening before! There's got to be something going on in there they don't want Arthur to see. I should get there quick if I were you. Well that's about it, Sgt Edwards, er... I'll leave it with you then?"

Mrs Battersly thanked the sergeant in his absence and put down the phone, satisfied that she had done her duty as a conscientious citizen. As an animal lover herself, Mrs Battersly had always taken it upon herself to not only learn the names and personal habits of her near neighbours, but also of their pets too.

Although his visit was not unexpected, Dave still expressed his surprise on greeting the peer in the hallway of his house, politely offering Lord Lovernock a drink in the same breath.

When Dave had first been told of Lord Lovernock's intention to call on him, given the nature of the weekend's activities, it was not something he would have encouraged. But after giving the matter some consideration, he thought there might be some advantages in getting better acquainted with the railway's patron, especially as he had shown such a keen interest in Sammi. Dave had formulated the rudiments of a plan to get the peer on-side. He might well prove to be a useful ally in the future.

The visitor took a moment to cast an eye around the room before answering. His attention was immediately drawn to the group of girls, particularly so after Sammi gave him a wave.

"Yes, why not, as there appears to be a something of a party going on here, may as well join in with whatever it is you're celebrating."

"...Oh, we're all just winding down after the weekend you know, and what a weekend it was eh?" responded Dave, anxious to take the conversation in a different direction.

"Indeed it was... all now resolved satisfactorily I'm glad to say – which incidentally brings me to the reason I called in to see you. I hope you didn't mind but that delightful Siamese girl... er Sammi is it? – We took tea together you know – said she thought you wouldn't mind me dropping in on you. I really wanted to thank you and the ladies personally on behalf of myself and the Worfe Valley Railway for all your sterling efforts in coming to its aid. From what I've been told, you all showed exceptional courage in confronting those ruffians.

"I must say though that's quite a black eye you received for your troubles, I hope you managed to return the favour."

"Well I was hit by a handbag actually, and as I understand it, the lady in question was only trying to help, I just put the mistake down to the fog of war," said Dave.

"I see, collateral damage as our American allies would call it.

But I was about to say, as a token of our gratitude, the Worfe Valley Railway would like to offer you all complimentary tickets for next year's steam extravaganza. I'd also like to present this bouquet of flowers to your good lady."

"That's excellent! And you're most kind, thank you," replied Dave. He called Galina over to take them from him.

"Thernk you very much, they are most beautiful," she said while exchanging a conspirital look with Dave. "I'll jurst take them through into the kirtchen."

"I'm sure we can make use of the tickets. It just so happens that the ladies fully intend to return again next year – for some more sporting action as it were," said Dave

"Excellent! Excellent! I'll arrange for the tickets to be sent out at the appropriate time."

"Thank you once again Lord Lovernock; another drink perhaps?"

"I don't mind if I do. I say, this Russian vodka packs quite a punch!"

"Ah yes, it's a lot stronger than our own you know. My partner Galina says it's the only one to drink. Have some nibbles as well"

"Thank you I will. Yes, I'm sure she's right. You know you must both come along and have Sunday lunch on the train, again courtesy of the railway. We have an exclusive dining car at our disposal for such special occasions. Tell you what, bring some of the girls along too, we could have quite a party."

"That's very kind of you, I'm sure we'd all love to. The girls said how much they enjoyed the weekend."

"Yes, they caused quite a stir you know. In fact, we've already received numerous requests from members asking for them to be invited back for a return visit. I was surprised to find so many of our members interested in ladies' rugby."

"Yes, well, life's full of little surprises isn't it? You never know when you're about to be given one – as it were. So come on drink up your Lord... er, ship, you know it's not polite in Russian society to drink alone!"

"Please, call me Hugh. Well I shouldn't really, but it's certainly hitting the spot I have to say... Whoa! That's enough!"

"Down the hatch then Hugh!"

"Yes cheers er... Dave!"

Just then a big roar of laughter went up from a group of girls huddled in the corner.

Lord Lovernock turned to cast further admiring glances in their direction. Sammi again smiled and waved at him. He waved back.

"You know, there's some damned attractive girls in this rugby team of yours, especially that Siamese girl... Sammi!"

"Ah yes Sammi, One of our best fu... er... hookers, always gives value for money!"

"I'm sorry?"

"I mean... always gives one hundred per cent. A team player you might say."

"Yes, I was telling your... Sammi earlier, I was quite a rugby player myself in my younger days, though I didn't have such attractive team members to play with – more's the pity what! Tell you what Dave, I wouldn't mind being a fly-on-the-wall when they have their team bath eh!"

"Too right Hugh, and with an all-girls team there'd be no fears about bending over to pick up the soap either eh?"

"Please Dave! Don't remind me of my public schooldays!"

"I say Hugh, you're nearly empty, let me top you up."

"Am I? So I am. Well if you insist, I shay I'm not starting to slur my words am I?"

"No, you sound perfectly sober to me!"

"It musht be me then!"

"Yes, it must be. You know Hugh, I can't help noticing, you seem to have taken quite an interest in Sammi over there."

"Ah yes, Shammi, yes, what a girl, and one of your best scorers you say!"

"That she is! You know I could tell you a very intereshting story about her."

Dave, having matched Lord Lovernock drink for drink, was now seriously inebriated himself, and couldn't stop himself from relating the salacious details of a story recently told to him by one of Sammi's colleagues.

"Really? I'd be most interhested to hear it," replied Hugh, edging closer.

"Well you shee, amongst her many talents..." Dave took a further gulp of his drink before continuing. "Shammi here is also a dab hand at ping pong too!"

"You don't shay! Well I'll let you into a secret too er... Dave, it just so happens that I was pretty nifty with a table tennis bat myshelf at one time. Of course, it's all in the wrist action you know."

"You are still talking about table tennis?"

The peer laughed out loud. "We men never lose that skill, do we Dave eh? No indeed. But you were saying shomething about Shammi were you not?"

"Was I?... Ah yes, I was wasn't I. Yes, I was going to say, that's the secret, she doesn't actually use her hand you shee!"

"Really?"

"Oh, no!"

"So what does she do with the ball then?"

"Well I'm jusht getting around to telling you aren't I? Look, before I tell you, this ish all in the strictest confidence... man to man like."

"Of coursh dear boy, goes without saying... absolutely"

"Well... and this ish between you and me remember... Well... she shoots the ball out of her..." Dave lent closer to the peer and whispered the details in his ear. The peer looked astonished.

"Good god! No! Is that true?"

Dave slowly nodded his confirmation.

"Well I'll be damned! I would never have thought it physically poshible," stated Lord Lovernock as he took another glance in Sammi's direction. The details, as revealed to him in the shared confidence, now begged a supplementary question. "So er... how far would she be able to, you know... project the... er... ball as it were?"

"Ah well, that's the big question isn't it? I would love to know myshelf! Didn't seem polite to ask though."

"No, no, you're right not to Dave. Would seem a trifle indiscreet to come out with a question like that at a drinksh and nibbles party. But one has to wonder at the range of her... well, you know what!"

"I'm told it's all to do with the power of the pelvic muscles! And from what I've heard, she's something of an expert at it. Now don't go quoting me on thish Hugh, but I have it on the best authority that back in Bangkok our Shammi here was the reigning pat pong champion of Ping Pong! 'Ang on, or was it the ping pong champion of Pat Pong... Anyway, it's one or the other. There'sh not many that have that claim to fame you know!"

"Yes indeed, what a girl! Makes you wonder what other tricksh she can perform eh?"

"My shentiments entirely Hugh."

"I musht say Dave, I've never heard the like of it before. I've obvioushly led a very sheltered exus... exhis... exshits... er, life. You know, this omission in my otherwise extensive public school education really needs to be addressed. So to fill in the gap – if you'll pardon the expression – what I propose to do is go over there right now and renew my acquaintance with the lady in queshtion, er… if that's alright with you old boy?"

"No, feel free, I'm shure there's no one better to learn from."

The Lord steered a hesitant course to the settee where Sammi was sitting. Florid-faced and beaming his broadest smile, he flopped himself down in the space next to her.

Before Dave had a chance to circulate, there was another knock at the door. He went to answer it wondering who else could be calling on a Sunday evening. Dave opened it to find the omnipresent Sgt Edwards standing there.

"Ah! Shergeant Edwards, I might have known. Is thish a social call, or is there some other compelling reason for a further visit from your good shelf?" he asked with just a hint of sarcasm.

The sergeant gave him an interrogative stare before speaking.

"Yes, good evening Mr Brand, I'll come straight to the point. We've all got homes to go to and it has been a long day. It shouldn't take long. Just a few questions related to the previous enquiry I was following on my last visit here. Never did get to the bottom of that little matter now did we? But that's... "

"Excuse me for interrupting, but you said shomething about coming straight to the point."

"Yes, well, we've had a complaint from a member of the public that men are being 'entertained', if I may use that expression, for monetary reward in this house, and of course we're obliged to investigate any such allegation."

Dave, with some deliberation due to the amount of alcohol consumed, looked up and down the pathway, before casting his eyes up to the landing window next door, just in time to see the net curtain drop back into position and a solitary figure step away from the window.

"No, I'm afraid you've been mishin... mishinfoamed Sergeant, we're having a party that's all. A party to celebrate our magnificent victory against those men from Yorkshire! Shurely you know all about it? The police were swarming all over the place arreshting the per... perp... perpletraitors!" Dave felt himself swaying, so braced himself against the door. "Anyway who's the we?"

Sgt Edwards was busily peering through into the house, trying to identify the persons attending and the reason for so much revelry.

"Sorry? Oh, er, it's just a figure of speech Mr Blond, just a figure of speech meaning the police in general. No, actually I was not one of those involved in the clearing up the criminal activity at the railway station. I was following up other lines of enquiry at the time."

He could have added that having been removed from the inquiry, he was now being investigated by the Police Complaints

Authority over his actions – or rather the lack of them during the man-eating lion incident. His one remaining hope now was to prove correct the long-held suspicion of his that a vice ring was being operating from the Bland household. His theory, if proven, would help to salvage his standing within the department and also his police career and pension.

"Well if, as you say Mr Bland, there is nothing that constitutes a criminal offence taking place, I'm sure you won't mind if I come in and just check for myself."

"So you don't believe me then eh? I have to shay Sergeant all this is beginning to look like you have a pershonal ven... venet... vienetta againsht me!"

"Not at all Mr Brand, not at all!"

At that moment, Lord Lovernock chose to walk through into the hallway accompanied by Sammi. Standing with his right hand firmly grasping her left buttock, he addressed the police officer.

"Good evening Constable, what sheems to be the trouble here?"

Sgt Edwards did a double-take on seeing a peer of the realm at the house. It was certainly not the sort of social gathering he would have expected someone of his standing to be found at. Unsure as to the exact nature of the relationship between the two gentlemen, and knowing the peer to be a personal friend of the chief constable, Sgt Edwards realised he needed to tread carefully, and so avoided any accusations as such when he restated the reason for his visit.

"No, I can ashure you officer, nothing whatshoever untoward is taking place within these walls…" He paused to give Sammi's rump another squeeze, making her squeal out loud. "…Well, not as yet anyway," he cackled. Sammi began to giggle too and brought a hand up to hide her mouth; her culture considered it unseemly to show amusement at such lewd behaviour.

Trying to remain focused, the sergeant laboured on. "Er, yes… quite. So am I to understand that all the ladies in this room are members of a ladies rugby team then?" He indicated with a sweep of his arm the ladies in question.

"That's correct, Shergeant," replied Dave.

"I have to say, they don't look the sort you'd normally expect to find playing a tough contact sport like rugby. Take this young lady here, she looks barely big enough. I mean, would she know what to do with the ball even if she managed to get hold of it?"

Dave and Lord Lovernock looked at one another and immediately fell about laughing. Sammi again had to mask her mouth.

"Something I said?" asked a nonplussed Sgt Edwards, looking from one to the other and back again.

"No, no, not at all officer, I'm afraid we're all just a touch inebriated, and things are getting rather shilly. Isn't that right Dave?" responded the peer.

"Absholutely Hugh!" he croaked.

"I have it on good authority Shergeant," stated Lord Lovernock, as he struggled to maintain his composure "that on the contrary, the young lady knowsh exactly what to do with a ball!"

Dave instantly cracked up again and turned away to hide his state of mirth.

Hugh continued, "As to the reason for your visit, it appears you have been seriously mishinformed. But make no mistake constable, if I do happen to be accoshted by ladies of the night seeking monetary gain in exchange for my body, you will be the first to know!"

Sgt Edwards tried not to react to the mocking tone, though his anger and frustration were clear to see from his face. He knew where the blame lay for this latest fiasco, and would be seeking immediate redress from the person concerned.

"So Sergeant, if there's nothing elshe we can help you with…" inquired Dave, trying to suppress the giggles long enough to bring the conversation to a close.

"Yes, right! Sorry to have troubled you I'm sure!" He turned to go.

"Not at all, Shergeant, not at all!" Dave replied

As he strode down the driveway, Sgt Edwards looked to next door, hoping to catch sight of the architect of this latest misfortune.

Unable to detect any movement behind the net-curtained windows, he headed for the front door and was just about to rap on it when a man opened it from the other side. Seeing another person standing there, the man pulled the cap down over his face and quickly exited the house.

Thinking the man looked more than a little furtive; the detective paused on the doorstep to observe him for a moment before stepping through the doorway into the house. Sgt Edwards was about to call out the woman's name when he noticed two middle-aged men seated in Mrs Battersly's front room. Both were reading magazines from a small pile on a side table. The scene reminded him of a doctor's waiting room. He was puzzled by the unusual situation and went to open the door to the adjoining room in search of the lady in question. One of the two men immediately called out to him. "Hey! You can't go in there she's got someone with her. Anyway, I'm next! Have you got an appointment?"

Now even more puzzled, he could only reply that he hadn't.

"Well, she won't see you without one."

The sergeant guessed she must be running some sort of home based business; one he'd previously been unaware of. As he sat down to wait for an opportune moment to question her, he ran through a few of the possibilities in his head: *chiropodist, clairvoyant, counsellor, drama coach...*

"Yes, Madam Whiplash is a very popular dominatrix you know," continued the man.

"*Dominat...* What! Did you say dominatrix?"

"Yes, I had to wait for a cancellation you know."

"You're kidding me?"

"No, Sunday evenings are always busy!"

"No, I mean about Mrs Batterslee being a dominatrix?"

Sgt Edwards couldn't believe his luck – or surprise. She was the last person he expected to be carrying out this sort of activity. If this was all true, it was just the sort of break he needed. Gleaning as much information as he could from the waiting client, he was able to piece together the type of activities being carried out on the premises. He learnt that the property had a cellar situated directly below them, fully-equipped with all the paraphernalia for disciplining clients. Customers set their own level of punishment and could choose from a selection of whips, canes and other assorted instruments of torture stored down there.

Once he'd heard the details, he revealed his identity to the two waiting customers who quickly decided to forego their booked treatment and promptly left. Sgt Edwards was not interested in such minnows. He was after the big trout down below.

Moving through the adjoining room, he looked around and found what looked to be the door to the cellar. When he put his ear up against the roughly hewn timber door, he could hear faint plaintive cries coming from somewhere down below. As quietly as he could, he lifted the latch and descended the steps one at a time. The cries grew louder with each step he took. Sgt Edwards winced when he heard the unmistakeable sound of a whip biting into soft flesh; all the while accompanied by the foulest abuse he'd ever heard from a woman's mouth.

Reaching the bottom step, he peered around the corner to see the outline of a small lumpish woman completely dressed in black leather, her bosom tightly bound with black criss-cross lacing. Her most noticeable feature were the prominent varicose veins protruding through the weaker sections of her black fishnet stockings. A leather mask hid her face, but it was the unmistakeable outline of Mrs Battersly alright.

She gasped and froze in mid-stroke when she saw the police sergeant standing there.

"How... how... did... you get?..."

"Never mind about that Mrs Baterjee. I'm afraid your little game is up. Madam Whiplash indeed! Yes it's a very clever operation you're running here. I must admit you nearly had me fooled, trying to divert attention from yourself by making all those accusations against your neighbour. But of course I never really believed that... No, I only played along with you long enough to gather the evidence I needed! You are a morally corrupt woman Mrs Butterly, who should really know better at your age!"

"But... but, I'm only providing a public service Sergeant. My clients need me!"

"A public service! These are sick people. I mean what sort of pervert would pay to be whipped and humiliated like this?"

"Er... Sgt. Edwards!"

The detective turned in surprise towards the tethered figure who had just uttered his name. The man was shackled to the wall wearing nothing but a blindfold and a rubber thong. A series of ugly red weals stood out prominently on the man's back – closely matching the colour of his freshly thrashed buttocks. But how did the man know who he was? Sgt Edwards was unable to make out his face in the dim light, though his voice sounded vaguely familiar. He moved to get a better look. The realisation stopped him in his tracks

"Super! Is that really you?"

"Yes, er... unfortunately it is er... Brian. It is Brian, isn't it? Well Brian, I know what you're thinking, and yes this is obviously very embarrassing for me – and of course for my wife and family if this should ever get out... Mavis has always been a bit old-fashioned about matters, well... you know. It goes without saying that I would be more than grateful if you were able to leave any mention of me out of the report you might make into all this.

"Look, it's quite difficult talking to someone when you're chained up with your face against a cold damp wall. Do you think you could get the keys off Madam Whip... er, Mrs Battersly and undo me, then we can have a little chat and hopefully get this matter sorted out – a private word in your ear, like."

Sensing that the situation was very much to his advantage, Sgt Edwards did as requested.

"Thank you Brian" As he began to rub the feeling back into his numb wrists, the superintendant made a proposal. "Right, promotion, now that's a word I'm sure you'd like to hear in your ear. It must be long overdue by now eh... er, Brian! I'm sure something can be arranged to that effect, what do you say?"

Sgt Edwards stood mulling the offer over. Although he may have picked on the wrong people initially, his nose for sniffing out criminality was rarely wrong and once he was on the trail, found he'd not lost his knack for cracking a case in minutes. Now getting over the shock of finding his superintendant to be one of Mrs Battersly's clients, he realised he was in a position to dictate rather more favourable terms than the ones so far offered.

"That would be much appreciated Super, also I was just thinking, you know that tiny office of mine..."

Lord Lovernock left the party with Sammi in tow some time later. Their departure was prompted by his chauffeur knocking at Dave's door after hearing nothing from him for several hours and expressing his concern for the peer's well-being.

With the last revellers gone and 'Rina having taken to her bed to sleep off the effects of the alcohol, the room was now empty, Dave had Galina all to himself.

Feeling more than a little tired and emotional after the party, he relished the opportunity to be alone with his Galina. He took her in his arms and led Galina in a faltering shuffle around the floor to the accompaniment of a love song compilation. He nuzzled the nape of her neck where more than one exotic perfume assaulted his senses. The feel of Galina's warm soft skin against his cheek initiated in Dave a strong desire to declare his love for her as they moved around the room – or was the room moving around them? Dave was not entirely sure any more.

Galina appeared highly amused by his repeated declarations of affection, which she knew was influenced more than a little by the amount of alcohol he'd consumed. It did though bring to mind a matter she had been meaning to raise with him when the moment was right. Judging him to be more receptive in his inebriated state, Galina took the opportunity to tackle him on a subject very much close to her heart of late.

"So how murch is murch then, Dave?"

"Sorree?" he said as he slowly lifted the full weight of his head from off her shoulder.

"You say how murch you lurve me, so how murch is murch Dave?"

Still befuddled, he was slow to interpret the underlying meaning of her question.

"Er, well, murch means a helluva lot in the English language. In fact it means I'm totally devoted to you in every way and that I really, really, really, really love you..."

To back up his words, Dave planted several wet kisses on her face and neck.

Galina remained enigmatically aloof. He looked at her puzzled for a moment before realisation set in.

"Ah yes! Actually, I have been meaning to address the question that I know is very much on your mind, and which you have dropped several hints about recently... but of course, we have been so busy!"

Dave, his voice now croaky after all the alcohol, cleared his throat and looked directly into her eyes.

"Darling! You would make me the happiest man alive, if you were to do me the honour of – inviting you mother over to stay for a month!"

A delighted Galina threw her arms around him. "Thernk you Dave, I am so graterfurl. She is a good woman. You will like her I know!"

"What is it about Russians and their families eh? Yes I'm sure I will, my darling! I'm sure I will – but even after four and a half weeks?"

"Yers of course! She will help the round house. My morther is very gourd cook you know, you wirl love her cabbage and potato soup!"

"Yes... er, sounds delicious."

"You are being sarcastic now, I know. But I make up to you in orther ways!"

"And what other ways would those be?"

"You know, I do not herv to spell it out for you, do I?"

"Yes you do… because I like to hear you say it!"

Some thirty minutes later, ablutions duly completed, Dave burst into the bedroom wearing nothing but his slippers and a rose snatched from Galina's bouquet; its stem firmly clenched between his teeth. Galina looked up from the cuddly toy cat she had been stroking and, trying to keep a straight face, said in a voice heavy with theatrical menace,

"Ah, Mr Blarnd! I've been expecting you."

"Do you expect me to talk?" replied Dave.

"No Mr Blarnd, I expect you to lie… jurst here and make passionate lurve to me – burt I see your lip is bleeding!"

"Oh… it's only a small prick!"

Struggling to keep a straight face, Galina cast her eyes down his body, "I… would never thirnk to complain though."

Both collapsed onto the bed venting shrieks of laughter. Their comic parody left them both helpless. It was some time before they could compose themselves enough to actually make love, but when they did, it was with a consuming passion.

Three days later, Ernie Blowfield was sitting at his office desk above his scrapyard in Postlethwaite reading his recently-delivered copy of the *Steam Railway Weekly*. He turned to the back pages, finding the obituary column sandwiched between a list of reproduction station signs, and an advert promoting a four-day overland coach trip to visit signal boxes in the Baltic States.

The notice was headed by the old British Railways' motif, which he noted, featured a lion sitting atop a train wheel. Ernie wondered whether its inclusion was intentional.

'Darren Isambard Pickersgill'

'Darren Isambard Pickersgill, aged 26¾, devoted son of Frank and Ellen Pickersgill. Taken from us on 21st September by a vicious predator while in the care of his father – who should have been looking out for him but was too busy playing trains at the time with that lot from the Postlethwaite Rail and Tramway Society. What a waste of a life!'

'Eaten but not forgotten'

'Rest in peace son.'

"Rest in pieces", more like, he muttered. Reading the details, Ernie was struck by the harsh tone of the notice; obviously written by a mother consumed with bitterness – unlike her son who was just consumed. He chuckled at his cruel mockery of Darren's fate.

Ernie's mood changed when he turned over the page and caught the headlines blazoned across the inside cover. As he absorbed the details, his increasing anger caused a pencil he had been idly turning over in his fingers to crack, then snap in two.

The cause of his ire was a feature on the Worfe Valley Railway's recent special steam weekend. It reported the unwelcome news that the malicious attacks had the opposite effect of what Ernie intended. Contrary to expectations, the weekend had turned out to be a huge success with a record number of visitors attending. This had resulted in the highest ever ticket sales for a steam weekend.

Ernie was not a happy man – not a happy man at all. He was making careful note of the people he considered to blame for the debacle and referred back to one of the people mentioned in the article.

"Dave Bland, eh? Now that's a name I won't be forgettin' in a hurry. Pity 'e never fell under the wheels o' one of them trains 'e was so keen on protectin'. Never mind, I'm a patient man, accidents will 'appen – eventually!"

Acknowledgements

Many thanks to my wife for her patience, and understanding that all the jobs that needed doing in the house, could easily wait a few more years.

My thanks also go to **Joe Evans:** http://quirkyjoe.com for his brilliant front cover illustration.

An Apology

My apologies to Yorkshiremen and trainspotters everywhere, no offence really!

Remembering

Clarice May Wightman, 1921 to 2013